Praise for *The Goblets Immortal* Series

'A promising series opener with a rich
supporting cast of characters. Packed full of
adventure and ending with a cliffhanger that
leaves readers anxiously awaiting a sequel.'
Booklist

'Fast-paced and can be read in a day –
perfect for a long airplane ride.'
SciFiMoviePage

'*The Goblets Immortal* is a very interesting
and unique fantasy story. It is fun and chaotic,
and I really enjoyed the read."
FanFiAddict

'I had a blast reading this compelling fantasy with a
wonderful, character-driven plot lead by a kick-ass
main character! I highly recommend this book!'
The Haunted Fae

'Immediately pulled me in and
wouldn't let me put it down.'
Jessica Belmont

BETH OVERMYER

DEATH'S KEY

Book Three in
The Goblets Immortal Series

This is a **FLAME TREE PRESS** book

FLAME TREE PRESS
6 Melbray Mews, London, SW6 3NS, UK
flametreepress.com

US sales, distribution and warehouse:
Simon & Schuster
simonandschuster.biz

UK distribution and warehouse:
Marston Book Services Ltd
marston.co.uk

Publisher's Note: This is a work of fiction. Names, characters, places, and
incidents are a product of the author's imagination. Locales and public names
are sometimes used for atmospheric purposes. Any resemblance to actual
people, living or dead, or to businesses, companies, events, institutions, or
locales is completely coincidental.

Thanks to the Flame Tree Press team.

The cover is created by Flame Tree Studio with
thanks to Nik Keevil and Shutterstock.com.
The font families used are Avenir and Bembo.

Flame Tree Press is an imprint of Flame Tree Publishing Ltd
flametreepublishing.com

A copy of the CIP data for this book is available from the British Library
and the Library of Congress.

HB ISBN: 978-1-78758-720-5
PB ISBN: 978-1-78758-718-2
ebook ISBN: 978-1-78758-721-2

Printed and bound in Great Britain by Clays Ltd, Elcograf S.p.A.

BETH OVERMYER

DEATH'S KEY

Book Three in
The Goblets Immortal Series

FLAME TREE PRESS
London & New York

Know what is to be; everything, you see:
Drink from the Goblet of Seeing.
Lighter than air, float without care:
Drink from the Goblet of Drifting.
Strength and survival, no beast is your rival:
Drink from the Goblet of Enduring.
Strategic and cunning, to war shall be running:
Drink from the Goblet of Warring.
Take what you can, banish at hand:
Drink from the Goblet of Summoning.
Luck is your friend, all others must bend:
Drink from the Goblet of Questing.
Immortality to he who drinks from one and the rest –
And a curse for the soul who was born as a Blest.

CHAPTER ONE

Aidan

The day's light gave way to night, and Aidan found himself no more certain of where he was or how he had arrived there exactly. Three things he did know of his situation, and those he had trouble accepting. Firstly, something was wrong with his traveling companion, Slaíne. She had remained unconscious from the moment they had rematerialized from Nothingness, the land between the living and the magical dead, waking only once to ask where she was. He couldn't even give her *that*.

Aidan raked a hand through his dark hair and continued pacing in front of the iron-barred window. The second thing he knew of their plight was that they were both captives of a wizard who called himself 'Hex'. Hex had materialized moments after Slaíne's collapse. He sent her ahead by some mysterious means before he took Aidan through a strange white portal that opened midair. Where the wizard was now, Aidan hadn't any idea. His Pull, the sense Aidan had of a person's or object's presence, had disappeared or changed somehow.

He looked at the door, as if that would force the being to return. Pacing was getting Aidan nowhere, so he stopped and sank to the floor, clutching his sore head in his hands.

Finally, the third and most unnerving of the facts Aidan repeated to himself, was that he had begun to hear a woman's voice in his head – only, no one else was in the room with him besides Slaíne, who was asleep. Granted, he had heard voices in his head before, such as the strange man Salem, who possessed the ability to inhabit Aidan's mind and take over his body from time to time. Salem was among the magical dead in the land called the Beyond, with which Aidan had a connection he couldn't explain. In the land of the living, there was Meraude, the mage, who had interrupted his dreams but had remained suspiciously silent since Aidan was stabbed by the nymph queen's ice blade. Meraude wanted all magic-kind dead and would use the Goblets Immortal to see to it, if Aidan didn't stop her in time. He tried to push those thoughts aside and focus on the present. The voice speaking to him now was different than Meraude's and Salem's; it was ancient.

Aidan...Aidan...Aidan....

Smashing his hands over his ears, Aidan let out a growl of frustration. If only that miserable wizard would return so Aidan could have something to do with his fists, though he knew a mere Blest such as himself would be no match for a being such as that. His own power was, after all, derived from a single wizard's array of abilities, as were all powers gained through a Goblet Immortal. From what he knew, there were five Goblets Immortal, magical vessels that gave their imbibers different abilities, and together immortality and great power. Whoever drank from the Drifting Goblet gained flight for a time, until the water left their body. If a woman drank of a Goblet when she was with child, her offspring would be known as a Blest and would have a magical ability for the remainder of their days. Maybe he and Slaíne, whose mother must have drunk from the Drifting Goblet, could fight the wizard together...if only she would wake.

The sun had sunk in its entirety now, and a night-crow let out its mournful shriek. This would not do, sitting on the floor and waiting. Aidan needed to do something. Anything. He pulled himself to his feet and approached the bed where Slaíne lay.

"Can you hear me?" Aidan asked, pressing a hand to her forehead. She was cold. Far too cold. Aidan looked not for the first time for means to start a fire. There was a great fireplace, but no wood, no kit, no tinder, nothing he could use. Again he tried finding his cache in Nothingness, the magical place objects disappeared to when Aidan Dismissed them. It was there, but when he tried reaching for it with his mind, his thoughts overshot it and he caught brief visions of the Beyond. Why had his ability to make objects disappear and reappear chosen now to change? He kicked at the wall and gave a shout of frustration.

That was when a fire burst to life in the fireplace.

Aidan leapt away. "What the devil?" The hairs on the back of his neck stood on end, and dread clenched his stomach as he stared at the green flames licking at the grate. The wizard must be near at hand, to have conjured a blaze such as this. Trembling with the need to act, Aidan reached for the iron fire poker and was surprised to find the metal nowhere near as repulsive as it might have been once upon a time. In the past, iron had always felt wrong to handle. It interfered with Aidan's magic, and he could neither Dismiss it – make it disappear into Nothingness – nor use any of his magical abilities on it. Silently, he prodded curtains, looked behind tapestries, and even peered inside the great wardrobe at the east end of the room. There was no one there, just him and Slaíne.

He felt the Pull a mere second before the wizard spoke. "Those are interesting flames." Before Aidan could lash out with the poker, it vanished from his hands and reappeared by the hearth, causing him to jump. "I know you have a lot of questions," Hex said, folding his arms across his chest. "I'm sorry I left you both alone for so long. I was dealing with…the aviary." His shoulders sagged, and Aidan noted shadows like bruises beneath his eyes. "If a person's angry enough, the transfiguration reversal process becomes very difficult."

"Where are we? She's—"

"Slaíne is going to be all right." The wizard motioned for Aidan to follow him to the door. "She'll probably be unconscious for the next few days." Hex shook his head. "It must be quite a shock."

Aidan opened his mouth to ask what he was talking about and demand to be released at once, but the wizard walked through the solid door and disappeared. After a moment, he returned the same way, wearing a look of confusion on his face before smirking. "Oh, right. Curses. You can't…." Hex laughed and pulled the door open like a normal human, then motioned for Aidan to follow. "She is perfectly safe where she is, Aidan."

"How do I know I can trust you?" Aidan demanded, still unwilling to leave his traveling companion at her most defenseless. She may no longer be cursed – something that had been done to her as a child and had prevented her from being away from whomever she called master – but that didn't mean she was safe.

Hex snapped his fingers, and at once they were no longer standing in the bedchamber but found themselves before a red fire burning bright and smokeless in a circular pit. The white brick room was vast, with windows reaching from floor to ceiling, and though it was dark outside, Aidan could hear and smell the roar of the salty sea.

Startled, Aidan nearly stumbled into the blaze, which spat green sparks at him as he righted himself. "What—"

"Maybe we should be seated for this." Hex waved his hand, and a chair materialized behind Aidan, knocking into his knees so that he fell backward into it. The wizard took his seat more gracefully. "Right. You wanted to know where you are. This is Vät Vanlud."

Aidan's shoulder prickled with cold, and he could hear the faint voice of Salem shouting, but could not decipher the words. Salem always chose the wrong times to attempt to contact him from the Beyond. He had been doing it for weeks now through their peculiar mental connection. Aidan couldn't remain too angry with him, however; Salem had saved him from Lord Dewhurst, Aidan's nemesis, by inhabiting his body temporarily, after all. "Vät Vanlud," Aidan repeated, pushing the voice of his inner friend aside. "What does that mean?"

"The House of Curses." Hex gestured around vaguely, sending a rainbow of sparks flying from his fingertips. At once the walls around them disappeared and it was as though he and Aidan had been transported to a sheer black cliff overlooking a raging green sea. "The island we're on – Trys Lanludd – is unreachable." He gave Aidan a meaningful look. "No one can come or leave here without my help." Perhaps sensing Aidan's growing unease, the wizard waved his hands again, and the walls reappeared. "Now, you must wonder how I know who you are." He opened and closed his mouth a few times, shook his head, and said, "I keep an ear to the ground for trouble in the land. When I heard your name and what you might be up to, I sent out one of my servants and had you followed. As for the why and how, that is really a question to answer when Sláine's awake, I fear." He gave Aidan a curious look, one that the latter did not care for in the least. It was a look of expectation and resignation, as though the wizard were waiting for Aidan to burst into flames so that he might extinguish them. After a moment, the look passed, and Aidan found himself regathering his wits.

Anger at being taken against his will bubbled hard in Aidan's veins. But he knew he must tread carefully with the wizard if he wanted to get out of this mess alive. "Who are you exactly?" he asked, his tone flat and brittle.

Hex seemed to consider this as he sat there and rubbed his bare chin. "You were expecting someone ancient-looking, with a long, tangled beard, I suppose."

Aidan did not dignify that with a response.

Hex chuckled. "I am the third of the Seven Great Wizards to once rule the Saime, what now is mostly wilderness and wasteland. It was once one nation, but now I see it divided." The wizard flicked a finger and a long reed pipe appeared in his tanned hands. Out of the tip of his pointing finger he produced a red flame, which he placed inside the bowl of his pipe, and began to puff meditatively.

A chill wriggled its way up Aidan's back. This wizard was most likely the one who had aligned himself with the rest of magic-kind against the cruel and controlling wizards in the Great War – a war between wizards and the rest of magical kind – making him well over five hundred years old. It had to be him; only two wizards had survived the war, from what Aidan had learned. Aidan had already met the other wizard the day previous, and he was insane. But how could this man be over five-hundred? The other wizard had looked ancient. Hex looked Aidan's age and not a day older.

Perhaps reading Aidan's thoughts, as wizards of lore were wont to do, Hex said, "Do not look so surprised, Aidan Ingledark. Magic always comes with a price." The smoke wafting from his pipe turned red and began to twist and writhe and form itself into strange shapes in the dim air. "The price I pay is immortality." He laughed but it was without humor. His gaze roved back to Aidan. "You must be famished. I'm sorry I left you alone for so long, but as I said, she's still fairly angry, and that makes this type of magic difficult."

Aidan frowned. He did not know how to respond to this, had no idea what the wizard was going on about, so he leapt to his feet. "This is ridiculous. The longer we sit here, the more likely it is that Meraude is going to get what she wants." From what Aidan understood, Meraude hated magical beings and wanted to assert herself as queen of everyone left after the dust of her conflict settled. Whether or not she had the allies to accomplish this remained to be seen.

Hex's expression darkened. "That is not entirely true. There is no Questing Goblet, after all."

The Questing Goblet, had it been made, would have given its imbiber luck beyond measure, and would have aided Aidan and Slaíne in their quest to destroy Meraude. If they could get their hands on the Seeing Goblet, they could look into the future and see the means to their revenge. Even the Summoning and Drifting Goblets might prove useful, though Aidan could not think of a good reason why at the moment.

"Yes, there is no Questing Goblet, but there are other Goblets to contend with." It took all his strength not to scream at this strange, calm man. "What if she has the Warring Goblet? Then she will have the war she wishes for."

But the wizard was shaking his head. "That is not how it works, Ingledark. I think you know that very well. You have, after all, imbibed from it."

Aidan blinked. For a short time, less than a full day, he had possessed the magical vessel. Before knowing what it would do, Aidan had drunk from it, and the only effect it had had was to clear his mind. No wars had sprung up around him, which of course would have been ridiculous. He did not admit any of this to the wizard, however, but he knew Hex was aware of his thought. "All right, but if she has it, then she will have the mind of a great warrior. Will anyone be able to best her?"

For a moment, Hex's eyes twinkled. "Meraude does not possess the Warring Goblet." He held up his hand and began ticking off on his fingers. "Nor does she have the Drifting Goblet, as you well know. She doesn't have foresight, and I believe she is too frightened to attempt to drink from the Seeing Goblet at the moment. The other Goblets, wherever they may be, are not your concern."

Anger flashed through Aidan, clouding his thoughts. "You decide what my concerns are, do you?"

Hex let out a long sigh. "You need to calm down, Aidan. I know it's hard. I was young once like you. Age will mellow your rage, but until then, it's only going to hurt you and those you care about."

Aidan was so furious he couldn't move or speak but stared into the flames, which seemed to jump in reaction to his rage. He felt a cold blast of air, and he at first assumed one of the windows had blown open. But he was

wrong: the windows remained closed, and Hex was lowering his hand, tendrils of red wafting from his fingertips.

He gave Aidan a sympathetic look. "It'll get easier."

"What will get easier? Being held against my will?" The heat, however, had gone out of Aidan's anger, and all he felt now was tired and empty.

The wizard's eyebrows shot heavenward. "Interesting. I thought you knew. Forgive me."

Before Aidan could ask Hex what he meant, a tray of food materialized before him. It was piled high with piping-hot mounds of roast beef, roasted carrots and red-skinned potatoes, green string beans, and baked apples with their skins melting tenderly off the browned and spiced flesh. As inviting as this all looked, Aidan could not bring himself to be much interested in consuming anything. He continued to stand.

Hex shook his head. "It won't do you any good to stand there and brood, Ingledark. You can't have eaten for a day at least."

It was tempting to insist that he would eat when Slaíne was awake, but the wizard made an interesting proposition: "I know what you are thinking. But hear me out: nourish yourself, and I will show you a magic trick."

Aidan bit down on a smirk. "Oh?"

"You think this was interesting?" The wizard gestured around him. "This was nothing to be impressed with. Sit, eat, and I will introduce you to some higher magic." He waved his hand, and a fine yellow bird in a gilded cage appeared in midair. The poor little beast was squawking away, a sound Aidan had heard many an irate mother bird make to keep predators away from its nest. But the bird's Pull was all wrong. It felt... suppressed.

The cage turned so the bird was now facing Aidan, and the creature's squawking became a screech. As it went silent, the wizard shot a bolt of white light out of the tip of his pointing finger. The light hit the bird in the back, and the creature began to glow and then slowly grew in size, transforming from a tiny feathered beast in a cage to a woman with deep blue eyes that were in great contrast to her jet-black hair.

At once the wizard took a step back, not afraid, but apparently nervous.

When the woman opened her mouth, her voice sounded strained, as though she had been screaming for some time. "Where is Quick?" The words must have been directed at Hex, but the woman was looking at Aidan, apparently befuddled.

The fire in the pit began to jump again, its colors shifting slightly. Hex's gaze traveled to Aidan, watchful again.

"Where is he?"

The wizard cleared his throat. "Jinn, your brother is in good health. Come, you're distressing yourself for naught."

"Where is he?" Still her eyes did not leave Aidan.

Hex snapped his fingers and another chair appeared, this one on the wizard's right; like Aidan, the woman did not choose to sit. "Quick is sleeping off a feast in one of the guest rooms. He has wanted for nothing and is at perfect ease. You may see him shortly, once I've explained a few things."

Aidan's discomfort increased as the two continued to stare at him while they were talking to each other. *What madness is this?*

"I didn't foresee— It's dark. So dark." She hiccupped, a sound bordering on a sob.

Shifting his weight, the wizard now looked at Jinn and frowned. "All shall be made known presently. For now…Jinn, allow me to introduce you to Aidan Ingledark. Aidan, this is Jinn. I thought, things being as they are, what with you both at last under the same roof, it would only be fitting for you to meet. There, be met."

At this the woman paled and would not quite meet his eyes. "Why are you doing this?" At last she stopped staring at Aidan like he was some strange specimen and turned to the wizard. Anger radiated off of Jinn in waves, and Aidan almost imagined he could see it.

Aidan shook himself mentally. One could not see emotions, he was being fanciful, and he never had much of an imagination.

It was a sight, the slight woman confronting the wizard, who seemed ready to run from the room. If the circumstances had been different, Aidan might have sat back and watched the two verbally spar. As it was, he was in no mood to put up with small talk. He needed to know what the purpose of keeping him here was and when they would be released. "Wizard, I do not care what your quarrel is with this woman or even *who* this woman is. Tell me what Sláine and I are doing here, or so help me…."

"That is a fair question," Jinn said, clenching her small hands into fists. "You have no right to detain us, wizard."

Hex shook his head. "You don't understand." He turned to Aidan. "And I think you will be very interested to know whom you share shelter with."

The air was charged, and the woman seemed to shrink immediately, as if awaiting some fatal blow. "It's – it's not what it seems. Don't listen to the wizard. You know they can't be trusted."

Now Aidan's interest was piqued, even if only slightly. "Go on," said he to Hex.

"This is Jinn, her brother is Quick, and they have been pursuing you for around a month now." The wizard placed himself between Aidan and the young woman then, as if fearing what Aidan might do.

Aidan was confused. His attention focused on Jinn, and he found himself scratching at the stubble on his jaw. Pursuing him? Was she some reward-seeker, hoping to turn him in for a bounty? He was, after all, still a wanted man for supposedly killing Lord Dewhurst's wife and child. Aidan's eyes flickered to Hex, who shook his head, and then back to Jinn again. "Yes, I am a wanted man. But if you think you'll be able to hand me and mine over for a bounty, you are sorely mistaken."

Of all things, the young woman looked confused. "I don't know what you're talking about. But maybe we can—"

Hex snapped his fingers, and Jinn disappeared. "Eat," he commanded, and Aidan decided it would be best now to oblige. The wizard's brow creased as they both took their seats, and the pipe that he had been holding earlier rematerialized in his large hands. "I turned her brother into a bird too." Perhaps that explained why the young woman was so angry with him. "That's right, you were there." Hex puffed on his pipe and then rubbed his eyes with the heels of his hands as the pipe floated in the air. "You live so long, you remember so much, and the more you remember the more there is to forget. It's quite maddening."

"I'd imagine."

The wizard frowned. "Eat," he repeated, and Aidan ate, though hesitantly. The two of them sat and regarded the fire. "Jinn and her brother have been sent after you, Aidan. They are not two people you want to befriend."

Aidan snorted. "And *you* are?"

That drew a low laugh from Hex. "No. I believe our goals are very different." He puffed red smoke for a moment, his expression vacant. "If only I knew more."

This would not do, the two of them sitting here, as if there were no greater worries in the world. Time was precious. Slaíne might wake up, find herself alone, and wonder if Aidan had abandoned her. "Why are we here?" he said after some time as he set the half-full plate aside. The wizard said nothing. "From what has been said, I believe you have both the Drifting and Warring Goblets. They are not yours."

Hex's hands tensed on his armrests. "And neither are they yours to take and do with as you see fit."

"My goal is to—"

"Your goal is childish and petty," said Hex, shaking his head. "You children and your quarrels."

A mere quarrel? That was going too far. Aidan's temper again uncoiled and rose to the surface. "Meraude had my parents murdered. You call avenging them petty and childish?"

"Bah."

The fire sparked green and red, the flames clashing against each other, warring for mastery. "Meraude is killing my kind, Vex, or whatever your ridiculous name is. She needs to be stopped." Both men were on their feet, standing head-to-head and toe-to-toe as the flames continued to dance. "You are heartless." It was with those words that Aidan felt a tightening in his chest, as though some great invisible hand were attempting to squeeze his heart through his rib cage. The green went out of the fire, and Aidan swayed.

"Careful, sapling," said Hex. "You would do well to remember not to question me and my motives here in the House of Curses."

The pressure in Aidan's chest released, and he collapsed, clutching the spot. "Meraude is—"

"Not your concern. I'll send you back to your quarters now. I grow weary of you." The wizard snapped his fingers, and the world glowed red as the room around Aidan dissolved.

With a none-too-gentle thud, he found himself back in the room with Slaíne, possessing more questions than answers.

*   *   *

Slaíne slept through the night, though Aidan attempted to rouse her at intervals. The green magic fire had gone out long ago. It was now an hour or so before the dawning, and he had given up hope of warming the room, but grabbed a blanket for himself and sat curled on the bed a ways away from Slaíne.

Something was different. Her Pull was all wrong; it was just as strong as ever, but its quality had changed. Aidan lay there, listening to the strange voice inside his head. Then he suddenly shot across the bed and landed against her with a thud, and was then tossed away as if by an invisible hand. "What the devil?" said he, picking himself off the floor. Half-awake and wondering how he had lost control of his abilities, Aidan crawled back on top of the coverlets and placed a hand on Slaíne's brow. She was still cold. He felt for a pulse, though he knew what he would find: a strong, healthy heartbeat that thrummed in time with his own.

Aidan.

He curled into a ball and shivered as he struggled to keep his eyes open. "What?" he said through a yawn.

You feel different.

Aidan cracked an eye open. Was he going insane, or was she somehow tapping into his thoughts? "*You* feel different." He shuddered violently as the wind outside picked up to a howl.

You're not insane.

He blew a strand of hair out of his face. "Wake up and tell me that. Then I'll know for certain that we're both mad."

The voice that sounded like Slaíne's sighed. *Nay think I can yet. Too tired.*

Aidan grunted. He knew the feeling. "I really have lost my mind. Nothing's been the same since the cave." In the cave where they had hoped to find the Questing Goblet, Aidan had been forced to Dismiss himself and Slaíne into Nothingness. Something strange had happened there. Slaíne had said something about him freeing her spirit, and then proceeded to take something out of his chest and put it into her own. He had felt so cold, so…empty. Then there was pain. Slaíne had taken something out of her chest and put it in his. When they had returned to Existence – the world where the living dwelled – she had fainted and Aidan was left wondering what exactly had happened. At the thought, something stirred in Aidan's chest. Again he let out a mighty shudder, and now could not keep his teeth from chattering.

You gotta let it take over, I think.

That did not sound promising. "Let what take over? The madness… or whatever illness this might be?"

Slaíne stirred, and Aidan sat upright, ready to help her if need be. Her eyes remained closed, and her chest continued to rise and fall at a slow, rhythmic rate.

Cold.

"I would try making a fire," he said, as though she could hear him in her sleeping state. "But there's no wood, and Nothingness is...." Aidan puffed out his cheeks and gestured widely in frustration. "I can't access it."

You're cold, Aidan, not me. Nay fret 'bout no fire. Crawl in next to me.

Now Aidan knew himself to be losing his mind. If she had been conscious, the Slaíne he knew would never make such an invitation.

Maybe I'm not what you knew. Maybe I'm more.

Aidan decided to ignore the voice in his head to the best of his ability, and curled up again on top of the coverlet with his back pressed against Slaíne's side. After some time, he drifted off and slept a dreamless sleep.

★　　★　　★

"There was a man
Sat at death's door
The girl he had
He loved no more
Now from her breast
She drew her light
Placed it to rest
In him, the blight
Loved not the wife
Not in her life
But in her death
Gave him her breath
And sealed her..."

There was a long pause, to which Aidan awoke with a frown. "Hello?"

"What rhymes with 'breath' but means 'fate'? Or maybe somethin' else...."

Aidan rubbed his eyes and looked over at Slaíne, and was surprised and relieved to find her eyes open, if only a crack. "Are you all right?" When she didn't respond but lay there, blinking at him, he repeated his question.

"Oh, I heard ya the first time, Aidan." She started humming, only to stop and start listing words. "Breath, death, deaf...deft? Nah, those aren't all true rhymes and none of 'em fit, anyway. Help me out."

He rolled onto his back. "You've been asleep for two days."

But she shook her head. "Nah, more like five. *You've* been asleep for two."

That made Aidan sit upright. "What do you mean I've been asleep for two days? What has happened? What's—"

Slaíne placed a distracting hand on his leg. "Calm down, Aidan. I'm not awake enough yet for ya to have a full-blown panic." She yawned large enough to swallow a pillow and blinked frantically before swearing. "I figure another ten minutes should be right." There was a pause, and she opened one eye further. "You know about it yet?"

Baffled, Aidan stared at her. "Know about *what*?"

She swore some more. "Ne'er mind. If I tell ya, you'll be upset."

It occurred to Aidan that she had said something strange moments earlier, something she had only ever said when she was under great duress. "Slaíne," he said after a moment. "When did you start calling me by my first name?"

But she had started to snore. *Upset.*

Aidan shook his head and then reached for Slaíne, only to be hit with a bolt of blue light in the hand. "Ack!"

Slaíne stirred and groaned. "You can nay do that right now, Aidan."

"What did you do? How...?"

"You startled me."

Now it was Aidan's turn to swear. "I've startled you before, and you never threw blue fire at me then." He held his hand where the light had struck him, which felt as though she had slapped it. This was getting to be too much for Aidan to cope with. What would she do next? Turn into a frog and leap out the window?

You're overreactin'. Her lips were unmoving. Was she speaking to him with her mind?

"Are you inside my head?" Aidan demanded, tapping his right temple and then daring to tap hers. This time, mercifully, she did not attack him.

"Of course I was inside your head," she said, taking his hand and holding on to it. "We're bound."

What was she talking about? "Bound to what?"

"To each other, you great idiot. Now, let me be a minute more." Slaíne tugged on his hand, effectively pulling him down next to her. Her brow puckered and her grasp on him tightened, but whatever had her worried, she did not voice it.

Aidan's pulse quickened as she rubbed small circles on his wrist with her thumb. Her Pull warned him a moment before her eyes flew open and bored into his. Once gray, they now were an unnatural blue. A thrill of terror and desire jolted through Aidan, and he didn't know whether he should flee or throw himself at her. He didn't get a chance to do either.

"I feel your fear," said Slaíne, placing his hand on her breast over her heart. Her skin was like ice, making him shudder. "It's natural for most to be afeared of me. But you ain't most no more. We are one, you and me." She released his hand, letting it rest on her bosom.

Her heartbeat was frenzied. The second rhythm in her chest, the one Aidan recognized as his own, had taken off as well. His hand steadied and he rubbed the spot there, eliciting a primal sigh from Slaíne. Delighting in the sound, Aidan traced his callused fingers across her collarbone and marveled at the silky smoothness of her skin. Her flesh warmed at his touch, or rather, Aidan observed, his cooled to match hers. He ceased caring that they were in the clutches of a dangerous wizard and he forgot about Meraude. Blood roared in his ears as he rose to his knees, searching her eyes for permission.

In answer, Slaíne grabbed him, effectively tearing his shirt and landing him astride her, right where he wanted to be.

★   ★   ★

After, they lay entwined, his clothes here, her clothes there. Aidan no longer felt the cold, though something told him the moment he let go of Slaíne, he'd be shivering again. "What happened in the cave?" Aidan ventured to ask, bringing her knuckles to his lips.

Slaíne was quiet for a moment, and then rested her head on his chest. "You say a wizard's got us?"

Aidan grunted. "Yes."

"He's not the only wizard in this place, Aidan." She said nothing for a time, as though letting the truth settle into Aidan's brain. When he remained silent for too long, trying to make sense of things, she sat up, her red waves cascading over her shoulder as she twisted to face him. "You understand me?" She smoothed his brow.

"How did I not know?" he asked. "Why didn't you tell me that you're a...wizard?" It made no sense. She had displayed no powers beyond being a Blest with the gift of flight. Why now? As she continued to stare at him, into him, Aidan's thoughts cleared. "After the cave, in Nothingness, you said the curse had been broken, and something about freeing your spirit. The curse—"

"The curse that was put on me kept my powers locked down. I nay knew I was a wizard 'til they was unlocked."

Aidan nodded, though he still found himself bewildered by the whole thing. "Well," he said after some time, "what does this mean for our plans to destroy Meraude?"

Slaíne groaned. "Well, we've a better chance at succeeding, to begin with." She gave Aidan an odd, expectant look, one that he would think about late into the hours of the night, before releasing him and sitting up entirely.

Just as Aidan had predicted, he again found himself freezing cold. "That is a boon, indeed." The words came out through his teeth, which were clashing together so hard, he thought he might knock a few of them out by accident.

"You nay started no fire? It must be cold in here for ya now."

"I tried," he reminded her. "There was a green fire in here earlier, but that went out quickly enough. I...." Aidan watched as she moved toward the wardrobe, opened it, and began rummaging through its contents.

First she pulled out a silky green tunic, which she pulled over her head, then a pair of men's trousers. Those she hoisted up to her waist beneath the tunic, securing the loose fabric about her with a sash. Satisfied apparently, Slaíne reached farther back and pulled out a shorter tunic and another pair of trousers, which were longer. "Here," she said, tossing them at Aidan. When he didn't move, she snapped her fingers, jumping when a blue blaze appeared in the fireplace. "Well, that answers that question."

With a shudder Aidan pulled on the trousers, which were much too thin to keep out the biting cold of the room, secured the sash around his waist, and then pulled on a brown tunic. "How did you do that – make the fire, I mean?"

Slaíne laughed. "Magic, I s'pose. But I can nay quite control it... yet."

Aidan did not know if he entirely liked the sound of that. "How are you going to learn to control it?"

"From our wizard host, of course." She reached into the wardrobe once more and pulled out a dark brown cloak, which she brought over to him. "Here. This should help."

"Thank you." Aidan threw the cloak around himself, marveling how at once his shaking and teeth-chattering ceased. He felt warmed through, as if he had been plunged into a hot bath. He followed Slaíne to the door, which she tried pulling on, before swearing at it.

"Well, that's rude."

He was tempted to remind her that being taken hence and held against their will was *beyond* rude, but now knew what she was potentially capable of and did not provoke her. "He walked through the door like it had no substance," Aidan said. "Can you...?"

Slaíne threw her weight against the door, and bounced off it. "Not very ruddy likely. Let me try something, though." She took a few determined steps back, and Aidan made sure to remove himself from her path, for she had raised her hands as if preparing to cast a spell. Shaking and clenching her jaw, Slaíne stared at the door with rapt concentration, and then made a throwing gesture at the knob. Nothing happened, except the blue flames in the fireplace began to dance wildly. Her shoulders hunched and she looked at Aidan, as if daring him to laugh.

He was not even inclined to give her a half-smile. There was nothing remotely amusing about their situation.

"Have you tried escaping?" she surprised him by asking.

Aidan shook his head. "The bars are iron," he said, pointing to the window, "and the door has been locked fast." He did not voice the fact that he had been concerned about her condition and had hoped that the wizard would help her.

"Iron don't feel dif'rent now?"

He considered that for a moment before saying, "It does feel different. How would you know?"

She did not grace that question with an answer but again threw herself at the door with a loud grunt before falling to the floor in a heap. With much cursing, Slaíne got to her feet and began pounding on the door with her tiny white fists. "Hey, you. Wizard. Let us out."

Now Aidan did feel the stirrings of amusement tugging at the corners of his lips, but didn't dare let a smile come into full fruition. "Perhaps I ought to tell you, the wizard's name is Hex."

"Odd, that."

Aidan nodded. "And there are at least two other prisoners here, and it seems they were trying to find us for some of our journey."

That caused Slaíne to cease her pounding and yowling at the door like a cat left out in the rain. She turned to Aidan, the strange blue light in her eyes flashing, before fading and leaving her looking almost human again. "The shape-shifter?" Before arriving at the cave, Aidan and Slaíne had noticed they were being followed, and one morning, they were awakened by the creature, who had attempted to kill them both.

The mention of the creature made the hairs on Aidan's neck prickle, but he brushed the feelings of terror aside and shared the rest of his information with her. "I don't think so. Larkin warned us that I was being sought. They must be the persons to whom she referred." Larkin was a Blest with the ability to see parts of the future and had hindered and helped him at different points in his journey.

Slaíne took to pacing, and as she did, sparks of blue fire flew haphazardly from her fingertips, though she did not seem to notice, until her tunic began to burn. She stifled the small blaze by putting the offending part of the sleeve in her mouth, much to Aidan's horror, and then resumed pacing. "That ruddy seer. She ought ter have told us more about what we would face."

"She said something about there being holes in a veil, and that our futures ended in darkness." He moved to the bed and perched on the edge of the mattress. "Perhaps she did not know our fate."

That caused her to laugh without humor. "Some ruddy good seer she is, then. If'n she told us what's true." Slaíne paused and whirled around to face Aidan. "Right. And you can nay feel anything in Nothingness?"

Aidan winced. "It's there, but I keep…overshooting it every time I try reaching into it." He studied Slaíne, who suddenly looked guilty.

"Your magic's changed."

It took great strength of will not to grind his teeth and growl. "We're going to need everything in our arsenal if we're going to escape this wizard." *And now I'm absolutely useless to us and our cause.*

"You're not useless," she said patiently. "You just gotta learn to adapt." She joined him on the edge of the mattress. "'Sides, like I said afore, I need to learn my magic from this Hex fella. Then maybe he'll set us free."

"To go on our merry way and kill Meraude?" It was Aidan's turn to let out a dark, humorless chuckle. "I'm afraid that's most likely not going to happen. Our wizard host has the Drifting Goblet and at least one other, the Warring Goblet."

Slaíne put a hand on his knee with a squeak. "He do?"

Aidan stared at her fingertips. "Yes, and he did not seem keen on releasing us or them when we last spoke." Why, though? What could he mean to do with them? Aidan's stomach clenched just as Slaíne's snarled, and they both looked at each other. "You haven't eaten in a week." They'd only had water available to them.

With a sigh, she removed her hand from Aidan's leg and rose. "You probably nay have either. Lemme try somethin'." Slaíne took her hand in his and pressed it over her heart.

"I have eaten." Aidan felt his half of a soul begin to writhe in her chest, and his heart began to race in excitement.

"Stop thinking amorous thoughts, Aidan. Try to focus on Nothingness."

He cleared his throat, closed his eyes, and began feeling for his cache in the land between the living and dead. Salem's confused face flashed before his mind's eye, then the mansion, then the orchard and fields beyond. "It's the Beyond again."

Something shifted inside him. Aidan felt a great swelling of power within, one that threatened to tear him apart. Then, before he could fully comprehend or reach for the source of this strange new strength, he felt the power leech out of him, until only the old, familiar one remained. Aidan sensed the Pulls inside Nothingness, those of food and cloth and tools. Still dazed, he attempted to latch on to only those Pulls that were edible, and succeeded in Summoning them to Existence, along with a few other things, he found upon opening his eyes.

"There," said Slaíne, her brow creased as she released his hand. When he was slow in removing it, she gave him an amused, albeit dangerous, look and Aidan let his hand drop.

The power that Aidan had felt surge through him pulsed again, before fleeing to some dormant, quiet place inside his chest. Eyes wide, he looked at Slaíne. "What was that?"

She shrugged. "Just some o' my power."

Aidan had more questions, but he would save them for later. Right then, the food was proving too great a distraction. They fell upon the small feast – leftover cuts of ham, some bread, and a slice of cheese – as civilized as they could, though both proved ravenous. It took a deal of willpower to override his instincts and let Slaíne have the first drink of the one and only water bladder he had managed to Summon. By the time it returned to him, the contents were more than half-gone.

Her eyes spoke her apology as she broke her fast in silence. Finally, after every morsel had been devoured, Slaíne sighed and then sniffed. "We both reek to high heaven. Maybe that's why that wizard will nay come near us." She laughed, and he managed a low chuckle in response. With a grunt, she was back on her feet. "Right. We should try somethin' else. I wonder if…." She worried her lower lip for a moment and gave Aidan another strange look, before closing her eyes and reaching out her hand as if grasping for something. "How do you do it?"

"Do what?" he asked, only to be immediately hushed. Frowning, Aidan watched her and was ready to ask her if she was all right, when he felt another strange stirring of power in his chest.

Slaíne groaned. "Do ya nay have any tools in Nothingness?"

His hand flew to his heart, which began to throb excitedly, as though he were running a race. "What sort of tools do you mean?"

"Like a hammer or crowbar or somethin' we could use to pry the door open." When Aidan did not respond, wondering if he was having a heart episode, Slaíne snorted. "No, Aidan. Yer all right. Just think of the tools in Nothingness. What do they feel like?"

Aidan tried to consider this, but the surge of power intensified, and he became aware that a strange presence was rummaging through his cache in Nothingness, one that was alien and at once familiar. "How are you doing that?" he asked in wonderment.

"Doing what?"

He grasped his chest and willed his heart to stop racing. For a moment he managed to slow its pace, but then he felt her soul-half within his chest writhe; it gave him a jolt, as if in warning.

Don't interfere, she said.

Aidan's temper flared. "What are you doing?"

Slaíne ignored him, and then…. "Aha!" She Summoned a copper

knife, nearly cutting herself. It sliced through the air and clattered onto the ground by her feet. "Ack!"

Had he not been so confused and startled, Aidan would have rushed to her aid. As it was, he sat there, gaping at her for a moment, before his eyes narrowed in suspicion. "How?"

"Lights above, Aidan, but ya've got to 'ave something better than this stored away. Concentrate."

Once again she shut her eyes and reached out her hand, but this time Aidan was having none of it. "Slaíne," he said, stumbling to his feet. As the stirring began again in his chest, he placed his hands on her shoulders. Both pulsing souls within his breast and within hers stilled for a moment, before a loud ringing filled his ears. It happened so quickly. One minute they were touching, the next they were on opposite sides of the room, a wall of red fire between them.

CHAPTER TWO

Jinn

It had been eight days since her arrival at Vät Vanlud, the House of Curses. Since then, Jinn had seen their host only twice, and she was beginning to wonder if he had been a figment of her imagination. The first time she had seen the wizard was when she was still a bird – a strange and humiliating experience that she did not wish to think about – and the second time was when he had succeeded in changing her back to human form.

Praise fate or any powers above, she had then been reunited with her brother, Quick, who seemed unharmed, albeit confused upon seeing her appear out of thin air. Food and drink had mysteriously appeared on the table in their room three times a day, but the siblings were alone. Quick did not seem to mind. This was the most luxuriously they had ever lived: there were beds, a fireplace with plenty of fuel to feed it, water to drink, water to bathe in, and every comfort they could wish for. But Jinn found herself anxious most of the time. When she was not pacing during waking hours, she was having a go at the door, which remained stubbornly locked.

"This cannot go on," Jinn said for the twentieth time that day. "We're running out of time."

Quick grunted. "Hmm. Sister, why worry? We safe."

"No, Quick, we are *not* safe. We don't know this wizard or what his intentions are. And as long as Mother continues to breathe...." Their mother, Meraude, had surely meant for them to die in their quest to find the Summoner, Aidan. Had the wicked mage suspected her children would run afoul of a wizard? Jinn snorted. "I doubt she knows of their existence."

"Huh?"

Jinn waved her brother's question aside and then paused. Perhaps that was the reason why Mother was building an army, for surely she would need all the help she could get in defeating the wizard. A shiver ran down Jinn's spine, and she gave an almighty shudder. As much as she fed the fire, it seemed to do little to dispel the cold. The cave they had grown up in was surely warmer than this wretched place.

"Magic is cold," Quick said sagely, pulling the blankets up to his nose.

That caused Jinn to laugh. "Right. Quick, would you not consider breaking down the door?"

Quick seemed to consider the question, before his eyes flickered closed and he began to snore.

Jinn groaned. "Well, your brute strength is proving useless." She stopped pacing and marched to the wardrobe, intending to add layers to what she was already wearing. Upon throwing the doors open, Jinn was surprised to find the collection of clothes had doubled, perhaps even tripled since last she looked. Among the trousers and tunics that had been there before were cloaks and strange-looking hats, and ever so many things that toppled onto the floor in front of her. Blinking for a moment, Jinn drew back in fear, making a clawed hand in front of her to ward off any evil. Then she felt silly. What evil could possibly come from a piece of furniture? "A wizard's wardrobe, though?" she muttered, still hesitant to explore.

After a moment, she gathered her courage and started sorting through the fabrics. Toward the bottom of the heap, she found a short blue cloak, which she threw around her shoulders and sighed as the cold was driven out of her body. "Well, that's better."

The wardrobe groaned, and the door swung farther open. *See what else I've got*, it seemed to say.

Ignoring her instincts, Jinn swayed and tripped through the mound of clothes and looked inside. She found a few more hats, a glass vase, and, of all things, a ring of keys. These she regarded for a brief time as though they might bite her, but she plunged her hand inside the wardrobe and snatched them up. The keys were heavier and colder than she had been anticipating, and she nearly fell onto the floor. "Quick!" she shouted.

Her twin grunted in his sleep, so she repeated her call for him.

"Jinn in trouble?"

"If I said I wasn't, would you ignore me and just go back to sleep?"

Quick groaned and sat up. "What wrong?"

"I found a ring of keys," she said, dropping them onto the floor, nearly hitting her foot. "They're really heavy. Can you help me try them on the door?"

Now her brother laughed. "Jinn is silly. Who would leave keys to room?"

"The same person who's arrogant enough to leave us alone for several days without checking on us."

But Quick was snoring again.

Jinn looked around the room for something to throw at him, settled on the vase, knowing it would not harm him – due to the invulnerability he had from the Enduring Goblet – and threw that at Quick's head. "We can at least try," Jinn said, once Quick had sat bolt upright in bed with a yelp. The vase had missed him, striking the wall next to his head instead and shattering.

"Why?"

That startled Jinn. "What do you mean, 'why'? I just saw the Summoner in this very castle. We need to get to Aidan, ally with him, and make our escape." Surely he was not so slow as to think they could stay where they were indefinitely.

With a grunt, Quick got out of the bed, shuddering greatly. He picked up a large brown robe and pulled it over his clothes. "That better. Now. Where are the keys that have Jinn so worried?"

Jinn pointed to them. "You try those on the door, and I'll see if I can find something to transport the remainder of breakfast in." And she did just that as her brother hefted the keys to the door. Their packs had been taken or left behind when they were turned into birds, and there was nothing that would readily work to transport items of necessity with them. Perhaps if they could convince the Summoner to aid them, he would be able to steal a few things and store them away. With that thought, Jinn gave up on her endeavor and joined Quick at the door.

"There are many keys," he said, shoving a large brass one at the keyhole, which was too small to accommodate it. "You are certain one works?"

She shook her head. "No, I'm not. But we need to try."

Quick sighed and shoved a tiny key inside the keyhole, but that key did not work either. "What we do if wizard finds us out? He'd be angry, no?" He shuddered and his hand slipped as he slid another key into the keyhole.

"Perhaps," she admitted.

"He hurt you?"

Jinn pulled her hood up in preparation of a quick flight. "Not if I can help it." She thought back to her first encounter with the wizard. Then she had had a magical knife, stolen from hags. It possessed the ability to block magic. If only she had it now....

The next key Quick tried turned in the lock with a *snick*, and the door groaned open an inch. "Oh. What now?"

"Keep your voice down," said she, easing the door open the rest of the way. In her books, Jinn had read about wards that wizards of old set up around doors and windows. Wards were all but invisible, but once you attempted to walk through one, you'd find yourself thrown back, burned, or worse. "Hmm." Jinn plucked a lacey white handkerchief from the floor, wadded it into a tight ball, stood back, and threw it at the entryway. The cloth floated through the air, caught in a draft, and blew right through the entryway without being impeded or singed.

The twins looked at each other. "Why that?" Quick asked, gesturing widely, his hand passing through the entryway.

Jinn's breath caught in her throat, but she need not have worried: there really were no wards. Quick withdrew his hand, which remained unharmed. "Right. Put your boots on." As he did just that, Jinn tried to recall everything she had read about wizards in her books. Iron did not affect them like it did the Blest and other magical creatures. Perhaps it was because their blood was made entirely of the metal. So the iron fire poker could not be used to their benefit. If only she had the hags' dagger still! "No use weeping over a slaughtered sow," she muttered. What chance did she have against a magic-wielder, especially when her foresight had been depressingly silent? There had to be some advantage she possessed. If only she knew what it was.

"Jinn must look ahead," Quick said simply, as if reading her thoughts. She shook her head. "I haven't had a vision since we came here." From time to time, Jinn caught glimpses of the future without trying, thanks to the Seeing Goblet's gift. When she concentrated, she could often experience foresight that way. Not now, though. With a shudder, Jinn drew her cloak more tightly about her. "This place must really be cursed." *Or the wizard has cursed* me. *Why else can I not see my future…or his, for that matter?*

Boots on both feet, Quick lumbered to where she stood waiting. "Well? We try to escape, no?" He surprised Jinn by being the first to leave the room, after looking both ways in a not-so covert fashion. Mercifully, no alarm was sounded, and the two fled from the room, shutting the door gingerly behind them to keep up the ruse of them being contained.

They trod past many rooms, none of which seemed like they would lead to the outside. The place looked deserted, which couldn't be true; there were the meals and well-tended fire, after all. If they were truly alone, how would the magic continue to run? "Anything might be possible with a wizard," Jinn said to herself as they rounded a corner, cursing herself for having not studied more on the topic.

Quick startled Jinn by grabbing her by the back of her cloak and tunic, lifting her, and drawing her back. Met with an incredulous stare, her brother put a finger to his lips and bent down to whisper into her ear. "Someone is here. Must be quiet."

Jinn shuddered. By stupidly talking to herself, she might have given them away. "Sorry," she mouthed. She frowned. How did Quick know anyone was here?

But her brother was already moving on, tiptoeing past a closed door as best he could manage. As it was, the floorboards protested something dreadfully, and Jinn cringed, waiting to be caught. Mercifully, no one seemed to hear them. They moved on.

In the span of twenty minutes, they had explored what felt like two castles, though they'd only remained on one floor. Every window thus far had been barred with iron and warped, impossible to see through clearly. Should they ascend? Or maybe descend, as they perhaps were not at ground level.

As if reading her thoughts, Quick moved to a window that ran from floor to ceiling and peered out. This one was clearer, though still barred. The sun shone brightly in the sky, and as Jinn drew nearer to him, she heard the calling of gulls and the splashing of waves against rocks. "How we find Summoner?"

Jinn's shoulders heaved. She had not thought this through very well. "To start with," she began, this time below her breath, "we find the exit and then we work our way back from there. Perhaps we should look for signs or listen at doors or...." She was grasping at straws, and they both knew it.

Quick shook his head. "One of us must look ahead."

"I was afraid you were going to say that." Looking about, she found a small corridor, where she pulled Quick and told him to keep watch. With dread gnawing at her stomach, Jinn closed her eyes and tried to find the Summoner's future. Darkness. The Summoner's future was one gaping maw of a hole like her own. She pushed farther, thinking she might have caught a glimpse of light, and she found the Summoner during the late summer season, standing at a crossroads leading to Mother. He was with his traveling companion, the redhead. There were three packs, but no third person in sight. Shaking, Jinn drew herself back to the moment. "It's no use. I see that the Summoner and his companion leave here someday, but I cannot be certain when." She swallowed. "A third pack was there, along with theirs. It might've been yours."

"Where yours?"

Jinn sighed. Instinctively she knew that the third pack was Quick's and not hers. But why would she be left behind? "It doesn't appear that I'm with you."

Perhaps that had been the wrong thing to say. Quick's brow furrowed, and tears began to well in his large tawny eyes. "Not leaving without you. Not again."

"I know," she said soothingly, remembering with guilt how she had tricked him into leaving her so as to keep him safe. They had been in pursuit of Aidan, the Summoner, hoping to enlist his help in destroying Meraude. When Jinn's foresight had ended in darkness, she assumed she was meant to die and didn't want to entangle Quick in the same fate. So Jinn had sent him away on a fool's errand. *A lot of good* that *did*. Her plan had failed, and here they both were in this mess. "Let me try again."

But Quick shook his head and puzzled Jinn by saying, "Maybe Quick can see where you can't." Before she could ask what he meant by that, there was a shout down the hall from where they had come, followed by swearing.

"He must know we've left our room. Quick, we have no time to find the Summoner. Do you think—?"

"Quick find exit?" Quick heaved a large sigh and shook his head. "Dunno. We try, yes?" He peered around the corner and motioned for Jinn to follow him.

The shouting continued. "Save your voice, Welch."

"It's a wonder I have a voice at all after the human stabbed me. You ought to have warned me that he possessed such a blade."

Jinn.

"What?" she turned to mouth to Quick, but while she'd been pausing to listen, he must have gone forward without her. Jinn swore below her breath and, finding a staircase leading abovestairs, she started to make her way to the next floor.

No, over here.

"Quick?" she asked, turning back and following her brother's voice.

Fifth door on the right.

"Lights," she cursed under her breath, hoping her brother had found the exit. She counted the doors, got to the fifth one, whence came nothing but silence. Her hand hesitated over the knob before she turned it and stepped inside.

At once the door closed behind her and the lock slid into place. "It's all right," said the wizard's voice. "Why don't you sit while I finish up with Welch?"

Cursing her own stupidity, Jinn tried the door, which grew hot beneath her touch, causing her to pull back her hand in haste. "Stay out of my head!" she shouted, her voice trembling with rage or terror, she wasn't sure which.

"Please, make yourself at home." The room was an impressive size, filled to capacity with lush furnishings, so much so that there seemed to be no room to walk. With a sigh, the wizard emerged from behind a privacy screen just then, the front of his pale tunic covered in splotches of dark red. "It will only take a minute more."

Jinn glowered at him, and the wizard's cheeks flushed slightly as his jaw set. His eyes, however, were laughing at her.

There was a stirring behind the privacy screen, and a second man peered out at her. "You have one under your roof now?"

"Manners, Welch." The wizard – Hex, Jinn remembered – pushed the other, shorter man out of view, waved his hand, which glowed red for a moment, and then stepped back. "You will not frighten or annoy the humans, understand me?"

"What, there are two or three of them even?" Welch rasped.

Hex glared at the smaller man. "There are…well, yes. I guess there are three. For now."

The funny little man gawped at the wizard. "Are you expecting more, sir?"

"Fewer," he admitted. "Can we discuss this later?" His eyes were on Jinn again.

But Welch wasn't through. Now donning an overcoat, the squat man waddled out from behind the screen and stood just behind the wizard, his eyes narrowing. "She was not with the other two."

"No."

"She smells familiar." He started forward, but the wizard grabbed him by his overcoat and dragged him back. "What? Can't I have a look?"

Jinn's flesh prickled. Something was strange about the creature, as though he did not quite belong to this world. Perhaps it was his eyes, which, even in the light streaming through the back window, were all pupil. Or maybe it was his nostrils, two slits in the middle of his face where a nose should have been. "What are you?" Jinn found herself asking, her gaze traveling to the red scar on his throat, which was fading before her eyes.

The wizard sighed. "Don't encourage him, Jinn."

She bristled at the familiar tone he had taken with her, and then inwardly chided herself for being so silly. Manners were the least of her problems now. "Where is my brother?"

"He is safe back in your accommodations." Not taking his eyes off Jinn, the wizard pushed the strange creature, Welch, toward the door.

"Oi, this is *my* room."

Hex looked at the creature, who trembled and murmured some apology, before scurrying past Jinn and out the door. "You should not have wandered around without supervision," Hex said after a moment. "Most of the creatures here are under my control. But Welch…well, he is changeable." He motioned to the array of seating choices, but Jinn continued to stand there, arms folded across her chest, trying to look braver than she felt. After a moment of awkward silence, the wizard said, "I'm sorry. I'm not used to having humans here. Do you not sit?"

The sincerity with which he had asked the question made Jinn want to laugh, but she stopped herself and settled on an icy stare. "What are we doing here?"

"I was afraid you were going to ask that." Again he motioned toward the seats, before walking past her and taking one for himself.

"We did nothing to provoke or warrant such an attack and subsequent imprisonment. You are obligated to release us."

Hex cocked his head to the side, a small smile touching his lips. "Do you always talk like that?"

"I'm not finished."

Now the wizard was grinning. "All right. Go on."

It was a stupid impulse, one that she would perhaps regret, but Jinn approached the settee, picked up a small round pillow and threw it at his head. "Don't be insufferable."

Hex let out a roar of laughter, causing Jinn to turn and march for the door. This was going to get her nowhere fast if he would not take her seriously. Perhaps wizards adhered to a different code of decency – if they had any decency at all – and though she was a prisoner here, she did not have to stand and allow herself to be mocked.

"I'm not mocking you," he said gently, causing her to pause. "It's – it's hard to explain, but I feel like I've known you for a very long time."

Jinn did not dignify that statement with a response. Instead, she repeated her former question, "Why are we here?"

The wizard shook his head. "All in due time. First, let me explain a few rules."

"You have a lot of nerve, you—"

Hex held up a hand to quiet her. "Please, humor me for a moment. I don't mean rules of *my* making that are to be obeyed or disregarded. The *house* has rules."

She stared at him. Perhaps he was mad.

"Everything has rules, and most everything has exceptions. No one can defy the pull of the force that keeps us aground. Except for some wizards and fewer still Blest. It is not their rule, but the earth's. Just as you will find it impossible to open certain doors here, but I will have no difficulty in doing so. Everything here is cursed to follow a code."

The expression on Jinn's face must have shown her confusion, for the wizard held up a finger as if asking her to let him think more on it for a moment. He then reached for a glass goblet on the table, his hand glowing red before throwing the drinking vessel onto the floor with great force. Of all things, the glass bounced off the floor once, twice, and then rolled to a stop at Jinn's boot, unharmed.

"See? The glass could not break because I cursed it not to."

"Isn't that a blessing?"

Hex shook his head and smiled sadly. "Being forced to comply though it goes against your nature or nature itself? No, that is not a blessing. That is a curse."

Jinn hoped no fear could be read on her face as she said, "So you can control anything?"

"No, not everything. Not Welch, for example. He's a shape-shifter, one that owes me a debt of loyalty. Well, I *think* he does. A blood oath only matters to a shape-shifter if the blood that was taken was come by in their natural form. As far as I know, what you saw is the creature's base state. And even then it becomes difficult." The wizard shifted in his seat, and Jinn became aware of her own legs growing restless. "If he were to take on another form, the oath becomes diluted."

"Why do you let him stay, then? He could slaughter you in your sleep."

Hex shook his head slowly. "No, he couldn't." He did not expound that thought, but shook his head and said, "I'm sorry I left you for so long. I had to track Welch down. Apparently your Summoner stabbed him in the throat."

Jinn blanched. *And I'd been meaning to befriend that very Summoner and help him escape.* She shuddered at the thought, recalling the scar she had seen on the shape-shifter's neck.

"Sorry, I didn't mean to upset you." Now the wizard worried his lower lip and his eyes shifted ever so slightly. "Right, the rules of the house. No object can be used to purposely or accidentally harm me here. That pillow you threw just minutes ago…if it had been something heavier, say a pitcher, it wouldn't have made it to my face before it disintegrated."

Well, that was good to know, should Quick or she try to physically attack him.

Hex seemed to have read her thoughts again. "Anything living would just be thrown backward."

She nodded. "I see."

"The second rule of the house: no human or Blest can purposely harm themselves or another guest. If you tried, say, hitting yourself, your hand would hit an invisible wall before it could make contact. And finally," he said, sitting forward, "no one's magic works directly against my magic here."

Jinn unfolded her arms and shifted her weight. She really should sit, but her pride and fear would not allow it.

Perhaps knowing this, the wizard gave her a wry smile. "You might want to pass that on to your Summoner friend."

She frowned. "He is not my friend. I don't even know him."

"I know you don't," Hex countered. "But that did not stop you from pursuing him and his mate." He said the word 'mate' with narrowed eyes for some reason Jinn could not fathom, but when that drew no response from her, his eyes widened again. "Why did you want to find Aidan Ingledark, Jinn?"

"Why don't you just read my mind?" she retorted.

Hex shook his head. "Wizards don't read minds, we read faces. And body language. And we can smell some emotions."

Wonderful. That is the very last thing I need. Jinn clenched her fists at her side.

"What can a Summoner do for you that your brother cannot?" He studied her intensely. "Or *will* not...?"

What if the wizard was allied with Meraude? She knew that a wizard had sided with mortals before the other Great Wizards' blood was drained and used to make the Goblets. Would he side with Mother and stop Jinn from destroying her? She could not risk him getting between her and the so-called mage queen. Jinn closed her mouth and said nothing.

The wizard's intensity lasted for but a moment longer, fading to a blank look as he seemed to realize that Jinn wasn't going to answer his question. He stretched out his legs in front of him and shook his head. "There is no Questing Goblet."

At that, Jinn's heart leapt within her breast, and the wizard gave her a curious look. "That's good, isn't it? That means that she— *no one* is invincible."

Hex frowned.

"Except you, of course," she amended.

Something seemed to pain him, but he shook it off like a dog ridding itself of fleas and when he spoke, it was as though he were thinking out loud. "Maybe it's nothing. Maybe there do not need to be six. But I

need the Goblets. All that there are. Maybe that will still stop…things."
He stared at Jinn with haunted eyes, and then looked away. "I think you
should probably leave now."

"Good. I'll get Quick and we'll be on our way."

Hex laughed. "I did not mean *that* far." He approached Jinn slowly,
stopping when she stiffened. "Right. You'll need to stay on the premises
while I figure out what needs to be done. It won't be forever. Don't see
yourself as a prisoner here, Jinn, just a…a…."

"Guest by force?"

The wizard's eyes twinkled. "If you like. Come, I'll return you to
your quarters."

Jinn didn't move. She did not want to be shut up in that room again,
as comfortable as it might be. She needed air, to be outside. She hadn't
seen the sun but through glass for days.

"We're overlooking a cliff on every side, I'm afraid. The land does
change from time to time, but going outside would be difficult at
the moment."

She nodded, swallowing down her panic and willing tears not to
form in her eyes. "Right." There had to be a way out of this place,
other than through this wizard. Unless he had some weakness she
could exploit. Looking at him now, that did not seem likely. He had
changed her into a bird without batting an eye. Turning her back
to human form had caused him some apparent trouble, though. Yes,
there was a chink in his armor. After all, her own magic, foresight,
wasn't perfect. This would be the hope she would cling to in the days
to come, Jinn decided.

Hex cocked his head to the side, most likely alert to her changing
mood. "Perhaps tomorrow I'll show you more of the house. It will be
safer then." He motioned for her to follow him to the door, and then
stepped through first, pausing and causing Jinn to run into him.

The shape-shifter was waiting just outside, staring and picking at his
nails. "What?" he said as the wizard did not move. "It *is* my room."

"For now," said Hex, putting himself between the creature and Jinn.
Welch relented with a huff and returned to his room, slamming the

door behind him, nearly shutting it on the tail protruding from the back of his trousers.

Jinn blinked in surprise but said nothing as the wizard took her lightly by the elbow and steered her back toward the guest quarters. As they walked in silence, she made sure to note where the unbarred windows were. Perhaps her captor was lying about the cliffs. She would see for herself, before she ruled out outright escape from her mind.

"I'm sorry for pitting the Summoner against you, but if I hand Aidan allies, he'll surely use them against me," Hex said as they arrived outside the room where Quick could be heard snoring. "Perhaps I could have used it to my advantage, rather."

"I'm used to being a pawn," she said bitterly. "You have an end in sight, though I don't know what it is. We're all playing a game, aren't we?"

The wizard regarded her for a moment, his expression unreadable. The door creaked open without either of them touching it, and he folded his arms across his chest. "'Game' is perhaps too light a word for the trouble we now find ourselves in."

What was she supposed to say to that? "All right, then." She turned and was about to reenter her prison, but his hand alighted on her shoulder, staying her.

"Forgive me," he said when she froze, letting his hand drop. "How did you get the lock open?"

"You're joking, aren't you?" she said, hugging herself.

The wizard smirked. "I'll find out eventually. It would be in your own best interest to let me know now."

"Are you threatening me?"

"No," he said. "I told you, it isn't safe for humans to wander around here without protection."

Jinn frowned. "The house rules...."

"Protect mortals from each other. They do not protect mortals from the house," he admitted. He leaned in, and Jinn drew back. "The house plays favorites. There hasn't been a human here in over five hundred years. I don't know yet what the house will make of you."

Well, that was disconcerting. "There were keys," she said, stopping him from entering the room.

Hex's eyes widened. "Where?"

"I found them in the wardrobe."

He stared at her, apparently disbelieving. After a moment, he did step past her and entered the room, then returned with the heavy ring of keys in hand. "If these turn up again," he said, his tone light, "please don't use them. But do tell me."

"All right."

"Promise me?"

Jinn sighed. "Fine. I promise."

Hex nodded, though his expression was wary. "Until tomorrow."

She did not dignify that with a response, but entered the room, stifling a sob when the door clicked shut behind her. Shaking, she turned and put her hands on the wood, which grew hot beneath her touch. "A ward? Curse you," she said, realizing he had not believed her promise… rightfully so. "There's got to be another way out of here."

CHAPTER THREE

Aidan

Once Aidan had come to his senses, he ran for the washing tub he had found earlier and tried lifting it. Full of water, the tub was too difficult to move without help, so he grabbed the pitcher sitting next to it, filled it, ran back to the blaze, and threw the water at it. The water evaporated with a sizzle and hiss as soon as it came in contact with the flames. The fire, oddly enough, was not spreading, but remained a steady, thick wall between him and Slaíne. "Are you all right?" he shouted, but the sound bounced back at him, and he doubted she could hear what he said. Knowing it to be fruitless, Aidan threw down the metal pitcher, which clanged on the floor, and watched as the blaze sputtered and snapped. He paced.

What might have been fifteen minutes passed, and the flames were slowly burning down to nothing. Aidan could see Slaíne on the other side of the wall of fire. He shouted a few times, and he saw her mouth working as well, but there was nothing to be done. Another fifteen minutes, and the flames were ankle-high. Aidan tried stepping over them, but the fire flared up again, and neither attempted approaching it until the blaze was nothing but sparks on the floor.

Slaíne's swearing was the first thing he heard as they flew at each other. "What was that?" she said as they checked each other for burns. "Are you all right?"

"Are *you* all right? How did you do that?"

"Me? I didn't do that," she said. "I thought...."

Relief at finding her unharmed was wearing off, and he found himself growing angry, something he could see reflected in her own eyes. "You thought that I somehow did that? Summoning fire is impossible."

Of all things, Slaíne laughed, a real roar of sound that grated on Aidan's nerves. But then she stopped and looked at him knowingly. "You angry?"

His mouth worked for a moment, opening and closing as if of its own accord, before he assessed himself, and realized there was no good reason for him to feel so. "I'm sorry. I don't know why I blamed you." The words were difficult to say, and they cost him what was left of his patience. He turned his back and walked to the other side of the room. *What is wrong with me?* Looking back over the past few weeks, he realized what had caused his previous moments of misplaced anger with Slaíne. This was not the same. This was different, alien. It felt... other.

He became aware of Salem in the Beyond, trying to reach him through their peculiar connection. That threw some cold water on his temper, but the rage was still there, simmering.

"It might've been me fault," she said, and it sounded difficult for her to admit. "But I s'pose 'twas neither of us. This house...it feels all wrong."

That sparked something in Aidan's memory, and his temper cooled a little more. He looked over his shoulder. "Hex called this place the 'House of Curses'. You don't suppose—"

"That this house is cursed? Maybe. I dunno."

Again Aidan faced the wall. He needed to think. If this house was cursed, it must have been cursed by a wizard – presumably, Hex, their jailer. But didn't something have to trigger a curse?

"Yes, somethin' usually triggers a curse," Slaíne conceded, reading his thoughts once again. "Least, that's what happened with my curse. Don't know if that holds true to all curses, but seems likely, don't it?"

Putting his mind to a problem drained the rest of his rage, and he turned back to face Slaíne and approached her with caution. "Right. So, what did we do that might have invoked a curse? And does it matter?"

Of course it matters, you great idiot, if you don't want a large fire erupting unexpectedly every now and again.

Slaíne snorted. "Right. It do matter." She waited a moment and then marched to the door, which she laid a hand on, speaking to herself. *No wards that I can feel.*

Aidan blinked, startled again at her having spoken directly into his mind. "How do you know?"

"Lemme answer your question with another. How does we know it were a curse and not something we— *I* did?"

"Well...I have no idea."

"Wards, from what the elves did tell, are hot to the touch. But this place...." She sighed. "This whole place is cold to you and not to me. Why is that, you think?" Her look was expectant, reminding Aidan of a teacher looking at a particularly promising pupil.

After a moment of thought, he said, "Magic?"

"Right. Wizard magic must be cold. I'm cold to ya 'cause I'm a wizard. The house is cold because it's under a wizard's magic – *curses.*" She worried her lower lip before continuing. "But that nay does explain the heat of a ward and the wall of flame that came up 'tween us." With a shout of frustration, she kicked at the door, only to be knocked backward. "Well, this keeps gettin' stranger."

Aidan nodded, his thoughts still churning, as Salem's voice died out entirely from his mind. "The two are similar – the heat of a ward and the hot fire wall between us. Then the wall might have been a ward." He sighed. "Ward magic must have heat. But as to what we did that would trigger a ward...." They stared at each other, willing the other to come up with the answer.

A smile twisted the corners of Slaíne's lips, not an entirely friendly one. "The wizard must be afraid, if'n he's puttin' up wards around us. That's something. We could use his fear to our 'vantage...."

"Or make him so suspicious he never lets us out of his sight."

"Maybe it's both," she said, and Aidan knew she was referring to something earlier in their conversation, but she did not elaborate, and he did not press her for information. After a moment, she shook her head and moved away from the door. "There ain't no ward on the door, but there's now some magic that weren't there before, keepin' me from hittin' it too hard."

Aidan approached the door. He tried focusing on the inner workings of the lock, but they felt like nothing he had ever encountered before. Combining that with the fact that his abilities had changed, he knew that he wouldn't be able to dismantle it…yet, at least. "What if I tried Dismissing us both?" He looked to Slaíne, who shook her head. "What?"

"Why don't you try just yourself?" When he opened his mouth to protest, she waylaid him by saying, "My power is too strange in Nothingness. 'Sides, there ain't a curse binding me to anyone no more. Won't hurt to leave me."

He studied her for a moment, and then closed his eyes and tried to focus on Releasing every object in the room. But every object, each an anchor holding him to Existence, proved to be too strong, and he found himself lying on the floor without knowing how he had gotten there. "Well, that didn't work."

Slaíne looked down at him. "It almost did. You faded for a moment."

A pounding headache was forming behind Aidan's eyes. He sat up and rubbed his brow, and noticed that Slaíne was doing the same. "I think I'll wait before trying that again." *If I try again at all.* He got to his feet and closed his eyes, feeling for his cache in Nothingness. As before, he had trouble latching on to any one object, but this time his reach didn't overshoot the place for the Beyond.

"Anything there to pick a lock with?"

Aidan was aware that Slaíne had closed her eyes and was joining in his search. He did not stop her, but clenched his fists and forced himself to ignore her. "There's nothing here that will do, save for the knife, perhaps." They both opened their eyes, their headaches abating by a degree. He took up the blade and approached the door, exploring the lock with a squinted eye rather than his extra sense. Then, with nothing to lose, he inserted the knife's tip and wiggled it around a little. "The blade is too thick. Could you try Dismissing the lock?"

"Me?"

"You're the wizard."

Slaíne sighed and said something unintelligible before approaching the door again. "I'll try, but you gotta come to accept and understand yer own powers, Aidan. Summoning and the like is a borrowed ability. It ain't common to my magic."

Aidan stared at her blankly.

It would seem she was in no mood to explain how she knew anything at all about her magic or his ability, but reached out a hand and closed her own eyes. "Put the knife away. Yer makin' me nervous."

After one failed attempt, Aidan managed to Dismiss it. "Stop straining your body. The power to Dismiss comes from your mind."

"Oh, hush. I'll learn meself," she snarled.

The stirring in Aidan's chest began again as she tried using his power, but this time he did not fight her. He was tempted to offer more instruction, but thought better of it and simply watched as sweat formed on her brow. *She's going to faint if she holds her breath any longer.*

Keep your thoughts to yourself, she pressed back. For a moment, instead of being Dismissed, it seemed that the door and its lock were bending their natures. Their Pulls had gone strange, and the quality was nigh liquid.

"You're not Dismissing," he said with a groan. "Slaíne, you're adding new properties to the lock and door. Please, stop before you hurt yourself." *Or make the door even more difficult to open.*

Cursing, she opened her eyes. Then, fingertips glowing and spitting blue sparks, she turned from the door and stalked away.

Aidan watched her a moment longer, wondering. Perhaps it was a foolish idea, but fire seemed to be tied to Slaíne's anger, the one thing she had some control over. As soon as the thought had formed, she heard it and turned.

"That sounds real dangerous."

"I know. It's a risk." He grimaced.

"An' what if this wizard's my one chance at learning magic? Can't risk burning us all to a crisp."

That was an excellent point. Aidan took to pacing, stopping when he heard a tiny popping sound. The door groaned on its hinges and opened a few inches. Not waiting to question why it had happened,

Aidan seized Slaíne by the hand and pulled the door the rest of the way open.

"Why'd it open?" she asked him, her voice bouncing off the walls as they stepped out into the hallway.

Aidan hushed her and looked around. There were no human Pulls in the near vicinity, though he didn't trust himself to be a good judge of this fact at the moment, what with his magic having changed.

This way.

The hairs on the back of Aidan's neck rose and he looked at Slaíne. She seemed to have heard the words as well. "Where did it come from?"

She pointed with her free hand down a corridor to the left. "It sounded like it was comin' from that way."

"Then let's go the other."

They passed suits of strange-looking armor the color of pitch, and rich tapestries that told terrible tales and seemed to whisper at them as they passed. There were many rooms in the hall that seemed to stretch on for miles, and when they finally reached the end of the hall and were forced to choose right or left again, they came upon the first window. Drawn to the sound of calling gulls and roaring waves, Aidan looked through the immaculate glass and found himself staring down the face of a cliff. So the wizard Hex hadn't been lying: the House of Curses was perched atop a sheer face of rock. Escaping would prove…problematic. Aidan turned to relate this fact to his mate, but again he heard the voice:

You can't run. Open the door, Aidan.

Aidan's attention was at once drawn to the left, where sat a round red door. He regarded it for a moment, and then turned his attention to Slaíne, a question on his lips.

They exchanged a glance before he reached for the brass doorknob and turned it.

The room was dimly lit, the floors a polished black that reflected what light there was. All the furniture – blood-red lounges and settees and an overstuffed chair or two – had been pushed to the side, making an aisle of sorts to a fireplace simmering with red flames. And by one obsidian wall stood the wizard. He stared at them both, his expression unamused.

After a moment of cool regard, Hex spoke. "I have lived many years, and in none of them have I sensed such a reckless use of magic."

At once Aidan's spine stiffened, and he felt Slaíne go rigid beside him. The air was charged with everyone's anger, and the flames in the fireplace began to dance as they had the last time Aidan had seen the wizard.

Much to Aidan's surprise, Slaíne said nothing to contradict Hex, but spoke directly into Aidan's mind. *Don't let him bait you.*

He shivered as the words curled around his thoughts and cooled his rage by a degree. "You've taken your time in summoning us."

Steady, Aidan.

Aidan surprised himself by snarling at her, baring his teeth before recalling himself and cringing. *What has gotten into me?*

"You haven't told him," Hex said, sounding puzzled. "Why?"

"He knows what I am," Slaíne replied, her tone measured.

Hex shook his head and some of the anger seemed to go out of him. "You," he said to Aidan, motioning to one of the chairs pushed off to the side, "sit. If you're not able to participate, you need to be off our field."

Confused, Aidan hesitated. "What do you plan on doing?" He found himself putting his body between the two wizards, though he realized it was perhaps not the wisest of moves.

The male wizard regarded Aidan, measuring him with his eyes. "Testing her mettle. It shouldn't take long. Then we'll discuss what is to happen here." He cocked his head to the side, listening to sounds that Aidan could not hear, and frowned. "This house is going to be the death of me."

Aidan looked to Slaíne, but she seemed no more enlightened than he was.

"Right. Out of the way. We have only a moment." Hex threw out his hand and Aidan found himself sliding across the floor and landing with a none-too-gentle thud in one of the chairs on the outskirts of the large room.

The two wizards stood facing each other, paces apart, a low growl rumbling in Hex's throat. Before either Slaíne or Aidan could react, a continuous bolt of silver light flew from Hex's fingertips and hit her in the chest. She screamed the most unearthly shriek Aidan had ever heard, her back arching as she contorted in apparent pain.

Aidan was on his feet in an instant, meaning to put himself between the older wizard and Slaíne, but Hex flicked his wrist, and Aidan went flying back. Again he was on his feet, knowing it was futile. Helpless, he was flung back once more as Slaíne continued to scream and her body took on a silver glow.

"Most wizards are half-human," said Hex. "Usually the mother is a mortal."

With apparent effort, Slaíne drew her hands in front of herself, attempting to stop the attack. She glowed all the brighter for her effort.

The older wizard's face twisted and he said quite calmly, "But you have no mother, do you, Slaíne, daughter of none?" The flare of light doubled in brightness. "Too much concentrated power. Too much instability. I should kill you right here and now."

"For pity's sake, stop!" Aidan cried, attempting again to charge at him, only to be thrown back yet again. "Both her parents were mortal. They were woodworkers."

Hex sneered at Aidan. "So she believes...so *you* believe. Her blood, however, is telling me a different tale."

Now Slaíne stopped screaming, silver blood leaking from the tips of her fingers. She whimpered once and collapsed.

Panting, Hex let the bolt of silver light evaporate, leaving his victim on the floor shaking and writhing. "No, stay where you are, Ingledark. She'll attack if you approach her now."

But Aidan would not listen. He ran for her, and indeed, she lashed out with a bolt of light of her own, missing Aidan by inches. The bolt hit the chair in which he had been sitting, splintering it to pieces.

Slaíne looked at him, eyes wild, as he froze. *I'm sorry.*

Heart racing and hands sweating, Aidan only nodded. He turned to the older wizard, who watched him with interest. "Let her go," Aidan said.

"She is too dangerous, Ingledark." Hex still seemed out of breath, which brought Aidan some measure of satisfaction. "A wizard of single parentage is not unheard of, but a *female* wizard on top of that? I need to study this."

"Slaíne is not some specimen in a jar to be poked and prodded for answers." Hatred filled Aidan's breast, and he found himself longing to destroy this wizard who had hurt his mate. So strong were his feelings that his vision began to blur around the edges, and everything around him seemed to take on a green hue. He closed his eyes and shook himself, willing logic and reason to return. He noticed a Pull approaching the door, and when Hex became aware of the new presence a few seconds after Aidan had, Aidan took advantage of the wizard's distraction and threw himself down by Slaíne.

"I wouldn't," she murmured as he reached for her.

Aidan ignored Slaíne's warning and lifted her partially into his lap. "Are you all right?" He felt foolish the moment the words left his lips, knowing well that she wasn't. "Is there anything I can do?"

Silver tears rolled down her cheeks as he stroked her hair. "He ain't gonna kill me, Aidan. Don't worry." The words came out a weak croak, and she only sounded half-convinced of their validity herself.

The Pull that Aidan had sensed was now at the door, which creaked open. The woman he had seen days before stood there, seeming uncertain of herself as she picked at the neck of her cloak with one hand. Then she looked down at Slaíne and swore.

"Jinn," said Hex. "It's all right. You can come in. Just don't get too near to those two." The 'they're not safe' was implied in his tone, as if Slaíne were some wild animal and not a wizard like Hex himself.

The woman hesitated a moment more before shaking her head and slipping inside. "What happened?" she asked.

"Nothing to be concerned about," Hex replied.

Jinn's gaze met Aidan's, a question reflected in her eyes. Before she could voice what she wanted to say, Hex interrupted.

"How did you get out this time?"

Her head snapped around so fast, Aidan swore he could hear her neck crack. "I'm sure you would like to know." No other answer was forthcoming.

Slaíne shuddered and attempted sitting up, only to collapse with a grunt. It would seem that she would not be running to safety any time soon, but at least with the woman Jinn here, Hex seemed unwilling to attack again.

"Jinn, I wouldn't...."

The strange woman ignored his warning and stepped fully into the room, hands clenched into loose fists. "Don't mind me," she said, her tone sweet yet somehow caustic. "Or should I go lock myself back up and wait for you to make up your mind whether or not you're going to kill us all?"

"No one's going to be killed, Jinn. I think you know that."

Jinn moved closer to the wizard, slipping her hands behind her back as she put herself between Hex and Aidan. "Why should I know that?"

Aidan blinked. Perhaps it was bravado, or maybe the woman was unafraid of the wizard, but Aidan sensed something strange was at work. *What is going on here?*

Having heard his thought, Slaíne stirred and spoke back into his mind. *She's the one who was after us, yes?*

"I think so," he murmured, causing Hex to look at him oddly.

Don't answer me out loud, Slaíne warned him. *I don't know if a wizard is s'posed to talk to other people like this.*

Fortunately, Hex's attention had returned to Jinn. "I'm sorry you feel that way, Jinn." He did not sound sorry. He sounded amused to Aidan's ears. Yes, something strange was going on here indeed.

Aidan, where she stands, I could stop her from e'er botherin' us again. I've got a clear shot.

He was about to answer, when he noticed the woman's hands start gesturing behind her back: one was open somewhat, though her fingers were curling around something, and the other hand was pointing to it. *Let's not be too hasty, Slaíne.*

That seemed to upset his mate, but she did not reply, nor did she attack.

There's something in her hand, he thought after a moment. *I'm having difficulty exploring its Pull. Can you sense it?* Indeed, judging from Jinn repeatedly pointing at her occupied hand, Aidan knew whatever it contained was meant for him.

Sláine snorted as the wizard and Jinn continued to argue about many different things, none of them making sense to Aidan. *I'm not used to Pulls an' how they make a body feel.* She hesitated. *Lemme help you, though.* Both of their eyes went to Hex for a moment, before she placed a hand over Aidan's heart and closed her eyes.

It was at that moment that Aidan's senses became heightened, and he was aware of a weak Pull in Jinn's hand. Delaying no longer, he latched on to the object's Pull and Summoned it into his own hand, swiftly tucking it into his sleeve and not a moment too soon: the wizard looked over Jinn's shoulder at him, frowned, and then returned his attention to Jinn, who seemed to take offense at something and stormed out of the room.

Hex shook his head and sighed. "I had hoped to have a meeting of minds, but mortals are so very unpredictable." The half-smile he had quirked faded and he approached. "I'm not going to hurt anyone."

Aidan grimaced. "It's a little late for that promise, don't you think?"

"I'll allow you time to rest and recover," Hex said, ignoring Aidan's words. "After that, we'll begin training." He held up a hand to waylay their questions. "There is nothing more dangerous than a wizard who has great power but no knowledge of how to wield it. I'll help you, but in return I must ask that you do not attempt anything foolish." His eyes narrowed. "Your door will remain unlocked and without a ward...for now. Just know that this house is not entirely safe for anyone.

"You'll find food and drink in your room when you return. I suggest you bolt your door." The wizard turned his back on them, and Aidan took that as their dismissal.

He helped Sláine to her feet, though she proved too weak to support her own weight, so he lifted and carried her back to their room. Once they were back inside their quarters, Aidan gave the door a kick in an attempt to close it and set Sláine down on the bed.

She sighed and her eyes closed. "You get the note?"

Aidan pulled his hand out of his sleeve and produced the piece of paper, which he unfolded. "It's in Abrish," he said, passing it on to Slaíne, whom he knew could read the northern language. "You can read it later, if you're too tired."

"I ain't too tired, but there's somethin' you ought to know afore anythin' else is said."

He smoothed out her creased brow as she studied the note. "What is it? What's wrong?"

Slaíne sucked in a deep breath. "I know him, this wizard what's got us, this so-called Hex." She hesitated. "I nay did want to say nothin', for fear what you might do. Promise me you won't do nothin' stupid."

The hairs on the back of Aidan's neck prickled as he regarded her. "How do you know him?" he said, reluctant to promise anything.

She shook her head and clenched the note in her fist. "Hex is the one who cursed me when I was a child."

CHAPTER FOUR

Aidan

Aidan felt his face reddening. His jaw clenched and his whole body trembled with barely suppressed rage. "Are you sure it's him?" He knew that Slaíne wasn't mistaken. He could sense the certainty and anger pouring off of her in waves – something that he did not stop and consider strange until later. Aidan turned from her before she could witness his loss of self-control and marched toward the door, which she slammed shut in his face with her mind.

"It's my job to avenge my own self. It's none of your doin'," she said, and Aidan realized she relished the idea, though why she was holding back now was beyond him at the moment.

He turned and faced her, feeling less and less human and more like an animal as the seconds passed. *What is wrong with me?* He became aware of Salem pushing his way into the back of his mind.

She's hiding something, his possessor said.

Slaíne's eyes flashed and she pointed a finger at Aidan's forehead, causing Salem's voice to quiet. Trembling, she propped a pillow behind her. "Your friend talks too much."

Aidan frowned. "If I'm not to avenge you, then why did you tell me?"

"Because I nay want ya trustin' him. And I need you angry right now." She gave him a meaningful look.

He tried to push the rage aside, but Slaíne seemed to be pushing it right back at him. "Why are you doing that?" he asked, clenching his teeth. "You're exhausted and hurt. Stop trying to provoke me if I'm to do nothing about the wizard."

Now Slaíne was panting, her will fighting against Aidan's. "I was goin' to give you time to come into it on your own, but you're too stubborn and some things need ter happen faster." He blinked, and she shook her head. "The note says that Meraude is building an army of Blest."

Aidan's blood ran cold. "An army of Blest?"

Slaíne took advantage of his distraction by pushing all her anger into him through their peculiar mental bond. The weight of it made Aidan's shoulders sag, and he felt something deep within stirring, something that froze his bones. Spots formed in the corners of his vision, and Aidan blinked furiously.

"Stop fighting me," Slaíne growled. "You need to accept what you are now."

"What I am now?" He grunted as the cold made his hairs stand on end, despite the warmth of the cloak he wore. Pain like he had felt in Nothingness ripped through his muscles, and he opened his mouth to scream. The two souls in his chest writhed as green fire rippled under his skin, catching his clothes ablaze.

"Sorry about that," Slaíne said, eyes rolling back into her head as she stilled.

Aidan ran for the washtub, flames billowing from his body. The fire licked at the tapestries, but they did not catch, nor did the wine-red curtains hanging from the window as he ran past. He fell into the tub, which was large enough for two people, took a deep breath, and then ducked his head under the water. Although he was on fire, Aidan shivered with irrepressible chills. It felt like someone was freezing him from within. *What did she do to me?* Behind his closed lids, he saw the fire still raging through him and from him.

This was worse than the experience in Nothingness. *Then* he had had Slaíne talking to him, soothing and reassuring him after she had plucked out part of her own soul and placed it inside his chest. *Now* she was silent.

The water around him began to freeze. His limbs became heavy, and sleep tugged at his eyelids. Aidan tried moving, tried rising to the surface to draw the breath his lungs were burning for, but his joints locked.

Slaíne! he screamed in his mind, hoping that by some miracle his words would reach her.

His eyes closed, the pain ebbed, and the water around him turned to solid ice. He shivered once, and his soul fled to the Beyond, the land of the magical dead.

Salem stood waiting for him, a grim expression on his face. "We don't have much time to talk, Aidan," said he. "I know your mate doesn't want us exchanging many words. She doesn't like thinking of you as possessed…which you aren't exactly."

Distracted from Salem's words, Aidan blinked. His body was rippling with a strange green light, and he felt energized as he never had before. At least, his mind did. His body, where he had left it, was probably going to suffocate by the time it woke up or someone found him. Aidan said as much out loud.

"No, Aidan. I don't think you can die that way. Not a fitting way for a wizard to go, that." He looked at Aidan knowingly and offered a weak laugh. "I always thought I'd be the powerful one. You – you be careful that you don't let it go to your head. We need you. More than ever before."

Aidan shook his head, trying to rid himself of the waves of energy pouring out of him. "So that's what happened when she put part of her soul in me."

"I see you're not going to let go of that easily." Salem sighed and motioned for Aidan to follow him to the barn, which had exploded in Existence when Aidan had first discovered his abilities as a Summoner. Here it was fully intact… and a lot smaller than Aidan remembered. "We don't want anyone else knowing you're here, especially the state you're in. Wizards are not quite welcome here, but not entirely forbidden…I hope."

"There are no wizards in the Beyond?" He shuddered and tried to think of himself as now belonging to that group, but found it difficult to believe, though each step he took threatened to consume the ground beneath him with power.

Salem gave him a pitying look and shut the door behind them. With Aidan lit up like a fireplace, they didn't need to light a lamp, which made the strange Endurer – a magical being who was extremely strong and mostly invulnerable to attack – chuckle. "You look like you've been hit by lightning," he said with a laugh.

Aidan narrowed his eyes. "You don't seem surprised at finding me this way."

The man shrugged and sat on a hay bale. *"I've been following most of your adventures through our connection, though it is harder to reach you now wherever you are."*

Aidan thought to tell Salem that they were in the House of Curses with the wizard named Hex, but something made him hesitate. *"Salem,"* Aidan said sharply, *"how much of our conversations stay between us?"*

A look of hurt crossed the other's face, but he smoothed it over and continued to speak in a light tone. *"Anything you say to me stays between us...unless I think Treevain needs to hear it. She's good, Aidan."*

Aidan had groaned at the mention of the she-elf, a miserable, ugly old creature who had tried to kill him shortly after their first meeting. Granted, he had stolen Slaine from her and her sisters, along with keeping the Warring Goblet, which he had been supposed to hand over. *"Treevain spoke with me, and she seemed to be on our side of things,"* he conceded, albeit reluctantly. *"There's something afoot here, though."* He grabbed a bolt of fire that had made its way toward Salem, stopping it inches from the man's chest, before it evaporated. *"You would tell me if there was something I ought to know here, wouldn't you?"*

Salem frowned. *"Of course. We're f-friends. You need to learn to trust me."* Aidan began to say something on that score, but Salem held up his hands and waylaid any comments, his now-nervous eyes never leaving the fire surrounding Aidan. *"Now that you're a wizard, our contact will become even more limited. So listen to me. You are with someone powerful – besides your mate – I can feel their power pushing through the barriers of the worlds. Get as far away from him or her as possible. We can't have anyone interfering with the plan."*

"The plan?" said Aidan with a scowl.

"Find the remaining Goblets and take them to the Seeing Pool in the north. There they can and must be destroyed. You did find the Questing Goblet, didn't you?"

Aidan hesitated. How much did he trust this possessor of his?

"Aidan?"

"No, I don't have the Questing Goblet. It – it wasn't at Cedric's grave." Half of the truth, though perhaps enough of it for the other to guess.

The man eyed him, his expression grim. *"Well, that can only mean one of two things, either you're lying or there is no Questing Goblet. Which would* mean...." He swore. "Cedric's alive, isn't he? Well, at least Meraude can't have complete success at everything she does. Though, that means exactly the same thing for us."

"What of the armies in the Beyond?" Aidan asked, watching the other carefully for any signs of deception. "What is the situation here?"

Salem tore his gaze away from the flames and looked straight at Aidan. "I can't tell you."

It was Aidan's turn to swear.

"Peace, friend. I can't tell you in case you're cap— well, you're already captured. But I can't tell you in case you're tortured or your mind's tampered with. Let's just say that there are ways to deal with Meraude now, and they're being put into place." Though Salem said the words with confidence, a shadow of worry and doubt crossed his features. He noticed the look Aidan was giving him, and smiled. "No one's really telling me much, but I have eyes and ears of my own to observe."

"What good is an army in the Beyond?" said Aidan as more power surged out of him. He felt boxed in, stifled, like someone had tied him up too tightly in heavy chains.

Salem stepped back, avoiding being struck by any of the green waves of energy emitting from Aidan. "The thing is...I think there might be a way to bridge worlds. They're calling it 'Death's Key'. The—"

Aidan's eyes snapped open in Existence. He was encased in ice, and Salem was silent in the back of his mind, his presence having retreated so far that Aidan could no longer feel him. With a grunt, Aidan tried breaking free from the ice, only to find himself too weak.

The flames that had engulfed him were gone, though Aidan still felt like he was ablaze. He tried taking a breath, which was his impulse, but found that nothing was entering his lungs, and with nothing in his lungs, he couldn't make any sounds. *How am I not dead?* He tried pushing a few thoughts at Slaíne, but she was strangely quiet. He could feel her there on the other end of their connection, and she was pure exhaustion and pain. Though he was tired himself, he reached deep inside and found his last shreds of strength, but instead of his arms moving, the ice around him shattered into millions of tiny pieces, responding merely to his thoughts.

Gasping, Aidan pulled himself out of the tub and fell over onto the floor, where he slipped into a deep, dreamless sleep, with no contact from Salem, only the distant impression that they were running out of time.

★   ★   ★

When he awoke, he was in bed, his head pounding. Aidan reached out and felt for Pulls, and was startled to find a very important one no longer in the room with him. He blinked a few times and groaned. As he had thought, Slaíne had left him alone.

Cursing, Aidan sat up and made to find her, following her Pull, but a wave of exhaustion overtook him and he lay back onto the mattress with a grunt. This was no good. He needed to find Slaíne and discuss the note from that woman – Jinn – along with the vision of Salem in the Beyond. Maybe she would have an idea of how an army of the dead might pass into Existence. *Death's Key*....

Aidan drew in a deep breath, braced himself mentally, and sat up. He groaned. While he'd slept, his clothes had been stripped away. They'd been burned and tattered from his conversion – or whatever one might call it – of that he was certain. But this spoke to something sinister. He had a feeling there was something else at play here.

He threw himself out of bed, and began searching for something to clothe himself with so that he might go after her. The thought of Slaíne facing the wizard, her curser, put a weight in Aidan's stomach, and he knew he would not rest easy until she was found. "Slaíne," he growled, finding the wardrobe empty. There were no chest of drawers, no compartments, nor nooks nor crannies, just the bed, the washtub, and the wardrobe. Tapestries hung from the walls, and there were sheets on the bed.... "I'd look a right fool, running around with one of those draped around me. What was she thinking?"

Maybe Slaíne wants to be alone. She has, after all, not been in true solitude since the curse took her, said the fair part of his mind. Aidan hushed the thought and went for the towel by the washing-up tub. After wrapping it around himself, Aidan approached the door and tried to open it. It was locked.

Cursing, he stepped away.

Are you awake? Her voice sounded surprised, though he felt a hint of amusement slither down their mental link.

Aidan shuddered. "Would you like to explain what's happening?"

Silence.

"Slaíne?"

There was some panting followed by a breathless laugh that caused Aidan to flush. *You should go back ter sleep, Aidan. I can feel yer exhaustion.*

He ignored that. "Where are you?" He grimaced. Being apart from her was akin to pain. Aidan hadn't realized how accustomed he'd become to the strength of her Pull, anchoring him and centering him. Now, with it no longer nigh at hand, he felt strongly deprived and irritable, something he hoped she couldn't sense.

Again she laughed. *I'm safe, love. Just workin' on my skills.*

Aidan blinked. "You're with Hex, aren't you?" When she didn't answer immediately, he closed his eyes and reached out and searched for human Pulls. As he had expected, he found one lesser Pull in the same vicinity that he sensed hers. But as he explored the Pulls, he realized that this one was not Hex's. "Who's with you?"

No one.

She was being honest; he could feel it through their link. "There is someone near you – someone within striking distance, Slaíne."

Slaíne swore. *I must get used ter these Pulls. Don't understand what half of these feelings mean.*

As he opened his eyes, he became aware of her Pull moving nearer, and sighed in relief. The other Pull, the lesser, somewhat familiar one, stayed where it was. Aidan didn't want to appear overly anxious, so he returned to the bed and covered himself before lying on his back. He mentally tracked her Pull, knowing she was nearing him as it grew in intensity, and sensed her hesitating at the door. Frowning, he sat up. He felt a strange shudder run down his spine, as though someone were raking a hot hand down the length of his back as the lock turned and the door opened.

After first bolting it behind her, Slaíne turned and looked at him strangely. Her eyes were that odd glowing blue again, and her face was red from exertion. Aidan assumed it was exertion, at least, because she was breathing hard and she was covered in sweat.

They regarded each other for a moment. Her thoughts were suddenly silent to him, but her feelings were not.

Aidan swallowed. "Why did you lock me in?" he asked as she padded toward him.

Slaíne flipped the covers down and crawled in bed with him. "So you'd do nothin' foolish." She stopped his words with a kiss.

He pulled back. "Nothing foolish? What do you think I am? Some liability?"

Her left hand roved over him, tracing his muscles lower and lower, until he snatched her by the fingertips. She grinned at him wickedly, the glow in her eyes intensifying. "Do nay look at me like that, Aidan Ingledark. Yer no liability. But make no mistake, you are mine, and I intend to keep what is mine safe." She leaned down and kissed the skin over his heart, and the place grew strangely hot.

"Slaíne, we both—"

She sat up and placed a hand over his mouth. "I'm sorry, all right? I's afeared you'd attack Hex while I was trainin' meself. I dunno how much power I gave you, but you ain't trained enough to use it, anyway." Slaíne replaced her hand with her lips for a moment, before settling down next to him. "Now, I feel you has got something to tell me."

He pushed her concerns aside; he did not want to think about the reason he needed training, let alone consider what she had truly done to him in Nothingness. "Salem paid me another visit."

She stiffened for a moment, but then relaxed and began tracing circles on his stomach. "What'd your friend have to say?"

Aidan launched into a summary of what he had been told, pausing when her hand became too distracting. He cleared his throat and tried again. "I have this feeling, Slaíne, that if we don't strike soon…. Well, whatever Meraude is planning, it's definitely not going to benefit us."

Apparently exasperated, Slaíne pushed away from him and hissed through her teeth at him. "If we attack afore we know what we can do, then she's definitely going to get her way. What'd ya have me do? There's enchantments on this place. I know ya can feel them. There's nay gonna be any easy way out of here."

He felt his temper rising to meet hers, and his fingers tingled with green flickers of lightning, catching the sheets afire. Swearing, they both jumped out of bed, and Aidan smothered the blaze with one of the feather pillows.

"See?" she said, gesturing to the burned mess. "You can nay control yourself." When he gave her a look, she rolled her eyes. "Yes, neither can I. I know. I know." Now Slaíne took to pacing, blue sparks of her own emanating from her hands.

Aidan sighed. "All right. Let's find out what we can from this wizard. Ease him into a false sense of security, and then you, Jinn, and I will combine our efforts and— What?"

The look Slaíne gave him was savage. "That Blest creature is up to no good. I feel it in me bones."

"'Blest creature'? Slaíne, you and I both are Blest."

"Nay, not no more. Not since I found out I'm really a wizard and made you one. Well, mostly." She huffed out a deep breath. "I don't like the idea of workin' with her kind. 'Sides, why was she lookin' for ya to begin with?" She stopped her pacing again and swiped at her wild mane. "Something's not right about this. She's hidin' something. I know it."

Aidan crossed his arms. "So the note she gave us was a lie? Are we not to trust it?" There was no argument in his words, only sincerity; thankfully, Slaíne received them that way and didn't start shouting at him…or worse, hitting him with the blue flames that were still crackling between her fingers.

That seemed to bring Slaíne up short. Her brow wrinkled and her shoulders heaved, the fire leaving her eyes and hands. "But what if it's a trap? Could she be working with Meraude?"

He went in search of clothes again, before remembering Nothingness.

Searching through his cache there, Aidan was pleased to find himself able to latch on to several cloth Pulls, which he meant to Summon into his waiting hands, but missed entirely. They landed on Slaíne's head instead. "Sorry," he said over her swearing.

The clothes he had Summoned were a mishmash of earth-tone tunics – some for men and a few for women – trousers, cloaks, and belts. But no shoes or boots – thankfully; that would have hurt. No wonder Slaíne was looking murder at him now: the pile had to weigh ten pounds.

After dressing himself in black trousers and a dark blue tunic, Aidan tied a brown belt around his waist and went for the iron-barred window. "We need to explore all our options," he said in response to Slaíne's raised eyebrows. "I'm not going to sit here and allow Hex or fate to decide what happens to us." At first he stood there, staring at the bars and exploring their Pull. Then he reached out and attempted to Dismiss them. The metal fought him as he tried to bend it to his will with his mind like he did with any other material. With a jolt, he was thrown backward by what felt like an invisible explosion, nearly knocking Slaíne over as he flew past. Grunting and feeling slightly singed, he sat up on the bed where he had landed. "Well, that's a ward."

Slaíne snorted. "Surprise."

Aidan glowered at her. "Is there anything the elves told you about breaking a ward?" When she just looked at him like he had sprouted a second head, he prompted, "You know, something like turning around three times in a counter-circle under a full moon in the blood of a dozen snow-white cattle?"

"Don't be ridiculous, there ain't no snow-white cattle in these parts." She smirked at him. "Wards are complicated magic…so said the elves. Ya gotta break the one who set them in order for them ter fail."

That did not sound promising. "So we have to kill Hex to break free?" He sighed. "It's a wonder he's willing to train you."

But Slaíne was shaking her head. "Train us. Nah, you nay have to kill him. Just debilitate or drive him to the point of distraction. It takes some conscious effort to power this type of magic…. Least, that's my understandin'."

"Then we will have to find a way to distract him…and then get off the cliff that the house is sitting on." The mere thought of it made him tired enough to collapse, though he knew the change that had taken over him might be partially to blame. Weary, he closed his eyes and lay back down. But as he tried to rest, he continued to worry. Besides needing to find a way to escape without smashing themselves on the rocks below, there was also the matter of finding the Goblets that Hex had and stealing them before they fled.

"You can prob'ly fly now, silly," Sláine reminded him. "That's how we'll leave here."

"Please don't listen to my every thought and criticize them." In response to his irritation – and perhaps Sláine's as well – the bed began to shake. He tried to calm himself.

Sláine lay down next to him, and the shaking ceased. "I've a feelin' that findin' the Goblets won't be a problem. You can nay hide magic like that. We'll sense 'em somehow."

Aidan grunted. "Then that is our first act. One of us will have to distract the wizard while the other searches for the Goblets."

For once she did not argue with him outright, though he could feel her reluctance to put him in danger. "We'll take turns. I'll start training, and you can search the house. Hex nay said anywhere was out o' bounds for either of us, just that it was dangerous. You find nothin', and I'll give it a go the day next while you train."

He cringed at the thought, and the whole room began to shake. "No, I'm not training."

"You'll be dangerous until you can control yer abilities." Her eyes narrowed. "You still don't think it affects you, do ya?"

Deep down he knew he was being ridiculous, but he couldn't help but feel bitter about being left out of the choice to become— well, whatever it was he might be now. "I don't wish to speak of it." As his agitation grew, so did the magnitude of his artificial earthquake.

"Calm down," Sláine warned him.

That did nothing to allay the pain roiling in his mind, warring for control of his senses. He fought for a moment, attempting to overcome the palpitations beating next to Slaíne's half of a soul in his chest. But exhaustion overcame him and he lost control. The power in him flew outward, throwing Slaíne off of the bed, pushing everything away from his prone form. He Repelled the sheets, the bed drapes, and sent them crashing against the far walls. Slaíne shouted above the roar that filled the room, her small frame pinned between his power and the wardrobe, bringing him to his senses. Exhausted, he Released her Pull, lay back down, and immediately fell asleep.

CHAPTER FIVE

Meraude

Meraude observed as three men, all of them tráined warriors, drank from the onyx-black Goblet. No one had informed them of whom or what they would face in the arena. Even she, the mage queen, did not know what lay behind each of the three closed dungeon doors. Fate would decide.

The woman on Meraude's right, Mai Tefta, one of her most trusted advisors, placed a hand on the mage queen's arm. "Milady, do you think it wise to subject yourself to their presence?" She nodded in the men's direction. "These brutes have killed women, children. They've raped, pillaged, plundered—" She grew silent as her lady gave her a pointed look.

"No one knows nor feels these men's crimes more than I do." Meraude turned again to face the devils, her resolve unwavering. "They have drunk from the Goblet."

Tefta worried her lower lip, a sign of her increasing anxiety. Meraude would have to train her to suppress such feelings, or to at least hide them in the enemy's presence. "Yes, they have imbibed. They have been told of the powers – in general terms," Tefta hastily added. "None know they come from the Goblet."

Meraude nodded once. "It doesn't matter. They will guess soon enough. Besides, we want the chosen creature to have no outside advantage."

"Yes, milady."

They watched in silence as the three men were sent to a corner of the small underground arena, separated from the mage queen and her advisor by wire and six of Meraude's guards. The ground down to the dirt battleground was sloped, affording the mage queen a good view of the proceedings over the heads of her guard.

Far from terrified, the three seemed excited at the prospect of battle, their war cries ringing in Meraude's ears. After their handlers had left the arena and filed into the safe area, the gatekeeper bowed to her lady and then prostrated herself facing the northern wall. She was entreating fate in the Old Tongue, requesting guidance in choosing the correct door. It was a mere formality. Fate would have its way no matter what. Finally the gatekeeper rose and walked with purpose to the middle door, the one painted blood-red.

"Ah, the color of battle," said Tefta. "Let's hope she chose wisely."

Meraude inclined her head, her eyes never leaving the arena. The door resisted being opened, as if it had not been used in some time. This was untrue, however. Something or someone held the door back, which should have been impossible, as it opened only from the outside. Meraude and her general exchanged glances as the gatekeeper continued to struggle.

"What is the trouble?" General Tindra demanded.

The gatekeeper turned, bowed, and explained, "Whoever is on the other side has gripped the door's bottom with their fingers. They are holding it shut." The woman looked at the general for direction.

Instead of offering advice, Tindra moved from among the ranks of soldiers, skirted around the fencing, and approached the door. Without preamble, she removed the hinges, stepped aside, and the door fell forward and onto the ground.

Fingers still gripping the wood, there crouched a young woman with close-cut dark hair and wild black eyes. Her gaze went right to Meraude, a plea.

The mage queen stared back, unyielding, as the general and the gatekeeper tugged the door away and exited the arena. If she were to build a second army, Meraude needed raw material. This girl looked about as raw as they came.

When the first man approached, fists raised, the girl crept backward, only to realize her mistake: she was trapped. As her attacker closed in, a high keening filled the air, the girl's anguish palpable. "I don't want this," she said in Abrish, before retreating into the darkness of the tunnel behind her.

Meraude held her impatience in check. This would play out as it was meant to play out. She needed to learn what she was dealing with.

The first man, dressed in a loincloth, his filthy, matted hair swinging in a braid down his back, disappeared into the tunnel. He emerged a moment later, dragging the girl by her arm.

His fellow warriors circled in closer, watching the apparently easy kill stumble to the ground. The first man kicked her in the side, the sickening thud echoing through the otherwise silent arena. The second and third men, both half the size of the first yet still twice the size of the prey, dragged her to her feet and held either arm, opening her up for the first warrior to have full access.

"I don't want this," the girl said again.

The one man punched the girl in the stomach, lighting horrified surprise in her dark eyes. She sought out Meraude, her eyebrows raised. So now she knew what she was facing. Before she could react, another blow was dealt her, then another.

Panting and crying, the girl continued to hang between the two men, an oak in the wind, unwilling to bend. "Please, don't—" She was silenced by a blow across her face. Blood dripped down her chin.

"This is not the display I was hoping for," Tindra said, picking at her nails morosely. "Perhaps you should have let me train her younger. Nineteen is too old." She tutted and then whistled her distaste through her browning teeth.

The mage queen held up a hand to waylay her general's complaints, which would be dealt with later. She watched the girl, whose eyes had closed.

The warrior men seemed to believe the girl had fainted. The two released her, and she collapsed in a heap. It would seem the men were victorious. One looked at General Tindra, disbelief and disgust written across his face.

"At least give us a challenge," he shouted, and his men laughed.

The general's hand went for her sword. "This has gone on long enough. Apparently this line is inferior."

Meraude's eyes roved emotionlessly to the men, who, despite claiming to have faced little challenge, appeared to be covered in sweat. Slowly, a small smile tugged at the corners of the mage queen's lips.

While the men were staring at the general for instructions, the crumpled form rose. The girl got to her feet, dusted herself off, her eyes now brimming with tears and determination.

Seeing that their prey was not so easily overcome, the men turned back to face her. The man in the loincloth came at her first, swinging his meaty fists at her head, but she moved around him expertly. On his fifth attempt to strike the girl, she caught the man's fist in her hands and pulled his wrist back, effectively snapping several of his bones. *Crack!* He screamed in anguish, and the other two warriors seemed less certain of themselves. She let the man drop and arched her back as the second man reached her, catching him by the throat, though she had to leap into the air to do so. He collapsed, his windpipe successfully crushed in the girl's fists.

The third warrior backed away when he saw this, his courage apparently waning. Fortunately for him, Meraude observed, the girl was busy with the first warrior, whom she kicked once in the head before he lay still.

Now with two fallen brothers-in-arms, the third one ran for the wires and tried pulling them down. But the Enduring Goblet's strength had left him through his sweat, and he was now helpless to the Blest's attacks.

The girl did not play with her attacker-turned-prey but ran for him, caught him midflight, twisted his neck, and was done. Shaking, the Blest girl dropped to her knees and stared at her hands.

Tefta hovered at the mage queen's elbow. "Should we clear the bodies?"

Meraude shook her head. "No. Let her live with what she has done for a while." She watched as the girl took a few gasping breaths and then stopped shaking. "There is hope for this line yet."

CHAPTER SIX

Meraude

The girl's name was Egreet, Meraude had learned. Eleven other Blest, females only, stood in the circular room, each taking covert looks at each other when they thought they weren't being watched. Like the lean Egreet, each had had their hair cut close and were dressed in flowing white linen trousers and fitted leather vests.

"Sit," Meraude said, motioning to the wooden benches in the center of the room.

Everyone took their seat at once, except for Egreet, who seemed ready to run for the door where General Tindra stood, hand clasped around the grip of the sword that hung from her side. The girl seemed to think the better of running, however, and took the bench in the back row.

Meraude studied them for a moment and then announced, "You must be hungry. Eat." She motioned to the feast that had been set out before them on the floor.

The girls hesitated, regarding Meraude with unbridled curiosity and then fell upon the feast without ceremony. All did this, except for Egreet. She did not move.

"It's not poisoned."

Egreet clenched her jaw and continued to sit there, undecided, then closed her eyes and frowned in apparent concentration. Her eyes moved behind their shutters, and her face registered several different expressions. She opened her eyes and looked at Meraude, cautious yet curious. Then, with a shrug, the girl rose and skirted the others, reached her hand in, and snatched a few slices of smoked ham, which she ate slowly.

Few talked and fewer still watched Meraude, only stealing glances at the general by the door. Those who did look at Meraude were curious more than anything. The look she trained on them in return was bored, though secretly she was on the watch for any signs of potential like she had seen in the arena the day before. *These had better be the best of the clans.*

Each clan was comprised of different Blest women and their keepers, and each came from a different school of thought and ability. Elsted, a girl Meraude observed snatching food out of the hands of others, was a trained warrior whose mother had imbibed from the Enduring Goblet. At the same time, the girl on her left, whose name Meraude had not bothered to commit to memory, was an untrained Sightful whose mother had drunk from the Seeing Goblet. Some of the Blest were second generation, their mothers being Blest themselves plus having drunk from a Goblet. Only two in the group were doubly Blest. There was Egreet, untrained and raw, and Ing, who had been trained to control her brawn if not her foresight. The latter regarded Egreet with a wary eye as she ate, as if sensing this girl, too, was special.

They had been allowed to eat in peace long enough, Meraude observed. It was time to test their dispositions. Closing her eyes, Meraude latched on to a girl's slice of bread and Dismissed it when she had looked away.

The girl glared at her neighbor, a trained Endurer, who was scarfing down her own bread. "That's mine," the first said, attempting to snatch it from her.

Meraude concentrated again and Summoned the bread onto the Endurer's lap.

"I took nothing from you," said the Endurer.

Egreet's eyes went to Meraude and she frowned. She started to speak, perhaps to inform the others of what was going on, but seemed to think the better of it and backed away.

"That's mine," said the untrained Sightful again as the other held the bread out of her reach.

"There's plenty to be had," said Ing. She had apparently not looked ahead, not like two other Sightfuls, who jumped out of the way.

Meraude did not need to possess the gift of foresight in order to determine what was to happen next: sixty years, three attempted armies, and two cleansings had taught her what to expect from the expression on the untrained Sightful's face.

After failing to get back what was hers, the girl lunged at the Endurer and started clawing at the other's face. A howl of pain went up from the Sightful, whose nails were now bent and bloody.

The Enduring child looked bored and without a scratch on her face. "I told you, there's plenty more."

Meraude focused for a moment and Dismissed all the food, eliciting a few screams from the girls, who had apparently heard nothing of the Summoning Goblet. All eyes went to Tindra, who quirked an amused smile.

"Don't look at me." The Endurer flashed her rotting teeth and the girls slowly turned their focus back to the front of the room opposite the door, where Meraude stood.

"How'd you do that?" Ing asked, her eyes narrowed.

"How'd you do that, *milady*," Meraude corrected her.

The child scoffed, something Meraude would handle later, and said, "All right. How'd you do that, *milady*?"

Meraude Summoned a chair behind her and perched on the edge. "What do you know of the Goblets Immortal?"

Most of them exchanged confused glances, though Ing's and Egreet's eyes met each other, their expressions unfathomable. The Endurer who had been attacked raised her thick arm after a moment, and Meraude pointed to her. "Goblets? You mean like drinking goblets?"

"She said they were immortal, dummy," said a trained Sightful. "That means they can't die."

Before the others could speak up with their ridiculous assumptions and ideas, Meraude raised a hand. Unlike the soldiers under her command, the children did not quiet. *They will have to learn the hard way, I see.* "Silence." Meraude flicked her wrist, and the one talking loudest suddenly found her jaw dislocated.

The girl screamed, and the others backed away from the example in their midst.

"When I tell you to do something," said Meraude, her tone measured and just loud enough to be heard above the injured girl's whimpers, "you do it without hesitation. You do not want me as your enemy. Understand?"

The others nodded mutely.

"General Tindra," Meraude said to the woman at the door.

The general stood more erect. "Milady?"

"See this chatty girl to the infirmary and then return to your post."

Tindra bowed and motioned for the girl to follow her. "Come, child. Dawdling won't heal you." She nodded once to Meraude as the girl scurried over. The child was clutching her face and whimpering, and only after the door had shut again did she continue screaming.

The group was unsettled, to say the least. Perhaps now they would listen.

"Would anyone else care to join her?"

All of them shook their heads, and a few muttered their dissent. "No, milady," said Egreet and Ing, avoiding her gaze.

Meraude hid her surprise, which was instantly followed by suspicion. "Good. Now, we were discussing the Goblets Immortal." She sat back in her seat and motioned for the girls to resume sitting on their benches, which they did posthaste. "There are six Goblets: the Seeing Goblet, which some of you have experience with, the Drifting Goblet, the Enduring Goblet – another one familiar to a few of you – the Summoning Goblet, the Questing Goblet, and the Warring Goblet. Each of these magical vessels was made from molten wizard blood. By themselves, each fuels whosoever drinks from them with different abilities. Unite all the Goblets, and the drinker becomes invulnerable and undefeatable, with powers beyond any wizard's for a time." *So, they haven't heard.* "Are you with me so far?"

The girls nodded and a few followed Ing and Egreet's example by murmuring a hasty "Yes, milady."

Meraude inclined her head. "There is a war coming," she said after allowing them to stew on this new information for a few moments. "Wizards walk the land again, and it is up to us, the Blest, to make certain the magical vessels do not fall into their dangerous hands."

Ing frowned and raised a hand, speaking once Meraude had nodded her permission. "What would the wizards need the Goblets Immortal for? Don't they already have enough power?"

She rewarded the girl with a sad smile. "The Great Wizards lost the Great War, but one fought with the rest of magic-kind. I believe he now regrets that decision and that he and the remaining, lesser wizards wish to rule us all again, like in the Dark Age. You see, magical beings are considered chattel to wizards, especially the Blest." Meraude rose and took to strolling about the room, the hem of her white gown whispering on the polished floors. "If they were to possess the Goblets Immortal, they would destroy them."

"So? What would that do?" an Endurer challenged.

Meraude smiled. "That is a good question, one that I never hope to have the answer to. No one knows what would happen if the Goblets are destroyed. No more Blest could be created, that is for certain."

Ing's hand shot upward again, and again Meraude called on her. "How would one destroy the Goblets Immortal?"

It would sound like a harmless question to anyone else, but Meraude knew there was no such thing. She ceased turning about the room and folded her hands in front of her. "Fortunately, the usual methods of fire and blunt instruments do not work. The Goblets, after all, are imbued with the powers of those who created them, and most wizards are difficult to kill."

A look passed between Ing and Egreet, one that Meraude did not like but did not acknowledge. The two had never spoken and yet they seemed to be in league with each other. *Cursed foresight.*

Egreet, who had remained silent, raised her hand and spoke without permission. "Has anyone drunk from all the Goblets Immortal?"

The room stilled. Girls exchanged concerned looks, but Egreet's eyes remained on Meraude, whose lips curled up into a sad smile. "Not to my knowledge, Egreet. We are still working on uncovering a few before the wizards can get their hands on them."

"Are you certain?" she said, her tone measured. She sounded innocent, too innocent.

"Quite. One of the Goblets has never been seen since its creation around five hundred years ago." Meraude Summoned a water bladder into her hand and took a swig. "As long as there have been wizards walking the lands of the Saime, there has been power too great for mere humans to handle."

A few of the young women frowned, and one said, "So, we aren't human."

Meraude inclined her head. "We are *more*. That is why we have to make certain the Goblets do not fall into mortal hands, not again."

"Again?" said Ing, dropping the pretense of polite deference. "What do you mean 'again'? This happened before?"

It would seem the situation was about to bubble out of control. *Good. Let them test me and see what I am made of.* She held up her hand, the way she had when she broke the Sightful's jaw, and the room quieted. "We shall discuss the Circle and their treachery another time. For now, know that humans cannot be trusted, nor can wizards or other magical beings. The former would use us for their own ends, and the latter would see us destroyed as abominations. "This," she said, lowering her hand, much to the group's apparent relief, "is the reason we must work together. We are all very much alone, apart from one another." She let those words settle over the room before taking her seat again. "Now, among you younger Blest there are five Endurers, products of the Enduring Goblet, and five Sightfuls, products of the Seeing Goblet."

One of the girls, the Endurer who had had her face scratched at, frowned and murmured something below her breath, and then raised her hand. When Meraude nodded for her to speak, the girl said, "But there are twelve— well, now there are only eleven of us." She cringed and Meraude knew she was thinking of the girl who had been sent to the infirmary. "What of the other two?"

"An astute observation," Meraude said dryly. At that moment, she sensed Tindra's Pull approach the door to the room.

The general knocked once, entered, and resumed her post with a slight nod.

Meraude ignored the gesture and continued. "Five of you had mothers who drank of the Enduring Goblet, which has imbued you with extreme strength and a thick hide, as you noted earlier." She looked at the girl with the bloody nails, who flushed bright red. "Five of your mothers drank from the Seeing Goblet, which has given you the ability to see parts of the future. But two of you, and you know who you are, had mothers who drank from both. You are doubly Blest."

Egreet, Meraude noted, had become restless and was ready to attempt something drastic. The girl did not like Meraude, not one bit. Ing seemed to feel the same way, but she was striving better to hide it. The former raised her hand. "I'm not feeling well, milady," she said, her tone gruff.

"General Tindra," said Meraude, "see this girl to the infirmary. We can't have anything spreading among the girls." She gave her head a subtle shake and pulled on her braid, a pre-arranged signal that Tindra noted and responded to in kind. "Follow the general, Egreet."

The young doubly Blest nodded and got to her feet. No one watched her as she left except for Ing, whose eyes had closed slightly, a sign that she was attempting to look ahead.

"Ing," said Meraude sharply, "eyes on me."

Ing jolted, her eyes opening wide.

"Thank you, Tindra." Meraude turned her attention back to the girls, catching glimpses of Egreet moving for the door as she continued teaching. "In a few minutes, we are going to divide into two groups: trained Endurers against Sightfuls. And just for a lark, I'll allow Ing to choose which side she feels she belongs in for the—"

There was a loud grunt and the sound of a body hitting the floor, followed by metal clanging. The class turned just as Egreet charged toward them, General Tindra's blade in her hands. The girls froze as the powerful Blest leapt over one of the benches and brought the blade down on Meraude, who sighed.

The blade shattered as it struck Meraude on the shoulder. Shards flew across the room, and those who were Endurers remained unharmed, and those who were Sightfuls had dove out of the way as soon as Egreet had snatched the blade.

Egreet stood there, staring at the haft in her hand and then looking at Meraude, curiosity burning in her eyes. It was a start.

Meraude snapped her fingers, and the remains of the sword disappeared. "Before you attack, be certain of who you're dealing with," she said calmly. "Know your opponent and adjust your plans accordingly. You have the gift of foresight. You could have avoided this humiliation if you had thought to look ahead, like Ing." She nodded to Ing, who lowered her gaze and seemed to be trying to make herself as small as possible.

All eyes moved to the other doubly Blest.

"Ing is more subtle. She was perhaps planning something not quite so dramatic, yet perhaps quite as ineffective. A poisoning, maybe?" The look on the girl's face betrayed her. "But you found out something, didn't you, Ing?"

The girl was sweating. Meraude swore she could smell it from where she stood, seven arm-reaches away.

"Answer me, Ing."

"The threads."

Meraude nodded once, and some understanding began to dawn on the faces of the Sightfuls in the room. The pure Endurers, however, frowned. "Enlighten the rest, child."

Ing looked at Egreet, who still hadn't recovered her wits from her failed attempt, it would seem. "There are threads that make up the Veil that separates past from present and future from both. Each thread is an element attached to a potential happening with hundreds of connecting threads that make up a possibility, which is perhaps a small patch in the Veil." She looked at Meraude, wonder in her eyes. "Past threads are dead threads and can't be accessed by any Blest. Present threads are alive and plentiful. The more threads you see, the more ways there are to get to one outcome or a totally different one.

"I tried looking at this – the threads surrounding her ladyship here, but they are very tangled. Too tangled. Which must mean...." She flushed. "Well, besides it being too risky to attempt to kill her outright, I don't exactly know what it means." Her eyes sought Meraude's, and the mage queen shook her head.

"That is for me to know and for you all to discover." Her attention turned to Egreet, though her words were for Ing, "I believe you deserve an extra food token, Ing."

Egreet scowled at that, and the others took to murmuring among themselves. Good. Meraude knew she had everyone's attention.

CHAPTER SEVEN

Jinn

The temptation to wander grew each day. But Jinn knew it was dangerous. That was the one thing she had believed immediately when the wizard had spoken to her about it. It was going on the second week of their captivity, and Quick was still sleeping most of the time, only waking to eat, use the chamber pot – which thankfully magically emptied itself after each use – and then return to resting. Jinn felt sleep tugging at her eyes during the day as well and wondered whether it was a way of coping for them both or if there were something more sinister like a spell in place, lulling them to sleep. She remembered the village, Gullsford, where everyone had mysteriously dropped what they were doing and fallen asleep. She still meant to ask Hex how he had managed it, if it had in fact been him, but she had been avoiding leaving the room, and the wizard hadn't sought her out. Perhaps he had lost interest in their presence here.

It had been several days since she had slipped her missive to the Summoner. She hoped that it had gone undiscovered by Hex and that it hadn't caused the Summoner any trouble. As time passed, she began to wonder if he had even read it, and if he had, what he had made of it. Abrish was a dying language, but it was the only one Jinn knew how to write in fluently.

The day gave way to evening shadows, and Jinn was about to give in to sleep, when the door creaked open, as it had not done since the day she had found the wizard tormenting the Summoner's traveling companion. Jinn hesitated for a moment. She hadn't even tried the doorknob for days, uncertain if she would find it unlocked or not. Now, bored out of her senses, she threw back the covers, pulled on a blue cloak and a pair of boots, and left the relative safety of her prison.

All was still and calm, save for the sound of waves beating against the rock beneath them and the occasional cry of a gull. Then, startling her, the door shut behind her with an ominous click. Terrified, she spun around and tried the doorknob. It was locked. Jinn cursed, knowing the house was playing a trick on her for some reason of its own. But she couldn't just stand here, waiting to be let back in or discovered by something unsavory. With a sigh, she tied the cloak's belt around her waist and ventured toward where she fancied she heard whispering.

The faint sounds led her farther away from her cell than she had wandered before. She passed flowing tapestries, dozens of doors of varying sizes and colors, elaborate sitting rooms with fireplaces three times her height and twenty times her width, and staircases that led to seemingly nowhere. One such staircase drew her attention. The steps were steep and narrow, and the wood they were built out of was a dark cherry, though Jinn was uncertain of how she knew this with such certainty. Drawings in her books could only teach a person so much about the flora and fauna of the world.

Down here, said a somewhat familiar soft voice that Jinn assumed belonged to the wizard.

Feeling stubborn, Jinn turned her nose up at the staircase and was prepared to go another way, when the voice hissed into her ear, *I know your secrets, Jinn, daughter of Meraude. You wish to deceive my master. I wonder if I should tell him. I wonder if I should leave you be. Is he foolish, or are you blinding him? I wonder....*

After sucking in a shaky breath, Jinn said, "Where are you?"

Me? Where am I not? Laughter trickled from the walls. *Be not afraid, Jinn. I am the House of Curses: nothing less and nothing more.*

Jinn considered this for a moment. A talking, sentient house? She supposed there were stranger things under heaven. Looking around, hoping to find the source of the voice, she said, "You've been leaving keys and clothes in the wardrobe and unlocking my door, haven't you?"

Again the house laughed. *You understand the matter more readily than he would have predicted.*

She stopped spinning in circles, having grown dizzy. "And whose side are you on?"

The house breathed in deeply, as if considering. *I am on the side of no mortal, child. But you are no mere mortal, are you?* Its voice echoed around Jinn.

Jinn swallowed. "Then whose side *are* you on?"

Patience, child. I am no friend to Meraude, if that is what you're asking.

Well, that was something. "And whose side is the wizard on?"

The house hesitated, and when it spoke again, its tone was dismissive. *If the Great One hasn't told you, why would I?*

She considered that for a moment and said, "For the same reason you've been going against his wishes and opening my door?"

That made the room shake, and Jinn wondered if she had gone too far. *Such cheek*, the house rumbled, though it sounded thoroughly amused. *Such daring. I have not had this good a laugh in six hundred years, and that is saying something.* As if to prove its point, the windows rattled.

Jinn suppressed a grin.

Why don't you be seated? I assume you have many questions, and since my maker has not expressly forbidden me from entertaining curiosity, there are a few answers I may yet be able to divulge. A plump chair that Jinn hadn't noticed before rocked in the corner on its stubby legs and settled, a clear invitation from the house for Jinn to make herself comfortable. The house sighed. *Now, I believe you asked whose side Hex is on.*

Jinn tipped herself into the chair and waited for the house to continue. When it was silent, she resisted the urge to press it for answers. The being was ancient and must be allowed to take its time. Though she did wish it would hurry; what would the wizard do if he found her sitting here, talking about him? The thought made her cringe.

The wizard is confused. The house creaked.

"These are confusing times," Jinn found herself saying.

They are indeed. And you demigods are making it all the more so. But suffice it to say, that no matter how confusing you find Hex's choices, they are not meant for your harm.

Well, that was all well and good for the wizard, to decide what he thought was best for everyone. Jinn wondered if the house meant what it said, or if it had been bidden to talk to her on Hex's behalf. Jinn murmured as much.

The house cackled, a menacing sound that set Jinn's teeth on edge. *I do not lie. I cannot lie. It is part of my curse.* The word 'curse' bounced around the house, ricocheting off furniture and ringing in Jinn's ears, which she covered.

"Can you tell me how to escape, then?"

Of course. I know the way out. There is always a way. But I don't think you'd like it.

She wanted to object, but the house cut her off.

And I don't think it's time to tell you. Not yet. You'll need the she-wizard's trust first. And her mate's, though I believe he is desperate enough to put his faith in anyone who makes the right offer.

"You mean the Summoner and his traveling companion?" The house was silent. "She's – a wizard?" If she had been told about the existence of a female wizard just a short month ago, she wouldn't have believed it. But her dreams had been interrupted by some powerful being weeks previous, trying to steer her path away from the Summoner. The being had been most definitely female.

Tread carefully there, the house warned. *Between the two of them, the wizards have more than enough power to help or destroy you.*

Jinn's brow wrinkled. The Summoner had seemed…different when they first met, stranger and more dangerous than she remembered from her visions. Was he more than what she had first thought? "Do you think they might eventually help me?"

Jinn, I am not the one with foresight.

That made her stomach churn. "I can't see anything in this place."

Nonsense, the house boomed. *You may not like everything you've seen, but there is only so much future the curser can blot out.*

"So Hex *is* the reason I can't see my own future."

The house settled on its foundations with a small groan. *Ah, perhaps I have said too much.* The being sounded far from penitent.

If Jinn was not mistaken, the house was perhaps at least leaning toward her side of things. Still, she knew she must tread cautiously and not foolishly place her trust in something so ancient. "I saw a future," she said after a moment of reflection.

Ah. And what was that future, child?

For a moment she hesitated, reluctant to commit the words to the air, but realized she needed to gain some of the house's trust in return. Jinn sighed and sank farther back into the cushions. "I saw Quick, my brother."

The house inhaled…if houses were able to do such a thing.

"He was with the Summoner and…the she-wizard, as you called her. They— There— I wasn't with them." Jinn brushed a few wrinkles out of her cloak and cleared her throat. "I don't know if that means I die here or not."

What were they doing?

That question made Jinn hesitate. They had been on the road to Meraude in that wisp of a future. One stray word from her, and the future could warp and change into something else entirely, endangering whatever chance her brother at least might have of leaving here alive. "They were fleeing. I couldn't say from what." Her cheeks warmed at the lie, and the house grumbled.

So that is how it shall be. Very well. Very well. I am too old to take offense at half-truths, and can read between the proverbial lines. You are very young, child, and need to understand something: Hex will not purposely harm you. It is against his…ah, against his nature.

Jinn shifted her weight. "It sounds like someone else might be speaking in half-truths."

If the house had a head, Jinn imagined it being shaken right then. *Trust him. Seek him out, whether he likes it or not. Your paths overlap. Of that I am certain.*

"I'll – think about it."

There was a stiff silence between them, and Jinn wondered if she should move on. There was plenty of house left to explore. If the being would not tell her how to escape, maybe she would be able to puzzle it out herself.

There are some dangers lurking inside me. I am not entirely tame, child, and though you seem comfortable with me, I would be careful in wandering without aim.

"What dangers?" The words had made her sit up a little straighter. "The wizard said something about the house— about *you* being dangerous."

The house was silent for a moment. *Beware the one who shifts his shape. He does not care for mortals, least of all the Blest. Also, there's the dungeons you'll want to stay clear of. They have a way of driving a person to...ah, driving them to distraction. And that is an understatement.*

Jinn pursed her lips. "And you're definitely not going to tell me now how to escape?"

No, I think not. You're not ready for that information. Good day to you, Jinn, daughter of Meraude. With that said, the house grew still and the chair that Jinn was sitting in tipped her onto the floor and disappeared in a flash of red light.

"Thank you for your help," Jinn murmured. "I guess." She stood and dusted herself off. What should she do? The sensible thing would probably be returning to the room she shared with Quick, but she remembered that the door had locked behind her – no doubt the house's doing. Jinn huffed. There was some hidden reason behind the house wanting her to befriend the wizard, if that is what it had meant. There must be some advantage it would give the house. "But what does a house need?" She shook her head. No, the advantage must be for Hex. He was, after all, the sentient building's master.

A wave of fatigue washed over Jinn. She had slept a lot as of late with little movement. No wonder she felt lethargic. Though she was wary of wandering now, Jinn decided that she might be safe exploring at least some of the floor she was on. The shape-shifter had been ordered to leave her alone, after all.

But there were other things to worry about. Like how was the wizard preventing her from looking ahead? The house had mentioned something about their paths being entwined.

"I need to try, don't I?" she said below her breath. There might be a glimpse of something she hadn't seen before. "Or maybe I need to stop looking at *my* future. Maybe I don't have one." The thought was depressing, but she pushed past it and closed her eyes.

At first, there was nothing, just blackness and the distant pull of a possibility. Jinn focused on that, a single green thread. The closer she looked, the more she came to realize that the thread was actually two: green and blue, entwined. She reached for them both, and they flittered out of her reach. Not one to give up so easily, Jinn chased the threads down with her mind just as a dull silver one appeared. The silver thread felt most familiar, and it was moving at a snail's pace, so she grabbed on to that and untangled it. As she had suspected, the thread belonged to Quick.

He was standing in a room that Jinn hadn't seen before, but was fairly certain belonged to the House of Curses. "I don't like," *he said to someone Jinn couldn't see.*

There was a pause, and her giant of a brother shook his head.

"Not leaving without you."

"Jinn?"

A wave of pain tore through Jinn, and the vision faded. Everything grew dark.

Again she heard a voice call her name, and, pushing away unconsciousness, Jinn blinked rapidly. Time seemed to stop, and a vision attempted to break through the barrier that had been preventing her from seeing. She squeezed her eyes against it, but it was too powerful.

Mai Larkin, the Sightful Blest Jinn wasn't supposed to know about, stood alone in Inohaim Tower, stooping over the Seeing Pool. As if sensing Jinn's presence, she turned and nodded. "You know what must be done," *she said, her voice echoing strangely.*

Jinn frowned. "What *must be done?*"

The Sightful stared right through her. "Bring the Goblets Immortal to the Seeing Pool. You will need Lord Ingledark and his mate for that." *There was a distant rumble of thunder, and she shivered. "And whatever you do, do not let Meraude take the—"*

"Jinn, are you all right?" asked the same insistent voice from the present.

Furious that her vision had been interrupted, Jinn swung out with her hands, catching only air. She thrashed and she struggled as someone grabbed her from behind and lifted her as though she weighed nothing.

"Let go," she said with a growl as the world spun and her stomach clenched.

The person carrying her sighed and set her down on something soft, and she immediately tried running away. "No, that's not going to happen. Sit still for a moment. You were having a fit and need to rest now."

Jinn blinked through the film covering her eyes, and pushed with all her strength against the force pinning her down. She needed to return to that vision. It was important. Whoever had interrupted it was completely blocking her foresight now, and she needed to get as far away from them as possible. Unfortunately, they were too strong for her. With an exasperated grunt, Jinn ceased struggling and shook the haze from her thoughts. Her vision cleared, and she found herself staring up at Hex, who was paler than she had remembered.

"Are you all right?" he asked again. When she didn't answer, he put a hand on her brow, which she attempted to shake off. "You're feverish. What happened?"

"Your house talks," was all she could muster.

Hex froze and gave her a peculiar look. "It talked to you?"

With a grunt, Jinn attempted to sit up, but the wizard was having none of that. He put a firm yet gentle hand on her shoulder and pinned her in place.

A shadow passed over Hex's face and he shook his head. "You tried looking at my future, didn't you?"

Jinn glared at him. "And?"

Hex sighed. "Jinn, that's not a good idea right now. You must have breached the boundaries and triggered the curse."

Those words made Jinn's insides turn cold. "What curse?"

For a moment he looked at her, torn, and said, "If you promise not to sit up too fast or run, I'll explain."

As if I could run anywhere right now. At length she nodded, though it made her vision blur and her head throb.

"I put a reverse curse on myself. Whoever tries to look at my future will either see nothing or experience a fit every time they try. I should have warned you. I'm sorry." He truly sounded it. "I thought after our last talk that you would leave the future alone, and didn't realize you had an interest in mine."

"Not *yours,*" Jinn said, regaining some of her wits and earlier annoyance. "I was looking at *mine*...at first." *I wasn't looking at mine at all. But I'm not going to tell him that.* Somehow, Mai Larkin had managed to get a message to her. It must have taken great power and energy in order to do so, and Jinn had paid part of the price for that.

Hex hung his head. "Our futures are more tightly entwined than I first thought." He removed his hand from Jinn's shoulder and sat down on the settee next to her. "But you seemed to have seen something. What was it?"

Jinn waved his question away and posed one of her own. "If my presence here is so important and I am not to wander, why, in the name of all that is dear, do I have to keep to one room?"

Hex jumped slightly, as if she had hit him. "Oh?"

"Lights, Hex. I don't know if wizards like confined spaces, but I am going out of my mind locked up like an animal in a cage." Now she managed to sit up, slowly, and since the world only spun a little, she attempted standing, thought the better of it, and sat back down.

"I'm sorry," he said, and he sounded sincere. "You're right: I'm not accustomed to entertaining humans." Hex sat forward and rested his head in his hands. "If I'm being completely honest, I would have to admit that I've been avoiding...that is to say, I've been...." His shoulders heaved, and he looked up at her. "I'm sorry. I'll try to be a better host."

Jinn nodded and looked away. Inside, she was seething, but she knew she had a part to play if she was ever to see the other side of these walls. Meraude remained undefeated, and if Hex was unwilling to stop her, Jinn would have to convince him to allow her group to attempt it. Arranging her expression carefully, she turned back to find the wizard watching her, wary. "What?" she asked, her tone sharper than she'd meant it to be.

His lips quirked into a half-smile. "You look like you could murder someone."

That made her cringe. "Mother always said I was a bad actor," she admitted, and at once regretted mentioning Meraude.

"It's a shame we don't get to choose our own parents," Hex said lightly. "If it makes any difference, you don't seem like a murderous dictator."

Jinn scowled at him, but he grinned in response.

"Since the house has introduced itself, maybe it's time for a tour." He looked at her doubtfully. "That is, if you're well enough?"

Well enough or not, Jinn wasn't about to give up this opportunity to find out more about her surroundings so she could plan an escape. "No, I'm fine." Slowly, she sat up and got to her feet. Jinn swayed on the spot for a moment, but Hex took her arm and tucked it into his.

"Here, let me help."

Jinn could only nod. She still felt like she might fall over at any moment, so perhaps rejecting the wizard's help would be unwise. "Where is the House of Curses exactly?" she asked as he led her out of the sitting room and into a hall she hadn't seen before.

The wizard was silent for a moment, as if debating whether or not to share the information with her. "We're on an island north and east of where you originate. Meraude cannot reach us here."

Jinn frowned. "I don't remember coming here on a boat." The memory of spending time as a bird made her grimace. How humiliating that had been.

Hex steered her around a corner, and they wound up at a window overlooking the sea. "That's because there was no boat. That's not how I travel." He released her for a moment, and they both stared out at the sun setting beneath the waves.

That's not how he traveled? That meant there was probably no boat to commandeer and sail away on. She would have to find out what method the wizard used for getting around. Before he could suspect her interest in the subject, Jinn tried to steer the conversation back to something she knew she should be harping on more. "If you're not on Meraude's side, why are you trying to stop me from destroying her?"

Next to her, the wizard stiffened and looked down at her from the corner of his eye. "I need the Goblets, Jinn. There's something I know I must do with them, and I can't have them falling into Meraude's hands."

"What do you need them for?" she demanded. "The Goblets shouldn't even exist. They need to be destroyed."

But Hex was shaking his head. "You don't know what you're saying."

"Oh, I think I do," she said, ignoring his stare as the day's last light plunged below the horizon. Its lingering orange rays peeked out from behind deep blue clouds, and the birdsong faded into the oncoming night. "It's the only way to stop her." She chanced a glance at the wizard, and was surprised to find him distraught.

"Do you know how the Goblets came into being?"

He had her full attention now. If she knew how they were created, perhaps she would have a better idea as to how they might be destroyed. "I know they're made of wizard's blood."

Hex nodded. "Yes, but how do you think the wizards were killed? Their blood was drained, yes, but killing one, let alone five, is supposed to be impossible."

Jinn shrugged. "I guess fate had different plans for them than they would have liked."

Taking her arm again, Hex led her away from the window. Jinn could still feel the sun's warmth on her back, though she felt cold suddenly when she saw the sad, torn look on the wizard's face. "The wizards, the six Greats, were cruel, greedy, and had very little respect for other magical life, never mind what they thought of non-magic folk." They walked down another hallway, and Jinn tried to take note of her surroundings while paying attention to what Hex was saying. "There was an uprising."

"The Great War."

Hex bobbed his head in acknowledgment. "It was lost before it was won. Many magical and non-magical creatures died at the hands of the Greats. Sadly, I was young and did very little to help…at first. I didn't think it was my place."

"At first?" A distant memory flickered in the back of Jinn's mind, something she had read in the history books. "You were the traitor I read about?"

The wizard nodded. "I wasn't on the council even. But there is an unspoken expectation among wizards that we will turn a blind eye when another of our kind does evil." He sighed and led her into a small room brilliant with candle- and torchlight. "Cedric the Elder was on the council, and he tried to sway the others to be more benevolent toward their so-called lesser magical kin."

"But they didn't listen," Jinn said, remembering more history.

Hex conceded with a grunt. "When I came upon a few of the wizards slaughtering a whole village of fey, I knew I had to do something. I confronted Melnine, but he wouldn't stay in the same room to hear me out. Nor would any of the others, save Cedric, and it was he who made me realize: the other wizards were afraid of me."

Jinn felt her brows knit together. "Why?"

That made the wizard chuckle. "You don't find me frightening?" He sounded hopeful, and that made the hairs on Jinn's arms stand on end.

She cleared her throat and ignored his question. "Why were they afraid of you exactly? I thought all wizards were equals."

"Well," he said slowly, weighing his words as though he were afraid he might scare her, "I'm the only wizard who has ever been able to curse another living soul, wizard or not." Torchlight flickered across his face, and his dark hair caught in a breeze that whistled through the cracks in the wall.

Jinn drew her arms about herself. "You cursed them?"

Hex's ancient eyes closed as if against the memory. "If I had known what the elves and sprites would do to them, I would have set stipulations. But, yes, I made the wizards powerless against the magical creatures. They executed the five Greats that I had cursed and they drained their blood, which the elves molded into the Goblets. Cedric escaped his fate, it would seem. It's my fault the Great Wizards died out, and it's my fault the Goblets Immortal exist in the first place." The words hung heavily between them as they stood there facing each other.

Jinn's thoughts raced in a hundred different directions, but she could form no words at first, and the silence stretched uncomfortably between them. If what he said was true, and she had no reason to doubt him about this, not only could he help them, he could curse Meraude and make the process even easier. "You can curse anyone?"

"Not just anyone," he corrected her. "I have to have them in my sights when I perform the curse."

"But how did you curse me from seeing you?"

He shook his head. "I didn't. There's a taboo on my future, that's it. It's a complicated magic, but it's not quite a curse, though I use the two words interchangeably." Before Jinn could ask him to explain, the wizard held up a hand. "I'm not proud of what I did, and I vowed to myself never to use that magic again. Meraude is awful, yes, but those wishing to kill her will have to do so without my aid."

That made Jinn scowl. Mother was right: she was terrible at hiding her emotions. "If Meraude gets her way, forms her army, and marches against all magical kind that oppose her, you might not get the choice. You must see this. Someone powerful has to stop her."

Hex seemed unmoved. "There's always a choice, Jinn. And it's not just about power. Power can come in unexpected shapes and forms: through understanding and kindness."

Unbelievable. "So, you're saying if I approached her right, showed her some kindness, she might stop her plans?"

"How much do you know about your mother?"

Jinn threw up her hands and groaned.

"No, I'm serious, Jinn. If you knew where she was coming from, why she is the way she is, maybe you could put a halt to her plans. She doesn't need to die to be stopped or destroyed."

"I'm the one who must stop her, Hex."

The wizard studied her, his expression inscrutable. "No."

"No? What do you mean by no?"

"No, you're not going to stop her, and you're most certainly not going to kill her."

Jinn didn't have much of a temper, but Hex was stoking the fire of what little there was within her. "And *you* get to decide that? The house was wrong; I shouldn't have sought you out. You're impossibly thickheaded and controlling." She turned from him, and was surprised to feel him gently snatch her by the arm before she could flee.

"Don't make the same mistake that I made, Jinn. Killing Meraude isn't the answer. It will only eat you alive for the rest of your days as you wrestle with what you have done and what might have been. Trust me."

She shrugged him off.

When he spoke again, his voice had hardened somewhat. "That's why I can't let you go. You're not going to defeat the mage. You're going to get yourself and anyone you take with you killed."

Her eyes filled with angry tears, and she was about to leave, but couldn't resist getting in one last word. "You asked what I knew about my mother's history without asking anything about mine."

"What about your history?" His tone had softened again.

Jinn did not turn to look at him as she continued, her tone brusque. "Our births were a secret, Quick's and mine. Only her right-hand woman knew about us. Thyla, our caretaker, raised us in a small cottage in the middle of nowhere until we were ten. She taught us – or rather, taught *me* – to read and to write and do many other things. The woman loved us, I think. She treated us kindly, and we never wanted for anything. We knew she wasn't our real mother, though we knew nothing of what ours was like.

"It was the day after my tenth birthday when I was Jolted into my abilities. I began to see visions of Meraude in my future, though I only knew her then as some terrible power that would swoop in and take us from our caregiver. There was nothing I could say to convince Thyla to flee with us, and the day came when Meraude showed up on our doorstep." Jinn took in a deep breath.

"She killed Thyla outright, and took me in chains, forcing Quick to follow. Meraude tortured me for a day, hoping to break my spirit so I would obey only her. She knew that Quick would follow. But when she saw it would take more than that to get through to me, she abandoned us in the cave she had taken us to, and didn't come back with food until a week later." She shook her head, trying to clear it of emotions. Hex needed to see what Meraude was capable of, and she needed to communicate it clearly, unclouded by emotion. "She then began training us for her army, but abandoned hope of making anything out of me after six short months. Meraude left us with one blanket and some supplies for two weeks, returning every so often with food and other provisions, which she left at the mouth of the cave.

"Quick and I were too young and naïve to attempt running away at first. But when we turned thirteen, I talked Quick into leaving. I didn't even bother looking ahead, believing that the mage had forgotten us at this point, as she hadn't been to see us for a month. It was the longest she had left us yet. We didn't know that she.... There were snares set up to catch us, should we attempt anything. Quick fell into a pit, and I ended up hanging from a tree limb by my ankle for an hour before he managed to jump out and pull me down." She swallowed, shaking her head at the memories rising up before her eyes. "Meraude knew that her traps had been sprung, and when she returned next, she didn't do anything to me. She – she went for Quick."

When she paused, trying to collect herself, Hex interrupted her. "What did she do?"

Jinn turned to look at him, her left eye twitching. "Quick absorbed my part of the curse that belongs to each Blest, but he wasn't always so...simple. Meraude burned and cut him, over and over again, and made me watch. This went on for five days, until it was obvious he could take no more. Only an Endurer can truly hurt another Endurer." Now she knew she was babbling, so she turned her back and cleared her throat. "You see, Meraude isn't just insane with power-lust, she's evil. Nothing is going to change her. If someone can do what she did to her own children, there is no hope for them."

They stood there for some time without speaking. The expression that the wizard wore was unreadable, and Jinn tried to keep hers neutral. She needed him to believe her, to sympathize with her cause. If she didn't get him on her side of things, she would have to work around him, which would only make things more difficult. There was no time for sneaking around, trying to find a way out. Meraude's plans were unknown to Jinn for the most part, though she knew it would involve the slaughter of much innocent life.

Finally, after what felt like an hour, Hex sighed and shook his head. "I believe what you say is true, Jinn. Meraude's sins are great indeed."

Jinn braced herself. "But?"

"I've seen things you haven't. If I were to allow you to have the Goblets, and you were by some miracle able to destroy them and then Meraude, what then? I've seen death, Jinn – death that the Goblets could prevent. What a waste to destroy them."

The air left Jinn's lungs in one great whoosh. "Deaths, many preventable deaths, will happen if the Goblets are *not* destroyed. You have to see that." She was nearing the end of her patience, and it took all her strength not to reach out and shake the wizard to make him see sense.

Hex's shoulders heaved and then he squared them. "I'm sorry, but there's no changing my mind about this."

Jinn's heart sank, and her careful mask turned into a scowl. "You're on her side, then."

That seemed to startle Hex. "No, I'm not, Jinn. Please don't say that." He reached out as if to take her arm again, but Jinn pulled away.

"Don't touch me."

"Please, I would help you if I could, but you don't understand what you're asking of me."

She turned and walked away, annoyed to find him close at her heels. "Leave me alone, wizard." Jinn felt the ghost of his hand reaching for her shoulder, and she quickened her pace.

"I know that you're angry, but you don't understand all the facts. You haven't seen what I've seen."

Jinn stopped walking and spun around to face him, and the two nearly collided. She swatted him away after he had righted her. "Then enlighten me."

The wizard seemed unwilling or unable to speak, his eyes pained. "Please, don't make me say it."

Unyielding, Jinn stared up at him, her temper simmering. "If you're not going to give me any solid answers, I see little point in continuing this conversation. Goodbye, Hex, and good—"

"You die, Jinn." The words came out with such force that Jinn took a step back. "That's what I've seen. If the Goblets are destroyed, there will be nothing to save you." His eyes closed as if against great pain. "Every time I lift the taboo around my future and I follow the path that leads to the Goblets being destroyed, I watch you die, helpless to do anything."

A great shudder rippled through Jinn's body, one that she was unable to stop. Was the wizard telling her the truth? And if so, what was it to him if she lived or died? Hex was lying. He had to be. "I don't think I believe you."

"Jinn, please."

But Jinn had had enough. She took off at a run, taking the path she was fairly certain would lead her back to Quick. This time, the wizard did not follow.

CHAPTER EIGHT

Aidan

When Aidan awoke, the room was dark, dancing in shadows cast against a blue fire in the grate. His stomach clenched with pain, and he realized he had not eaten or drunk anything in quite some time. He smelled the remnants of a meal, and wondered if he had been asleep for days or merely hours.

The air was charged, causing the back of his neck to prickle with dread, though there were no signs of immediate danger. Still, it felt like he was being watched.

Aidan took catalogue of what he observed. Slaíne slept next to him in the bed, her Pull reassuring and strong. Last they had spoken, they had fought. Aidan shook his head at the memory. Was he being too stubborn and unforgiving? *I'm not.* His feelings for her remained unchanged, but it would take a long while before he accepted what she had done to him. He moved his attention away from her and looked about the room. Even though the room was dim, Aidan could make out every detail of his surroundings, something he credited to his strange new abilities that he had not sorted through yet. Everything was exactly as he remembered it. Nothing had moved. And yet something was wrong.

He sat up and dangled his legs over the edge of the bed. A breeze met his toes, which he curled, before lowering his feet to the floor. Careful not to wake Slaíne, Aidan padded toward the window. The drapes had been left open, letting in extra cold air. Not that it bothered him. Still, he took one look into the dark, listening to waves crash against the rocks below and the wind whistle through cracks between the windowpanes, before closing the heavy curtains and turning back to face the room.

"Who's there?" he said more to himself than anyone else.

In her sleep, Slaíne mumbled something and reached out to where he had been lying. When her hand met no resistance, she rolled over to his side and at once began to snore.

Aidan took to prowling about the room. There were no human Pulls that he could find, but there lay a heavy presence nearby, one that was most decidedly unfriendly. Summoning the silver sword into his hands, Aidan moved toward the door. Something or someone was out there.

The door shook on its hinges, startling Aidan and nearly causing him to drop the blade. He drew in a steadying breath and closed his eyes, seeking the source of the Pull. Ah, it was a weak one, and it had changed in substance since he had last felt it, but he was certain he knew it. His eyes flew open, and he considered opening the door and facing the creature, in whatever form it might choose to take, but he remembered that he had not just himself to think of. "Slaíne," he said.

She stopped snoring but said nothing.

Aidan looked over his shoulder and saw that she had sat up, but her eyes were barely open. *I don't know how, but the shape-shifter has followed us here somehow*, he thought at her, hoping his words would reach.

Slaíne groaned. "That's not likely. Come back to bed. Or better yet, eat somethin'. You was asleep all day yesterday after your...fit." She frowned in the darkness.

Ignoring her concern, Aidan approached the door, one hand outstretched to open it, the other holding the sword, ready to strike. There was a gentle rapping at the door across the hall where the Pull had retreated.

"Lord Ingledark?" asked a woman's voice, one that Aidan recognized. "Are you in there?"

A floorboard creaked beneath Aidan's bare feet, and the Pull across the hall moved closer. "Who's there?" Aidan asked, keeping his voice steady as he unbolted the door and prepared to turn the knob.

"Aidan, what are you doing?" Slaíne demanded.

Before he could open the door, it flew open and nearly hit him in the face. He was thrown backward, as if by an invisible hand, and missed hitting his head against the wardrobe by a hand's breadth. He sprang to his feet, Calling the sword back into his hand, as he had dropped it during his fall.

There, standing across from him, was the wizard Hex. But the Pull was all wrong. The creature leapt at Aidan, who lashed out with his sword. The being was fast, but he didn't have Aidan's skill set. Without hesitation, he Summoned his copper knife and Repelled it away from himself directly at the other's chest. The knife froze inches from the shifter's face— no, *Slaíne's* face.

"Aidan," the real Slaíne screamed.

The shape-shifter mimicked her cry perfectly, turning Aidan's skin to gooseflesh. It reached for the knife that hovered midair, but Aidan Dismissed the blade. "No, Slaíne. Don't engage it. I know this creature's Pull." *You won't be able to tell the difference should he take my form.*

Once more the creature shifted its shape, now taking on the form of Jinn before changing its mind and transforming into her giant of a brother. He lashed out at Aidan with great strength and speed, nearly striking him.

Aidan felt the breeze the creature's fist had made. He swung around with the sword in response, but again the blade was blocked by an unseen hand. Cursing, Aidan Dismissed the weapon and charged at the shifter-giant.

The creature caught him midair by the throat, and tossed him aside like he was a rag doll, and went for Slaíne. There was a knife in the shifter's hand now, a thin cruel blade that had no Pull.

Aidan stumbled to his feet and latched on to the creature's Pull, attempting to Call him. It had only ever worked with Slaíne, something that didn't seem to have changed now. He only managed to slow the shape-shifter, having successfully latched on to the Pull of a glove on his hand. That gave him enough time to run and launch himself at the creature, only to be flung back. "Run, Slaíne. I can't stop him."

Slaíne threw herself out of bed and flew right up to the ceiling, drawing a frustrated huff from the shifter.

"Watch out," Aidan cried as it threw the knife at her. The blade missed her by a foot and embedded in the wall behind her.

Seeing that its one weapon was out of play, the creature looked at the door and began to flee. Aidan was going to let him go, but the door swung shut and barred itself.

"Why did you do that?" Aidan and Slaíne asked each other at the same time.

Now the shape-shifter was trapped with them. It grinned before shifting back to Slaíne's form, prowling slowly toward Aidan. "Wrong wizard," it said, cocking its head to the side. "It will have to suffice."

"Stay up there," Aidan warned Slaíne, trying to think of something, anything he could do. For some reason, he had been unable to land any blows on the being, who seemed to have no such limitation. If he could not attack, then Aidan knew he would have to at least defend himself until help could arrive.

"Aidan, you need ter—"

Whatever Aidan needed to do, he did not hear over his own ragged breathing and the roar of the shape-shifter who came at him in Slaíne's form. Aidan Summoned the sword again, effectively blocking the creature's fist from connecting with his head.

The shape-shifter skidded backward, as if repulsed by the blade.

It was disconcerting seeing such hatred and malice in Slaíne's likeness, but Aidan tried not to let that distract him. Experimentally, he held out a hand and tried Summoning a curtain rod at the shape-shifter. Like the sword before it, the object landed harmlessly inches from the creature's feet.

With a great snarl, the shape-shifter lifted the rod and tried using it as a weapon against Aidan, who simply Dismissed it. "You'll tire soon enough," the shifter promised.

Aidan did not doubt that. Being turned into a wizard had taken its toll on his body, and he knew himself to only just be on the road to full strength. He needed to think of something quickly.

Fly, you great idiot, Slaíne shouted into his mind, disorienting him for a moment. A moment was all that it took for the creature to get past his defenses.

The shifter kicked the sword out of Aidan's hand and punched him in the stomach, knocking the wind out of his lungs. As Aidan tried to launch himself at the ceiling, hoping that this time he would be able to make flight work, he was seized by the leg and thrown against the wall. Stars swam before his eyes as he tried Summoning the sword.

Again he lashed out and the blade skidded off harmlessly. Aidan was going to Dismiss it and then Summon it, but the creature's hands were around his throat, strangling him.

Slaíne shrieked and made to fly at the attacker, but Aidan held up a hand and Repelled her back to safety. The creature might have been able to land physical blows and block air from reaching Aidan's lungs, but it was not having quite the obviously desired effect.

It was strange; he was not breathing and could feel the pressure on his neck, but it did not hurt. No spots formed in the corners of Aidan's vision. His lungs did not burn.

With a furious scream, the shape-shifter released Aidan's throat and shifted into a new shape that had knives for nails and tried stabbing him.

Uncertain if the blades could harm him or not, Aidan threw up his arms to protect his neck and face, and a blinding flash of green light filled the room. He blinked and lowered his hands, wondering why the creature hadn't attacked. What he saw confused him.

The shape-shifter was suspended mid-jump in what appeared to be a large bubble, which pulsed green and shot out strange little bolts of light every time the being attempted to move. "Strange," Aidan mused as he pulled himself to his feet.

"He manages impossible magic and all he can say is 'strange'?" Slaíne scoffed as she lowered herself from the ceiling. "Not a wizard, my hide."

Aidan ignored that. "Do you think Hex sent it to kill us?"

The beady-eyed man's mouth worked furiously as he tried to wriggle free from the small prison. Aidan felt a slight prickling under his skin every time the shifter attempted to move, and it occurred to him that it was his own magic actively powering the transparent cage.

"Doubt Hex had anythin' to do with it," Slaíne said with a shrug. Her eyes narrowed. "Though, I'd like ter know what we're doin' under the same roof as it."

Aidan couldn't agree more. "What should we do with it?"

"If we can't kill it, we should at least take it to Hex and demand he do something. Can't go 'round all the time with one eye o'er our shoulders, can we?"

"Agreed." He reached out a hand toward the bubble, which responded by floating away a few inches. "I guess that answers the question of how to move it."

Despite the late hour and the peril, Slaíne gave him a smug smile and led the way out of the room and down the hall, where they were met by the wizard, who appeared most disheveled. "How did he get past me?" were his first words.

Slaíne glared and pointed her finger in his face. "Keeps company with a murderously evil creature and wonders where he went wrong."

Hex's face darkened, but he did not rise to Slaíne's bait as Aidan knew he would have. "Forgive me. I thought I had him under control." Before Slaíne could hurl more insults and accusations at him, the wizard reached out and tapped the bubble, which faded from green to red. "Welch, you're henceforth banished from ever setting foot in the House of Curses. Should you attempt to interfere with me and my company again, may my deadliest of curses be on you."

The creature seemed to shrink and then disappeared with a loud popping sound.

"He was meant only to keep you from breaking the curse," he said to Slaíne, earning a low growl from the she-wizard. "He failed there." Hex gave Aidan a rueful glance. "He wasn't supposed to try killing anyone, though."

It was Aidan's turn to urge caution. *Slaíne, remember that we don't know all he's capable of.*

She gave him a sideways glance. "Why'd you do it?" she demanded, ignoring Aidan's concern. "Why curse me and then set that creature against me?"

"Because I didn't know how else to deal with your power," Hex said evenly. "By the time I found out you even existed, you'd nearly killed your adopted parents twice. In fact, I thought you were responsible for their deaths, until I discovered Meraude's involvement."

Slaíne began to shake. "I nay ever hurt them."

Aidan watched Hex and was sad to see the truth in his eyes.

"It was an accident," Hex reassured her. "But you were too dangerous, nonetheless." He motioned for them to follow him into the adjoining room, but neither Aidan nor Slaíne were inclined to move. The wizard's shoulders sagged. "I meant to raise you myself and used the curse as a precaution." He sighed heavily. "You got away from me shortly after, and the elves were there. I tried getting you to come with me, but the elves took advantage of the terms of the curse."

Tears rolled down Slaíne's cheeks, and she did nothing to wipe them away. "You sayin' I went with them o' my own will?"

Hex nodded then frowned. "We had fought, if I recall correctly. You were only five and five hundred years—"

Aidan's eyebrows rose in alarm. "Five hundred years?"

The wizard put up a hand to waylay Aidan's questions. "You were very young and wanted your own way. The elves seemed to promise that, so you chose to go with them. I had no choice but to flee before they, and you with them, could overwhelm me."

Slaíne regarded him for a moment, and the tears stopped flowing. Now she swiped at her nose angrily, and looked over at Aidan, who didn't know what comfort he could offer such suffering.

I'm sorry.

If she had heard him or not, Aidan was uncertain. Slaíne's expression hardened and she turned away from both of them. "So ya sent your shape-shifter to keep watch o'er me? No, that ain't right." She clenched her hands into fists. "You made sure I stayed cursed so I could harm no one else, is that it?"

The wizard was quiet.

Slaíne turned, and her eyes glowed an unnatural blue. "Tell me!"

"You were and are a danger and a menace," he said without emotion. "You're lucky that what you did to Aidan didn't kill him."

"I knew it wouldn't," she spat back. "I know my own power."

Hex stared back at her, unmoved and unconvinced, apparently. "Transferring part of your soul should not have worked. It never has even been attempted before." He shook his head. "You are too young and impulsive. Aidan didn't deserve to be put through this hell, no matter what you feel for—"

Aidan's hand shot out as if of its own will, and a blast of green light flew out of his fingertips, stopping half an inch before the wizard's face as it pulsed threateningly. "Don't," he growled, "attempt to speak for me."

The wizard's face paled in the light, and his eyes grew wide with surprise before narrowing. "So you've accepted your fate? Welcome." He pushed the ball of light aside, and it faded away as Aidan realized he could not harm Hex. "Go back to bed. You both begin training in the morning."

★　　★　　★

Aidan slept very little that night. When he did manage to rest, he dreamed of Slaíne wandering alone, weeping as she wiped blood from her hands that could not be cleansed. Weary and wound tight, he rose before the sun.

The thought of training as a wizard made Aidan ill at ease. He could refuse, surely. *But why would you want to do that?* asked a nagging voice in the back of his mind. Deep down he knew he should use every advantage he had against Meraude and Hex. "This isn't natural," he found himself saying and then felt foolish. Nothing about him had ever been natural.

When the nymph queen had stabbed him in the shoulder with the ice knife – Nitchoo – Aidan had seen visions of his past. If those visions were to be believed, Aidan had been conceived and born inside the confines of the Circle, a cult that had apparently bred men and women to have offspring with magical abilities from the Goblets Immortal. His parents and uncle had escaped somehow, but Aidan was the product of that treachery. Meraude had found them years later and killed Lord and Lady Ingledark, along with Aidan's younger brother, Samuel. At least, Aidan had believed this to be true. Now, pacing the room, he had time to piece together facts that he had had little time or inclination to before.

After defeating Lord Dewhurst, the man who had framed Aidan for murder, Aidan had found Lord and Lady Ingledark's somewhat decomposed bodies on the estate. "How were they only partially decayed?" he wondered aloud, causing Slaíne to stir slightly. More than twenty years had passed since their deaths. The bodies ought to have been dust.

Aidan Summoned a water bladder and took a swig of tepid drink. Then he froze. Had Dewhurst kept them alive that whole time? But for what purpose? He knew that Meraude and Dewhurst had forged some kind of alliance. If the Ingledarks had been kept alive that whole time, Aidan had failed them worse than he had at first imagined.

"My fault," he gasped, and the pain was too great to bear. He collapsed to his knees and clenched his hands into fists.

It was there, despair washing over him as he tried to find release in tears that would not come, that his inner friend gave him a gentle nudge. *Aidan.* Salem's voice was faint and yet hoarse, as though he had been screaming for some time. And then, it was silent.

Aidan shook his head and Dismissed the water bladder, which had dropped onto the floor. Morose, he watched as the water from the vessel pooled on the floor. *This is why you need to train. If you don't keep busy, your thoughts will eat you alive.*

Swiping angrily at his nose, Aidan stumbled to his feet. But his thoughts were not done with him. He could still see his mother lying there in Dewhurst's stables, her honey-blond hair splayed out around her.... How was it possible that she had looked so young? A new idea came to Aidan, one that made his stomach churn but at the same time lifted a weight from his shoulders. When Slaíne had killed the guards holding them captive at Lord Dewhurst's manor several weeks ago, Aidan had Dismissed their bodies. He was unable to Dismiss anyone that was alive – save for himself and Slaíne – but once a person's life force left them, they had less of a Pull anchoring them to Existence. Perhaps Meraude had murdered his parents all those years ago and Dismissed their bodies for some reason. Nothing decayed in Nothingness.

But how did they end up on Dewhurst's estate? Meraude was nowhere near us at the time…or was she? And was Meraude also a Summoner? Maybe Hex would know.

Now he felt a little better, though there were still too many questions paddling around in his mind for him to get back to sleep. He looked back at Slaíne, who remained in a deep sleep. He could feel the whispers of her troubled dreams lap against his own thoughts, but was able to shut them out without too much difficulty. There was nothing to be done here in this room, and now that Slaíne's curse no longer set a boundary of how far they could be apart, Aidan needn't worry about hurting her in that way. Perhaps it was time to do some exploring of his own.

But Aidan hesitated. Last night, he had unbolted the door, accidentally letting the shape-shifter in. If he left now, there would be no way to keep Slaíne safe from whatever remaining horrors lurked in the House of Curses. The solution came to him almost instantly. With one more look at his mate, Aidan closed his eyes and relaxed, Releasing all of the Pulls around him. He first focused on detaching himself from the small, inanimate things: the blankets on the bed, the rugs on the cold floor, and then moved on to bigger things, such as the bed and the washtub and wardrobe. Then there was Slaíne's Pull to contend with. It was stronger now than ever, and Aidan had trouble for a moment as he tried separating from it. Then, grasping success quite unexpectedly, Aidan left Existence and entered Nothingness.

In the past, he had never been able to see or even move in the land between the mortal realm of Existence and the land of the Beyond, but now he found himself standing in what appeared to be a large storeroom full of all the things he had sent there. In a tidy stack sat the papers he had managed to take from Dewhurst's manor: clues and maps to the different Goblets Immortal. Those were perhaps useless to him now, as Hex had two of the five at least. Aidan turned from the papers and looked around. There was the silver sword, the bronze sword, which he had taken from the shifter when they had first met weeks upon weeks ago, and odds and ends strewn among hay and tanderine blossoms. With sadness, he remembered his horse, Triumph, which had been taken from him by goblins.

Now that he had taken catalogue of what he had in his cache, Aidan focused on returning to Existence, outside the door. When he had returned from Nothingness with Slaíne the other week, there had been little difficulty in landing exactly where he had planned. This time, he felt a strange pressure in his chest as he tried to return, and put a hand over his heart. Slaíne's soul-half was writhing just there, causing him pain.

Aidan returned to the room in Existence with a great grunt. He was startled to find Slaíne standing right in front of him, awake and screaming his name.

"What happened?" she said with a great sob upon seeing him, and then threw her arms around his neck.

Bemused, Aidan returned the embrace and patted her awkwardly on the back. "I didn't mean to wake you."

Slaíne stiffened in his arms. "What?"

"What?" was all Aidan could think to say in return. Apparently he should have offered something more than that, because Slaíne pulled back and glared at him.

"Ya *wanted* to scare me?"

Confused, Aidan shook his head. "No." He stretched the word out for an uncomfortably long time, earning him another dirty look.

She swore at him. "Then what were you doin'? Where were you?"

"I Dismissed myself."

Her expression shifted to confusion. "What? Why?"

"To keep you safe," he said, feeling dumber with each spoken word. Aidan shook his head. This was going poorly. He tried again. "After the shifter attacked last night, I didn't think it wise to leave the door unbarred, and since I wanted to explore…." The look on his mate's face made him stop.

"So you were goin' ter leave me without warnin', attempted to Dismiss yourself to the other side o' the door, and nearly gave me a heart episode in the process? Blimey, Aidan, what were you thinkin'?" She reached out and grabbed him again.

Well, that was irritating. "So you're allowed to leave me sleeping and locked in, but I attempt anything similar, and there's hell to pay?" Anger bubbled hot in his stomach, and he found himself trying to pull away. "I think there are a few things we need to sort through, Slaíne."

But Slaíne was having none of that. She held him tighter still, as if reassuring herself that he was not gone for good, though he could feel the heat of her anger in the kiss she pressed against his lips. "You could have warned me."

If he were not so angry, perhaps he would feel guilty. As gently as he could while still seething, he extricated himself from Slaíne's embrace and stormed toward the door.

"What are you doing?" she shouted, her relief giving way to rage, apparently. A wall of flames burst forth in front of Aidan, forcing him back.

He shot a glare over his shoulder at Slaíne, who was shaking, her face drawn and pale. "I'm sorry. I didn't mean...." As she spoke, the blue flames sputtered and died out into nothing, leaving behind a metallic tang in the air that tickled Aidan's nose.

Aidan didn't spare her another look before stepping over the thin pile of ash on the floor, his spine rigid and his steps louder, heavier than what was necessary. He ignored her, even as she called his name, storming through the doorway before slamming the door shut behind him. Only when he heard a raw, tortured sob from the other side of the door did he hesitate. His anger cooled for a moment, before the embers of it were fanned into flames again. She had made him what he was, and now she sought to control him.

She loves you, you idiot, whispered the fair part of his mind. *You worried her.*

He brushed the thought aside. Since he had become...whatever it was that he was now, Aidan had noticed his temper rising to the surface oftener. It was as if something inside him had broken and was trying to bind itself together again with whatever strong feelings he could find within himself. There was the very strong compulsion to strike something.

With a frustrated grunt, he continued onward, blind to the riches surrounding him. With each step he took, it felt more and more like he was wading waist-deep in honey. Slaíne's Pull, normally a comfort, now chafed at him. His pace quickened. He needed to get away and sort through things.

Suddenly he stopped. He had become aware of a Pull nearby, one that he recognized slightly. Unaware of whether or not the familiar presence was friendly, Aidan darted behind a marble pillar, and waited for it to pass.

"Hello?" asked a deep, rumbly voice. "Jinn? You behind pillar? Please don't play games."

Aidan knew that voice, but he couldn't place it for a moment. Covertly, he peered around the pillar and at once remembered the giant of a man who had attempted to capture him after the whole ordeal at Cedric's tomb. Last Aidan had seen him, the giant had been turned into a bird by Hex. *Ally or rival?* Aidan couldn't decide.

"Jinn? Please." The giant's Pull was moving closer to Aidan's hiding place; he needed to make a move quickly.

Rage all but forgotten, Aidan ducked around the pillar and into clear view of the large man. "I don't think we have properly met."

The man blinked and stared. "You're the Summoner."

How should he respond to that? Aidan nodded. "You grabbed me."

"Yes, Quick did. Where sister?" As he did not make a move toward Aidan, Aidan did not Summon a weapon or Dismiss himself.

"Is your sister Jinn?"

"Yes," said he. "You know where she is?"

Aidan shook his head. "Not at the moment." It was alarming, the height of the man. He had to stand over seven feet tall. Aidan was not used to being the shortest person in a situation. "Why were you and Jinn looking for me, Mr....?"

"Quick," he rumbled in reply. "You are…?"

"Aidan." Aidan extended his hand, the giant stooped, and the two clasped forearms. Aidan repeated his first question, earning a shrug from Quick.

The giant gave him a suspicious look for a moment, and that emotion ironed out into confusion. "Quick doesn't know. Jinn always makes plans." He scratched his head. "Quick thinks it is about Mother. Jinn does not like Mother."

"Hmm," Aidan murmured in what he hoped was a consoling tone. "Mothers can be problematic."

Quick nodded with enthusiasm. "Oh, yes. Mother is a *very* big problem."

This isn't going anywhere. But Aidan remained, knowing that the man's sister was a potential ally. "What do you know of Meraude?"

For a moment, the man stood there blinking and looking this way and that. "What else were we talking about?" He considered Aidan through squinted eyes. "You are not very bright."

Aidan sighed. "I've been accused of worse, I suppose. We were talking about Meraude, were we?" The gears in Aidan's head turned. "Wait. Meraude is your mother?"

A great blush crept up Quick's face and neck, and he hemmed and hawed a bit. "Was not supposed to tell you that. Oh dear. Don't tell Jinn that Quick told." He looked about, as though his sister might pop up out of nowhere and scold him. He leaned down and whispered in a conspiring tone, "Mother's bad. Jinn says you won't help us if you know." The giant leaned back and regarded Aidan for a moment.

That complicated things. If he was telling the truth, and he seemed too simple and honest to speak anything else, why would Jinn seek him out? Why tell him about Meraude's army? It made no sense. "So Meraude *is* your mother."

Quick looked away.

"Not a very good mother, I'd wager," Aidan said, testing the waters. When the man did not answer but cringed ever so slightly, Aidan tried a different approach. "Do you love her, your mother?"

The giant shrugged and looked down. "Quick supposes."

"Quick?"

"Yes?"

This would have to be said with care. "I need to know what side you're on. If you stand with your mother, we might— you, your sister, and I might stand at odds." What a strange conversation to be having in the middle of a cursed house. It almost drove his fight with Slaíne out of his thoughts – *almost*.

Quick's brow furrowed, and as he began to speak, his overlarge hands swung through the air in a frantic gesture. "Quick loves Jinn more. Jinn does not love Mother." His shoulders heaved. "Jinn thinks Quick is stupid."

Aidan waited as patiently as he could for his potential ally to speak, all the while aware that he needed to make better use of his time exploring the house. Anything he said, however, might break the spell of the moment, so he kept his lips pressed together.

At length, the man said, "Jinn wants Mother dead."

"And what do you want, Quick?" Aidan asked, trying to keep his tone neutral.

Quick seemed to consider that for a moment and said, "You are the first to ask that." He hesitated. "Quick does not know."

That was enough to work with. Aidan felt around, making certain Hex's Pull was nowhere nearby. He could sense it, right next to Jinn's, but it was faint, meaning the wizard was far enough away. "And what do you know of the Goblets Immortal and the Blest?"

"Quick is Blest. Jinn is Blest. You are Blest too, Quick thinks."

Aidan nodded; he would not get into how complicated that was now. "Which Goblets does Meraude have?"

For a moment, the man hesitated. "Would Summoner be angry if Quick didn't know?"

"That is a shame, but I wouldn't—"

"Drifting and Enduring," he said, ticking the two off on his fingers. "Mother wants Questing Goblet." Quick pulled a face. "Then Mother will do whatever it is she wants."

Thank any powers above that there was no such thing as the Questing Goblet. Aidan did not mention it, however; some cards should be played close to one's breast. "And what is it your mother wants to do?"

The question seemed to bring Quick up short. He regarded Aidan with a wary eye and then shrugged. "Jinn not know, Quick not know. Summoner does not know either?"

Aidan sighed. "I can guess. She hates all magic-kind, besides herself, so why not kill all of us?"

Now Quick was laughing, a great booming sound that echoed down the empty hall, causing Aidan to wince. "She not hate *all* magic-kind. Just bad ones."

"Bad ones? And who, to her, are the bad ones?"

But it would seem he had lost the giant's interest. Quick looked around, a frown upon his face. "Where is sister?" He walked past Aidan and began to call out.

At once Aidan hushed Quick, earning an annoyed look in return.

"Why be quiet?" the man asked.

Aidan frowned. "I don't think we should be found together. In fact, tell no one but your sister that we met."

"All right."

Thoughts racing, Aidan started again to ask Quick for more information about Meraude and her plans, but the man was walking away from him. With a frustrated grunt, Aidan gave up trying. "Your sister is the other way," he said, causing the giant to pause. "You're going the wrong way. Jinn is with the wizard, and they are quite a ways down this hall."

Slowly, the man named Quick turned on his heels and trudged in the direction Aidan had pointed him in. "Thank you, Summoner. Happy meeting," he said with a tiny wave.

Aidan left the giant and hurried down the hall in the opposite direction, for the first time trying to take in his surroundings better. The floors were a polished onyx, and though early day's light streamed in through several windows, torches sputtered and stuttered in their sconces on the walls.

We are on a cliff, he reminded himself. The way that they had come to the island was peculiar: Hex had picked a doorknob out of somewhere, placed it in front of him, turned it, and opened an invisible door into a blinding white hallway. *Is that the only way to get here and leave? If so, where does he keep the doorknob?*

Strange Pulls tugged at him left and right, all of them nonliving but still almost just as much a distraction. Aidan ducked into a small sitting room full of ruby-red chaise lounges with gold thread spun along the borders. He closed his eyes and reached out, searching for anything that felt like a doorknob. Unfortunately, doorknobs, like most other nonliving objects, had no real different Pull from that of an inkwell or something else of a similar size. He might be able to tell the difference between a coatrack and chair, but without being familiar with the specific item's Pull, there would be no Summoning or Dismissing it without study. With all the rooms in the mansion, there were surely many doorknobs. Finding the right one would take patience and a thorough investigation of the place. As it was, he didn't have the time. The sun had cleared the horizon, and morning had arrived; Slaíne would become even more worried, and Hex would be perhaps sending for them both.

Still, Aidan was reluctant to return, the memory of the fight churning his insides once more, though not as strongly. He kicked at an area rug in frustration, exposing the worn floorboards beneath. Aidan cocked his head to the side. His temper cooled again as he tried to take in what suddenly nagged at him. The area surrounding the boards didn't seem heavily traveled. Why was this square area so worn?

Aidan kicked away the remainder of the rug and trod across the exposed boards. They creaked beneath his weight, and he could swear where there ought to be the Pulls of supporting beams beneath, there was only empty space. He frowned and got onto his hands and knees. Squinting, he could only just make out the outline of what might turn out to be a trapdoor. There was no time to go exploring, however. Aidan stole a quick look around and re-covered the area. The next time he was alone, he would have a look; now, to learn some magic and perhaps make amends with Slaíne.

*   *   *

When Aidan returned to the room, Slaíne was not there. He sensed her Pull a ways down the hall but did not pursue her. It was *she* who should seek *him* out, after what she had done. Telling himself he was glad to have some time alone, Aidan stripped and took a cold bath in the new tub in the corner of the room. Having toweled off and dressed, he found a shaving kit in the wardrobe and gave himself as close a shave as he could. And while he was at it, he took a knife and cut a few inches off of his hair so that it was now just below his ears.

Feeling human once more, Aidan decided to ignore Slaíne's absence and the wizard's promise to train him, in favor of exploring again. He had just tugged on his boots and was approaching the door, when he noticed a folded bit of parchment lying in the entryway. That was strange. He hadn't noticed any human Pulls approaching the door while he'd been cleaning up. Wary suddenly, Aidan nudged the parchment with his boot toe and picked it up. It read:

Breakfast is in five minutes. Follow your senses to the dining hall. Tardiness is frowned upon. Looking where you ought not is punishable. – Hex.

As soon as he had read the signature, the parchment began to crumble into dust in his hands and then blew away on a sudden breeze. Aidan turned from the door. Something deep within him rebelled at the thought of answering a summons as if he were some mere dog. On the other hand, he hadn't eaten a decent meal in a while, and there might be answers over shared bread.

Hunger won over pride, and he went in search of Slaíne to convey the message to her. He followed her Pull to another room a few doors down and knocked. There was no answer. "Slaíne?" he said, trying the doorknob. The door didn't budge. "The wizard has sent for us. We are to eat breakfast and then you can train." There was no response, nor any stirring within. He hesitated and swallowed even more of his pride. "I'm sorry my temper got the better of me." Now he was beginning to worry. Again he tried the door, this time throwing his shoulder against it, wondering if it was merely stuck. Then he heard a low sigh, and he knew that she was at least conscious. Troubled, he pressed his ear up against the door but heard no other sound. "Come, let's forget this morning and break our fast together. Surely you're famished."

Sweet relief flooded him as he sensed her Pull moving nearer to the door. He thought she would open it and emerge, but her Pull stopped.

"Slaíne? Are you hurt?" Should he break down the door and make certain she was all right?

Hearing his thoughts, Slaíne hastily said, "Go to breakfast. I need some time alone."

Aidan frowned. "You sound…odd. Is everything all right?"

Again she sighed. "Yes. Go. Just go."

"All right." Still he hesitated. Was this some sort of test? If so, he was bound to fail it, no matter what he did. His heart gave him a painful twinge, as though he had something to feel guilty about. What that might be, he couldn't imagine.

He turned his back to the door and went in search of Hex, aware that more than five minutes had passed since he had received the note. The House of Curses sprawled out in many directions, one hallway connected to another, leaving Aidan in doubt that it ever ended. Though his sense of Pulls had changed, he still was able to pinpoint the wizard's and followed it around the corner from where he had left Slaíne, down a long hall, and up a short flight of stairs past empty suits of armor and flowing tapestries, to the outside of a closed wooden door. He raised his fist to knock.

"You're late," said a voice on the other side of the door, which creaked open. "Come in and be seated."

Teeth clenched, Aidan fought his misgivings and forced himself into the room. The room was three times the size of the one he was staying in with Slaíne, and had a full wall of windows on the southern wall on the left, giving him a clear view of the ocean. In the middle of the room sat a dark wood table with high-backed chairs seated around it. Hex faced Aidan and thus the door, his expression wary. On his right sat Jinn, arms folded and face stony, and on his left sat Quick, who was too busy stuffing his face full of eggs and ham to wear any expression whatsoever.

"You've met Jinn," the wizard said as Aidan continued to stand there. "And I wonder if you have met her brother, Quick."

"A pleasure," Aidan muttered as dread dropped down into his stomach like a stone. The air prickled with magic and danger. His hairs rose on end and he fought down an animalistic growl that was clawing its way up his throat.

Hex's eyes seared into him and then looked back at Jinn, as if he were trying to solve some difficult puzzle. "Please, be seated."

Slowly, Aidan moved and took a seat on Jinn's other side, hoping to remove any suspicion that he had been talking with her brother. "Thank you."

The wizard waved his hand, and Aidan's plate filled itself. "I take it she isn't feeling well this morning?"

Aidan stiffened. *Please, no small talk.* "Slaíne's as well as one could imagine." *After your man tried to murder us both last night.*

Hex inclined his head and lifted a small chalice to his lips, regarding Aidan over the rim. "Will she be joining us for training?"

Aidan did not like the way the other was watching him, and his questions nettled. But he knew he needed nutrition if he wanted to remain strong and able to escape at a moment's notice. Unless the food was drugged or poisoned....

The wizard was still watching him and let out a humorless laugh. "Eat. I haven't poisoned anything." He looked meaningfully at the giant, who was downing a tankard of something that might be small beer. "Besides, poison is a woman's method."

Next to him, Jinn let out a huff and gave Aidan an annoyed look. They both knew that the wizard was trying to pit them against each other.

Still, Aidan explored the Pulls of the ham, eggs, hash, toasted brown bread, and beans. Nothing felt out of the ordinary, so he reluctantly raised a forkful to his mouth and chewed with trepidation.

Hex sighed. "You really do trust no one, don't you? Well, except for the she-wizard, and look where that has gotten you."

Aidan narrowed his eyes and swallowed the piping-hot mouthful of food. *He's testing your temper. Training a rage-filled wizard would be dangerous.*

Biting back a retort, Aidan explored the Pulls in his own tankard of small beer and, finding them to be safe, he took a small sip.

The wizard gave him a curious look and drained his chalice. "What did you two fight about?"

"What business is it of yours?" Aidan said coolly. *Stay calm. He's baiting you.* Aidan was then hit in the face with a spray of small beer, which had just exploded from the tankard in front of him. Shocked and dripping, he turned a glare at the wizard, who merely shrugged and refilled his own glass as if nothing had happened.

Jinn, however, was staring at Aidan as though he'd sprouted another head. Even Quick gave him a dubious glance before attacking the remainder of food on his enormous plate.

"I heard you two shouting, felt a pulse of magic leave one of you, and then there was much stomping of feet and slamming of doors. You really ought to keep a check on that temper of yours." He gave Aidan a meaningful look and took a bite out of his toasted bread. "What happens under this roof is my business, you see."

Mind games, Aidan thought with a rueful sigh. It was too early to attempt to match wits. Wiping the sticky beverage from his face with his sleeve, he froze when the wizard said, "Dismiss it."

Aidan blinked and said without thinking, "Liquids don't have Pulls."

Hex shrugged and took a sip again from the chalice. "You're thinking like a Summoner, Aidan."

"I *am* a Summoner."

"No," said the wizard calmly and slowly, as though he were speaking to a particularly dense child. "That's not even half of it. Try."

When he realized Hex wasn't going to relent until he at least attempted something, Aidan shook the remaining small beer from his hair, closed his eyes, and was about to search for the liquid's non-existent Pull, when something hot and greasy hit him in the face. His eyes flew open, and he looked down at the sausage now sitting on the table in front of him. "What are you playing at?" He swiped at the spot where the meat had struck him.

The wizard gave him a puzzled look and returned to eating. "Are you unwell?"

Quick let out a bark of a laugh, pounding the table and sending the plates jumping. "This is amusing. Do it again."

Jinn looked back and forth between Aidan and the wizard, her expression confused. Apparently still subdued, she said nothing and took a dainty sip from the chalice in front of her.

Now Aidan kept his eyes open and on Hex as he tried to Dismiss the small beer from his face and shirt. At first he could sense nothing besides his shirt and his own body, but after a moment he could swear there was something else. He blinked and tried to Dismiss whatever strange Pull he was feeling, but a piece of buttered bread collided with the side of his head, effectively distracting him. *Calm. Remain calm.* Aidan Dismissed the bread and was prepared to Dismiss the butter from the side of his face as well, when the ham on the platter in front of him rose slowly in the air before him. Before it could strike him, Aidan Dismissed the meat as well, only to feel something cold and wet spill down the back of his neck. He didn't have time to register what it might be when all manner of food and drink started to fly at him. Some Pulls he Dismissed, others he Repelled, trying to be mindful of the other guests at the table so that they would not be struck. But as soon as he sent an object away, another filled its place.

Finally, having had enough, Aidan slammed his hands down on the table, and everything froze. Bacon was suspended midair, along with a stream of small beer and globs of red jam from a golden tureen. Plates and specks of food hung between him and the other guests. Aidan let out a stunned breath, and everything vanished, except for the sharp knife he felt hurtling toward him. Aidan reached out and plucked it from the air before it could strike his neck.

Sticky and bewildered, Aidan looked over at the wizard, who was studying him approvingly. "Now Dismiss the small beer," said Hex, handing a clean napkin to Jinn, who was also covered in the morning's meal.

Rising, Aidan did as the wizard said without batting an eye.

"That is all for now. Training will resume this afternoon." A slow smile spread across Hex's face. "I suggest you clean up some time between now and then."

CHAPTER NINE

Aidan

That was humiliating, Aidan mused as he returned to the room he shared with Slaíne. With a grunt he moved to the washtub, sending the door slamming shut with a thought. For the second time that day he stripped and washed off in the tepid water, which mercifully – and perhaps magically – had been changed since earlier that morning.

After washing quickly, he dried off with a towel and found new clothes to dress in: a slate-gray tunic and a pair of black trousers, suitable for prowling around the sprawling mansion later. The wizard had made it clear in the letter that he would be in danger of punishment if caught poking his nose in places he ought not. *What is he going to do? Lock me up?* Aidan sat down on the edge of the bed so he could tug on his boots.

His stomach growled. He'd only managed to get a bite of poached egg and a bit of toast. This would not do. Slaíne must also be famished, he realized, and the notion propelled him to focus on his cache in Nothingness. Sadly, the food from the breakfast table was not where he thought he might have sent it, and there was nothing else there to be eaten but the strange apples he had been given in the Beyond.

Aidan got to his feet and decided to go in search of the kitchen. Perhaps he would find more clues as to the magical doorknob's whereabouts, or he could poke around some more at the potential trapdoor he had found earlier.

As he wandered, he sent a thought to Slaíne, telling her what he was doing. When he received no response, Aidan took a step to find her, hesitated, and corrected his course for where he assumed the kitchen might be. *If she's angry, I'm probably the last person she wishes to see right now.* He descended a set of stairs at the end of the hall, following his nose just as much as his sense of Pulls.

When he reached his destination, Aidan was surprised to find a fire glowing in the hearth with no one there to tend it. *What did you expect? You haven't felt any other living Pulls here besides those whom you've met.* The yeasty aroma of freshly baked bread met him and he inhaled deeply, his mouth watering. A covered pot over the low blaze bubbled and belched as Aidan passed, and as he watched, the lid lifted by itself and a long wooden spoon materialized out of thin air and began to stir the pot's contents. *Everything's bewitched.* Aidan tore himself away from the strange sight and went in search of something that he could take that would not be missed.

On the workstation in the middle of the room sat a bowl of fresh fruit – apples, pears, some orange and yellow fruits that Aidan had never seen the likes of, along with plums, peaches, starberries, and strawberries. Aidan Dismissed a few of the starberries and several plums and turned to the loaves of fresh bread sitting nearby. He explored the loaves' Pulls and Dismissed two of them and moved on to the sausages next to them. *Sláine will be hungry when she returns.* So he explored the Pulls again and Dismissed enough for the both of them, along with a jug of small beer and a handful of dates. Satisfied, Aidan left the warmth of the aromatic kitchen and returned to the bedroom.

Sláine had not returned.

For a moment Aidan thought of trying to send another thought her way, but decided to wait. He went about cooking some sausages over the fire that now burned blue in the grate, using his patera that he stored in Nothingness. As the juicy meats sizzled and sputtered, Aidan ate half a loaf of bread and a plum.

Twenty minutes later, the sausages were cooked. Aidan reached out with his senses, searching for Sláine. *Where are you?* he thought at her.

There was no reply or sense that she had even heard him. Perhaps she *had* heard him but was still stewing over things. Hunger overrode any objections he could form to eating more, so he ate a sausage, and another, wiping the grease that had dribbled down his chin with a sleeve.

After he'd finished and drunk a few sips of small beer, doubt and worry began to eat at Aidan. What if she was in trouble and was waiting for him to help her? *Unlikely. She can handle herself just fine now.* Still, what harm would there be in seeking her out? Aidan Dismissed the remainder of breakfast, leaving out his patera, which he knew he ought to clean properly.

He walked the halls unchallenged and uninterrupted. Hex's Pull remained in one part of the house, so Aidan kept as far from there as possible. Slaíne's Pull was moving again, and Aidan hastened to catch her. Distracted, he nearly missed the two human Pulls up ahead and to the left. Aidan skidded to a halt. The Pulls belonged to the giant and his sister. He could hear their voices from where he stood, raised and arguing apparently.

This might be the perfect opportunity to glean intelligence, to see in a candid moment whether he might be able to truly trust the pair. Aidan took a few silent steps forward and hesitated outside their door.

"—with you," the giant was saying.

"You need your rest," Jinn said, frustration obvious in her voice.

Quick laughed. "Have slept long enough. 'Sides, you need alloy."

"You mean '*ally*', Quick. And I know you will always have my back, but if I'm caught sneaking about, I don't think I'll get in as much trouble as you would."

There was the creaking of boards, and someone let out a heavy sigh.

"Then we both don't sneak."

She groaned. "Quick, don't be difficult. We need to find the Goblets Immortal." Jinn lowered her voice, but Aidan found that he had no trouble hearing her next words. "I need to look ahead again...or at least try. That vision from Mai Larkin makes me think we're running out of time."

Aidan's ears perked up. *Larkin. Could it be the seer that I know?* It had been said to him before that deep called to deep, that one magic folk would be attracted to another. But there must be other magic folk named Larkin. It wasn't that uncommon a name.

"Jinn, you get sick again if you look. Bad wizard makes it so."

Deciding he had heard enough, Aidan moved forward and knocked on the door, which groaned open under his touch. On the other side of the door, the two siblings stood wide-eyed for a moment, and then the brother made to shut the door in his face.

"Quick, it's the Summoner. This might be our chance." Jinn pushed Quick aside and opened the door more fully. "Please, come in before you're seen." She looked around him, as if expecting the wizard to pop up out of the woodwork.

Aidan did as she asked, saying, "The wizard is far from here. Though, if he has means of magically observing us, I am uncertain."

Quick grunted. "How you know he's far from here?"

Aidan blinked. "Well, I can feel his Pull and it's not strong right here, so I know he's far away."

"That's how his magic works, Quick," she explained, moving away from the now-closed door. She gave Aidan a curious look. "I've only ever read about your kind."

"Jinn loves books," her brother added fondly. "There is library in this palace. Wizard said that Jinn can read there sometimes."

She nodded with apparent impatience, and something prickled at the base of Aidan's neck, some intuition. Aidan didn't know what it meant, but he would explore this inkling later. There were much more pressing matters to deal with now.

"Let us get right to it," Jinn said. "What do you want with the Goblets Immortal? I know, with my foresight, that you've been seeking them."

Aidan eyed her warily. "What else do you know?"

"Well, that you hate Meraude, and that you've been looking for a way to stop her." She gave him a curious look. "Let me get to the point; would you use the Goblets Immortal for your own personal gain, or would you see them destroyed?"

Someone else who doesn't talk in riddles. I might just get along with these two...if they don't turn out to be my enemies. "I have no use for the Goblets. Immortality is overrated."

"Yes," said Jinn impatiently, "but there are other things you could do with them. Such as—"

"Build my own personal army?" he finished for her. "I have no need of an army, save, perhaps, to confront and destroy Meraude."

The tension in the room dissipated slightly, and Quick let out a loud belch. "You know where Goblets are?"

Aidan shook his head and paused. "Their Pulls were strange to me before. They both attracted and repelled me. Now…well, I haven't really felt anything since…." *I became a wizard.*

"Since what?" Jinn prompted.

"Since things have become complicated," was all he offered. He shifted his weight as Quick took a seat in a chair in the corner of the room. "I'd have to be around at least one of the Goblets to re-familiarize myself with their type of Pull."

Jinn nodded. "I see."

"You see what? Quick told you not to look ahead," said her brother.

Aidan cleared his throat, reminding the man that he was still there. "Could you, though? Look ahead and see where the Goblets are kept here?"

But the woman was already shaking her head. "No, I can only look at futures directly pertaining to a person. And right now…well, I can't see my future and I can't see Hex's. Everyone else's futures go on outside of this place, when they've escaped."

"Then we will manage to escape?" Finally, some good news. But why did the pair seem suddenly troubled?

Quick gave Aidan an unhappy look. "Jinn cannot see herself. That could mean bad things."

Aidan frowned and looked to Jinn. "Like what?"

"Like she dies," said the large man, his voice cracking. "We can't have plan that makes Jinn die. Quick say we stay here. It's not all bad."

"It's not all *good* either," Jinn said. "And do you really want Meraude to kill the whole magical world? We might be able to prevent it."

"So that is definitely her plan?" Aidan asked.

The two siblings exchanged a look and the giant shrugged. "No knowing. She not tell us her plans." The chair creaked beneath him as he began to fidget. "Quick has bad feeling. We should stay."

Jinn let out a frustrated groan. "Mr.—"

"Aidan," he finished for her.

"Very well. Aidan, what does your…where does your friend stand in all this?"

Reluctant to work with you, apparently. But goodness alone knows why. "Slaíne doesn't want the Goblets."

"And Meraude?"

He laughed bitterly. "If Slaíne had her way, she would get to end Meraude herself."

"She'd have to get in line," said Jinn below her breath and gave Quick a concerned look.

A bit behind in the conversation, apparently, Quick blurted, "What is Slaw-thing?" He looked over at Aidan, and then Jinn. "Slav-ya? Slock-a?"

"*Slaíne* is my…friend." He grimaced at the word. "She was the unconscious redhead you saw when you grabbed me."

Jinn frowned. "He grabbed you?"

Quick shifted his weight, and Aidan could swear the chair wouldn't be able to take much more of him. "Sister was looking for him, so Quick…impoverished."

"Improvised, you mean," she said, her voice weary. Jinn shook her head. "I wonder if there's any way the house would tell me where the Goblets are." Her shoulders heaved and she made a face. "The house is sentient, apparently."

"Pardon?" Aidan asked, wondering if he had misheard her.

Jinn gave him a rueful smile. "You heard me right, and I'm not crazy. But…I had a conversation with the house. It seems it might be on our side."

I've heard and seen stranger things than this. Aidan remembered the door closing of its own accord the night previous when the shape-shifter had attacked. If what Jinn said was true, it very well could have been the house's doing. "Right," he said slowly as he continued to process the information. "So it didn't tell you where the Goblets are?"

"No. I didn't get a chance to ask."

They were silent for a moment, and Aidan felt like he was forgetting something, something that would help them. Something to do with the Beyond....

Quick yawned hugely. "We talk to house now?"

As one, they all started looking around the room. Aidan didn't sense any living presence, other than themselves, Slaíne, and the wizard, whose Pull Aidan was alarmed to notice was much closer than it had been moments before. "He's coming," he said below his breath. "I must go at once. The wizard mustn't know we've communicated."

"Agreed. How close is he? Perhaps I could head him off and give you a chance to slip out."

Aidan nodded. He'd been foolish, ignoring the Pulls around him for as long as he had. Perhaps he could Dismiss himself, though the last time he had tried disappearing and then reappearing, it had worried Slaíne too greatly. He followed Jinn to the door and waited for her to open it.

Jinn moved away from the door, cursing. "It's locked now."

The wizard's Pull was drawing closer. "Then I'll have to hide."

"Where?" She was right, of course.

It was a bright day, so the curtains were blocking out the sun to keep the room from overheating. If Aidan were to hide behind them, his silhouette would be seen. The beds were low to the ground, so there would be no hiding under either of them. He ran to the wardrobe, but it was stuffed to overflowing with cloaks and miscellaneous items of clothing. A pile of that on the floor would be suspicious. Troublesome though it might be, Aidan knew he would have to Dismiss himself.

Hex's Pull was fast approaching. Aidan needed to act now. "Try not to move," he said, closing his eyes.

"Jinn?" asked Hex on the other side of the door. "Are you ready?"

Aidan's eye twitched as he desperately tried to release all the Pulls surrounding him. The hardest thing to Release was Slaíne's Pull, though she was several corridors away.

"N-not right now. I'm in my underthings," Jinn called out. "Please give me a moment."

"What is he doing?" Quick asked.

"What are you doing here?" Jinn asked, obviously trying to cover for her brother.

Aidan slowed his breathing and Released Slaíne's Pull and was about to wink out of Existence, when she latched on to his own Pull and would not Release it. Wherever she was in the house, she must have sensed his intentions and was preventing him from doing what he needed to do.

At the door, the wizard cleared his throat. "I told you I'd be coming for you at this time. Is everything all right? You sound distraught."

"Oh, I'm fine," Jinn said, and she did not sound fine at all.

Silently cursing himself, Aidan reached out and sent a desperate thought at Slaíne. *I'm in danger. I need to escape quickly, and you are preventing me from doing so. Please Release my Pull.*

At the back of his mind, he felt Slaíne's alarm. *I'm in the west wing, by the tapestry of the bloody fountain.* And with that, she stopped preventing Aidan from Dismissing himself.

And not a moment too soon. Aidan heard a ring of keys jangling as the wizard said, "You don't sound all right. Cover yourself, I'm coming in."

As the key slid into place in the lock, Aidan at last slipped out of Existence and appeared inside Nothingness, leaving Jinn to make up whatever lies she needed to say. He didn't know where the tapestry of the bloody fountain was, so he reentered Existence in the guest room they were staying in with a none-too-gentle thud.

Aidan left the room and followed Slaíne's Pull, knowing that he had a lot of explaining to do and that she might not be receptive to all of it. She had, after all, told him in no uncertain terms that she did not wish to work with the Blest siblings.

As he walked through empty halls, Aidan became more aware of the tenor of Slaíne's thoughts, which he still couldn't hear entirely. She was distraught and angry. Every few minutes, he would see a flash of the tapestry in his mind, followed by a feeling of gnawing dread in the pit of his stomach. Aidan shook these feelings aside and at last came across the door behind which he knew he would find Slaíne. He hesitated a moment, wondering if he should knock, but decided against it; she would be able to tell he was there just by his Pull. So he opened the door and stepped inside. "Slaíne, I'm sorry I…." He stopped and gaped at the fifteen-foot tapestry that hung on the far wall.

Nothing could have prepared him for the scene depicted in the intricate weaving of reds and blues and whites. It indeed pictured a fountain full of blood, just as Slaíne had said, but what she had failed to convey was the sheer savagery. A woman stood in the middle of the fountain, her head thrown back in a fanged laugh as blood spewed from her fingertips. In the blood surrounding her flowing white gown floated the lifeless bodies of men and women, their faces an unearthly shade of blue. The fountain was surrounded by men wearing horrified expressions at the bolts of azure light stabbing them in the chest. But that was not the most disturbing part. The woman strongly resembled Slaíne.

"Ghastly, ain't it?" said she, causing Aidan to jump and unwittingly form a ball of green fire in his right fist. He hadn't seen her standing there in the corner, looking out a tall, thin window.

Coming to his senses, Aidan turned his hands away from Slaíne and let the fire escape into the empty hearth on the east side of the room. He swallowed, hard. "Is everything all right?" Aidan watched her staring at the tapestry, her back ramrod-straight. When she did not respond, he cleared his throat and repeated himself.

She shook her head and turned away from the scene on the wall. Her face was white, and her eyes were red-rimmed, but she ignored his question altogether. "What danger was you in?"

"I was exploring and found the room where the Blest siblings are staying." He waited, watching her for some reaction. He could feel rather than see that she was displeased. "We know that two of the Goblets are here somewhere, we just need to find them. And then—"

"Did the wizard find you?" Though he felt her ire, she sounded calm enough.

Aidan shook his head. "He almost discovered me, but I managed to get away without being seen or heard."

Slaíne nodded absently and scratched at the back of her neck. "Any thought as how to escape?"

"The wizard brought me here through some strange portal that he opened in the air with, well, a doorknob. I've been looking for where it might be stored." He watched her closely, unease bubbling in his veins. Something had changed, but he couldn't put his finger on what was wrong. Aidan turned to hide his expression, which would give away his frustration. "I've been searching for similar Pulls, but the house is so large and there are so many doors."

"All with knobs," she finished for him. With a sigh she walked away from the tapestry and stood next to Aidan. "Right. Find anythin' else?"

He thought for a moment. "The house is sentient, apparently."

"I know."

Aidan did not ask how she knew. "The siblings seem to think it is on our side." Chancing a glance at her, Aidan was relieved to find that her expression had changed from unemotional to interested.

"And what say you ter that?" She grabbed his arm and pulled him out of the room with her, much to Aidan's relief; but he swore he could feel the woman in the bloody fountain staring at them both as they left.

"I've not encountered anything like this, but...." *Why would the house take our side when it is Hex who built it?*

Slaíne nodded, her jaw set. "That is a thought. Sounds ter me like a trap. Maybe not o' Hex's making...." *But perhaps it is of the house's,* she added in her thoughts. *We can nay trust anythin' it might say ter us or our potential allies.*

"Agreed. We'll have to rely on our own wits and abilities if we're to ever see the other side of these walls. Though, the girl is a seer, and she said she foresaw us escaping." He caught Slaíne's profile out of the corner of his eye, and he noticed that her posture had become rigid. But as she did not say anything, he let the matter pass. "I feel there is something I am forgetting. Something we could use to our advantage."

At those words, she tightened her grip on his arm, steering him as he began to take a wrong turn. "Was it somethin' magic-like?"

At first he shook his head, but then shrugged. "I think it must be. But I can't for the life of me recall it." The idea was there, just out of reach, teetering on the edge of oblivion. It felt as though if he were to take one false step, think or speak one wrong word, it would fall beyond his reach.

"Well, try not ter think too hard about it. I always find that if I think too hard on somethin', it gets all slippery like a bar o' soap and I can nay tackle it." They had arrived outside the room they shared and she hesitated.

Knowing something was on her mind, he turned her to face him. Another fight was coming, sooner or later; they might as well get it over with. But when he lifted her face to look at him, he was puzzled by her mischievous expression. "What is it?"

"Did the wizard really throw a sausage at your face?" Before he could ask her how she knew, Slaíne rose up on the tips of her toes and stole a kiss. "I woulda liked ter see that."

CHAPTER TEN

Meraude

The Blest under Meraude's instruction were slowly blossoming into something deadly. It had been a month since they began training, and no one was showing as much potential as Egreet and Ing. The two girls were evenly matched, and at the moment, it appeared either might one day rule in her stead. But Meraude knew time was running out.

Now as she watched, the two were sparring. Their right fists had been wrapped for protection, while their left, dominant hands remained vulnerable. It was interesting to watch Egreet, who struck out with both, while Ing, the more hesitant and cautious of the two, kept her left behind her back, easily dodging her opponent's blows at first. At the moment, Ing was allowed to use her gift of foresight while Egreet was forced to rely on brute strength alone. Meraude wondered what Egreet would do if she were given the advantage of seeing ahead for this fight.

As that thought crossed Meraude's mind, Ing struck out and hit Egreet in the lip, knocking the other doubly Blest a few steps backward. Furious apparently, the bleeding girl closed her eyes. "Open them," Meraude said.

"But—"

One look from Meraude was enough to quiet her complaint. The girl scowled and approached her opponent.

Ing was waiting for her to get within range, and as soon as she was within striking distance, she brought her left and vulnerable fist forward and with an upper cut with her right, sent Egreet flying through the air.

"That's – not – fair," Egreet groaned as she gasped for breath.

Meraude smirked. "Do you think a prejudiced mortal would be fair if you were to come up against one? Or how about a wizard? Life isn't fair, child. Your enemy will as soon gut you as look at you. Start thinking like a Blest and less like an emotional child."

The girl stumbled to her feet, huffing and not quite meeting Meraude's eyes.

"All right."

"All right *what*?" Meraude prompted.

The girl spat. "All right, milady."

While they'd been talking, Ing had stood there with her eyes closed, a small smirk spreading across her face as she took in the future. "Are you done sulking?"

Egreet glowered at Ing. "If I were allowed to use foresight, we'd be carrying you to the infirmary right now."

"Tough words for a weakling like yourself." Her taunting had the expected effect on Egreet, who charged at Ing and dealt a flurry of blows, all of which Ing blocked and dodged successfully. Soon the smile left Ing's face, and Meraude hid her amusement and curiosity. Something must have slightly altered the course of the near future, for it was apparent Ing had not foreseen the ferocity of her opponent.

Egreet was relentless. What she lacked in finesse she made up for in energy and passion. She moved so quickly that Ing was unable to block one of her blows, which sent her flying several yards.

Meraude waited for the girl to rise, but a few moments passed and Ing was still. Nothing had changed with the girl's Pull, so Meraude knew that she was merely unconscious or faking having been knocked out.

"Are you all right?" Egreet called out to Ing. When Ing did not respond, she took a few tentative steps closer. "Ing? Did I hurt you?" Foolishly, the girl was now within range of her opponent. "Say something."

Before Egreet could react, Ing kicked Egreet's legs out from under her, knocking her to the ground. Within moments, she was astride her opponent and choking her.

"Enough, Ing," Meraude called out.

But Ing either did not hear her or did not heed her. She continued to strangle the other, whose hands were trying to pry away her fingers.

"Ing, I said to stop." Meraude approached the two with a pitcher of water, which she threw at them as one would two fighting tom cats.

Still the girl did not release Egreet, whose face was turning blue as her eyes rolled back in her head.

Meraude threw her arms around Ing's torso and heaved. At first the girl didn't move, but Meraude applied the full force of her Enduring ability and was able to throw Ing several feet away and came between her and Egreet. "What was that about?" Meraude demanded, only just managing to keep the ire out of her voice.

Ing clambered to her feet, rubbing her middle where Meraude had grabbed her. "You are doubly Blest as well." It was not a question.

Ah, so they had been testing her. A small smile tugged at the corners of Meraude's lips. "When did you first suspect?"

"When the sword didn't work on you," Ing replied. "We wanted to make sure we were right. Well, that and to make certain you weren't a wizard."

Meraude could have rolled her eyes. "And your conclusion?" Behind her, Egreet was regaining consciousness, coughing and moaning intermittently.

"That you can't be a wizard. You would have just used your mind to throw me away."

That caused the mage queen to laugh without humor. "Dear child, what you know of wizards is faulty. Firstly, female wizards are very rare, if not a myth altogether. Secondly, not all wizards can toss people around like dolls using only their mind. You have a lot to learn."

Ing's expression grew thoughtful. "And all wizards are bad?"

Meraude nodded. "That is correct. The Blest will cleanse them and all other tyrants from the earth. They seek to control us, Ing, to destroy our source of strength."

"Lights above, fate was stupid to make them in the first place."

"Fate," said Meraude as Egreet sat up with a grunt, "is not to be questioned or molded to suit our whims. We are to listen to the signs and allow it to have its way."

The girl watched Meraude closely. "Is fate what told you to start all of this?"

"All of what?"

Ing gestured around her widely. "Your army, the trainees, the breeding grounds. People say it was all your idea, that you started it."

The mage queen hesitated for a few beatings of her heart. "I did not start this. But I intend to finish it."

★   ★   ★

Later that afternoon, Meraude dismissed her guards for two hours, something she had been doing for the last few days. Her old fears were fading, and new ones were creeping in.

Mai Larkin has been gone longer than she ought. What if she has formed an alliance with Dewhurst to work against me? She had voiced that concern with her most trusted Sightful, Mai – or, as some might say, 'Madame' – Bly.

"The future surrounding that Sightful has blurred," Mai Bly had said in response. "She is trying very hard to remain unseen." When the mage queen regarded her shrewdly, Bly quickly closed her eyes and took another look. "She is close and the blood oath still compels her actions. You should see her in the wood before the week is through."

Now, leaving the grounds to Tindra's control, the mage queen donned a pale blue cloak and sneaked out of the town, making for the southern gates. She passed few women on the way there, making certain to steer clear of the men's accommodations. Only once was she stopped, produced her traveling papers without showing her face, and was allowed to pass across the moat on the guarded drawbridge.

Then, making certain no one was watching her, Meraude stepped into Inohaim Wood. The trees were burgeoning with summer's bounty of leaves, slightly browned and wilted in places from the few days of rain. Some said it looked later in the season than it really was, but Meraude paid little mind to the flora and fauna of the wood.

This was the fifth day she had wandered, waiting for her servant to return. *Mai Bly had better be right about this.*

An hour passed, then two. The shadows were lengthening, and Meraude knew she ought to return to the safety of her gated community. But a breaking twig and the appearance of a human Pull caused her to stop in place. Slowly, she reached for the dagger she kept hidden up her sleeve.

Meraude almost let out a sigh of relief when Mai Larkin, face drawn and cloak filthy, emerged from the brush. "Oh. It's you." She made a face and pulled back her own hood. "I thought I told you to bring me the Summoner." *My other Sightfuls could not tell me where he was.*

Mai Larkin glared at her and then threw back her head and laughed, exposing the browning crowns of her teeth. "Just as you sent your twins to find him?" She gave her mistress an annoyingly knowing look. "Wonder what might be taking them so long. Jinn has the Sight as well."

Meraude's blood seemed to freeze in her veins, and she couldn't help but hiss below her breath. "Speak not of the two to me. You're not even supposed to know of their existence." The two stood, staring at each other. At length, the mage queen broke the silence, her temper once again under control. "Any rumors to report, seer?"

The blasted wretch pulled back her own hood and exposed her recently shaved head. "Milady is surprised."

Though inside she was fuming, Meraude managed to keep the emotion out of her voice when she answered. "You've made a vow." Typical. The woman was always searching for a way to get out of her blood oath. Not that any vow was more powerful than blood, but it still might spell trouble for Meraude's plans.

"Dewhurst is dead."

This was news. *What else have my Sightfuls been keeping from me?* "So I have gathered from reports," she lied in return.

"He found a way around his vow. I assume you did not know that."

Easy, Meraude. "And I assume that *you* found a way around *yours*?" She waited, striving desperately to keep her expression neutral.

"The one you forced on me? Might have done. Might not have

done. But one thing is for certain: Dewhurst betrayed you. He has withheld information from your people."

Enough of these games. Meraude's control on herself snapped, and she took a step toward her servant. "I compel you to tell me all." She pulled the dagger from her sleeve and pointed it at the rough-looking woman.

The Sightful backed away. "He has the maps now," she spoke, though she was obviously trying to stop herself. "He is coming for you." She cringed.

"Dewhurst's corpse is coming for me?" Meraude said. There were no known necromancers among wizards, but that did not mean there weren't any hidden among their ranks. It was within the realm of possibility.

Mai Larkin was really fighting her oath now, her face contorted as though she were in pain. "The S—" She stopped herself just before the word could come out.

Meraude heaved a dramatic sigh and tutted. "You know, Larkin, I will find out anyway. But let me hear it from your own lips."

"Su – mmoner." Larkin gasped and collapsed to her knees, panting. Then, before her mistress could ask another question, the Sightful reached out her hand, and Meraude's dagger went flying. Before Meraude could stop her, Mai Larkin drove the blade through her own throat. She lay there, sputtering blood for a moment.

Meraude watched her servant with annoyed surprise, and hefted her over her shoulders to bear her to the healers. All these years, she had not known Mai Larkin to be anything but a Sightful. *How did her Summoning ability slip my notice?* "You always have to do things the hard way, don't you, Larkin?" She ran with her back to town, not worrying any longer about being recognized.

The guards at the gate were alarmed to see her in that state with the bleeding woman on her back, and they let her pass without demanding to see any papers. By the time she arrived at the healer's station, Larkin's Pull seemed to change ever so slightly, indicating she was moments from death.

Meraude burst through the door, pushed her way past an alarmed woman in flowing black and laid the Sightful on the bench. "This woman has information I need. Tend to her."

Trembling, the healer approached her new patient and examined her throat. "Milady."

"Mend her."

"The wound is deep, milady. I'm sorry. This is beyond my skill."

Sensing that the woman's words were truthful, Meraude took a few calming breaths. "At least try something." But as she said it, the Sightful's Pull lessened in substantiality and into something that could be Dismissed.

The healer confirmed what Meraude felt after taking her pulse. "She's gone, milady. Was she someone important? Should I—" The healer screamed, for the body had vanished in the blinking of an eye.

"You have never witnessed a Blest death, have you?" Meraude said with a sigh. "She is at rest in the Beyond now. It would seem her soul has been accepted." *At least she can do no more damage there.* Meraude turned to leave.

"Milady," said the healer. "Your cloak, it's covered in blood."

Pausing, Meraude undid the clasp and removed the soiled garment. "See to it." She balled up the cloak and threw it at the healer with perhaps more force than necessary. Dewhurst had betrayed her and Larkin had broken part of her oath. Why hadn't her Sightfuls foreseen any of this?

Unless they, too, have conspired against and betrayed me. Meraude thrust the dagger into its sheath up her sleeve and left the healing station, aware that her presence would attract more attention than she wished for right then. She needed to process this all, to gather her thoughts. There were certain Sightfuls she needed to question.

CHAPTER ELEVEN

Jinn

The Summoner disappeared not a moment too soon. As the doorknob turned, Jinn knew she had to make it look like she had been dressing as she said she had been, so she hastily unfastened her belt and was just refastening it with shaking hands as the door creaked open.

"Oh," said the wizard, turning away. "I am sorry. It sounded like you were in distress."

Jinn rolled her eyes. "No, I wasn't."

Hex turned, a frown on his face. "Why do I sense magic in here?"

He must be sensing the magic the Summoner performed in Dismissing himself. Think of a lie, any lie, and fast. "I was—"

"Quick tried looking ahead," Quick said glumly. "Now have big headache. Don't think Quick can walk today." He leaned back in the chair and closed his eyes. "Would be better if you left now."

The wizard narrowed his eyes as he watched Jinn.

"You didn't say *he* shouldn't look ahead," she said, her heart racing. Did he believe the lie? It wouldn't do for the Summoner to be under the wizard's suspicion.

Hex's eyes went to the curtains, and Jinn was glad she hadn't suggested that Aidan hide there; the wizard would have seen him instantly through the semi-sheer fabric that was letting in the sun. Frowning, Hex turned back to look at her. "Do you still wish to go for a walk?"

Jinn wasn't sure what she wanted. She had been cooped up in the room since that morning after breakfast, but the wizard's presence still unnerved her, and she found herself arguing with him more than what was perhaps ladylike. But she needed to gain his trust and learn more about the House of Curses, and how to escape, not to mention the location of the two Goblets that the wizard kept.

The wizard must have noticed her indecision, for he cleared his throat and said, "I had something a little different planned for this afternoon's walk. It's a place you haven't seen yet."

That had Jinn's attention. "Oh." She waited a moment and sighed. "All right." She started to walk toward the door, but Hex caught her gently by the arm.

"Sorry," he said, releasing her. He did not sound sorry. "It's this way."

Jinn frowned and watched as the wizard approached the windows and threw back the drapes, letting in the blinding sun. She blinked against the sudden burst of light and raised a hand to her eyes. When her vision had adjusted to the new level of light, Jinn squinted and approached the window, and then raised an eyebrow at Hex.

The wizard held out his arm, which she regarded with confusion. "You'll need to hold on to me in order for this to work."

"For what to work?"

He grinned. "You'll see."

Now more curious than annoyed, Jinn reached out a tentative hand and rested it on the crook of the wizard's arm. She flinched when he put his hand over hers, and started to pull away.

"Don't let go, Jinn, until I say it's safe, otherwise you might get stuck," Hex warned her. He grabbed Jinn's hand in his own and tugged her forward.

Jinn stumbled and fell right through the solid window and the stone masonry surrounding it, landing on grass as her hand slipped from the wizard's. She swore. "Lights above, you could have warned me." But the words came out breathier and less angry than she had meant them to be.

Hex threw back his head and laughed, flashing his brilliant teeth. "You said you wanted to go outdoors. So, here you are."

They were standing in a small garden just outside her room. Jinn hadn't realized there was anything outside but cold, spraying sea and jagged rocks.

The air was damp and held an unnatural chill. It smelled of salt and wet things, and gulls cried overhead, diving beyond the edge of the garden down to what must be the sea below. She knew she was supposed to be admiring the garden, in which bloomed fragrant bushes of crimson, white, and yellow roses, but Jinn's only thought was escape. The wind whipped at the cloak she always wore in the House of Curses, stinging her cheeks and causing her hood to blow back and her hair to fly around her. "It's lovely," she said, her voice dead even to her own ears.

Beside her, Hex sighed. "I know you don't want to be here."

Their argument from the other day still rang in Jinn's ears. Hex thought she was going to die if there were no Goblets to save her. But what did it matter to him? What a feeble lie to make her believe he was on her side. "Does it drop straight down?" Jinn brushed past Hex and made for the edge of the garden, her feet slipping on the wet grass.

"Jinn, be careful." He caught her gently by the elbow and steered her away from the edge, though not fast enough for her to miss seeing the small, treacherous footpath that led down to the churning sea. Hex gave her a knowing look. "You would break your neck if you tried taking that path."

Silently cursing, Jinn turned away from the path and resigned herself to the fact that this was not a safe means of escape. Unless there was another way down. She glanced in that direction and her hopes sank. If she were to escape, first she would have to find a way to break through the window in her room – which was probably protected by a ward or some other kind of magic. Then, if she and Quick could fit through the narrow window and manage the steep, treacherous path, there were the waves to contend with and the fact there was no boat to be seen. Not that she knew how to row. Nor could she swim.

"Maybe this was a bad idea," said the wizard, startling Jinn.

If I can't escape this way, at least I can have some fresh air. Being kept inside had begun to remind Jinn of all those years she spent living in the cave, with no sun and very little to do but read. It had been a hellish nightmare, and the thought of being trapped caused bile to rise in her throat, which she quickly swallowed. "No. It's fine." She turned to look at the wizard, and frowned at his concerned expression. *I'm not some delicate flower to wilt at the first signs of adversity.*

Hex moved closer. "Are you sure? We could go back in."

Jinn laughed, a forced, hysterical sound to even her own ears. "No. That is, I would like to stay out a bit longer. It feels like I haven't seen the sun in months." She spun around in a slow circle, taking in her surroundings more thoroughly than she had before. The small garden was perhaps the size of the room she shared with Quick. Jinn never had cared much for flowers. They were useless, except for the occasional one with healing properties, and died all too easily. Herbs were her preferred plant, so she was delighted to see a small patch of them growing among each other on the edge of the garden. Aware that Hex was watching her closely but following at a slight distance, Jinn approached the tiny green cluster of plants and plucked a fragrant mint leaf and rubbed it between her fingers. The cooling aroma of menthol tickled her nose and cleared her thoughts. A handful of these leaves, crushed and steeped in hot water, would make a lovely treat. But these were not hers. She was a guest here. *A guest by force*, Jinn reminded herself and then began plucking as many of the leaves as she could carry.

Behind her, the wizard laughed. "Here, do you want something to carry them in?"

Jinn turned just in time to see Hex conjure a small brown wicker basket, which he held out to her. As the vessel exchanged hands, their fingers accidentally brushed. His hands were like ice. "Thank you." She quickly pulled away and began filling the basket with other herbs: lavender, thyme, and lemongrass being among them. As she plucked away at the small assortment, Jinn began to grow warm from the exertion and soon grew tired. The sea breeze tugged at her hair, and Jinn got a mouthful of it several times. Soon her basket was full to the brim, and she rose from a squat. Then she saw it, a small path leading around the corner of the house. "What's that way?"

"I was rather hoping you would ask." At first Hex extended his arm, offering it for a brief moment but wisely dropping it to his side after gesturing for her to follow him.

The path was just wide enough for two people to walk side by side, if not comfortably. On the right was the side of the house and on the left was a drop-off onto the rocks below. Jinn nearly hugged the building as she turned the corner, the winds buffeting her enough to make her leery of venturing too close to the edge. In a patch of barren ground there sat a lone hawthorn tree. She recognized the tree by its red berries and scaly bark, though she had never seen one in person. Jinn approached the tree, her hand outstretched, and she rubbed the tips of her fingers against the trunk. A bunch of insects scurried out from a few of the many nooks and crannies, quickly seeking shelter elsewhere.

"Legend tells that fairies planted the first hawthorn trees," said Hex from behind her. "They're considered good luck by many superstitious folk, and most farmers won't cut them down for this very reason."

"*Are* they good luck?" Jinn asked, only half-serious. She removed her hand from the base of the tree and looked up. The tree was heavy with its fruit, which Jinn knew it wouldn't shed until the following spring, or until birds picked it clean.

Hex studied her. "Do you need luck?"

"There's no such thing," Jinn said dismissively and went back to looking up at the branches. High above her was a small nest, no doubt empty since spring had passed. Still, she wished she could peek inside. She'd never seen an egg in her life, not until this morning where a plate of boiled brown shell sat before her. It had been startling and somewhat disappointing.

"There was a lovely family of wrens living there weeks ago, but they're long gone. If you want to look inside the nest, I could fetch it."

Jinn's shoulders heaved in a silent sigh. "I thought I told you to stop reading my mind."

"I can't read your mind, Jinn," he reminded her. "I can just guess your thoughts by the tenor of your feelings."

"Then stop reading my feelings," she said, heat rising in her face and in her voice.

Hex shook his head. "I'm sorry. I can't help it. Your feelings are—they're very loud. Louder than anyone's I've ever experienced."

That made Jinn pause and think. If her feelings were so obvious, it wouldn't be easy to escape. The wizard would always be one step ahead of her, knowing what she was plotting and planning. "Oh."

"I'm sorry. I didn't mean to make you upset."

Jinn smiled, in spite of herself. "No, I guess you can't help what you sense." *What am I saying?*

"Is there anything I can do? To make your stay here easier, I mean."

All the air seemed to leave Jinn's lungs in one great whoosh. She turned her back to him and continued studying the tree, then set down her basket and kicked at the dirt with the tip of her boot. "How tall is it?"

"The tree? It's going on thirty feet high. It's fully grown at this point."

The lowest branch was perhaps ten feet up. Even if Jinn stood on the tips of her toes, she wouldn't be able to reach it.

No doubt sensing her intent, Hex moved in closer. "The outdoors agrees with you," he said.

Puzzled, Jinn turned and studied him. Was he mocking her? It was difficult to tell. She was ready with a retort, but when the wizard waved his hand, a swing swung down from the lowest branch. Swearing, Jinn jumped and backed away, only to laugh at herself, approach it slowly and take a seat. She had never operated a swing before, but she faintly recalled a drawing in one of her books from when she was a girl. Imitating what she remembered, Jinn pumped her legs once and then stopped.

"Go on." When she didn't move, the wizard said, "It's all right to distract yourself sometimes, you know."

Distract myself from escaping, you mean. She nodded once, her teeth clenched, and pushed off from the ground. The sensation of coming back down made her lightheaded and her stomach seemed to drop. She closed her eyes tightly, her fingers digging into the ropes. Again and again she pumped her legs. *Higher, higher.* Jinn remembered the short time she had spent as a bird. Was this what it would have felt like, had she been allowed to stretch her wings and fly? Dizzy suddenly, Jinn allowed the swing to slow, her toes scraping against the ground as her eyes flew open.

The wizard, she was startled to find, was staring at her, a confused look on his face. And for the second time since arriving at the House of Curses, a vision overtook her.

It was nighttime, and she was creeping through the halls of the house, followed closely by the Summoner, his partner, and Quick. "Note this tapestry," her vision-self said, pointing to a scene of three golden stags locking antlers against a turquoise background. "There are three Goblets and they're hidden somewhere around here. That's what the vision said."

The Summoner and the she-wizard exchanged a look. "Are you certain you want to go through with this?" Aidan asked.

Jinn's vision-self looked at Quick, who would not meet her eyes. "Yes, I'm certain. This is the only way."

Blinking, Jinn sat up. She was now on the ground, and the wizard stood where she had seen him moments before, his eyes strangely unfocused. Jinn pulled herself to her feet and dusted dry grass from her knees. *I saw myself.* Somehow, the taboo had been lifted, allowing Jinn to see her own future, which the wizard claimed was too tightly entwined with his own to be foreseen. Eager to see more, Jinn closed her eyes and attempted to latch on to her future again, only to be met by darkness.

"Are you all right?"

Jinn opened her eyes again and looked up at the wizard, whose expression was unreadable. "I'm fine. Just a touch of a headache. Maybe it would be better if I went back indoors." She was talking far too fast, she knew, but if Hex thought her behavior to be strange, his face did not betray it.

"Perhaps that would be best. I fear a storm is approaching." His eyesight must be far superior to her own; the skies were a clear, cheerful blue, and the few clouds there were seemed harmless enough. "I'll send the herbs ahead to the kitchen to be dried…if that's all right with you."

"Might I have some in the room?"

Hex scooped up the basket and motioned for her to follow him back around the corner. "If you would like."

Hope and dread buoyed up inside of Jinn as she returned to the room and bid a hasty goodbye to the likewise distracted wizard. If her vision was to be believed, there were three of the Goblets Immortal near the tapestry of the three stags. It would be better if she could gauge how far in the future the vision might be. For all she knew, the wizard rotated where he kept the Goblets on a daily or weekly basis. And something else bothered her. Why had the taboo ceased working in that moment, allowing the vision through? And why had the wizard seemed as though he were experiencing a vision of his own? She would have to talk these questions through with someone who might know, and there was no better person to talk about them with than a wizard. The problem would be getting to the Summoner's mate without being caught.

CHAPTER TWELVE

Aidan

The early afternoon passed, and the wizard did not summon Aidan or Slaíne to train, but left two trays of hot food at their door with a note. *Tomorrow after you have broken your fasts*, was all the small piece of parchment said.

After they had brought the trays inside their room, Slaíne spread a hunk of brown bread with butter and tore off a massive bite with her teeth. "Something's changed. Did you feel it earlier?"

Aidan nodded and took a sip of small beer. An hour prior, when the sun was higher in the sky and Slaíne was resting, there had been a sudden change in the pressure in the air. Gooseflesh had broken out over Aidan's arms, and he had felt as though some great power had been leeched out of the room. It was a strange thing to describe, let alone understand. "So it wasn't my imagination."

"Somethin' powerful went out like a light," she said through a mouthful of herbed chicken.

That was perhaps too simple a word for something that had left Aidan feeling as though his lungs had been constricted and were suddenly allowed to inflate to their fullest. The sensation had lasted a minute, and then the oppressive pressure had returned.

Aidan chewed in thoughtful silence. "What do you know of curses?"

"Them's my words, Aidan," said Slaíne, amused. Indeed, those had been among the first words she had ever spoken to him. "I know a fair bit…well, as what was told me by the elves, and them you can nay truly rely on. Why?"

"If the wizard needs to consciously power the curse that he put on this house, what if something distracted him, just as we talked about before?"

That made Slaíne pause, chalice to her lips. She took a quick sip and set the drinking vessel down. "That was a theory. Not sure how much stock to put into what them elves told me about curses. Lemme try something, though, afore we give ourselves too much hope." After scrabbling to her feet, Slaíne approached the fireplace and threw out her hand toward it. Blue sparks flew out of her fingertips and filled the empty grate. "Right. I feel the magic it's takin' to keep the fire goin'."

"Because there's no fuel in there to feed it," he said, standing as well. "What does it feel like?"

Slaíne gave him an incredulous look. "Aidan, you've been using magic a long time. An'— my, can't ya feel this now?" She put her hand over his soul-half in her chest, and Aidan focused on that. After a moment of searching, he could feel a slight pulse there, a bit of a strain that would have tired him out after a while, had he been a regular Blest.

"I concede the point. How do you make it stop?" But he already knew the answer. He could feel it, a tremulous thread tying Slaíne – and by extension, himself – to the blaze. One would sever the connection as one would sever a lock of hair with a pair of scissors. Or, in a wizard's case, a mere thought.

She gave him a knowing look, blinked, and the fire went out. "That don't explain Hex, though."

"Indeed," Aidan murmured. "What could make a wizard unconsciously choose to stop the curse surrounding this house? The thought contradicts itself."

"Ayé. Unless it's like accidentally cutting off yer finger."

Neither of them could come up with a satisfactory answer, so they finished their meal in relative silence. As soon as they were done, their trays disappeared, no doubt sent to be washed by whatever magic was running the kitchen.

After a time, Aidan grunted. "We didn't get to talk much earlier."

Slaíne stiffened. "Oh?"

"I discovered something, I mean," he hastily added, aware that they still needed to have a difficult conversation about her behavior earlier. "I think I found a trapdoor."

She didn't make a comment at first, seeming lost in thought as she approached the grate. Again she lit the fire by magic, and this time she let it burn. "You nay went through it, did you?"

"No." He gave her a challenging look. "Would it have been a problem if I had?"

Slaíne glared at him before her expression smoothed over into one of indifference. "Would nay have been the smartest thing to do. And goodness knows what ya might find down there."

"I might find the Goblets," he protested. "Or the means out of here."

"Or you might've been stuck down there with no means of gettin' out again and some great horrible beast nippin' at yer heels." Her chest was rising more and more quickly, and her gray eyes had begun to glow that unnatural blue again.

Aidan knew he needed to calm her down quickly before she did something dangerous, whether by accident or design. "But I didn't go down. All is well."

Her expression crumpled. She looked sad, hurt even. "You're right," she said. "We just gotta be careful, 's all I'm sayin'." A moment later, her breathing seemed to slow and the strange light went out of her eyes. "Right. We should probably do some trainin' of our own, if the wizard is too distraught to do it himself."

"You think Hex is distraught?" he asked, concerned with how she was now circling him. "What are you doing?"

Slaíne laughed. "'Course he must be distraught. Why else would he cancel trainin'? Keep your hands up."

"What – why?" Before he could react, Slaíne lunged at him, knocking him off of his feet and onto the bed.

Eyes twinkling, she pulled away. "Try an' catch me!"

"This isn't training with magic," Aidan complained. "This is just tiring ourselves out."

"Thought you nay wanted to train with magic, anyhow." She

feinted lunging at him again, and then took off running in the opposite direction. "C'mon. What're you waitin' for?"

"We shouldn't. What if we hurt each other?"

Slaíne Called a pillow to herself, which first hit Aidan upside his head. "Can't. The rules of the house forbid it."

Aidan stared at her, earning him another face-full of pillow. "How do you know that?"

Her expression soured and she went for the door. "Catch me or not. I need to run."

But Aidan used his magic to slam the door in her face. "Are you certain that's true? That the rules of the house— Slaíne!"

She had Summoned the copper knife and slashed it toward her left thumb, only for her hand to freeze mid-strike in the air. "See? Can't hurt no one here."

"Put that away. You could have really harmed yourself."

Slaíne wasn't listening to him. "Then how could the shape-shifter attack us, if no one can hurt themselves or another here?" She tried the door again, but Aidan held on to it with his mind. She turned around, her expression thoughtful. "He must not've been bound by the curse put on this house."

"Slaíne, put that blade away or so help me—" He lunged for her, but she danced under his arms and around him, evading his reach.

"Or maybe the curse only works on mortals and Blest." She was panting now, running with the knife, point facing upward. "Guess I've got Blest in me, your soul-half." Slaíne Dismissed the blade just as Aidan grabbed her by the arm and pulled her to himself.

"Enough."

She gave him a knowing look and pulled away. "Not fun, is it? Worryin' about what trouble the other might get into."

Aidan folded his arms across his chest. "This is different than you worrying about me."

Her eyes darkened. "How? Come now, enlighten me, Aidan."

"Well, *I'm* not trying to *control you*," he blurted out before he could stop and think his words through.

Again her eyes lit up with blue light, her hands balling into fists. His soul-halves both in his chest and in hers warned him before she Dismissed herself into Nothingness.

Furious with himself and Slaíne, Aidan threw up his hands and yelled. A powerful wind kicked up around him, swirling from his toes up to his head. The world began to glow green, and his feet left the floor. He was startled, the heat went out of his anger, and he fell backward onto his tailbone. *I'm sorry. I didn't mean it*, he thought at her.

There was no response.

Aidan sat up and rested his head in his hands. Any time he'd Dismissed himself, it had always taken an hour for him to return to Existence. Maybe she couldn't hear him in Nothingness and he would have to wait to mend things until she reappeared…if he wanted to be there when she did. If *she* wanted to see *him* then, even.

He got to his feet and approached the fireplace, where the blue fire had died out.

"This is far too complicated for my liking," he said to his reflection in the mirror over the mantle. Wishing to distract himself, Aidan stepped back and cast his hand out toward the grate as Slaíne had done. At first, nothing happened, so he tried again, this time putting his anger into it. Green flames burst to life in the fireplace as they had his first night in the House of Curses. He examined the thread of magic connecting himself to the fire he had made and turned away. Even with the fire out of sight, he could sense it licking the walls of the chimney, rising to meet the air above. What would distract a wizard enough to lose their grip on that thread?

Aidan tried thinking of different things. He thought of his adventures that had led him here, of painful things such as the loss of his father, mother, and brother, Sam, and let himself feel the hurt as if it had happened yesterday. But throughout it all he was aware in the very back of his mind that there was a magical thread actively attaching him to the blaze. Swearing, Aidan turned. Indeed, the fire was still burning.

He had created a fire by accident his first night there, but it had been extinguished when he had returned to his room. There was a faint memory in his mind of severing it somewhat consciously. He had been angry when he created the blaze. But what about when it had been put out? He could not recall.

Sorrow and anger were strong emotions, good enough to help create magic, apparently, but perhaps not good enough to sever magic by accident. *Maybe it varies from wizard to wizard.* He took to pacing. *If I were Hex, what would distract me?* It was a ridiculous question, seeing as he knew next to nothing about the wizard.

All these thoughts had somewhat taken his mind off his second fight in one day. Sláine was impossible, maddening, and perhaps more stubborn than he was. The thought that she would try to control him made him seethe with rage again, and he saw the fire responding to his feelings. Aidan had been getting on just fine until she had shown up and shoved her magic at him.

Was I fine, though? He'd been on the run with little direction, just trying to keep himself alive.

The fire sputtered.

Maybe he wasn't being fair. Being a wizard was as new to her as it was to him. If she felt half the rage he had been experiencing, it was a wonder they hadn't quarreled oftener.

Aidan grimaced. He had said all the wrong things, provoking her. Some of it had perhaps been true, and though that thought was bothersome, he knew the more they allowed themselves to be divided, the easier it would be for them to remain conquered. Besides, he did not like seeing her hurt.

There was a tug in Aidan's chest, and the thread that attached him to the fire snapped. Startled, Aidan blinked his eyes to reconfirm what he already knew: the fire had died without him consciously severing the magic.

★　★　★

Aidan waited for Slaíne to return from Nothingness for an hour, but once that time had passed, he felt her Pull return to Existence on the other side of the house. *So much for making amends.*

The hour grew late, and he retired for the day. After a while, he felt Slaíne's Pull nearing, heard the door creak open, but remained silent as she pattered across the floor and then crawled into bed next to him. He was tired of arguing, so he did not attempt any conversation. His revelation about accidentally severing magical threads would keep.

Soon Slaíne's breathing slowed, and Aidan knew her to be asleep. He tried to sleep himself, but as the hours dragged on, all he could do was stare at the ceiling and try to tire himself. At what might have been midnight, he decided he'd had enough.

The House of Curses was still and silent as Aidan climbed out of bed. The moon was in its waxing and had yet to reach its fullness, but as he crept to the window, dark clouds scudded overhead and soon masked the light. He Summoned a bit of parchment and some charcoal and scrawled out a hasty note, informing Slaíne of his whereabouts, should she awaken and miss him. This he placed on his pillow and then crept toward the door.

Slaíne moaned in her sleep and rolled over, causing Aidan to stop. Was he wrong in leaving her? *I'm being overly scrupulous*, he chided himself as he slipped through the door and bolted it from the other side with magic.

There was a chill in the air, one that Aidan had not felt since his new powers had manifested. Every creak and whine the house made seemed to suggest approaching footsteps, and every whistle of the wind was a cry being taken up somewhere in the house. These Aidan tried his best to ignore. He sensed no human Pulls near him, so he knew it was safe to proceed.

He tried following the path he had taken earlier, the one that would lead him to the trapdoor. This proved difficult, since he had found it before when distracted and angry. Aidan took a left and then a right, thinking that perhaps the portrait of a bowl of shriveled pears looked familiar, only to find himself at the end of the corridor. So he turned and went another way.

The house was dimly lit by torches in sconces on the walls here and there. As he passed, the flames would flicker from red to green, making Aidan feel like he was being watched. But as Hex did not materialize and stop him, Aidan kept moving.

Another hall led him to another intersection. *Did I really make this many turns?* He thought not, so he returned to where he started, using Slaíne's stationary Pull as a guide.

There was a presence, not human or animal, but neither was it lifeless. Aidan tried to ignore it, guessing it was the house…if the house was, as Jinn and Slaíne claimed, sentient.

He hurried straight down a hall leading north, shivering as a cold breeze breathed down the back of his cloak.

What are you about, wizard? asked a disembodied male voice.

Now used to voices in his head, Aidan ignored it and continued on his mission, using Jinn's and Quick's familiar Pulls to guide him, since they were closer to this spot than Slaíne. His footsteps echoed loudly as he went, and Aidan couldn't help but wonder if the house or its magic was affecting his attempt at speed and stealth.

I wouldn't go that way, said Slaíne into his mind.

Tentatively, he reached out with his mind. *Don't be angry I—*

Aidan, what are you doing?

Cursing silently, Aidan moved from the room and hastened his steps. By now he had put perhaps half a mile between himself and Slaíne, whose Pull he still felt back in their room. That soon changed however, and he sensed her Pull on the move. So much for finding the trapdoor and not worrying her.

Aidan stepped into the hall and began exploring the Pulls below his feet. What he found was peculiar. It was almost as if there was nothing beneath the stone under his feet, not where he stood, nor as he moved to where he sensed the presence of wood. He had reached another rug and stopped.

Slaíne's Pull was fast approaching.

Determined to at least have proof of a trapdoor when she arrived, Aidan rolled back the heavy rug, which chafed at his hands and resisted him as he moved it about, exposing the square space of wood in the floor beneath. After kneeling, he rapped on it with his fist once and then again. It sounded hollow and he couldn't feel any Pull directly beneath the wood, so he began searching for a way to remove the board.

He tried placing his fingers in the groove between the board and the stone surrounding, but it was a tight fit and he couldn't find purchase. Frustrated, he stood.

"What are you doing?" Slaíne asked as she rounded the corner. "Thought I said tryin' the trapdoor was a bad idea."

Aidan rolled his eyes. "This is too good an opportunity to pass up. What if the Goblets are down below? Or maybe the magical doorknob that brought Hex and me here?" He explored the board's Pull and Called it to himself. The wood resisted and groaned, so Aidan raised his hand over it and moved it with a thought, raising one side of the board from its apparently invisible hinges. Triumphant, he caught the door before it could slam shut. "I'll need something to prop it open with."

Slaíne shook her head. "Aidan, this is nay very smart."

He ignored her and felt in his cache in Nothingness for something to keep the door from closing on him when he went below. Finding nothing suitable, he searched the hall around him and settled upon a broomstick that was longer than the hole in the floor was wide. The door was old and heavy. He would have to hope that the broom wouldn't snap and trap him down there, but that was a risk that he needed to take. Besides, he could always use magic to escape, if needed.

"Please," she said. "At least lemme come with you."

That gave Aidan pause. Hex had said the House of Curses was dangerous. Should he risk Slaíne coming down with him and them both becoming trapped? He shook his head. "Why don't you stay up here?"

She gave him a withering look.

"In case the door doesn't stay propped open. One of us should be up here to let the other out." They could always Dismiss themselves, should they run into trouble, but the thought of putting Slaíne in potential danger as well made omitting the full truth easy. Thankfully, she didn't think of it. Besides, Dismissing was magic Slaíne still hadn't mastered and wouldn't for a long time. She might end up becoming a liability, should the need to make a quick escape arise.

Slaíne swore. "All right. Just please be careful, 's all I'm sayin'." She took the broom from Aidan and held the trapdoor open for him. "You hear or see anythin' dangerous, call me."

He nodded, very much doubting that he would find anything more dangerous or exciting than perhaps a few rats. "It'll be fine. You'll see." After first giving her a quick kiss on her cheek, Aidan removed the torch from its bracket on the wall and began his descent down a set of smooth stone steps.

The light he brought with him did little to illuminate much of the path before him, so Aidan took slow, cautious steps. He could sense rather than hear Slaíne's unease behind him and sent a few comforting thoughts her way, which either she did not receive or chose to ignore.

Pushing through cobwebs that crackled as they met the flame of his torch, Aidan reached out with his abilities and was rewarded with a faint pulsing sensation, a nonhuman Pull in the distance down below. The steps curved, and where there had been a wall on either side, there was suddenly only a long drop on the right. Disoriented, Aidan put a hand on the wall to his left to reassure himself it was still there, though he could both see and sense it.

As the steps continued to wind in one large circle, they began to slowly narrow. The air cooled considerably at this point of his descent, and he was met with a slight breeze, which caused the flame of his torch to sputter. Dust tickled his nose and he fought a sneeze. His eyes watered and burned.

Aidan stepped on something that cracked and gave way beneath his left boot. He looked at what he had trod on, and discovered strange bones, like those of no creature he had seen before. They seemed to glow a poisonous green as he directed the torch at them, and crumbled to dust and blew away in a draft.

What's happening down there?

Aidan jumped and nearly dropped the torch as Slaíne pressed the words into his mind. *Nothing very exciting*, he thought back. *Just crunchy old rat bones.*

Oh. Lovely.

Aidan grinned and continued downward. The pulsing sensation increased the farther he traveled, but he knew himself to be quite a ways away from it. Frustrated by his slow progress, Aidan quickened his steps. He now had to be at least half a mile beneath the House of Curses. The air was close and damp and smelled of seaweed, and the occasional gurgle of water could be heard in the distance.

It was dizzying, the descent. When he was perhaps a mile below, Aidan paused and took a rest. He had grown weaker during the past few weeks, having had little exercise. His endurance was not quite what it had been, so his legs were already protesting.

The Pull below pulsed again, and Aidan closed his eyes and tried to explore its properties. It was not quite like anything he remembered feeling before. The Pull felt both alive and not alive at the same time, a contradiction that Aidan could not figure out. *There might be someone down here*, he thought at Slaíne, Summoning the silver sword into his right hand after passing the torch to his left. Yes, he did sense something alive. Something…malevolent. No, not malevolent, but perhaps something not entirely benign. Aidan shivered, impressed suddenly with the urge to turn around and the thought that he was trespassing. But he'd come this far. Perhaps it was some sort of trick Hex had put on the house, to keep him away from any hidden Goblets. He opened his eyes and took another step.

I'd turn back now if I were you. If it hadn't been before, the voice was most definitely unfriendly now.

Aidan shook his head as an unwanted, unbidden image of himself falling to his death flashed through his mind. "Hello? Is someone down here?" He forced himself to peer over the edge to his right and was hit with a wave of panic.

This is your last chance, strange wizard.

Yes, no doubt Hex had cursed the house to say this, to drive any trespassers back. There was something down there, something important. There had to be. Gathering his courage, Aidan took another step, and the world around him went dark as his torch fizzled out. He reached for the wall and collapsed in a fit of fiery pain on the steps. He dropped the sword, which he Dismissed ere it could fall into the abyss beside him.

Aidan, what happened? Slaíne's thought was muffled and panicked. *Maybe you should come back up here.*

Trembling with sudden fatigue, Aidan attempted to send comforting words her way but found he couldn't think clearly. He tried to ease himself to his feet, but his legs would not support him.

The pulsing below became audible, and the air around him took on a red glow. A woman screamed from the bowels of the earth. He knew that voice.

"Slaíne?" he whispered, his teeth chattering. When she didn't answer, he shouted her name, wondering how she could be down there and yet above him at the top of the stairs at the same time.

Again she cried out, and this time the sound ended in a strangled sob. Through the red haze that hung before him, Aidan saw his love running toward him, her hands and chest coated in something dark and thick.

He reached out for her, but she looked through him, her eyes vacant as she fell at his feet. "What happened? Are you all right?"

"Why? Why'd ya do it?" she gasped.

It was then that Aidan noticed the dagger protruding from her stomach. Slaíne plucked the blade out before he could stop her. She was covered in her own blood. "No," he said and tried to stanch the flow. His hands, for some reason, passed right through her. "Slaíne, what trick is this?"

The light left her eyes and she breathed her last. But it couldn't be Slaíne; whatever fiend this was, it did not have her Pull. It hadn't any Pull at all.

Aidan blinked and tried to clear his mind, but every time he closed his eyes, he could still see her lying there, pale and dead. He shook his head. "What magic is this?" Movement beyond the fake Slaíne caught his eye and he looked himself fully in the face.

It had to be the shape-shifter. The being had a demonic glint in his eyes. He did not stare through Aidan as Slaíne had, as though he were not really there. This creature looked straight into him, right to his heart. "Our anger did this," he said savagely. "We killed them. We killed them all. Meraude and Sam and every Blest." The being threw back his head and let out the most raucous laugh, which turned Aidan's insides cold. It stepped over Slaíne's still form and knelt in front of Aidan, touching him on the forehead.

The strangest of sensations came over him, as though he had been plunged into an uncomfortably hot bath. His temper flared and he lashed out at the shifter, only to find the creature matching his own movements. "Stop that," he snarled, as did the shifter. Their fists shot out at the same time, meaning to strike the other across the face. Aidan realized too late that he was now staring into a mirror and that the shifter was his own reflection. His fist went right through the glass, which shattered into thousands of pieces, and he now was the one covered in blood and falling forward. Down, down he went, through Slaíne's body, which vanished into thin air, and to the edge of the stairs. He looked over and the red light faded, leaving him in darkness once again.

Just a little farther....

Yes, just a few inches farther and he'd be dead.

It's a faster way down. An easier *way out.*

Aidan became somewhat aware that his name was being shouted, that a familiar Pull was nearing him. But when someone grabbed him by the shoulder, he couldn't help but lash out and try to escape their grasp. His fist connected with air, and something struck him across the face, hard, as a woman screamed his name. Again he was slapped, his face still stinging from the first strike. He blinked furiously, trying to clear his vision to un-see the broken mirror before him, which he knew deep down to be an illusion.

The scene before him shifted and he was staring at his cache in Nothingness. Dead bodies littered the floor in that space, and Aidan sent them all back to Existence. Or rather, he tried to. Every time he Summoned something, it was at once sent back.

"No, we gotta keep that secret," the woman's voice was saying, trying to reason with him. "Aidan, look at me." She swore. "Your eyes won't focus, will they?"

A Truth Apple…. My, I have not seen the likes of this for so long. Perhaps I shan't have to betray him after all, said the male voice belonging to the house.

Images flashed before Aidan's eyes: a tapestry depicting three golden stags with their antlers locked, three Goblets – Drifting and Warring, which he knew by sight, and Summoning, which he knew in his heart – then a shiny yellow apple, one Salem had given him from the orchard in the Beyond.

"These ones draw out the truth," Aidan remembered Salem saying. *"They're a cross between the Memory Apples and the regular red variety. Don't bother taking a bite; they taste mostly like any ordinary apple. Catch."*

The house began to whisper. *His weakness. Find his weakness, strange wizard.*

"Weakness?" Aidan echoed as he tried to cling to consciousness.

"Aidan, hold on. I'm going to get help." It was Sláine. Her hand rested on his shoulder, and this time he did not attempt to attack her.

"No," he said firmly, shaking sleep from his thoughts. "He mustn't know – mustn't know we were down here." Aidan grabbed her gently by the wrist and stayed her.

She fought against him. "I don't think I can carry ya, and yer in no shape to travel back up the steps. We gotta fetch someone."

"Quick," Aidan said, his eyelids fluttering. "Find Quick. And hurry. I know how to escape."

CHAPTER THIRTEEN

Jinn

The time was late, and Jinn couldn't sleep. For the last four hours she'd tossed and turned, trying to make sense of her vision and how she'd come to have it in the first place. Something had broken the taboo the wizard had put on those wishing to see his future. But what? Nothing out of the ordinary had happened in that moment by the hidden garden. Lying in the canopy bed, she went over the details in her mind for what felt like the hundredth time, but nothing revealed itself. *I'm missing something important. Maybe something that Hex did not wish me to see.*

With a groan, Jinn threw off her bed coverings and slipped on the boots lying in wait. Maybe some good old-fashioned walking – well, *pacing* – would clear her mind.

There had been no visions since the incident, though she had looked further and harder for them than usual, resulting in a headache and a nosebleed. She had almost told Quick about what she had seen, but was afraid he might try to look ahead himself, something that was particularly dangerous for him to attempt. There was a reason that male Sightfuls and seers were nigh unheard of, as the ability took a greater toll on that gender. And, to make matters worse, Quick had absorbed her part of the curse, a curse that belonged to and yet differed with every Blest – in his case, a childlike mind.

As if in answer to her silent worrying, Quick let out a great sigh and turned over. "Sister can't sleep either?" he asked as his eyes blinked open. He yawned and sat up. "Something on Jinn's mind?"

Jinn tied her cloak around her and shook her head. "It's nothing important, Quick. I'm sorry if I woke you."

Quick chuckled. "Quick has slept enough." Again he yawned. "Magic here makes Quick sleepy. Does Jinn—" He sat up abruptly, his hand to his ear.

"What? What's wrong?" But now she heard it too, a woman's voice calling to someone.

Help me. The words echoed again and again in Jinn's mind.

"Jinn hears it too?" Quick asked, getting out of bed and reaching for his boots. "Could be trap, no?"

She hushed him.

Down below. Hurry, the voice was saying. *Don't let the wizard discover you.*

Jinn hurried to the door with Quick at her heels. She expected to find the lock in place and a ward up, especially after that moment she'd experienced in the garden, but the door opened soundlessly on its hinges and she passed a hand through without scorching herself.

Hurry.

"It very well could be a trap," said Jinn, hesitating.

To her surprise, Quick gave her a gentle push and moved around her. "It's the she-wizard," he said. "Summoner is in danger."

"What?" Jinn asked, trying to keep up with his long, sure strides. "What makes you say that?"

Quick did not answer at first, but led her through a series of turns that she had never taken before. The house was still and silent. All was bathed in moonlight, as the clouds obscuring the night's eye had parted. If Hex emerged or the house alerted him to their midnight journey, they would be easily seen.

Please, hurry.

"Slow down, Quick. My short legs can't keep up with your pace."

With a long-suffering sough, her brother slowed his steps and allowed her to catch up. "House is alive."

"Yes, I know, Quick. It was I who talked to it."

He nodded. "Summoner trespassed. House of Curses is angry."

Jinn wondered at her brother. She wanted to ask him how he knew, but was prevented from doing so when he yanked her around a corner and put a finger to his lips.

"Hello?" It was Hex. They must have been making too much noise, and now they would be discovered.

She had to make a decision and a quick one, at that. The wizard was doing nothing to soften his footfalls, and every moment drew him nearer to their hiding place. Jinn tapped Quick on the arm and gestured what she meant to do: head toward the wizard, leaving Quick behind.

At first she thought he was going to put up a protest, but was surprised instead to find him nodding. He would help the Summoner and the she-wizard.

Jinn braced herself and left the nook they were hiding in. She walked several paces toward where she'd last heard the wizard, and still jumped in surprise when she saw him emerge from the shadows and into the moonlight.

Afraid he would drag her back whence she had come, passing and most likely finding Quick's hiding place, Jinn straightened her back and took a sharp right and kept walking. *I hope Quick hurries. I don't know how much time I can buy him.*

As expected, the wizard followed her; she could hear his feet clapping against the flagstones behind her. "You shouldn't be out tonight." His tone was colder than she had been expecting, but Jinn did not allow that to frighten her. Instead, she approached a window facing the east.

The glass was as clear as crystal, and Jinn pretended to study the night's sky through it. "I couldn't sleep," she murmured. That much was true.

Hex stopped where he was, a few yards behind her, and sighed. "The house is not safe. Especially tonight."

Jinn shrugged.

"It's angry for some reason, but it won't tell me why." This he seemed to say to himself, so Jinn ignored it entirely. "Jinn?"

Say something, idiot. Think of an excuse for him not to drag you back to your prison — or worse, magic you back. "I used to think the moon was pretend," she found herself blurting. As soon as the words had left her lips, Jinn cringed. Why, of all facts and thoughts had she chosen to relay something so embarrassing and stupid?

"That's not something to be embarrassed about…or afraid of." He sounded confused at the last part.

That's right; he can smell emotions or some other nonsense. I'm embarrassed by my candidness, but what fear is he sensing?

Hex was still talking. "I would imagine that after living most of your life in a cave, many things would seem unlikely and frightening." He took a step forward and her heart began to race. "But I have a feeling, a slight intuition, that you did not escape your room to watch the moon set."

No, don't panic. Think of a lie. A good lie.

"I couldn't sleep."

He moved next to her, scarcely making a sound. "So you said." Some of the coldness had returned to his voice, which sparked Jinn's anger.

"So sorry to inconvenience you, but you know you don't have to follow me around like some watchdog. I can take care of myself." *Easy, don't let him rile you. You're supposed to be distracting him, not picking a fight.*

Of all things, the wizard chuckled. "Oh, I don't doubt that. But the house—"

"The house hasn't harmed me." She chanced a look at Hex, and was surprised to find the wizard staring at her, his expression unreadable.

"Yet," he said. "The house hasn't harmed you *yet*."

Jinn threw up her hands in disgust. "I don't think it would. And besides, how is the room you have me stashed away in any different or safer from the rest of the rooms or corridors?"

Hex was already shaking his head. "It's not that the rooms are safer, it's more that I know exactly where you are, just in case. I won't have to waste time trying to find you if something goes wrong."

"What does it even matter to you?" Jinn went back to looking out the window. "You don't want me to kill Meraude? Well, I can't do it locked up *or* dead, so you win. Congratulations."

Hex stilled beside her. "What did you say?"

"I think you heard me." She squared her shoulders. "It's foolishness thinking I'm not willing to risk everything in order to escape." A thin cloud flitted in front of the moon, momentarily dimming the room. Jinn didn't know how much more of this conversation she could take. Each word drew her temper closer and closer to the surface, and the stars above only knew what might happen if she provoked the wizard much more. It was selfishness, she knew, that caused her to act. Quick needed more time to find the Summoner and his companion, but Jinn turned away from the window and started back to her prison.

"Jinn," Hex said.

Startled, she turned.

"Do you take delight in professing words and assigning them my name? Must you always misunderstand me?" His eyes glittered dangerously, and Jinn shivered. "I did not say I wanted you dead. Haven't I declared the opposite?" He moved slowly but surely toward her.

Tempting though it was to take an equal measure of frightened steps back, Jinn held her ground. How to parry words she didn't entirely understand? "I did not say that you or anyone wanted me dead," she said, quickly sorting through the conversation thus far in her mind.

"Yet you implied indifference on my part, which is the next worst thing." Hex stopped three feet from her and the intensity in his eyes made Jinn look away. "Will you make me say it?"

"Say whatever it is you need to say, and perhaps we can be done with this conversation for the night," Jinn said, though without heat or malice. Her shoulders were suddenly sagging under the weight of the day, and she knew she would sleep as one dead once she was able to.

Hex was unrelenting in his pursuit of closure. "I have seen the future, Jinn, and I have since been desperately trying to prevent parts of it, not knowing why events might come to pass or why I would care if they did. And yet, over these last few weeks, especially the last few days, my eyes have slowly begun to open. And I now know what will happen to me if things are allowed to continue on their predetermined course." He took a small step toward her and then another. "You are wrong in assigning indifference to my motives. My motives are quite selfish." He was mere inches from her then, one hand reaching out to take hers.

Jinn watched in silent surprise as he clasped her palm in his and brought her knuckles to his lips. Her fingertips tingled, and a great shudder rippled down her spine.

For the second time that day, the taboo lifted unexpectedly, filling her head with flashes of strange visions from the future. One moment she foresaw herself alone and wandering, and in the next she was laughing and walking hand in hand with the wizard, an unfamiliar glint in her eyes. The visions came too quickly for her mind to process, as though her foresight was making up for lost time. Soon the whole room seemed to spin. Jinn tried to block the visions or at least slowing them down, but they were powerful and insistent.

Fortunately, or perhaps unfortunately, depending on how Jinn chose to look at it, the wizard seemed to come to his senses and released her hand. At once the taboo snapped back into place with an audible bang. She had seen so much and understood so little. It was tempting to ask the wizard to let her look again, though she knew he wouldn't. Instead they stood there, each of them breathing hard as her vision began to clear.

"I think I should go," Jinn found herself saying, her voice distant to her own ears.

Hex nodded, his expression inscrutable. "Yes, that is probably for the best."

Jinn gave him one last confused look before turning on her heels and hurrying back to the room she shared with Quick. Her brother was not there when she burst inside, and she wondered if she ought to sneak out again and make certain he went undiscovered. The thought of seeing the wizard again just now was unbearable. She needed to distract herself. So, dazed and trembling, Jinn took to doctoring the fire, which had burned down to its embers. *What did that all even mean?* Jinn shook her head. *No, don't think about it. Just work.* Fistfuls of kindling went in first, along with knots of dry grass. Was that a footfall she heard outside in the hall? No, it was her imagination. She took a quarter of a dry log and tossed it in toward the back of the fireplace.

After ten minutes of attempting to clear her mind and revive the blaze, the door burst open, causing Jinn to jump and nearly tumble into the flames. "What happened?" she asked as Quick set the moaning Summoner on his bed.

"He's got on the wrong side of the house, that's what," said a crisp voice from the entryway, just after the door had shut behind her. The redheaded she-wizard was paler than in any of Jinn's visions, and the circles under her eyes made it look like someone had hit her, hard. She brushed past Jinn and went to the Summoner, who startled them all by crying out, "Death!" He began to thrash about like a madman, clawing at the air.

"Summoner keeps saying that," Quick said, holding Aidan down with ease. "House hurt his mind, no?"

The she-wizard wrung her hands. "I nay know my magic well enough to reverse it. Maybe we should get the master o' the house."

"No," Jinn said quickly. "Let me think."

The she-wizard – Slaíne, Jinn recalled – actually growled. "No one's stoppin' ya from thinkin'. He needs medicine."

"We need to assess him first," Jinn said, sorting through information in her mind. She had read plenty of magical medical texts in the cave as a youth and a new adult. Well, as often as she could without wasting candles. "Quick, hold him still. I need to look at his eyes."

Her brother hesitated. "He fairly strong. Quick doesn't want to break his bones."

"We'll deal with broken bones if we need to. The mind is more important. Do as I say. And you, sit down, you look like you've suffered an attack too."

Slaíne got in the way, as though attempting to shield her mate, but Jinn easily pushed her aside. "What's wrong with him?"

Jinn hushed her. "Aidan, can you hear me?" She lifted his lids and was surprised to find the pupils tiny pinpricks in the dim light.

"Dead. S-so many dead." The Summoner's words were slurred, and he renewed his struggle against Quick.

"Summoner uses magic. Is cheating."

After feeling for his heartbeat – racing – she then smelled his breath. "That's odd. It's like he's been poisoned. Did he eat or drink anything?"

"Down there?" Slaíne said, her voice high and cracking. "In the dungeons? What would he eat or drink down there?" The she-wizard swore. "Could ya make an antidote, if it is poisoning?"

"Magical poisoning is different than medicinal poisoning. Hex said the dungeons would drive a person to distraction. It's probably a curse."

Slaíne let out a strangled sob. "We've got to fetch the wizard." She got to her feet and went for the door, but hesitated. "What do you know of tanderine blossoms?"

Jinn looked at her sharply. "They're an antidote to most poisons, yes. Do you have any?"

The she-wizard nodded, closed her eyes and swayed on the spot. "Curses, it's harder than he makes it look. Can nay focus on nothin'." She approached Jinn, her eyes glowing a strange blue. "Lemme through."

"Of course." Jinn stepped aside and murmured to Quick, "If she faints, catch her."

"Looks ready to drop," Quick concurred.

The she-wizard bent over her mate and tore his shirt open and placed her hand on his chest. The Summoner continued to lash out until she commanded him to be still in a voice that was not quite human. At once he ceased moving.

Magic crackled all around them, causing Jinn's hairs to stand on end. The air smelled like it did just before a lightning storm, so she retreated to what she hoped was a safer distance. Quick followed suit.

"Where have you got them?" Slaíne asked Aidan.

The Summoner spoke some nonsense and then moaned as the room took on a brilliant green glow.

"Dontcha fight me, Aidan Ingledark," she ordered.

There was a great flash of blue light, and Jinn was forced to look away. *Thud!* She stifled a scream and opened her eyes. Swearing, she looked at the mess of hay, papers, clothes, food, and weapons that littered the floor.

"They've got to be in this heap somewhere," Slaíne said as she rolled up her sleeves. "Don't just stand there. Help me find the ugly blighters."

"Remind me what they look like," Jinn said.

Slaíne rooted through a pile of hay, tossing it over her shoulder and onto Quick as she went. "They're yellow, shriveled – sorta remind me of a creature with a skin fungus. If'n I could remember what their Pull felt like, maybe I could Call them...."

"This it?" Quick asked, holding up an orange flower.

Jinn shook her head. "No. Keep looking."

They tore through the disaster that was now the room, throwing everything into one pile at the she-wizard's suggestion so she would be able to easily Dismiss it all later. The hay in particular kept fooling Jinn's eyes and making her think she'd spotted the flower. Finally, what was probably only five minutes later but felt more like twenty, Jinn caught sight of something yellow poking out from behind a sheet of parchment. She lifted the document and was rewarded with a fistful of the flowers. "I found them."

The she-wizard was at her side in moments. "Bless. Ya know how to make an antidote, yes?"

"I'd feel better if I had an open text in front of me," Jinn confessed, picking bits of hay out of the bouquet she had formed. "Take that patera and boil some water in it."

Slaíne lifted the patera and carried it toward the fire, which was clinging to life. "Where...?"

"There's a pitcher on the table near the window. Quick will get it."

From the bed, the Summoner began talking nonsense about death and blood. He still seemed to be under the she-wizard's spell, thankfully, as he did not thrash around or attempt to rise.

"Water," said Quick, bringing the pitcher.

"Start boiling it," Jinn ordered as she separated the leaves from the petals and stamens. No part of the tanderine plant was harmful, from what Jinn could remember, but she wasn't entirely certain what parts were helpful, so she crushed the whole plant between her left palm and her right knuckles. "Move," she said to Quick, who was standing in the way, empty pitcher in his large, trembling hands. Jinn dumped the flowers into the patera, rubbing all the pollen she could from her fingers. "The fire needs to be hotter if we want the water to boil any time soon."

Slaíne nodded. "Hold this."

Jinn crouched and took the patera's long handle from her hands, sloshing a little bit of the precious mixture onto the embers. "Not too high," she warned.

Moments later, the she-wizard threw back her hands and cast a ball of blue flame into the fireplace. The logs took at once and began crackling merrily, a great contrast to the grave circumstances.

"Not to a boil," said Quick, surprising Jinn. He shrugged. "Bad things happen at a boil. Jinn's books said."

"All right. Not to a boil, though I don't know how you remember that."

He chuckled, a jarring sound in such a tense environment. "Quick and Jinn were fifteen. Quick was bored, so Jinn read. Quick remembers most stories." He tapped his large forehead.

Soon, the water had approached a boil, and Jinn removed it from the flames. She peered at the liquid, which had turned a deep yellow that bordered on brown and smelled like the citrus fruits she had once tasted.

"Summoner don't look so good."

Slaíne, who had been cradling her mate's head in her lap for the last five minutes, sniffed. "He's tougher than he looks."

Jinn watched as she stroked his hair and whispered his name, but soon looked away. It felt like an intrusion of their privacy even being in the same room, seeing the way the she-wizard so obviously loved him. Her mind wandered back to Hex's near declaration and the strange visions that had followed. What was the wizard's game? And what was her future-self thinking of, falling for it?

"Is it almost ready?" Slaíne startled Jinn by asking.

Trying to control the tremors in her hands, Jinn nodded. "It needs to cool a bit more or else it will scald his throat." She could still feel the pressure of Hex's cool lips on her fingers, still see his deep, dark eyes boring into her own…. *No, don't think these thoughts. You're only going to upset yourself. Besides, the future is subject to change. Distract yourself.* "What were you both doing down in the dungeons?" She blew on the water's surface, sending steam puffing away from her face.

The she-wizard didn't look up from her love, whose breathing had slowed. "He was lookin' for the Goblets Immortal. I know he's told ya the wizard here's got 'em."

Remembering her vision of the tapestry with the three stags and what she knew, Jinn cringed. Could she have prevented the Summoner's troubles if she had sought him out and told him? "Quick, fetch me a cup." She dipped a finger into the elixir, testing the temperature, and then shook her hand dry. "What made him think the Goblets were down there?"

Slaíne hesitated. "He thought he felt somethin' down there. Plus, I mean, the wizard ain't been too forthcomin' about their hiding place." She watched as Jinn took the wood chalice from Quick and carefully poured the flower water into it. "Time's runnin' out. He and me need the Goblets and to get out of here as fast as we can. Afore it's too late to stop...." She pressed her lips together.

"To stop Meraude. I know," Jinn said, easing herself to her feet. "I'm trying to stop her as well." She wondered for a moment if the she-wizard knew of her relationship to Meraude. Something made her think that the Summoner had not told her, and for that she was grateful. "Here, pour this slowly down his throat."

"Thanks." The she-wizard took the chalice and put it to Aidan's trembling lips. "You gotta drink this, Aidan."

The Summoner sighed and said something unintelligible, then he choked on a mouthful of the elixir. He coughed and sputtered and began to thrash again.

"Hold 'im down," Slaíne said. She sounded drained of energy, and Jinn again wondered if the she-wizard might have suffered at the house's hands as well.

With Quick pinning him down by his left arm, and Jinn pinning him down by the other, the liquid slowly made its way down Aidan's throat. Several more times he lurched and heaved against them. They held fast, putting all their weight against him. It wasn't until the last mouthful that the Summoner ceased struggling altogether. He lay still, the color creeping back into his face.

Slaíne shook him by the shoulders. "Don't ya ever do that to me again, ya hear?"

Again Jinn felt like she ought to look away. "Check for his heart rate."

"It's good now," Slaíne said without making a move to feel for his heartbeat.

"How do you know? You should really check it."

The she-wizard did not answer. "Thank you...?"

"Jinn. My name is Jinn." She waited for the she-wizard to properly introduce herself, but she did not. "Quick, would you carry him back to their room? We don't want Hex to find them missing."

Quick grunted.

"Wait," said Slaíne. "You think he ought to be moved? An' what if the wizard finds us?"

The last part made Jinn pause. Some instinct told her, however, that Hex would not be roaming the halls for the rest of the night. *He'll give you your space.* She flushed and hoped that no one in the room noticed. "I don't think he will be a problem tonight, but we really should return your— Aidan to your room before morning." She scrutinized the she-wizard. "Are you all right?"

She was pale and drawn, her eyes tight with some worries or unknown horrors. "I'm fine." Her brittle voice suggested that she was not, in fact, fine, but it also brooked no argument. "Let's be done with it."

Quick, who had been watching the exchange, gently lifted the slumbering Summoner, and carried him to the door, which Jinn ran ahead to and opened.

"He said he found it," said Slaíne, startling Jinn. "Right before his fit started. Said he found a way for us all to escape."

Jinn's heart leapt within her bosom and sank to her stomach like lead. "Oh?" was all she could manage to say before Quick, the Summoner, and the strange woman disappeared into the dark halls.

A way to escape? This was good...but why was she suddenly so worried?

CHAPTER FOURTEEN

Meraude

It was the 501st anniversary of the Great Wizards' defeat after the War, when their blood had been drained and used to form the Goblets Immortal. For this occasion, Meraude found herself obligated to host a handful of her most important advisors, and other important Sightfuls and Endurers, inviting them to enjoy a small feast in celebration. As a treat to her warriors in training, Meraude also invited her two most promising pupils, who, besides Meraude herself, were the only ones in the company who possessed more than one trait of a Blest.

The air of the small dining hall was heavily spiced with incense and cinnamon. Blood-red swags of cloth had been artistically twisted and draped over the windows, making the late sun's light look as though it were bleeding to death on the worn wood floors. Meraude cleared her head of the mere thought of blood. She needed to keep her thoughts detached and her actions spontaneous tonight.

Five times she had sent for her Sightfuls, and each time they had managed to avoid her call. Not tonight…unless they had fled Inohaim. No one would dare turn their nose up at such an affair as this without fear of appearing sympathetic to the wizards who had perished.

Meraude snapped her fingers, and a servant dressed in green linens scurried out of the shadows and bowed. "Milady?"

"Light the candles and summon the guests."

"Yes, milady." The servant bowed again and began giving orders to her underlings. Soon the room was plunged into a cheery orange light from the fragrant beeswax candles.

Meraude smoothed her black hair over her right shoulder and let it cascade down the length of her back. Fixing a warm smile on her face, she greeted her general, Tindra, who was the first to enter, as was her right per rank.

"Milady," Tindra said, bowing, and then kissed the ruby ring on Meraude's right hand. There was a question in her hazel eyes, which always assessed any room she entered for threats. She sniffed appreciatively as the door to the kitchens opened, allowing in the scent of roast boar. "Tonight promises to be exciting."

To that, Meraude quirked an eyebrow. Something was afoot and the general was warning her. "As it always is at such an important occasion, General. I trust that the troops are celebrating in their encampments?"

Tindra made a displeased face. "Yes. Some drink to excess, I fear. Even the Sightfuls among them could be caught blind and with their trousers down on a night like this."

Meraude nodded her dismissal of the general, who then bowed her head once and approached a servant offering drink. Next to enter were four Sightfuls, who looked perfectly at ease. "Milady," they choroused, before each in turn kissed the ring on the mage queen's right hand.

"You'll have to forgive the others of our caste," said the fair one with the red eyes whose name always escaped Meraude. "There has been a stomach ailment that we've been passing among ourselves."

"I see," said Meraude with a shake of her head. "It is a shame. I had wondered why I'd seen so little of you all as of late." She smiled indulgently, knowing that they would see through her calm exterior no matter how hard she tried to hide her pain and anger within herself. *I trusted you.*

The four quickly bowed and moved out of the way of Meraude's advisors, who were chiefly made up of Endurers. They greeted Meraude in their own boisterous way, going nearly as far as to be disrespectful, though the mage queen could not find it within herself to be offended. The ten of them also moved out of the way and on to the drinks, and all who remained to be greeted were her two chosen pupils: Ing and Egreet. The two stood out among the other, more formally dressed, women. They wore the black skintight trousers that were a part of all trainees' dress uniform, paired with the common blood-red tunic and black cloth belt. Both young women looked uneasy about something.

"Ing," said Meraude as the taller of the two bowed. She waited for the other girl to bow before addressing her.

"Milady, something's wrong," said Egreet, her eyes roving over Meraude's shoulder.

Ing hissed something below her breath. "There is too much iron in the Sightful barracks."

Meraude tried to hide her alarm. Iron was forbidden from entering the training grounds, as it interfered with the work they did. "Who put it there?" she demanded.

The two Blest girls looked at each other. "We do not know for certain," said Egreet. "But there are rumors it was done under General Tindra's orders."

Yes, something was afoot, indeed. But Tindra had nothing to do with it. "It's a ruse," she said, smiling to her other guests and pulling Egreet aside. "Ing, tell the general. And be careful."

Mouth set in a grim line, the girl did as she was asked.

Meraude turned to the remaining Blest. "Have you used your foresight today?"

"The – the iron has been interfering, so I haven't," she stammered. Her dark, intelligent eyes seemed to register Meraude's unease. "Someone plans to harm the Sightfuls?"

"No," said Meraude quickly. "Something bad is meant to happen here. I need you to look ahead, Egreet. Look closely for the other Sightfuls in this room. You can identify them by the green sashes."

Without hesitation, Egreet's eyes closed and she began looking into the future. "So you are not a Sightful yourself," she said below her breath.

"Focus," Meraude commanded. "But go to a corner of the room. Make it look like you have a headache. When you see the danger, tell General Tindra." She patted the girl on the back and returned to her guests. Strategy was not Meraude's strongest gift. Perhaps her mother had drunk little of the Warring Goblet, or perhaps Meraude's other abilities merely overcrowded it. As her mother had died in childbirth, and the Elders had scattered, Meraude would never know. Gifted warrior strategist or not, instinct told her not to turn her back on any of the women in this room. She nodded toward the assembly, and they all gathered in a semicircle, keeping their mage queen front and center.

"Welcome, honorable, distinguished guests," said Meraude, raising her voice as the others quieted. "We celebrate tonight the defeat of our enemies and the rise of a new empire that we build together. Every one of us possesses within us the gift of magic." She paused, looking individual women in the eyes. "Some are gifted with foresight, while others still possess great strength and the ability to withstand attack. Every one of you, Endurer or Sightful, is more than worthy to stand in this new order, and have made it possible by your sacrifice. It was not long ago, however, that the hated men, the Elders of the Circle, ruled our kind." At the words 'Elders' and 'Circle', the crowd let out the expected jeers and cries, which at once ceased when Meraude raised her hand. "We must remember our past, if we are to prevent it from happening again." Resolutely she kept her eyes from seeking out Egreet and Tindra.

"These men, these humans, possessed no power themselves." There were a few appreciative laughs. "They claimed they were among the order who destroyed the Great Six, the wizards whose blood powers the Goblets Immortal. We know no mere mortal was responsible. Elves and hags and other such creatures destroyed the wizards and drained their blood.

"Now, some say I hate all of magic-kind." Again she paused and looked individuals in the eye. "That is simply not true. Every last magical being has a purpose and is useful…if they are controlled by the right people."

"Hear, hear," cried out one of her Endurers.

Meraude smiled lightly in response, though her stomach was churning. *What are the Sightfuls planning, and why hasn't Tindra made a move yet?* "Victory, total control is near, my friends. The throne of

Inohaim will soon bear a ruler." The room stilled at these words. "And we will all live in perfect harmony."

A servant hurried to her side with a tray, and Meraude plucked up a crystal goblet. "To our health, to the death of our enemies, to total dominion, and to the end of the human race. Raise your glasses."

They did as one.

If I were a Sightful with no other ability, I would be more than on an even playing field in this room. She scanned the room of confused faces, and the mood shifted slightly. *Don't think. Your thoughts are your weakness in this game, to the advantage of a Sightful. Thoughts become decisions, and decisions become actions. Speak, they're waiting.* "Forgive me, this is an emotional moment."

At those words, Egreet pushed her way through the ranks of the crowd and put a hand to her own throat. A warning.

Without hesitation, Meraude blurted out, "No one drink the wine. It has been poisoned. Seize the Sightfuls in our midst."

All was chaos and noise as the few Endurers who were not stunned elbowed their way to the Sightfuls. The four women could not overpower the Endurers, but with foresight on their side, they easily outmaneuvered them. There was nowhere for them to go, however, except to Meraude.

"Milady, 'tis a lie," said one of the Sightfuls. She clutched Meraude's cloak. "Why would we try to poison anyone?"

Meraude shook the creature off and crouched to her level. "Why would you withhold information from me?" she countered in a whisper, rising again to her full height. Her strategic mind began processing the events. A party was a perfect time to attempt to poison Meraude's general and the other Endurers. But Endurers were not easily killed, by any means. The Sightfuls knew that. It was a ruse. "Egreet, Ing."

The other three Sightfuls struggled in vain against the Endurers holding them in place. "No, don't tell her anything," one of the women pled. "She's mad. You can't trust her."

Meraude nodded to Tindra, who then buried her fist in the Sightful's side. Ribs cracked audibly, and the woman fainted.

"Ing, tell me what the other Sightfuls, the ones not here or in training, are going to do next. Egreet, while your sister-in-arms looks ahead, I want you to take this knife." Meraude Summoned a silver dagger and presented it to the girl, who took it from her and tested its weight in her hands. Once Egreet was done examining it, the mage queen continued. "The creature here at my feet has chosen to side with the humans."

Egreet's face darkened.

"The other Sightfuls," said Ing, her voice trembling, "I can't find them." She choked on a sob. "I think they're dead."

"Look at me, Egreet," said Meraude. "What sort of creature kills one of their own kind without being provoked?"

The Sightful at Meraude's feet began to crawl backward, but Meraude stepped on the hem of the woman's cloak. "Clemency, milady. Please."

"You want me to kill her?" asked Egreet, her voice full of hate.

"No, Egreet. I don't want you to kill her. I want you to cut out her right eye as slowly and as painfully as you can manage."

A grim smile spread over the young warrior's face. "Hold her, Ing."

"Let this be a lesson to you all," said Meraude over the cries for mercy. She Summoned two more daggers and Repelled them away from herself, sending them as close to the other two Sightfuls as she could without piercing flesh, letting the blades hover in midair before their throats. "No more lies."

And that was when the screaming began.

CHAPTER FIFTEEN

Aidan

If you can hear me, follow my voice. There was laughter, and then there was nothing.

Aidan was aware of having been moved from the stairs leading to the dungeon, and of having been forced to drink something foul. Now he felt lost. There was a human Pull nearby that he thought was familiar, though he couldn't be certain. Other than that, there was nothing with which to orient himself.

You're not lost. I've found you. The voice in his head belonged to a woman, and he thought he knew her, but every time he tried putting a name to the voice, the word would drift away. His frustration was mounting.

Other voices crawled around inside his mind. There was a man, somewhere far off, who was trying to reach Aidan, but a wall lay between them. Soon that voice quieted, and the woman began singing some nonsense about a winding path and two star-crossed lovers on opposite shores. He blinked furiously at the sound, but his vision was fuzzy, so he closed his eyes again and drowsed for what felt like days, only to snap to consciousness with a start.

When he opened his eyes again, the room he found himself in was dark. "Hello?" he asked the void, his voice a dry croak. He sensed rather than saw that someone was with him.

There you are.

Aidan shook his head and a wave of nausea overtook him. "Who's there?" A blue light fell over the room.

"I've been practicin'," said the voice that he knew but couldn't place. It was melodic and entrancing, a shrewd serpent ready to strike. "Afore you ask, you've been asleep for five days. I've had to make up all sorts of excuses to Hex as to why you weren't showin' up to training or meals with the rest of us."

He let the name roll around in his mind and then his mouth formed it into a spoken word. "Hex?"

There was a deep sigh and someone sat down next to him. "You're more lucid than the last seven times we've had this conversation. Don't think no permanent damage was done. Your soul don't feel no different."

Aidan fought to see through the haze that was clouding his vision. And there was suddenly a name in his mouth. "Slaíne." He shook his head and groaned.

"Don't fall back asleep, Aidan. We've been waiting too long for answers."

"Answers?"

"Yes. You said you knew how to get us out of here."

"Here?"

The voice that belonged to Slaíne swore. "You really need to pay attention, love." She snapped her fingers in front of his face as his eyes once again began to close. "Aidan."

"He needs the bath?" asked a second, slightly less familiar voice. This one was male, all dull tones and strange intonations, albeit with hints of hidden intelligence. Aidan knew he would not be able to listen to it long without losing his patience.

"The water's frigid, just like you asked for," said a third voice, this one female. If the second was dull, this one was as tightly strung as a bow. The intelligence there was not hidden. He would have to tread carefully with her.

The first voice, the powerful one – Slaíne, he reminded himself – startled him by growling. "Careful, both of you, he ain't himself. Might lash out, if'n we're nay careful."

"Water?" asked the male voice again.

"All right," said Slaíne. "But if'n I tell you to drop him and run, you do so without hesitation, understand?"

The two remaining voices were silent, but Aidan sensed a change in the room. Something was about to happen – something involving him and cold water. Before he could figure out what that might be, a hand gently took him by the shoulder. He reacted without thinking, throwing out a fistful of green fire at the unexpected intruder to his personal space.

Aidan, it's just me, said Slaíne, deflecting the flames with ease. *It's all right. I'm going to help you, but you can nay struggle.* The words crawled and coiled around Aidan's mind, and he fought their seductive power, lashing out this time with his fists as his vision darkened once more. Again his moves were anticipated. The hand holding his shoulder moved away as an invisible wall rose between him and the person trying to calm him.

Slaíne, Aidan reminded himself. *Mate. She's your mate.* He ceased lashing out and was still, waiting to see what might happen next.

For that, he was rewarded with a soft kiss on the lips. "All right. Quick, lift him."

What? That was it? He reached for his mate again, but she was no longer there. In Slaíne's place were two overlarge hands that snatched him up by the front and bore him against his will across the dim room.

Don't struggle, Aidan, Slaíne said lovingly into his mind. Aloud she said, "When I say so, drop him and run."

There was a lull in movement, and Aidan felt his eyes slamming shut.

"Now!" said his mate, and Aidan left the grasp of the two giant hands and plunged into a small expanse of frigid water.

He thrashed and struggled to rise to the surface, furious at the betrayal, but some invisible force pushed against him. The more he struggled, the more his vision began to clear and the less tired he felt, a strange energy pumping hard through his veins. He gave a shout, and the washtub he was in exploded in a flash of green light, and whatever had been holding him down ceased doing so.

Blinking against the water dripping down his face, Aidan made out Slaíne, Jinn, and Quick, who stood on the opposite side of the room, their expressions wary. They, too, were soaking wet.

"Welcome back," said Slaíne, taking a tentative step toward him.

Aidan growled, but she did not seem the least bit impressed with his show of anger. He pulled himself to his feet, his legs shaking beneath him. "What," said Aidan gruffly, "did you do that for?"

Slaíne snorted with impatience. "You slept long enough, Aidan. We need answers, an' last thing you said to me was that you had them." She gave him a pointed look.

Aidan's thoughts began racing. Yes, he knew he had information about something important, but every time he tried to latch on to it, it skittered away from him. The more he tried, the more frustrated he became, and the more frustrated he became, the more his thoughts wouldn't co-operate.

Apparently noting his struggle, Slaíne approached him with a towel, and said, "We'll tell ya what we know, an' maybe that'll help ya remember." She threw the towel, and he caught it.

"That sounds reasonable." He dried off his face and moved back toward the bed, where he sat on the edge.

To his surprise, Slaíne conjured three chairs out of nothing, and the others sat. "Right. So, after you went down to the dungeons, I tried rescuing you, but you're too heavy."

"Needed Quick," said the giant.

Slaíne nodded. "Does any of this sound familiar?"

A hand went to Aidan's throat as he remembered being force-fed some horrible potion. "Yes." Slowly, details were starting to come back to him. "But before that, the house spoke to me." He closed his eyes and let his mind relax, and instead of chasing the memories, he let them come to him. "There are three Goblets here."

"We know that," said Quick, and the two women hushed him.

Aidan grimaced at the interruption. "We're supposed to find the wizard's weakness. And there's something about a Truth Apple." He opened his eyes again as the pieces began to fit together. "If we can get him to eat a Truth Apple, he'll tell us where the Goblets are and where the doorknob is kept."

"Truth Apple?" asked Slaíne.

"Doorknob?" asked Jinn.

Aidan launched into a short explanation of how he and Hex had traveled to the House of Curses, using a magical doorknob that opened a portal. "The Truth Apple," he said, "is something Salem gave me weeks ago. It tricks whoever eats from it into telling the truth."

"So you give Hex the apple and he'll unwittingly help us," said Jinn. "That's wonderful."

But Slaíne was shaking her head. "He ain't gonna eat anything Aidan or I give him. He's always got his guard up around us."

"And we have no reason to give him food. He has a larder magically full of it. If we knew his weakness, maybe we could use that instead."

"His weakness?" asked Jinn. "What makes you think he has one?"

Slaíne gave Aidan a curious look. "You ever figure out why the house's magic stopped working the other day?"

Aidan put up a finger. "Give me a moment." He was quickly growing tired from this interview and knew he would not be able to continue for much longer. When he had regathered his strength, he continued. "The other day," he said, directing his words to Jinn, "or rather, the other week, there was a great change in magical power. It felt as though Hex's magic that he uses to operate the House of Curses was overcome by some force. Slaíne and I were speculating about what might have caused it, so I did some experiments with fire." At this point, he remembered the fight he and his mate had had, and he cringed.

"You ran an experiment," Slaíne prompted once he had been silent for a few moments.

Aidan cleared his throat. "I lit a fire by magical means, knowing the only way to extinguish it would be to sever the magic. I guessed that the same principle would be true for any magic, great or small. But why would Hex sever the magic on purpose? It makes no sense. So I decided it must have been an accident. Something distracted Hex successfully enough that he unwittingly stopped all the magic powering the house.

"I tried different things to distract myself, wondering if anger or some other strong emotion would do. Nothing worked...until I started thinking about Slaíne." His eyes traveled to hers briefly, but then returned to Jinn, whose face had paled considerably. "Love effectively distracted me enough that I unwittingly released the thread of magic that kept the magical fire going, and the blaze died at once."

"Oh," said Jinn, her voice very small.

Aidan looked back at Slaíne, who looked less than impressed. "What?"

"That's all well and good, but how are we to figure out what this wizard loves? While you was sleepin', I trained with him. That wizard loves nothin' but himself, mark my words."

"What makes you say that?" Aidan demanded, feeling another different sort of tired now. "Everyone loves something. Or someone."

Slaíne's laugh was like hot lead striking cold water: a sharp burst that fizzled out at once, causing everyone in the room to jump. "You remember how he said he ought to kill me?"

The mere thought of it stirred white-hot anger in Aidan's stomach. "Well, yes, but…."

Quick leaned forward in his conjured seat, which protested beneath his weight. "Wizard is perhaps bad."

"That's an understatement, ever there's been one made," Slaíne said, slamming her fist on her leg. "Why, you shoulda seen him training me. Threw all sorts of magic at me that I'd rather not think of again. No one that horrible is capable of love."

Throughout this, Jinn had been quiet. Now, she stood up, clearly agitated.

"What wrong?" asked her brother.

Aidan watched her closely. "The house said for me to find Hex's weakness. He has one. I know it. And I think Jinn knows it too."

The woman brushed at her sleeve. "I don't know what you're talking about."

"What?" asked Quick, clearly distraught. "Is Jinn all right?"

"Be honest with us, Jinn. We haven't much time," Aidan said, impatience seeping into his voice.

Without warning, Jinn turned her back and fled from the room.

"Jinn," Quick called out after her. He rose and followed her, making enough noise to draw anyone nearby.

Aidan sighed. "I'm thirsty."

"Turns over a wasp nest and he says he's thirsty," said Sláine. "Unbelievable." Nonetheless, she Summoned a waterskin and threw it at him. "You think that horrid wizard is in love with...Jinn?"

After draining the waterskin, Aidan wiped his mouth with the back of his hand and nodded. "If not entirely yet, he's going to be."

Incredulous, Sláine stared at him. "That was fast. Are ya certain?"

Aidan shrugged. "You didn't see the way he treated her when she and I first met." He almost chuckled at the memory. "He was terrified of her."

"And that means he loves her?"

"Sláine, why else would an extremely powerful wizard be scared to death of such a small, slight Blest with her powers under arrest? He either loved her at first sight...."

"Bah!"

"Or he *foresaw* that he was going to. Either way, I think Jinn just confirmed my theory by running out of here."

Sláine shook her head and got to her feet. "Men are strange. An' since when did you become that observant?" She approached and sat on the bed next to him.

Aidan grinned. "Perhaps I've learned a thing or two since meeting you."

At that Sláine merely rolled her eyes and allowed him to kiss her on the cheek. "An' how exactly is Jinn gonna get this wizard of hers to eat a Truth Apple?"

"However she manages it, it will have to be soon." Aidan yawned, throwing an arm around Sláine. "And once she's done it, we'll need to be ready to go at a moment's notice."

★   ★   ★

It took a few days for Aidan to feel himself again, but at least he didn't sleep more than he ought. Sláine left him to train every day at the same time. She wouldn't be able to make excuses for Aidan much longer, she claimed, and that the wizard was becoming more and more suspicious of his absence.

"I told him your fever broke," she said one afternoon, bringing Aidan a meal as she had been since he'd woken up.

Aidan tore into the bread she had just handed him. Recovering from the house's attack had left him ravenously hungry. "Any news from Jinn?"

Sláine shook her head. "Haven't seen her." She, too, began stuffing her face with food. They were quiet for a moment, chewing their meal and draining a jug of small beer. "You gonna give her the apple?"

"I will when I know she'll go through with our plan."

"And if she don't?"

Aidan drew in a deep breath. "Then I'll have to find a way to trick him. He's an ancient being, though, and has seen much in his life. If I were to attempt any trickery, he probably would know something was afoot." No longer hungry, he put the remainder of his meal aside.

"Then there's the matter of gettin' out."

He looked at her, confused. "What do you mean?"

Sláine finished swallowing the remainder of the beer and wiped her mouth with the back of her hand as she set the empty jug aside. "We'll need him to be distracted when we escape."

"But the doorknob—"

"I know. It opens a portal. But what's ter stop Hex from making it impossible to use in the house when he's got it under his control?" She stared morosely at the remainder of their lunch, and then Dismissed it. "An' that's another thing. What makes ya think there's only one of these portal-makers? Maybe we have to get the right one."

There were many factors to take into consideration. Unfortunately, it all hinged on Jinn. "We'll have to make a list of things Jinn needs to ask Hex when she gives him the apple."

"If she can get him to eat it. I really have a bad feeling about this all."

Aidan nodded. "Yes, but let's not give in to despair too soon. We could always have Jinn distract him and destroy this place before he has a chance to know what's happening." *And probably kill ourselves in the*

There was no arguing with that. They would need every advantage they could get.

CHAPTER SIXTEEN

Jinn

For the last day, Jinn had avoided leaving the room she shared with Quick. She did not want to see that insufferable Summoner – what a suggestion he had made! – nor did she particularly care to deal with the she-wizard. Slaíne was beyond frightening. Well, as was Aidan. There was power there in both of them, and Jinn didn't think either of them truly realized what they might be capable of. More than anything, Jinn admitted only to herself, she was thankful that Hex had not sought her out since their last encounter. The mere thought of having to hold a conversation with him again after the Summoner's suggestive remarks was unbearable.

Unfortunately, Quick was also perceptive. "Sister not well," he said often. "Wizard do something bad?"

"No," Jinn said again, a day and a half after Aidan had woken up.

Usually, at this point, her brother would give her a concerned look and then let the matter go. This time, however, Quick surprised Jinn by saying, "Was Summoner right?"

"Right about what?" she asked, nearly dropping the goblet she had been pouring water into.

Quick muttered something unintelligible and took the pitcher from her. "Wizard is…dangerous. I don't want Jinn to get hurt…." There was an implied 'but' in the statement, but he didn't finish the thought.

Ignoring what hadn't been said, Jinn was already shaking her head. This was not the conversation she wanted to be having, least of all with Quick. "There is no chance of that, Quick. Everything is going to stay as it always has."

He quirked an eyebrow and gestured around the room.

"Yes, we'll have to escape first, but then it'll be just you and me again. You'll see." She downed the water with a shaking hand, which she hoped Quick didn't notice. When she'd drained the goblet, she glanced at him again and was disconcerted to find him looking thoughtful. "What is the matter now?"

Quick downed his water in one large gulp and then set the glass down with force. "Jinn knows where the Goblets are?"

"Not exactly," she said, relieved that the subject had changed. "I just had a vision of myself showing you where they are."

"By a tapestry with the three golden stags?"

"Well, yes. In all I've seen of the house, though, there hasn't been one like that."

He nodded, a thoughtful look on his face. "The background was a green-blue." Something had changed in his voice.

She looked at him sharply. "You've seen it, haven't you?"

"Yes. And no."

It took all Jinn's self-restraint not to leap upon Quick and start throwing questions at him. Why hadn't he told her? And what did he mean by 'yes' and 'no'? "When did you see or not see the tapestry?"

Quick held up a finger. "Jinn must make promise first."

Jinn gaped at her brother. "What? Why?"

He seemed hesitant to answer. When he did, he nearly broke Jinn's heart. "Jinn never wants to hurt Quick. Always worried for him. Too worried. Quick can take care of himself."

"Quick, I never said that you couldn't. I just—"

He waylaid her words by holding up a hand for her to stop. "Please. Needs to be said. Jinn is always taking care, but maybe not treating Quick like equal."

With difficulty she swallowed. "I'm sorry, Quick. I didn't know you felt that way."

In response he grunted softly. "'S all right. Everyone thinks little of Quick." He smiled sadly for a moment, and then his expression changed. "Before Quick says anything about the tapestry, Jinn must promise to trick wizard."

That didn't seem like too much to ask, especially if it would mend any hurt feelings between the two of them. "I will."

But Quick was shaking his head. "No matter cost."

"Cost?" she repeated. "What possible cost could there be?" Her stomach churned uncomfortably. She recalled that night the other week, the vision she had had of her holding Hex's hand. He had seemed happy. *She* had seemed happy. What could this mean? The water in her stomach threatened to make a return, and she swallowed, hard.

Quick smiled. "Still promise?"

For the life of her, all Jinn could do was nod.

"Quick did not see tapestry…not himself."

"You had a vision," she guessed, to which her brother nodded. "Quick, how could—" She stopped herself mid-sentence. How could she scold him just after apologizing for treating him like a child? Jinn shook her head and willed herself to be quiet so he could continue.

He grinned. "Because Quick is innocent, Quick can see wizard's future." Quick paused, letting the fact sink in. "House told Quick that's how Quick can break wizard's hex. That magic does not work on Quick."

"Wait a moment. If you can break a wizard's hex because of your… innocence, why can't you break the magic surrounding the house? We could have left here long ago." It was hard to keep the exasperation out of her voice.

Quick sighed. "Only good on simple magic. Curse on house? Powerful. Hex on Hex? Simple." He laughed at the play on words.

"All right, so you were able to see into Hex's future. I presume he was accessing one or more of the Goblets?"

"Yes," he said. "Tapestry is next to Hex's rooms. Hex reaches through wall, wall disappears, and Hex says strange words. Big flash of light, and Hex pulls hand out. The wall is there again."

Her stomach having settled, Jinn took to pacing the length of the room. "But where are Hex's quarters? They could be anywhere in the house. We might not be able to get near them."

"Jinn can find out," he said simply.

That made Jinn groan. "Do you think the Summoner really has one of those apples?" Part of her hoped he did, another part hoped that he did not. How would she trick Hex into eating one, anyway?

"Summoner has the apple," he said decidedly. "Jinn gives Hex apple, and Hex tells Jinn where rooms are, where he keeps doorknob, and how to get Goblets out of hiding place." Quick took a seat on his bed, looking rather pleased with himself.

Jinn stopped pacing and approached her brother. "Do you have any ideas of how I'll get the wizard to eat this magical apple?"

"With feminine wiles," said Quick sagely.

Jinn looked at him in disbelief and horror. "I hope you don't expect me to throw myself at him."

Quick laughed, a loud, booming sound that bounced off the walls and made Jinn's ears ring. "Jinn is amusing. No, no throwing. We talk to the wizards. They will know."

"The wizards?"

"Used to be Summoner and mate. Now wizards."

That gave Jinn pause. She knew they were both powerful and that Slaíne was a she-wizard, but that they were *both* wizards? "I suppose that explains why they're so intimidating."

Quick gave her a dark look. "Indeed."

★   ★   ★

For the last few nights, Jinn's midnight wanderings had been unhindered. She, and sometimes Quick with her, would visit the couple's room, helping Slaíne try to rouse Aidan before strolling the halls for a little while and then returning to their own quarters. Now, like those nights, she did not worry too much about making noise and did not hurry. Perhaps Hex was ashamed of his near declaration and was leaving her alone. That suited Jinn just fine. Well, if not for her plans. Whatever the case, Jinn had not been worried about meeting Hex around some corner in the dark, so that made nearly running into him now with her note in hand all the more startling. Clutching her heart, Jinn choked down a scream.

"I'm sorry," the wizard said, stepping back. "I didn't mean to startle you."

Jinn swore and tried to slow her breathing. "I didn't— I didn't expect to run into you." *Quite literally.* She swallowed and self-consciously pulled her cloak more tightly about her.

"You still aren't taking my warnings to heart," he surprised her by saying. He sounded troubled, and his face bore a frown that Jinn could just make out in the light of the torch in the wall bracket.

"I'm all right."

"I'm not talking about the house this time, Jinn. I know you've been seeing the wizards. They aren't safe. Why would you put yourself in danger like that?" He sounded angry.

"He was sick, I have some healing knowledge, so I was helping," she said, her own temper rising.

"Wizards don't get truly sick. He didn't need your help." The wizard closed his eyes and pinched the bridge of his nose with his left hand. "But you couldn't have known that. It was admirable that you wanted to help, but foolish."

Jinn was ready to shoot back a retort, but remembered she needed the wizard lulled into a false sense of security if she was going to get him to eat that apple. So instead she let out a frustrated growl and stalked away.

"Wait, Jinn. Please, I'm sorry."

Shoulders heaving with the effort to calm herself, Jinn waited a moment and then turned. "All right."

"But I do have to ask, if Ingledark is well now, why were you going to his and Sláine's room?"

"Who said I was going there?" she blurted, her anger still simmering.

Hex raised his eyebrows at that. "Oh. I thought…where were you going then?"

He can smell emotions, she reminded herself, knowing he would be able to tell if she lied. *But maybe I can fool his senses by masking one emotion with another.* Jinn was quiet for a moment, allowing herself to think of all the different things that had enraged or even merely annoyed her since arriving. When she spoke again, she practically spat, "I don't know where your quarters are, if you must know."

The torch's light stuttered momentarily as the wizard stood there, the expression on his face blank. "Why would you need to know that?"

The rest wouldn't be lying...not per se. Perhaps she could tone down the annoyance and rage. "Our paths haven't crossed for a few nights now, and I thought— maybe I thought...."

He did nothing to help or encourage her to continue, but stood there, his face giving away nothing of his thoughts, though his eyes did twinkle slightly.

"So," she said at last. "Would you like to go on a picnic?"

"A picnic," he parroted.

"Yes, that. You know, where people sit out of doors and eat?" She waited, and first it seemed like he wasn't going to say anything. Then, after what felt like ages, he nodded.

"Why?"

She threw up her hands, nearly dropping the note, which she quickly tucked into her cloak's sleeve. "If you don't want to, just say so."

Of all things, he laughed. "All right. What exactly did you have in mind?"

Now she needed to think fast and act as though she had actually taken time to plan this. "Let's go outside, near the cliff where we were that one day." Was it her imagination, or did he seem suddenly uncomfortable? "Or we could stay indoors...."

His face smoothed over. "No, outdoors is fine. When did you have planned?"

I have nothing planned. "Three days hence – in the late afternoon? If the weather is nice."

"I'll decide what the weather does," he said simply. "Three days, outside, sunny skies. Anything else I need to know?"

Nothing I can tell you. Aloud she said, "Um, well...where is the kitchen?"

★   ★   ★

Three days later found Jinn in the kitchen, trying desperately to figure out how to cook and bake. She had never had a chance to use a woodstove, having cooked all meat and veg over open flames the years she had spent in the cave. "You're not helping," Jinn snapped as her brother popped an egg she had just boiled into his mouth.

Quick shrugged and took a seat on one of the stools. "Where Summoner?"

"I don't know. He should be here by now. Why don't you go and fetch him?"

Just then, there was a knock on the kitchen door, which opened. "Need some help?" asked the she-wizard, stepping into the room.

The countertops were covered in ingredients, most of which Jinn had never seen the likes of in her life. She had gone digging through cupboards and bins, dumping whatever looked good onto the work surfaces, along with pots and pans. Now, standing there in a state of disarray, Jinn could only nod as she fought back frustrated tears.

"What're ya fixin' to make?" Slaíne asked. She approached Jinn, a shiny yellow apple in hand.

"I don't rightly know."

The she-wizard tossed the apple once into the air and caught it, her eyes never leaving the vast array of food. "Why don't ya start with the most important part?"

Jinn took in a calming, deep breath. "Right. The apple." She eyed it dubiously. It looked like an ordinary piece of fruit. Could it really force whoever ate of it to tell the truth?

As if reading Jinn's thoughts, Slaíne extended the apple to her. "If'n ya doubt, you can always try a bite."

"No, thank you." Jinn ran her hands down the length of her trousers. There was no need for a cloak in here, what with the woodstove burning away, along with two different fireplaces. Plus, she had been running around madly for the past hour, so that had warmed her up considerably. "What should I do with it?"

Slaíne polished the apple on her sleeve then cleared a space on the worktable with her arm. "I nay think cookin' it'll affect the magic. Maybe you could make tartlets."

"Right." Jinn looked around her.

"What is tartlet?" asked Quick.

The she-wizard looked from one sibling to the other. "It's a small sweet pastry with a filling. Are ya sure you can manage this by yourself?"

"No," Jinn admitted after a moment. "I have no idea what I'm doing."

Smiling reassuringly, Slaíne rolled up her sleeves. "You'll need to find flour and lard, though butter'd be better." She tossed the apple to Quick, who caught it and stared at it with wide eyes. "Don't ya eat that. We've only got one other, and I reckon Aidan's misplaced it in Nothingness."

Quick held the fruit away from himself.

"I haven't seen any flour," said Jinn, going back to the pantry. Perhaps it was there but she had missed it.

"Why don't ya let me? Though, you'll want to stand very still, as I'm nay quite good at this yet."

"Good at what?"

Slaíne flashed her an annoyed look, closed her eyes, and reached out her hands. "Where are ya, you pest?" Her fingers furled and unfurled, and she swiped her right hand from side to side, as though she were sorting through a pantry shelf and one by one discarding ingredients. "Ah, you feel like you might be flour. Are ya?" She flicked her wrist, opened her eyes, and only just caught a sack of flour that had materialized in front of her. "Right. Now for the butter...." The she-wizard went on like this for a few minutes, reaching out and feeling for objects she needed and then bringing them into Existence before her. Most of the time it worked. But some of the times she would wind up with the wrong ingredient. Slaíne seemed particularly upset when she brought forth a radish when she had meant to get a potato. And Jinn learned some new and colorful words when the she-wizard dropped a large kettle that clanged noisily on the ground. "Blimey, that was loud," Slaíne said with a scowl.

"What should I do?" Jinn asked as she watched Slaíne throw flour into a bowl by the handful.

The she-wizard nodded to Quick, who remained standing stock-still, watching the Truth Apple as though it might grow teeth and bite him. "Slice that up nice and even. I'll make the pastry shell." She cut up butter with a cruel-looking knife and began to work it into the flour with her fingertips. "So, you remember all you're gonna ask?"

"What? Oh, you mean…." Jinn stopped herself from saying anything about the Truth Apple or what they were up to, just in case there were unwanted listening ears near at hand. "Yes, I have the list in my head. Do I need to peel this?"

Slaíne shook her head. "Nah. The color'll give it a nice look, don't ya think?"

"Where did you learn to bake and cook? Did your mother teach—"

"Mother died afore I was old enough to learn to cook," she said shortly, attacking the dough with sudden vigor. "Your mother not teach you?"

Why did I have to bring up the subject of mothers? "No. My mother was not exactly the maternal type."

The she-wizard grunted. "Pump some water for me, would ya?"

Jinn had finished coring the apple and was trying to cut it into nice even pieces, hoping it would look pleasing enough to eat. She stopped what she was doing and picked up a pitcher sitting precariously on a side table.

"My former mistresses taught me to cook and bake," Slaíne surprised her by saying.

Not knowing how to respond, Jinn remained silent and pumped water from the pump in the corner of the room.

Slaíne sniffed and paused her work. "Nasty creatures, them elves. But they did train me well. Only thing I can really thank 'em for."

Jinn weighed her words carefully as she handed the water to Slaíne, who poured a bit into the bowl with the butter and flour. "How did you come to, er, be in their service?" She peered into the bowl and nearly caught an elbow in the throat as the she-wizard started working the crumbs into a dough.

"Oh, your wizard cursed me, so I had to have a master and was able to be only so far from 'em." She said it so casually, but Jinn could tell from the tightening of the woman's jaw that she did not take the matter lightly. "Take this over. You just add enough water 'til you can roll it into a ball without lots o' pieces crumbling off."

"Right." Jinn took over, trying not to show how much she was reeling from what she had heard. "And he's not *my* wizard."

Slaíne cleared her throat. "Sorry."

"He isn't. That's horrible that he cursed you." *What am I getting myself into?*

The dough was formed and Slaíne instructed her to let it rest, and then covered it with an oiled cloth. "Yes, he is terrible. But you can't always choose who you'll wind up lovin'."

That was annoying. If Jinn had hackles, she knew they would be raised. "Now see here! I don't love him. I *won't* love him. You don't know anything."

For a moment, the she-wizard's eyes lit up a strange blue color. "Careful," she said, though it seemed she was speaking to herself. Slaíne shook her head, and the light faded. "Any idea what else you're gonna make?"

Jinn took a deep breath and tried to regain her own composure. Desperately she looked about her, hoping the ingredients would somehow inspire her. There was too much, and she was beginning to feel even more overwhelmed.

Slaíne seemed to notice this and began sorting the food into piles. "You'll want light food, somethin' ya can eat with your fingers. We ain't got time for bread, but I see you've got some here already." She picked up a loaf of brown bread, tossed it back and forth between her hands, and dropped it onto the counter. "Oh." A hand flew up to her mouth.

"What? What's wrong?"

The she-wizard shook her head and held up a finger. She groaned and ran for the basin near the pump in the corner of the room, where she retched once, and then twice. Shoulders heaving, she stood there, shaking slightly.

"Are you all right?" Jinn asked, leaving the counter and approaching her nervously.

She turned and looked at Jinn. Her face was a sickly green and she continued to tremble. "Must've et somethin' bad."

"Would you like me to pour you a glass of water?"

At first Slaíne shook her head, but then nodded. "Yes. Thank ya."

Jinn hurriedly searched for a cup and filled it with the remaining water from the pitcher. After handing it to Slaíne, she pulled up a stool for her to sit on. "Are you sure—"

"Yes, thanks," she snapped. She sipped the water in silence for a moment and closed her eyes. The color had all but drained from her face. "Don't tell Aidan. He'll worry." There was a stretch of awkward silence as the she-wizard continued to sit there, taking a small gulp of water every now and again. When the glass was empty, her cheeks grew somewhat pink. "Why don't ya chop some vegetables? An' there's got to be smoked meat around here somewhere." She did not move from her spot on the stool, and continued to instruct Jinn as to what she should do and how she should do it for the next two hours.

By the time they had finished, there was a basket full of fresh fruit, chopped vegetables, smoked ham, an assortment of cheeses, fresh bread from the pantry, and the apple tartlets, which had taken seemingly forever to cool. Jinn stared at all she had put together. It looked tempting enough to her, though there was no saying if it would be so for the wizard.

"It looks great," Slaíne said, climbing from the stool. "Ya just need some wine and you'll be set."

Jinn smoothed her hands down the length of her tunic. "Do you think he'll eat it?" The pastries had turned out a little darker than Slaíne said they should be, and that had Jinn worried. Everything rested on this plan.

Slaíne stretched her arms over her head and yawned. "Well, if he don't, there's still more where that came from." She was referring to, of course, the Truth Apple, which both of them had been careful not to mention too much in case Hex had means of listening in on them. With everything prepared, the she-wizard grabbed a purple stoppered bottle off the far workspace and handed it to Jinn. "Don't pressure him to eat it. Just let things unfold natural-like."

"Right." *Easier said than done.* She hefted the overflowing basket into her other hand and they walked to the door.

"An' for goodness' sakes, watch yer feelings."

Jinn looked at her, surprised. She hadn't told Slaíne about the wizard's ability to sense her emotions. Perhaps the she-wizard possessed the same gift.

Quick, who had been sitting quietly in the corner, got to his feet. "Carry that for you?" He nodded at Jinn's full arms.

"No, I have it, thanks." *I hope.*

*   *   *

When Jinn returned to her room, Hex was waiting for her outside the door, leaning casually against the frame. "Do you need help?" he asked, straightening up.

She didn't, but it occurred to Jinn that men liked to be of use, so she nodded and handed him the basket. Quick had remained in the kitchen, so he was not there to witness her awkwardness. That was something, at least.

"Shall we?" Hex led the way into the room, and Jinn followed at a distance. When he got to the far wall of the room, he waited until Jinn had taken his arm, and they passed through the stone and glass, emerging outside. As promised, the weather was sunny but slightly overcast, so it was not unpleasant.

Jinn's stomach did a nauseating flip as he waited for her to walk at his side instead of trailing behind. *Watch your feelings. He knows them.*

A look of concern passed over the wizard's face, but he said nothing about whatever emotions he was sensing from her. "The weather is fair, is it not?" He actually winked at her, and Jinn felt her face flush.

"I heard it was going to be a fine day," she surprised herself by rejoining. "Though, in some parts of this land, forecasting the weather can see you hanged."

"Mm."

"Or stoned."

Hex laughed. "Imagine *making* the weather. What would happen to such an unfortunate fellow?" He motioned for her to go ahead of him on the narrow path leading to the other side of the house.

"Oh, I doubt much harm would befall any such person." She walked a few paces ahead and was amused to see he had already set out a cloth on which to picnic.

"And why is that?"

Jinn had to remind herself that they were talking about weather and wizard-craft. "They would be too scared out of their senses to go near enough to this 'weather-maker' in order to do him any harm."

"Well said."

Jinn bowed her head in recognition of the compliment and set the bottle of wine on the blanket. Her hands were so slippery with sweat that she had almost dropped it several times in the span of the last two minutes alone.

"And what of the house?" he asked as he set the basket in the shaded half of the blanket. "Has it been behaving itself?" The words were said lightly, though Jinn knew he was still concerned. He didn't need to know that his own cursed abode had found a way to work against him.

"Vät Vanlud has failed to live up to its meaning, if that is why you ask."

"You remembered its proper name." Hex seemed pleased at that, and Jinn couldn't help but roll her eyes.

"Don't be too happy. I've always had an impeccable memory."

Hex merely smirked at that statement. "Don't let the house hear that you remembered. It would become impossible to live with, so puffed up with pride." He waved his hand and two cushions materialized on the blanket, across from each other.

"I suppose it would," Jinn said, trying to keep her voice and emotions even. *Do your job, Jinn.* "It's amazing, the things I found in your larder." She took the blue cushion, the one nearest her, and reached back for the basket.

"Here. Allow me." Hex waved his hands and the different food items floated out before them, hovered, and then arranged themselves on their plates atop the blanket. With that done, he took the red cushion and lifted the wine bottle.

Jinn forgot herself and swore, causing Hex's eyebrows to shoot up. "I forgot the glasses."

"No problem." With a snap, two wineglasses materialized in front of them. Hex cut the wax seal from the wine bottle and set it aside. "We'll let it breathe first," he said, perhaps noting her confusion.

"Oh, right." She was trying very hard to look at something, *anything*, other than the two plump tartlets sitting on fine rose-colored plates. *Calm yourself, Jinn. Think of something that makes you happy.*

Hex startled her from her thoughts by asking, "Are you unwell?"

Again she felt her cheeks warm. "Oh. No. I'm honestly fine. I just—" *What should I say?* "I guess I'm just hungry." There. That wasn't a lie either. When Hex continued to look concerned, Jinn picked up the loaf of bread and tore a chunk off. While she chewed on it, the wizard ripped off a piece for himself.

"And what is your brother up to this fine, rainless day?" He bit into the bread and flicked his wrist. The wine bottle rose in midair and, tilting, poured some of its purple contents into each of the glasses, one at a time.

Jinn brushed her hands together and reached for a small cluster of red grapes. "Probably mulling around the kitchen, though I don't think he will find much food there, as I have clearly cleaned it out." She gestured around her and bit lightly into a grape, careful not to bite down on the seed she knew to be lodged in there.

"Oh, the kitchen takes care of itself. It has no doubt restocked its cupboards by now." He reached for his glass and took a small sip. Dipping his glass, he said, "You needn't worry about seeds. There are none."

She had to laugh. "Magic also?"

Hex smiled and shook his head. "Perhaps it is a secret." When she narrowed her eyes at him, he just shrugged and took another swig of wine.

The meal went on like this, both parties making light conversation, dancing around the fact that one was little more than prisoner in a grand house. Magical politics were brushed against, though the subject quickly changed once again to the weather. From there it roamed to books that had been read, poems that were favorites – the likes of most Jinn had never heard – and places that had been traveled to. They did not run out of topics to discuss until it became time for afters. Or, rather, they did not run out of topics at all. Jinn merely ran out of nerve. Though she had barely touched her wine throughout the meal, now she found herself taking a large gulp. At first she sputtered, and then she choked before spitting what she had back into the glass. "Sorry," she said. "I've never tasted wine this strong."

"But you're all right?"

Jinn could only nod. She nudged one tartlet toward him, the one she had grated less spice on to identify it. Secure in the knowledge she had given him the right pastry, she picked up the other one for herself.

"I don't remember ordering the kitchen to make these," Hex said, eyeing the tartlet with apparent confusion.

"That's because I made it."

He gave the pastry a tentative sniff. Brow furrowed, he met her gaze. "What is it?"

"A tartlet."

He looked at her meaningfully. "I know it's a tart. But why are you so nervous about it?"

"I've never baked before," she said, choosing her words with care. "It might be rubbish." *That is perhaps not the best way to sell it, Jinn.* Indeed, he was looking more and more skeptical by the second. "But the she-wizard was helping me, so maybe it's good."

At that he set the tartlet down. "She baked this?"

Oh dear. He's not going to eat it now, is he? "She looked over my shoulder and barked instructions at me, if that counts as baking." Waiting for a response was torture. Any wrong look from her or a stray feeling could put the wizard onto her plan.

Slowly, though, his expression transformed from suspicious to amused. Again he picked up the tartlet and began to bring it to his mouth, only to pause, eyes roving to Jinn, who was trying to look preoccupied with her own, normal treat, which she was suddenly too queasy to attempt to eat.

Why does this plan have to hinge on me not making a mess of everything?

Hex laughed, startling Jinn from her thoughts. "Truly, everything has been good so far. Why wouldn't this be?"

Jinn shrugged. "It's honestly the only thing here that I made. Is it bad?"

"Why don't you try a bite and answer for the both of us?"

Willing her stomach to behave, Jinn took a bite from the tartlet. The pastry itself was a bit tough. Sláine had warned her about overworking the dough to fit it in the molds. The filling was heavy on the spices, but not inedible. As she ate, she was aware that Hex was taking his first bite.

"This is good," Hex said after swallowing a small mouthful.

Silently Jinn wondered how much of the baked Truth Apple the wizard needed to eat in order for it to take effect. Would it even work on a wizard? How long would the fruit's powers last? She was working with a lot of unknowns, and it was unsettling. "Finish it or you'll hurt my feelings," Jinn found herself saying jokingly.

Hex laughed and started to put the pastry down teasingly, before picking it back up and taking another bite. "The apple is quite delicious. I do not believe I've ever tasted something so tart and yet so sweet."

Jinn shrugged and set her plate down under the guise of taking a small sip of wine. "Can I ask you something?"

"What is it?" Hex took another bite, a larger one, and swallowed as Jinn watched. "You really are nervous. Why is that?" He lifted his glass to his lips and took a drink. "That's a bit salty." At once he looked horrified with himself. "I'm so sorry. I shouldn't have said that. I don't know what's come over me."

Well, if that's an indication that the apple is working, I'd better talk fast. "I know that you have three of the Goblets Immortal, Hex. Where are they?"

For a moment, it did not seem like he was going to answer her. Hex sat there, frowning for the longest time, until, finally, his dark eyes glazed over. "They're by my room – the far east side of the house – in a magical vault. It's behind a tapestry with—"

"Yes, I know that. Tell me how to get the Goblets out."

"That's no simple task. My magic runs the house, and there's a strong charm attached to that magic protecting the vault. I would need to be very much distracted in order for it to drop."

That was what I was afraid of. "How might someone distract you?"

"You did the other week. I think you would probably manage to do it again." The way he talked was all wrong. It was toneless, without feeling.

Jinn couldn't wait to get this interview over with. "And what would be an effective way to distract you, so as to stop your magic from running the house?"

"Please don't ask me that."

Sensing she had little time left and a good idea as to how to distract him, Jinn asked, "Tell me what you know of the Goblets Immortal and how they might be destroyed."

Hex drew in a deep breath and began. "There are six— well, now we know there are five Goblets. Each has its mate and its opposite. The Drifting Goblet and the Summoning Goblet are mates, for example, which would make their so-called offspring very dangerous."

"You mean Aidan and Slaíne?"

He nodded. "If Slaíne had been the daughter of say, the originator of the Seeing Goblet – the original Summoner's rival – she and Aidan would be repulsed by one another. Completely incompatible."

"And how can we destroy the Goblets?"

A look of pain washed over the wizard's features, and it seemed he was trying very hard to overcome the effects of the Truth Apple. "Any good blade will do. But not here. Not in the realm of the living. No mortal or immortal walking the earth shall be able to destroy something so powerful."

"Aidan mentioned a doorknob opened a portal that brought him here. Where is it and how do we use it to escape?"

Again he tried fighting the Truth Apple, but there must have been enough in his system to overpower his will. After a short struggle, he spoke. "The portal-makers are in the vault. Any of them will take you— take you away from here, if a wizard uses it. They will know how." He was growing agitated, blinking fiercely and shaking himself.

Jinn knew she didn't have much time left with a completely open and unwittingly honest Hex, so she spoke quickly. "Tell me about Aidan and Sláine. You've said they're dangerous."

There was silence as he attempted to resist answering. "Yes."

"Why are they dangerous?"

Hex shook his head and shut his eyes in a grimace. "Their powers, if fully joined, could mean chaos for us all."

Jinn's heart beat faster. She had not been expecting this. "How so?"

"Changes in weather patterns, floods, famines, earthquakes to begin with. Untrained, their joined and untamed power is…well, it's not something I want to see." Blinking, he seemed to return to his senses, before taking another bite of the tart. "I've had to put up several powerful wards to prevent them from realizing their full potential in my home, training them just enough so they can control themselves without doing too much damage."

Cold dread came over her as she whispered, "They're that powerful?"

Hex nodded. "Oh, yes. Sláine's powers are beyond deadly. And Aidan must have been born with a magical inclination beyond being Blest, judging by how well he's taken to his abilities. They'll feed off each other." He finished the tartlet in another bite. "You really didn't need to worry about the pastry. It's a bit dry, but it tastes good enough."

"Will you remember telling me all you have?"

He looked at her, apparently confused. "If you gave me a Truth Apple? No, probably not. I should probably be furious for your trickery, but am rather too drugged to enjoy such an emotion to its fullest, so what is the purpose? I'd probably forgive you the next day, anyway."

Dare she ask more? *No. Let him keep some of his dignity...even if he did insult my pastry.*

CHAPTER SEVENTEEN

Aidan

"How do you think the interview is going?" Aidan asked Slaíne, who had just returned to their room. She had told him to stay away from Jinn, as he was likely to say something wrong and make her even more nervous.

Apparently weary, Slaíne clutched her back and used magic to help herself out of her boots. "Dunno. Strange word for it, Aidan. '*Interview.*'" She dragged herself over to where he was reclined, and sat on the edge of the bed. "Unlace me, would ya?"

Aidan sat up and slid his fingers through the ties binding her dress together. Then, slowly, he reached inside the fabric and ran his fingers over her shift, smiling when he drew a small gasp from his mate. He kissed where neck met shoulder, and trailed his lips down to her arm. Inside his chest, both her soul-half and his own began to hum to life, and he was delightfully aware of everywhere his skin touched hers.

"It's the middle of the day," she said breathlessly as he pulled her toward himself and out of her dress.

He lay back with her and kissed her throat. "If that is your only objection…." With a sigh, Aidan sat up and yet continued to hold her close to his breast. "Your half is loud today."

"My half?" She sounded amused as he kissed her jawline.

"Your soul. And— My, you are pale. Are you unwell?" Pulling back to look at her better, Aidan noted the dark circles under her eyes, which greatly contrasted with the pallor of her skin. Panic gripped him, and he held her a little more tightly. "What is wrong, my love?"

Slaíne leaned her head against his chest and made a contented noise.

"Nothin'. I think I et an egg that had gone bad. Tasted odd, and then I was a bit sick earlier."

Aidan stilled and sniffed her hair. *She has secrets*, her scent seemed to say. Again he inhaled, and the same impression was made on his mind. Hadn't Jinn warned them that Hex could smell emotions? Why, then, could not any wizard?

"Aidan Ingledark, are you smelling me?" She sounded so indignantly mortified, that Aidan had to chuckle.

"Promise me that you're well."

Slaíne looked up at him, her eyes narrowed. "All right. I swear that I'm well. Why?"

Nothing about her scent seemed to say she was lying, so Aidan shrugged. "I don't know. But you would tell me, wouldn't you?"

"'Course I would," she said briskly. There was a charged pause before she spoke again. "An' *you* would tell *me*?"

He started to answer, but she interrupted him.

"You'd tell me if you was afraid?"

That brought Aidan up short. He mused over her question in his mind, trying to discern what she could possibly mean by it. "Afraid? What would I be afraid of? Meraude?"

She sighed. "Forget it."

"No, tell me. What do you think I would be afraid of?" He waited for her to answer, but when it became clear that she wasn't going to, Aidan tilted her head back to look at him again. "Slaíne?"

"Dunno. Just bein' silly, I s'pose." Slaíne began picking at her shift with her fingernails. "What if'n I was dangerous?" She lowered her head and leaned back against him. "Would you love me just as well then?"

Aidan was quiet as he let the question sink in. Questions from Slaíne seemed often to hold deeper meaning. He knew he must answer with care. "I would still love you." A kiss on top of her head might have solved other matters, but it did not this time.

She squirmed. "But can you truly love that which you fear?"

Perhaps she was thinking of their quarrels over the past few weeks, of him feeling controlled by her. But that had had nothing to do with fear.

Then he recalled that moment in Nothingness, after the fire had filled Cedric's so-called tomb. He had feared Slaíne. She had been terrifying in all her power and splendor. "Slaíne," he said carefully, "I have been scared witless by you."

For a moment she struggled against him, but he would not let go.

"Allow me to finish. Despite being absolutely terrified, it does not follow that I loved you any less. It was perhaps the opposite."

With a sigh, she ceased thrashing. "You nay saw what I saw."

"What did you see?" He kissed her cheek.

Her voice was very small when she spoke again, and she nearly sank out of his grip. "The house, it— Well, when I went to rescue you from the stairs, it showed me things about meself. Things I'd rather not've seen."

Now it was becoming clear. "Ah, it played tricks on you as well."

"But they wasn't tricks," said Slaíne. She sat up now, and her hair came free of its loose knot, spilling down her nearly bare back in ringlets. "I did horrible things with my magic, Aidan. Things I'd rather not say. And I enjoyed e'ery moment of it." Her tone was so sad and defeated, it made Aidan's heart ache. "I'm afeared that it'll come true. That I'll lose myself in this new power and destroy everything an' everyone around me." Her shoulders slumped.

Silence reigned for a moment as Aidan tried to sort through everything she had said and what he might himself need or desire to say. There were many possibilities, ways their world could turn. But that was not what she needed to hear in the moment. It was not what he wanted to *say* in the moment. At length he murmured, "Whatever happens, I'll love you through it."

Slaíne shook her head. "What good is love gonna do when I wreak havoc on the natural world?"

"Not '*when*', Slaíne. Our destinies aren't carved in stone." He leaned forward and kissed her shoulder. "And you've been learning to control yourself."

"Have I?"

"In your lessons with Hex."

She laughed without humor. "I've been *taught*, yes, but have I *learned*?" Before Aidan could think of a response, she said, "And *you*? Are you worried you'll lose control of your magic and do somethin' horrible?"

He tightened his hold on her. "Honestly? I haven't given it much thought...not as much as I perhaps ought to have. But I can't control tomorrow. I can only dwell in this moment and strive to be the person I should be today."

"When did you become so wise?"

Aidan changed the subject back. "When first I met Hex, he said time would mellow my rage."

"Then let's make sure we have that time," said Slaíne. "If we—" She got no further before there was a frantic knocking at their door. "I think it's Jinn. Hope nothin' went wrong." The knocking turned into banging, and Slaíne wriggled out of Aidan's arms.

"I'll get it," he said, reluctant to leave the bed and the conversation. He had felt the Pull and knew it belonged to Quick, not Jinn. When he threw open the bolt and opened the door, he was met with a strange sight.

The large man was standing there, crying.

"What's wrong?" Aidan demanded, thinking perhaps Jinn was in peril. "Is your sister all right?" Behind him, Aidan was aware that Slaíne was slipping back into her dress. He stepped outside, pushing the giant aside and then leading him to a room across the hall. "Did something go wrong?"

Quick shook his head. "Sister...Jinn is going to leave Quick. It is Quick's fault. Stupid, stupid fault."

Aidan tried to get the man to lower his voice and stop his crying. When that did not work, he motioned for Quick to sit on a bench in the nearly empty room. Moments later, the door creaked open and Slaíne joined them.

"What's happened?" she asked. "Did somethin' go wrong at the picnic?"

"I don't think so," said Aidan slowly as Quick produced a

handkerchief and blew his nose in it. "I'm trying to get to the bottom of things, but as you can see, our friend here is too distraught."

As if to punctuate the point, Quick sniffled loudly and moaned. "All Quick's fault. Told her to help, no matter what. Now Quick has seen…." He broke down again, nearly wailing.

"You've had a vision?" Slaíne said, taking one of the man's hands in both of her tiny ones. "What did you see, Quick?"

For a moment Quick quieted, his eyes growing large as they stared at his one hand in Slaíne's. "S-sorry. Quick is sorry."

"I nay think there's anythin' here to be sorry for. Why don't ya take a moment ter collect yourself." She patted his hand. "I find if I think of somethin' I like, that calms me right down."

Quick nodded and sniffled again. After a moment, he seemed to calm some more, drew a deep breath, and said, "Jinn is going to stay."

Aidan and Slaíne exchanged a confused glance. "Stay?" Aidan asked. "You mean, as in, she's not going to be able to escape with us?"

Slaíne leveled a stern look at Aidan. "Say it in yer own time, an' in your own way."

"Jinn chooses to stay. Makes Quick leave her. Says it's only way."

Aidan looked at the man thoughtfully and then chanced a glance at Slaíne. "If Hex is in love with her, she would make a good— Well, she might be the only distraction we have at our disposal."

Slaíne hissed. "I do nay like it, but Aidan may be right, Quick. If yer sister is willin' to give us a chance to defeat Meraude, oughtn't we honor that?" She squeezed Quick's hand and tilted her head back and looked him in the eye. "Wouldn't ya do anythin' for yer sister? An' wouldn't she do anythin' for you?"

Quick sobbed.

"You don't have to decide right now," Aidan said. "Take some time to think about it."

"An' it's not like you would nay e'er see Jinn again."

That only made Quick sob harder. "Quick should stay with Jinn. Summoner and she-wizard should kill Mother. Not Quick."

Slaíne frowned. "Mother? We're going to kill whose mother?"

She looked over at Aidan and swore. "They're Meraude's children, aren't they?" As one burned, she dropped Quick's hand. "And you knew?"

"Yes," Aidan said, realizing she would look through his thoughts to ferret out any lies. "I should have told you. I'm sorry."

She swore some more. "Yes, you ought to have. Aidan, how can we trust these two? We've told 'em far too much already. What if they're her spies?" Slaíne took to pacing the room.

"Mother is bad," said Quick. "You stop her."

Ignoring the giant's words, Slaíne stopped her pacing and leveled another glare at Aidan and then at the door. "She ought ter 'ave told me. The nerve of her."

"Maybe she knew you'd react this way."

Slaíne growled. "I'm surprised *you* did not." She threw her hands up in the air. "When I get my hands on her...."

"No hands," Quick said, causing the room to shake as he leapt to his feet. "No hurt sister. Jinn is—"

Whatever Jinn was, they didn't get to find out. A voice called out across the hall, outside the bedroom where Aidan and Slaíne were staying.

"No," said Quick.

But Slaíne had already thrown the door to the side room open and was taking determined steps toward Jinn, who turned around just in time to be lunged at. "Meraude's child, are ya?"

Aidan groaned. "Slaíne, get off her." He went to his mate and, throwing his arms around her waist, wrestled her off Jinn's prone form. "Calm yourself. They're the both of them harmless, I'm sure." To his dismay, she continued to writhe and lash out, though thankfully did not resort to using any of her magic.

Quick helped Jinn to her feet and tucked her behind his body. "No hurt sister."

"Quick, it's all right," said Jinn, pushing around her brother. "Slaíne, I truly am sorry. But I didn't think you'd trust me if you knew about my heritage."

"An' ya think I wouldn't ruddy find out?" She stopped struggling in

Aidan's arms but spat at the other woman. "Meraude killed my family. She ruined the beginnings of my life."

Jinn sighed. "Yes, Mother had a way of doing that to people. But it was my *mother* who did that, not *I*." The woman's shoulders heaved and she swiped at her brow with the back of her hand. "I daresay I hate her more than you do...sorry, Quick."

Quick shrugged and backed away, perhaps noting the look Slaíne was giving them both. Aidan didn't have to see his mate's face in order to know she was giving rather dirty looks to the twins.

"She killed his parents as well," Slaíne continued, her voice rising. "We found the bodies in Breckstone not three months ago, right in her ally's stables. Tell me that be coincidence."

A confused frown stole over Jinn's features. "That's— that's not possible. Mother was nowhere near you at the time."

"An' why should I trust you when ya say that?" Again Slaíne spat. "You've told naught but lies. You's no better than yer wretched mother."

"Slaíne," Aidan warned, tightening his grip on her.

But Jinn seemed to be taking no notice. "My mother might have killed your parents, Aidan, but she did not leave the bodies in Breckstone. Someone else did." Her expression grew thoughtful. "I don't know who did it, but believe me, you've got another enemy to worry about."

Aidan thought back to what good shape his parents' bodies were in when he found them. They'd been missing for twenty years, and yet they hadn't seemed to be older or to have been decomposing for more than a week. "There's another Summoner," Aidan said, the wheels in his head turning. "When a body is Dismissed into Nothingness, it doesn't decompose. Someone's been holding on to the bodies in their own cache for two decades. But why?" Certain at last that Slaíne was no longer going to attack Jinn, Aidan released her and stepped away, his thoughts churning.

"Is yer mother a Summoner?" Slaíne asked, her tone sharp but no longer at such a high volume.

"Yes," Jinn answered. "But she was at the caves up north when I last saw her in the flesh. And in all of my visions, she's been in Inohaim

– near Egethberem. She stays north. My mother's never traveled south that I've ever seen."

They all looked at each other in bewilderment. At length, Aidan broke the charged silence.

"We'll return to this subject shortly, but I think we should hear about how your interview with the wizard went."

Jinn shook her head and motioned for him to be quiet. "He's sleeping off the effects of the Truth Apple in his room, but in case he wakes let's discuss this matter in your chamber." She led the way into the room, giving Sláine a wide berth.

Once they were all inside and the door was shut and secured, Jinn told them what had come to pass during the picnic, how Hex had eaten the apple tartlet and told her everything she asked. Her voice was near monotone, and Aidan silently observed that she seemed despondent. He made no mention of it, however; her feelings were her own, and they had needed her to do what she'd done.

When Jinn got to the part about distracting Hex and did not clarify how, Sláine made an impatient noise and interrupted. "What do ya mean you nay asked him how?"

Jinn gave Sláine a fierce look. "He told me not to ask him, and I felt bad enough about deceiving him up to that point. Why not save some of his dignity?"

Sláine swore. "His dignity? Lives are on the line an' you's worried about the wizard's *dignity*?" She turned to Aidan, her look appealing. "You can nay trust her. She must be working with the wizard."

"What makes you say that?" Jinn demanded. "I've been nothing but helpful."

"You've been nothin' but deceitful, that's what."

Aidan groaned. "Sláine, please don't make this more difficult than it already is." At once he regretted saying those words.

His mate turned her wrath on him instead. "An' what makes you take her side o' the matter, Aidan? You take an eager interest in her doings."

That brought Aidan up short. What was she going on about now? He spoke with care. "I take no interest in her doings, except as far as

they concern our escape and Meraude's defeat. Please, let's calm down."
Again that had been the wrong thing to say.

Slaíne's eyes lit up blue and her hands began to glow as well, causing everyone but Aidan to back away.

"Slaíne," he warned, approaching her cautiously. "Your hands."

It took her a moment to seem to understand what he was saying, but when it apparently dawned on her, she shook her head and covered her face. She took a few loud breaths, and when she looked up at Aidan again, the light had faded. Her hands took a few moments to follow suit.

"You doubt Jinn and Quick," said the giant, his voice a thoughtful rumble. "What if wizards need not doubt?" He looked at Jinn sadly. "Truth Apple."

Jinn made a face. "I don't know, Quick."

Aidan put his arm around Slaíne's waist. "I do have another Truth Apple in Nothingness. We could have one or both of them take a bite, if that would put your mind at ease." He kissed the side of Slaíne's head.

What rage was left seemed to go out of Slaíne then, her expression sheepish. Into his mind she said, *Sorry. I don't know what came o'er me.* She looked up at Aidan and then at the twins. "Never mind that just now." She pulled away from Aidan and paced again. "The Goblets are in a safe by his room, you said?"

"And we now know where that is," Jinn added. "Quick, why don't you be on the lookout, in case Hex awakens and tries to find us?"

Her brother made a face but nodded, leaving the three of them in the room. "Don't hurt sister," were his parting words, which echoed down the hall.

Jinn went to the door and shut it again. "I didn't want my brother to have to hear this part." She looked at the door and hesitated, as if afraid he might be outside, attempting to overhear them.

"He's gone," Aidan said at length, and the woman sighed.

She thanked him and nodded. "I'm going to have to stay behind. Quick's not going to like it, but I'm the only one who can properly distract Hex enough for him to release the magic operating the house."

"He knows," said Slaíne.

Jinn's eyes widened. "Well, that saves me some trouble. But that means he looked ahead again. Quick knows that's not good for his constitution."

"And you're certain you're up for the challenge?" Aidan asked, trying to steer the conversation back on course.

Of all things, the woman turned scarlet. "Yes, I'll do my part. I must."

"Your brother couldn't stay with you?" Slaíne asked, though not unkindly. Perhaps she was trying to make amends for her earlier outburst.

For a moment, Jinn seemed to turn this over in her mind. "I don't think he should stay with me. What if he turns up during the wrong moment and ruins the distraction? I love my brother more than anything, but he does have the worst timing."

Aidan nodded. "That settles it. If you can get him to leave with us, do it. We might have need of brawn. And we'll need a guide, if he's familiar with the land."

"He is. Like myself, Quick has had access to Meraude's maps. He'll be able to get you there, once you've left this place." She began to rub her hands as though warming herself and told them the rest of what she had gotten out of the wizard. But there was something she was hiding, Aidan could tell. Whether or not Slaíne discerned this as well, he did not know.

All he could do was hope that she did not...and pray they were trusting the right people.

CHAPTER EIGHTEEN

Meraude

The bodies of the Sightfuls in training had been easy enough to find. The poor things hadn't stood a chance, having been surrounded by iron, the one metal that could block their abilities. As best as General Tindra could figure, the guilty parties had poisoned the girls inside the barracks. Their bodies had been found buried in a mass grave not far into Inohaim Wood. Unfortunately, the Sightfuls responsible had then fled into the night, leaving no trail behind them.

But Meraude still had four Sightfuls left, plus Ing and Egreet. The latter two were young and inexperienced. Meraude needed answers, and she needed to know they were reliable. Torture had proven ineffective. She had questioned them each individually with Tindra at her side, and while their answers had matched for the most part, there were subtle discrepancies that alerted Meraude to their lies.

Tindra had suggested that Meraude drink from the Seeing Goblet. But that would be risking madness. Thankfully, there was one more method available, and it was nearly safe from all chance of failure.

Five days after the party, once it had become clear the torture and questioning weren't working, Meraude gathered six Endurers, the four traitor Sightfuls, and her two top pupils, Ing and Egreet. The traitors were chained together and forced to walk behind the cart that bore Meraude, Tindra, and the pupils for several miles.

It had not rained for many weeks, so the roads were dry and passable. The horses pulling the cart walked at a steady clip, whinnying happily from time to time. When the cart passed out of town, the roads became somewhat uneven, and the passengers were jostled. Finally, when it seemed the silent journey would never end, the driver called the horses to a halt and the cart stopped.

Tindra was the first out, helping Meraude to the ground and leaving the pupils to jump down by themselves. The prisoners were still being unchained from the cart, but it was just as well; that would give Meraude and her companions time to finish their journey on foot and catch their breaths before the others arrived.

In the distance, thunder rumbled, and the smell of rain filled the air. The women looked up at the sky hopefully, but Meraude called them away.

"You know the weather has already passed north and will not reach us. Come." And with that said, she led them into the woods. The cart driver remained behind with the horses, bowing to Meraude as she passed.

The small procession picked their way through thigh-high grasses and low-hanging branches without difficulty. Meraude did not venture here often, and when she did, it had always been with a Sightful to assist her in her communications. With the use of the Seeing Pool, operated by a skilled Sightful, Meraude had been able to visit the Summoner in his dreams. That had worked well...up until a few months ago when the connection that had been forged seemed to break for some unknown reason. Larkin's information, if it was to be believed, meant that Aidan Ingledark had indeed betrayed Meraude and was even now moving against her.

"You've the Goblet?" Meraude whispered to Tindra for the third time.

Her general nodded and patted at the bag strung over her shoulder. "Yes, milady. It is safe."

"Good. Tell none of the other Endurers what we are doing. The fewer that know, the better."

"Very good, milady," said Tindra, her lips barely moving.

Meraude breathed an inward sigh of relief. She knew she could count on Tindra, at least. The woman had as much reason to hate humans as Meraude did. The general would not betray her nor let her down in any way.

Fifteen minutes later, they emerged in a clearing, where sat the tall white Tower of Inohaim.

"I saw this in the distance once," said Egreet, craning her neck back as she shielded her eyes. "I didn't think it was this big."

"Come," Meraude said as the two girls continued to gawk. "We have a ways to climb." She led the way with Tindra close by her side, approaching the tower with care. This part of the wood was not guarded as well as others, and anything or anyone might be lying in wait for them there. Muscles tensing, she reached out with her mind, feeling for any unwanted presence and then, finding nothing, relaxed a little and hastened her step.

They walked up to the base of the tower and Tindra held up her hand to stop the girls from running into them. "Only one may pass through at a time."

Meraude noted the girls exchanging a confused look and fought a smile herself. The two were in for a surprise.

"Milady?" asked Tindra.

"You shall enter first," Meraude replied.

With a nod, the general eyed the smooth white stone, stepped forward, and vanished. "The way is clear," said the general's disembodied voice as Egreet and Ing squealed in surprise.

"After you two," said Meraude, gesturing toward the wall.

The two paled. "We just walk through the wall?" asked Ing.

"How?" Egreet asked at the same moment.

Meraude now did grin. "For magic-kind, there is no wall, here or at the top. But I must warn you, your abilities will be useless beyond the invisible barrier."

That did not seem to sit too well with the two young Blest, but they nodded tightly and, to their credit, did not complain but stepped one after the other through the stone. There were more squeals of surprise as they passed through, and the sound of them running into each other.

After first bracing herself for the familiar feel of her magic being temporarily ripped from her, Meraude stepped through the wall. For her, she knew, it would be more difficult than it had been for the merely twice-Blest girls. She had four different abilities to shed. With a great tremor, she felt them ripped from her and tried to keep her nerves together. Her powers would return once she took the throne.

The climb to the top of Inohaim Tower took a perilous twenty minutes of walking in a giant, ascending circle with only the wall to their left to lean into. The right opened to the abyss below. One wrong step, and there would be no Blest gift to save them.

At last, the journey to the top ended. Panting and clutching pangs in their sides, the two young Blest collapsed in the open throne room in front of the Seeing Pool. "That was dreadful," said Ing below her breath.

"Never again do I wish to do that," panted Egreet.

Tindra, who had physical prowess beyond being a Blest, seemed to be faring better than the two young women.

Meraude was quite winded herself from the climb and the loss of her abilities, but she tried to maintain her dignity and did not collapse. Instead she approached Tindra, hands outstretched.

"It's heavy," Tindra murmured in reminder as she held the sack out to the mage queen.

Meraude did not acknowledge the statement but took the vessel in its bag from the general and limped with it toward the great glass throne on the other side of the Seeing Pool. Her body ached and she was eager to be seated, though she knew she must delay relief. In silence she waited for the guards and the prisoners to arrive.

It took the better part of an hour, but soon Meraude could hear the telltale signs of ascension, and the remaining women fell through the wall on the other side of the room with great cries. Apparently these Blest had never been to the top of the tower before and thus hadn't known what to expect.

The three prisoners who were not too badly injured huddled together there on the floor, while the fourth one lay sprawled out, her bandaged chest rising and falling rapidly. She moaned in apparent pain.

Unmoved, Meraude made certain the Seeing Goblet was out of view and said, "Since you have refused to answer my questions truthfully, my hand is forced. This is your last chance. Tell me where the Summoner is and what he is planning."

No one answered, though one of the Sightfuls spat in her direction. That was all Meraude needed to know.

She braced herself then took the throne. A jolt of pain shot through her bones, but Meraude did not cry out nor did she flinch. "Rise," she told the Sightfuls, whose expressions went slack.

The four plus the two doubly Blest girls rose.

Meraude gripped the armrests of the throne with her slippery hands. "Foresee and tell me, where is the Summoner and what is he planning?"

As one, the six Sightfuls closed their eyes. After a moment, they spoke together. "The wizard will escape a great foe, a wizard with an iron fist."

"The wizard?" Meraude interrupted. "I told you to look for the Summoner." Sweat poured down her neck and she fought for control. "Ing, tell me what you mean by this."

The girl stepped forward, her eyes glassy. "The Summoner has changed. He is a powerful foe and very well could defeat you, he and his mate." Her voice was monotone and her expression emotionless.

Meraude asked Egreet, "Who is the mate?"

"The only she-wizard to walk the earth this age," said the girl. "She carries the wizard's child and will be a considerable challenge to defeat."

Meraude leaned forward on the throne, her hands aching from gripping the armrests so hard. "But she can be defeated?"

"Yes," chorused the six women.

"Egreet, tell me how."

As bidden, the girl said, "In the Tower of Inohaim, she and her mate will have no power that you cannot control. When they come hence, you may destroy them both."

"And they will come to me?"

The women said, "Yes. Soon they will escape and seek the Tower of Inohaim. You must be waiting. Then, you shall make your move."

Satisfied yet exhausted, Meraude held on to the power the throne and the Seeing Goblet provided together. "Ing and Egreet, go to the far wall and start your descent. Do not listen to me again until we are back on the ground, and then you shall forget everything that has happened here."

The two girls nodded, turned, and disappeared through the wall, the Endurers stepping aside to let them pass.

"Milady," said General Tindra, who was not under the mage queen's control, for she was not a Sightful but an Endurer and there was no Enduring Goblet present.

"Silence," Meraude commanded and was obeyed of free will. "Sightfuls, it is your duty to serve your queen. Over there is a ladder. Climb it, and then throw yourself off of the Tower."

The Endurers' expressions were grim as the four Sightfuls hurried to their deaths. And it wasn't until the last one screamed no more that Tindra seemed to find the courage to speak again. The faithful Endurer ran to Meraude and helped her from the throne. "Are you all right?"

Meraude nodded weakly. "Yes."

"Your hair, milady."

"I know." What once had been jet-black and lush, now was brittle and full of streaks of white.

"What shall we tell the people?"

Meraude straightened. "We shall tell them that the missing Sightfuls returned and attacked me, but I prevailed. This," she said, holding one silver strand, "is the price I paid to win."

CHAPTER NINETEEN

Jinn

A week had passed since Jinn questioned Hex at the picnic. She had seen the wizard every day since then, and as no mention was made of her trickery, Jinn was certain he had forgotten everything.

It was late in the afternoon and the world outside was overcast. Thunder boomed in the distance, and the air itself crackled as though with dread. Jinn had told everything to Aidan and Slaíne – everything that they needed to know to succeed in their escape. They didn't need to know she doubted her decision to go through with this, that perhaps the wizard and she-wizard should not be allowed their freedom. It was too late to go back now. Or was it?

Quick stood near the window, watching rivulets of water run down the glass panes. The weather reflected his mood well.

"Please talk to me," said Jinn for the tenth time that day. "You can't still be angry about my decision."

Her brother shrugged and continued to stare at the rain. "Jinn makes her own choice. Quick does not have to like it."

Jinn shook her head and stepped forward. "I'm not choosing anyone over you, Quick. We'll be together again soon. Surely you must know that I would never leave you forever."

Lightning struck somewhere nearby in one brilliant flash, followed by an immediate resounding boom that caused the twins to cover their ears. A moment passed, and Quick got to his feet. "Quick does not know future. Getting...harder to look."

Jinn gave him a sympathetic nod. "It's always been hard for you. I'm sorry for that."

"Not Jinn's fault." Quick sighed and went to the fire, which continued to crackle merrily, its light dancing across his face. "No one's fault. Honest."

With a shiver, Jinn pulled her house cloak more tightly about her. Quick wore a dressing gown over his traveling clothes, in case Hex caught sight of him. Aidan and Slaíne would have packed food and replenished their waterskins by now, and would be lying in wait for Quick.

"You ready?" Quick asked, though he would not quite meet her eye.

Jinn nodded once, tightly. Again the role of deceiver and distraction fell upon her shoulders. This time...no, she did not want to think about this time and what danger it might bring. "It will all go well. You'll see." She was telling herself this as much as she was her brother.

Quick turned the full force of his gaze on Jinn. "And if it doesn't?"

"He won't harm you, if you're discovered, if that is what you mean."

"Will he hurt the wizard and she-wizard, though?" he demanded.

Jinn looked at the door. "They know what they're getting into." *Lights above, the waiting is the worst part.* She knew she needed to get a handle on her emotions. If Hex were to walk in right now, he would immediately know that she was up to something treacherous.

But Hex was not scheduled to arrive for another ten minutes, and he was never early or late. "I'm going to take a quick walk," she announced after a moment. "My nerves cannot bear much more of this."

At once Jinn wished she could call the words back. It was too late. Quick's face fell and he looked back at the fire. "You know what I meant, Quick."

He made an uncertain noise. "Be careful."

Jinn tried to think of the words to make peace with her brother. She settled instead on running to him and giving him a squeeze. "I love you, Quick."

Quick nodded. "You know Quick," was all he had to say on that score.

Before she could say anything more to accidentally wound him, Jinn turned and left the room. The halls were darkened from lack of sunshine that day. Many of the torches were lit in their brackets, changing the quality and atmosphere of the house to something sinister. Jinn drew her arms around herself.

Shadows danced on far walls in strange shapes. Jinn swore she could feel the house itself watching and waiting, and she wondered why it had never sought to communicate with her again. Perhaps it was unable to interfere with matters anymore. Maybe Hex knew what had been done and had punished it…if one could actually punish a house.

Again the house rattled with thunder, this time startling Jinn to the point she thought her heart might stop. *I thought Hex controlled the weather here. Why is he allowing it to behave in this fashion?*

Outside the wind picked up. Trees scratched their bony black fingers against the windows, setting Jinn's teeth on edge. So great was the storm now, Jinn dared not go near any of the windows, in case a branch punched its way through the glass panes.

It was nearing the agreed-upon meeting time, and Jinn had wandered far, so she turned on her heel and hurried back to the room she shared with Quick. The wind screamed and moaned as she ran. Waves, she imagined, crashed against the face of the black cliff on which the House of Curses sat. Could the house tumble over into the sea? *Don't be fanciful.* Jinn scolded herself for allowing her thoughts to wander in such a direction.

She rounded a corner and ran straight into Aidan. "What are you doing here?" she demanded. Jinn looked the wizard up and down. He was not wearing his traveling clothes. "What's happened?"

"Something is wrong with the wizard," Aidan said hastily. "I can feel his despair. Can you?"

Jinn shook her head. "No, but I am no wizard."

Aidan made a face but otherwise did not respond to that statement. "The magic powering the house has flickered several times now. You might be able to come with us. You just— you need to look ahead first."

"His and my fates are too closely entwined. The curse on those who would foresee his future cloaks me as well."

"With his magic ebbing today, perhaps you will have a chance."

Aidan sounded doubtful. "Well, if you will not go with us, this is perhaps the opportunity we have been waiting for. I shall fetch your brother, if you have said your farewells."

Jinn reached out and put a hand on his arm to stay him, and was surprised when his image flickered, revealing a different version of himself, this one wearing traveling attire. "Is this magic?"

Aidan grimaced. "Yes," he said hastily. "Hurry. I don't know how much time we have."

Mind reeling, Jinn watched as Aidan ran toward the room where her brother would be waiting. "This is going too fast," Jinn murmured before turning and seeking out Hex.

The storm raged on. Jinn swore she could hear the house groaning as if in pain, but it still said nothing to her. She took a sharp turn and hurried up a set of stairs, pausing when she remembered she wasn't supposed to know where the wizard's quarters were. Could she claim she had gotten lost? Perhaps Hex would chance upon her in the hall and then…. *And then what?*

She swallowed hard, turned the corner, and then forced herself to walk up a shallow set of stairs. There were several doors leading to nowhere, all of them the same hue of red. Jinn had first discovered these when she had taken a drugged Hex back to his quarters. The floorboards creaked ominously beneath her weight, and Jinn froze, staring straight ahead.

At the far end of the hall sat the tapestry depicting the three stags. She had scarcely taken time to study it before. Something about it seemed wrong, but she could not quite think of what that might be. Perhaps the colors were too brilliant. Or maybe…no, but that wasn't possible. The edges of the decoration seemed to shimmer. As one mesmerized, Jinn found herself gliding toward it, only to stop herself just a yard away, shaking her head, and turning toward Hex's room, which sat next door.

His door, unlike the others, was black. It had not been that way before. She reached out a hand and was about to knock when she heard a groan from within. Again her eyes were drawn to the wall holding the tapestry, but there was nothing there but a gaping hole. Jinn blinked hard and, turning away from the door once more, she studied the place where sat three of the Goblets Immortal. *They look so ordinary*, Jinn mused. *How can such ordinary looking items cause so much trouble for the world?*

She took one step in that direction, but the tapestry returned with a flash and hung there as though it had never moved. Jinn scowled at it, waiting for the thing to disappear or flicker again, but as it did not seem inclined to do so, she went back to Hex's door, which was now a dismal shade of gray. She waited a few beatings of her heart, listening for any signs of life within.

Silence reigned, but Jinn swore she could feel a presence on the other side of the door. Ere she could knock, a loud clanking noise sounded from within the room and the door whined open a crack. *So much for the element of surprise.* With a grimace, she put out her hand and nudged the door open a bit more so she could slip inside.

At the foot of a great canopy bed sat Hex. He was on the stone floor, his head in his hands. By his feet there was a tankard of what might have been water, but for the smell. Hex had been drinking, and by the look of him, he had been at it for a while.

Disgusted, Jinn began to have second thoughts about going through with her plan. *Maybe he doesn't know I'm here. Maybe I can just quietly turn heel and leave....*

As if sensing her thoughts, the house let out a great rumble, and the wizard's head shot up. He was pale, and his eyes were red-rimmed and blurred with apparent tears. Or perhaps that had been Jinn's imagination. She blinked and the tears were no longer there. "How did you find my room?" Hex asked in a monotone.

A shiver ran down Jinn's spine. Something was wrong with the wizard, indeed. "I just— I heard moaning and thought I might help?"

Of all things, Hex laughed, a cruel, mirthless sound, but stopped himself. "I don't deserve your help," he said, so softly Jinn might have imagined the words. He looked over at his tankard, went to lift it, hesitated, then drained the rest of what was in it.

It was hard not to judge him in his piteous state. The only thing that kept her from leaving the room was the memory of the vision she'd had of herself and him, hands entwined, their faces lit with happiness. Surely there was some meaning to that bit of foresight. That's what Jinn held on to as she approached the wizard, who warned her to come no closer. "Why?" she demanded, her impatience spilling into her words.

Hex looked up again, and it was startling for Jinn to see into his eyes. The man was not drunk, not if the keenness in his gaze was anything to go by. This was a man in deep pain.

Jinn's heart thudded anxiously as she lowered herself to the ground a ways away from him. "What has you so upset?"

At first it did not seem that Hex was going to answer. But after a moment of staring at her, his gaze lowered to her hands and he said, "I have had another vision."

Jinn studied him as he studied her boots. Hex's already dark hair looked almost black, so filthy was it from apparent neglect. Jinn was surprised she hadn't noticed it the day previous. His clothes clung to his body with sweat, the odor of which reached Jinn, who tried her best not to wrinkle up her nose in disgust. His feet were bare and his hands were picking morosely at a hole in his right trouser leg.

Jinn gave him a few moments, allowing his words to echo around in her mind. At last, when she could stand the silence no more, she gently prodded him by saying, "What was your vision about?"

His picking ceased and he stilled. "Things I'd rather not have seen."

A sobering thought occurred to Jinn: what if Hex had looked ahead and foreseen his captives' escape? It took all her self-control to sit there and not run to warn the others. Little good it would do them now. "Can they be avoided?" Jinn tried to keep her tone neutral, but she knew he would be able to read the dread coming off of her in waves.

At last he looked at her again. "Did you have any visions?"

"No, not today." *What is eating away at him?* Part of her wanted to reach out and touch his hand, to reassure him that he was not alone. The other, more sensible, part remembered that they were yet enemies, so she remained where she was.

Hex adjusted his position on the floor as if meaning to rise, but merely recrossed his legs, left over right. "Do you ever wish you were not cursed with the gift of foresight?"

"Hex," she said, and he closed his eyes. "What is going on?" *Lights above. Why am I digging into his problems? I'm supposed to be distracting him.*

He laughed, this time a more sincere sound. "Please, answer the question. Do you see foresight as a gift or a curse?"

Cocking her head to the side, Jinn paused and gave the question thought. "I suppose both," she said slowly after some time. "All Blest are cursed…in their own ways. Quick took the curse meant for me in the womb, along with his own. He'll never be able to focus or fully understand things the way an adult understands things."

Hex shook his head. "That is not his curse."

"Oh, and you would know?"

"I am the reason the Goblets Immortal are cursed, Jinn. If not for me, Quick would not have the pain of knowing too much. It is the pain of knowing that causes his innocence. That's how his mind copes."

Jinn processed that in silence as Hex continued.

"Aidan's curse, I sense, is that he loses that which he loves eventually. Meraude's curse is the opposite, and just as unfortunate – she eventually gets everything she wants." Hex paused and let out a long sigh. "But you asked me what my latest vision was about and I have danced around the subject. How very rude of me." Again he uncrossed and recrossed his legs.

Now Jinn did reach out and take his trembling hand. She was startled to find his skin as cold as ice, and nearly dropped it. "You can tell me."

But Hex shook his head. "I found out what kills you, in the end."

That was not what Jinn had been expecting to hear. "Oh?" she breathed. Odd, how the thought did not frighten her, how her breathing did not hitch nor did her body tremble. She had brushed against death many times in her life, and it had always terrified her before.

Hex looked at her hand as though he couldn't fathom what it was. "Jinn," he said, his voice a plea. "I…." He left the thought unfinished but looked deep into her eyes.

Now Jinn's breathing did hitch, for an entirely different reason. It had been her plan to throw herself at Hex, to seduce him and thus trick him into releasing the magic powering the house. But she did not need to.

Eyes determined, Hex pulled Jinn toward him until her knees were touching his right thigh. "Maybe we can alter the future," he murmured, cupping her face with his free hand. His thumb stroked her jaw and his eyes closed as he leaned in and kissed her softly on the lips.

Jinn's own eyes fluttered shut as she yielded and kissed him back. Around her she could feel changes, small ones at first, but it didn't register in her mind what was happening.

Soon Hex's kiss deepened and his lips became more demanding, forcing her to choose: answer or pull away. She chose the former, kissing him back with as much passion as he was showing her.

Visions began to fill Jinn's mind, but she was able to ignore them for the most part. The fact that her plan had worked barely registered with Jinn, and soon she found herself in his lap, their bodies entwining.

Whether Hex was having visions of his own, Jinn was uncertain. Everything else ceased to matter, until the wizard froze.

Startled, Jinn pulled back to look at his face. Hex's eyes were unfocused, and his whole body trembled. Before she could pull away, the wizard lashed out with a wall of pure white light, knocking her out of his lap and across the room with its force.

A ringing sound filled Jinn's ears as fire filled her veins. The last thing she saw was Hex looming over her, the color drained from his face as he shouted her name. *Oh*, she thought as her consciousness ebbed.

CHAPTER TWENTY

Aidan

Slaíne was waiting for Aidan when he returned with Quick in tow. Without a word, she handed out two of the three packs she had made ready, before throwing the last one over her own back. The plan was for them each to carry a Goblet in their sack, since the magical vessels could not be Dismissed. "We ain't got much time," she said briskly, leading them out of the room.

"Does it work?" Aidan asked Quick as they hurried through the empty halls.

The giant's expression was tight. "Quick has seen success. But...." They rounded a corner and found the staircase leading up to the wizard's room. Quick lowered his voice. "There is failure there too. Hard to see." The fifth step complained beneath their combined weight, and he urged Aidan to go before him.

"Your job'll be to keep an eye on the future," said Slaíne in a loud whisper.

Quick nodded. "Quick knows, he knows. Stop reminding him."

Aidan and Slaíne exchanged a worried look. *Are you sure he's on our side?* she thought at him.

Yes, or this is a very elaborate, pointless performance, he thought back.

They arrived at the top of the stairs, and Aidan was uncertain of which way he should turn, but Quick led them left, and so they followed him that way. Light shone beneath one door that was changing colors as Aidan watched. He could feel two different Pulls on the other side, but all was silent. Slaíne gave Aidan's arm a tug when he hesitated, and he tore himself away from the strange sight, his heart racing when he spied a tapestry depicting three stags.

Time was of the essence now, according to Quick, who motioned for them to hasten their steps. When they arrived at the tapestry, Aidan reached out his hand to simply feel it, but Quick slapped him away and shook his head.

The giant's lips formed the word, "Trap."

Aidan lowered his hand to his side. They all stared at the tapestry, and as they did, the image of it flickered several times, and it all but disappeared once, then glowed bright red, and...nothing happened. They waited. Still it remained.

A few times, Slaíne reached her hand out and drew it back. Her gaze was on the giant, who seemed unmoved by the lack of activity on the tapestry's part.

Again Slaíne seemed ready to speak her mind, but Quick frowned at her and put a finger to his lips. Her temper, Aidan could sense, was rather close to the surface. He could smell her nerves getting the better of her, and if they didn't do something soon, not only would his mate blow a hole in the wall, she would also blow a hole in their plan.

Let's wait a few more moments, he thought to her, though his own nerves were wearing thin.

Slaíne turned her face to glower at Aidan now. *What if this turns out to be a trap? They're Meraude's children, Aidan.* She threw up her hands in silent frustration. *Maybe I should have had him eat the Truth Apple.*

Aidan scoffed. *This is our only chance to escape. Let's not lose sight of our plan.*

Slaíne ground her teeth, her body shaking. *It might just be the last plan we'll e'er make. What is taking her so....*

Quick nodded to them both and started counting on his fingers. His mouth began to move, counting backward from nine. When he had reached one hand, he pointed at his eyes, then at Aidan, and then at the tapestry.

There was the murmur of voices from down the hall, and Aidan became aware of the two Pulls moving. Aidan tensed, prepared to run if he had to, but he did not take his eyes from the tapestry, which shone brightly for a moment, and disappeared altogether.

Aidan did not hesitate. He thrust his hand through the new hole in the wall, grabbed one Goblet, passed it to Slaíne, reached in and pulled the other two out and handed them to Quick.

"Hurry," Quick urged below his breath, for at the back of the safe there sat eight or nine doorknobs.

Aidan managed to Summon three of them into his waiting hands before there was a great cry from the other room. The tapestry flashed back to life, and the three of them fled as a desperate voice began to shout in the room behind the color-changing door.

There wasn't time to run back to their room, nor was it a wise idea; that would be the first place Hex would look for them. Aidan took the lead and threw open the door at the end of the hall, which had nothing behind it but a brick wall.

"Come on," Quick whispered as the shout in the distance became a mournful wail. He led them down the stairs, which they took two at a time, making enough noise to rouse an army, and then opened a door at the foot of the stairs. The giant ushered Aidan and Slaíne inside and closed and bolted the door behind them. "What was noise about, Quick wonders?"

Not daring to look at Slaíne, Aidan shook his head and stared at the white doorknobs in his hands. "Jinn knows what she's doing." He pocketed two of the knobs and held the remaining one up to the light filtering into the room – a large broom cupboard, by the looks of things. What a magic house would need with such a thing, Aidan couldn't say. "Let's hope one of these works."

"Hurry," Slaíne urged him, taking up a fighting stance as she faced the door. *Something's gone horribly wrong.*

He nodded and imitated what he had seen Hex do when they had first met. The wizard had taken out one of the doorknobs, held it in the air, and twisted it. Aidan tried this now, but no portal formed.

"Wizard said you would know how," Quick said, though his tone was doubtful.

"Aidan, love, not to discourage ya, but you nay have had any lessons. Your magic's fledgling, at best."

That grated on Aidan's nerves, but this was no time to let his pride get the better of him. "Maybe you should try, then." As he said it, Aidan felt a tingling in his dominant hand and a stirring of power in his chest. Instinctively he pictured a doorway standing before them in the middle of the room, one large enough for the giant to fit through as well. Then, relaxing, he thrust the doorknob into where he imagined it ought to go, and turned it. With a satisfying click, an enormous brown door opened in midair before him.

Apparently stupefied, Quick put a hand on Slaíne's shoulder. "Summoner better wizard than Quick and she-wizard thought."

"Let's celebrate later," said Aidan, motioning for Slaíne to pass through.

"Where does it lead?" she demanded.

"I think we're about to find out. Quick, after you."

But the giant hesitated. He looked back over his shoulder at the door, whence came a furious cry and many pounding footsteps. "What if bad things happen to sister?"

Slaíne swore. "Then we'll send ya back. Later. Right now we need ya." She ran to the giant and, after first taking his hand, pulled him through the doorway.

Aidan pushed them ahead of him, shut the door, and removed the doorknob, which had popped through to his side. The sounds of Hex's approach faded entirely, and Slaíne led the way as they walked, single file, through a narrow white hall with no end in sight.

"Give me the portal-maker," Slaíne said after some time. "I nay think you should open it from your side." She reached around Quick and took the doorknob out of Aidan's outstretched hand. "Do ya know how to open it again?"

Quick had begun to tremble. "No like tight spaces. Feels like cave where Quick lived. Feels like being trapped."

This would not do. The giant of a man had stopped walking and stood there, breathing heavily. "Slaíne," said Aidan, "could you walk faster? Our friend here is having trouble."

Unable or unwilling to turn around in the narrow space, Slaíne instead took a few steps backward. "We're almost where we ought to be, Quick. Take my hand, I'll guide ya."

"Deep breaths," Aidan said reassuringly, patting the giant on the back. *Do you have a sense of where we'll end up now?* he thought at his mate.

Slaíne let out a shaky laugh as the walls seemed to narrow even more, forcing Quick to walk sideways. *Nay think I can take much more of this.*

Don't tell our friend here that.

Wasn't planning on it, she thought back. They took inch by inch, pausing when it seemed Quick was going to panic, and talking him through the worst of his fears.

"Can't breathe," the giant said several times, pulling at his tunic neck. "So hot in here." At length, Quick would not move at all and began crying for his sister.

Slaíne, who seemed to be nearing the end of her patience, swore and raised the portal-maker. "This ought to be close enough," she said, thrusting the doorknob into an invisible slot in the air before her. A large brown door materialized before them, and the travelers stumbled through it, landing in a heap in the middle of a forest. "Geroff!"

With some difficulty, Aidan managed to pull the giant off Slaíne's prone form, then took the doorknob from her and closed the portal she had made. Wherever they were, the sun was setting, the sky was clear, and Aidan knew they would soon have to make camp and figure out their current location. "We need to put some distance between ourselves and this place," he found himself saying.

His words were met with a grumble from Quick. "Need to go back. Jinn in danger."

The two wizards looked at each other. It was Slaíne who first spoke. "I'm certain she would nay want us to go back and ruin her plans."

Quick frowned, great tears rolling down his ruddy cheeks. "I look ahead."

"No," said Aidan hastily, worried about what the Sightful would find. "We need you to scout with us and help us figure out where we are exactly."

Sláine took the giant by one of his hands. "I know I brought us somewhere north. Not sure where, though."

The great man sniffed, obviously trying to hold back more tears. He pulled his hand out of Sláine's and tramped ahead, leaving the two wizards no choice but to follow.

Quick studied the sky for a moment, then circled a few trees, his fingers scraping against pale bark and moving on to a shrub with silver leaves. "This familiar."

"You know where we are, then?" asked Aidan.

But the giant did not respond at first. Instead, he continued on a few paces, turned left onto a somewhat worn path, and pointed at a sign. "Inohaim Wood that way." He shuddered. "Quick not safe here." He looked at his traveling companions. "Wizards not safe here either, Quick thinks."

Aidan studied the sign Quick had pointed to. "I can't read it," he admitted. "It looks like Abrish."

"Says, 'Turn back'," said the giant. "Maybe we should."

"We're in Meraude's territory now," Aidan said to Sláine. "Let's travel a ways farther tonight."

Quick groaned. "Bad idea."

"How far off do ya figure we are?" she asked the giant, who shook his head.

"Wood familiar. Caves in area." He looked at the sky. "Maybe thirty miles? Maybe fifteen?" That was not a very encouraging or definite answer. "Could look ahead." The offer did not appeal to Aidan; what if Quick looked and found something wrong with his sister? That would make getting him to co-operate even more difficult. And as much as he felt for the Sightful's plight, there would be no turning back to save her now if something had gone wrong.

We can't stop him forever, Sláine said into Aidan's mind. *I've got a bad feelin' 'bout his sister's fate.*

Aidan nodded and led them onto the semi-worn path. *As have I. We must treat Quick with caution.*

They picked their way around raised roots, through thickets of inedible berries and a few patches of thorns, which Slaíne was able to fly over. The prickling plants did not bother Quick, for his skin was too thick. But Aidan had more trouble and ended up accidentally blasting them with green fire, which he only just managed to put out before it could start a large blaze.

"Quick could carry wizard," the giant offered doubtfully, but Aidan refused.

By the time they were ready to make camp, the air had grown colder and their stomachs were snarling. The sky was now slate-gray, and a few stars twinkled opposite the fading sunset. It was strange, feeling the cold but not being affected by it. But Aidan did note that Quick had begun to shiver. "We'll have to chance a fire," he announced as they set down their sacks. "Neither you nor I produce any warmth, and our friend here is chilled to the bone."

"Fire draw bad people?" asked Quick.

Slaíne answered, "We'll have to chance it. Won't do no good if'n our guide freezes to death."

As Quick made no argument against that, the trio hastily gathered wood and tinder to make a fire. It was a convenience, having their strong friend carry wood and break it apart into logs with his bare hands. Within no time, Aidan had managed to light a non-magical fire and began roasting potatoes he had filched from Hex's kitchen.

"Quick looks ahead now?"

"After we've eaten," said Aidan. "The potatoes won't be ready for another hour yet. Why don't you gather some more wood?"

The giant grunted and got to his feet, though he did not seem happy about it. "You send Quick back if things are bad." It was not a request.

What do you know about setting up alarms? Aidan said into Slaíne's mind.

She didn't look up but continued to tend to the fire. *Ya mean like bells on strings and that sort of thing?*

Aidan shook his head. *No. I mean something that would alert us to magic being used nearby or a portal opening.*

Her head jerked up sharply. *You think the wizard might follow us through some means?*

"There were several portal-makers in the safe," Aidan said aloud, seeing that Quick was now out of hearing range. "It wouldn't hurt to have prepared something for Hex, should he show up." He waited as she ruminated over the matter.

The fire spat sparks at Slaíne's hands, but she brushed them away absently and got to her feet. "I dunno. The elves spoke on such things but they nay ever told me how to set one. 'Twould take power to do so, an' they nay knew I had it."

A twig snapped, and the pair looked up. But it was nothing to be concerned about, Aidan discerned from the retreating Pull – just an elk or some creature of a similar build. "Do you know if you— if *we* have foresight?" he asked.

Slaíne shrugged. "Dunno. Hex an' me did nay cover that in training."

That piqued Aidan's curiosity. "We never talked about it, but what exactly did you do in your training sessions?"

"He tested me mostly. Had me try dif'rent things, like Summoning. Said that all came from you. Then flight and conjuring – ya know, making something out of nothing." She poked at the logs with a long stick she fetched from the ground. "Fire creation and manipulation, rainmaking."

"Rainmaking?" Aidan repeated.

"Oh aye," she said. "Seems as though you an' me can control the weather to some degree."

Aidan scratched at the stubble on his chin and stared into the blaze. "That's a lot," he said after some time.

She startled him by throwing back her head and laughing. "That really ain't the half of it, Aidan. Hex discovered all sorts of interesting things when he was testin' me. Breathin' under water, talking to animals, empathy, spell-casting." Slaíne made a face. "He nay did seem very happy when he discovered the last one, nor the weather one. Seemed, I dunno, afeared or something."

"Is that why you asked me if I was afraid of you?" Aidan looked up from the fire and watched her, hoping he hadn't said the wrong thing.

But Slaíne's face gave away none of her feelings. "I guess."

Not one to pry into others' matters, Aidan turned away from the blaze and Summoned a water bladder, which he partook of briefly. He handed the vessel over to Sláine. "Our friend is nearby. It would seem he is taking longer than he ought." He took the water bladder back and Dismissed it, then Summoned his copper knife and thrust it into its sheath at his side.

You think he'd attack us? Sláine followed Aidan into the woods surrounding, making nary a sound as she passed over yesteryear's leaves and twigs.

If he's upset, anything is possible, Aidan thought back. He held up a hand for Sláine to stop, and then pointed to the base of a large elm.

Quick lay sprawled out on the ground, his whole frame shaking as he moaned, "No." He lashed out with his long limbs and continued to cry out, his voice getting louder and louder.

"We need to silence him," Aidan said, moving around the giant with care. "He could draw anyone within a few miles."

"So could the fire," said Sláine, though her brow was creased with worry. "What's wrong with him?"

Aidan shook his head. "I don't know. He's distressed over something. Other than that…." He got no further with that thought when he was hit with a blinding headache. The world around him disappeared, and he saw peculiar things.

Jinn lay on a bed, her face pale, and her chest barely rising and falling. The wizard Hex stood over her, speaking some strange words that were meant to revive her, as the scents of guilt and desperation rolled off of him in waves. On the front of the Sightful's tunic was a large singe mark that reeked of magic.

"We've got ter do something," said Sláine.

Still in a trance, Aidan tried shaking himself back to the moment they were in. "You saw it too?"

Before his eyes, an image of Jinn's and Quick's past selves rose. How he knew it was from the past, Aidan couldn't say. The twins were sleeping beneath the shelter of a large tree. Aidan sensed rather than saw that present Sláine had begun projecting words and images into the Sightful's mind.

"Don't trust the wizard," said Sláine.

The slumbering Jinn cringed and tried to shy away from the vision. "The wizard? There are no wizards in the Saime," she said, still sleeping.

"There are four. I am the third, there are yet three others. Do not ask me to speak their names. Names possess power."

"What are you doing?" Aidan shouted at Slaíne, but knew his words were in vain. He blinked furiously, trying to end the vision for himself so that he might see what was happening in the present moment. "Do you want to alter the past and possibly ruin the future?"

She ignored him and attached herself to Jinn's mind. "You're strong," said Slaíne. "But there is always a price, Blest One. I don't think you paid yours."

"Slaíne!" Aidan shouted. "This is madness. You can't save her. You're going to destroy the one chance we have left."

"Never mind that," said Slaíne to Jinn. "All Sightfuls lose their minds eventually."

"What am I supposed to do?" Jinn spat.

"Find the Goblets Immortal. The rest will play out as it should."

The Sightful sneered at the image of the she-wizard, who continued to glow a bright, unnatural blue. "How can I know you're not some dirty sprite? What makes you think I can trust you or anything you have said?"

"You're just making things worse, Slaíne," Aidan said with a growl. "Come back to me. Come back to now."

Slaíne continued to ignore him. "Jinn. For someone with that sort of name, you had better watch whom you call a dirty sprite. You think my *present* self is speaking to your slumbering mind?" She threw her head back and laughed. This was no longer a warning meant for the Sightful. Slaíne was drunk with power.

Aidan had to find a way to stop her. He shook himself out of the vision and, returning to the present moment, was startled to find Slaíne hovering in the air, her body glowing that strange shade of blue. Instinctively, he reached out a hand and Called her to himself.

She gasped and fell backward into his arms, screaming the words, "Destroy them all!" before her voice returned to normal, and her light faded.

Furious, Aidan nearly dropped her. "What was that about?"

Slaíne staggered out of his arms, turned, and glared at him. "I don't know. I didn't mean to do it. It just happened."

Rage melted at once to concern. "What do you mean?"

"It's like I said, like I've been trying to warn ya. I ain't always in control, Aidan." She sank to the ground, her green cloak pooling around her on the brown grass. "My magic does what it wants." Tears ran freely down her cheeks and she stared at Aidan, as though she thought he might turn and run from her.

This was no time to worry over things that were out of their control. Quick had ceased thrashing about and was still, his rising and falling chest the only sign he was still with them. "It's all right," he said, though he knew most certainly it was not. "We'll figure this out together. But right now, we need to get our guide back to the fire and try to revive him."

Sniffling, Slaíne nodded and got to her feet. Her expression was grim as they approached the unconscious Endurer. "How do we move him?" Absently she tapped at the soles of Quick's boots with the tips of her own.

Aidan scratched at the back of his neck. "Magic?"

But Slaíne was already shaking her head. "We nay can Call him." She cocked her head to the side. "Guess we'll have to drag him."

"Sorry, Quick," Aidan offered as he took one leg and Slaíne took the other. With quite a bit of difficulty, the two managed to pull the giant back to the fire, huffing and sweating as they struggled.

"Why couldn't we get Enduring abilities?" Slaíne panted as she collapsed next to Quick.

That made Aidan laugh, albeit half-heartedly. "It sounds like we have enough power as it is."

At that Slaíne sighed and lay back, her eyes closing. "I think the potatoes are probably done."

Once the meal had cooled, the wizards partook of the plain fare, neither of them very hungry but knowing they needed to keep up their strength. "Just give 'im time," Slaíne said as they finished up. Quick had not regained consciousness, though his face was a better color than what it had been before. "Whene'er I triggered my curse, time always did the trick." She seemed in better spirits, and neither of them mentioned their fears, though Aidan sensed she was trying not to think about them.

★   ★   ★

The night air was cold when Aidan awoke, though it did not affect him as it once would have. Disoriented, he looked around their small campsite. Slaíne was curled up next to him, her face bathed in the dying light from the fire. As if sensing he was staring at her, the she-wizard's eyes flew open.

"Something's wrong."

Aidan grunted in agreement. They both looked over at where they had left Quick, but the giant was no longer there. And that wasn't the only thing missing.

"The Goblets," Aidan said at once, and they both scrabbled to their feet.

"Can you sense him?" Slaíne headed into the wood surrounding, until Aidan took her by the arm and directed her the other way.

"He's not far."

Indeed, Quick was making slow progress heading north-east, picking his way blindly through thickets and stumbling over roots, when they caught sight of him.

Aware that he was being pursued, the giant let out a startled cry and dropped the sack containing the three Goblets on his foot. "Can explain."

Aidan crossed his arms over his chest. "Talk."

When Quick hesitated, Slaíne came at him, hands raised as though meaning to cast a spell. And by the looks of her, it wouldn't be a very nice one. "You're taking them to Meraude, ain't ya? Knew you could nay be trusted."

"Meraude the other way," the giant said, his voice trembling as he cowered, arms over his face. "Don't hurt Quick. Was just trying to help."

"Help *who*?" Slaíne demanded.

The giant sighed and reached to pick the Goblets up, took another look at the enraged she-wizard and hesitated. "Jinn in trouble. Hurt. Goblets can make her better."

Aidan shook his head and walked past Slaíne, intent on the sack. "What happened?" he asked, snatching the package up.

"Wizard accidentally hurt Jinn. Jinn got in way when he cast spell." He pointed to the Goblets in Aidan's hands. "Goblets have healing power. Maybe if she have them, Jinn get better." Quick's lower lip trembled. "Wizard looks for them."

Slaíne groaned. "Quick, we need ter destroy them."

"Why?" Quick demanded. "So can have revenge on Mother? Destroy her army?" He snorted. "Bad idea."

Aidan stole a look at Slaíne. "If we destroy the Goblets, her army will be powerless." It was just a hunch, something he had mulled over, but now as he stood there, he became certain of it.

Quick stared. "How you know?"

"Call it magical intuition. If we destroy the Goblets Immortal her army will lose its powers, won't it? No more Blest can be made, and she won't have the power to kill all magical kind as she so desires."

But the giant was shaking his head. "No." He made a leap for the Goblets, but Slaíne was ready for him, casting a blue-tinged magical net at him. Caught in her spell, Quick froze mid-jump, a look of piteous despair written all over his face.

"You jus' watch yerself," Slaíne said, her eyes flashing as she let the magic drop.

Quick fell to the ground in a sobbing heap. "Sister."

The wizards looked at each other. Was what the man said true? Could the Goblets save Jinn? "Quick," Aidan said, measuring his next words before he committed them to the air. "How many Goblets would it take to help her? You seem to know more about them than I had first thought."

Perhaps scenting hope, the man's head snapped up and he stopped crying long enough to say, "Quick does not know. Might take all six that exist. Might take one...the Enduring Goblet."

"There are only five Goblets Immortal," Slaíne corrected him. "An' none of these that we have are the Enduring Goblet."

Aidan cursed. "Meraude has the Enduring Goblet. Hex said as much."

"Please," said Quick. "Jinn needs Goblets."

"We can nay go back," said Slaíne, wringing her hands. "That wizard'll never let us leave if'n he gets his hands on us."

Aidan took to pacing, the hairs on his arms standing on end. The air was charged with everyone's overexcited emotions and he needed to clear his thoughts. He was not heartless, nor was Slaíne, he knew. But there was no way of both saving magic-kind from Meraude and saving Jinn from her injury. At length his pacing slowed, the acrid tang of despair faded to a musk of muddled emotions, resignation being most prominent among them.

"I'm sorry, Quick," said Slaíne.

The man sniffed. "But sister."

"There is one thing we can try," said Aidan, holding up his hands for Quick to quiet. Once the giant had settled down, Aidan continued. "If you come with us, we can take the Enduring Goblet, destroy the others, and then find a way to send you back to your sister and Hex."

But we nay know if the Enduring Goblet alone can save her, Slaíne said into Aidan's mind.

We can't tell him that, I'm afraid, he thought back. *We'll have to take a chance, or more than just Jinn will die.* He forced a lie of certainty through his teeth, "I'm convinced the Enduring Goblet will be enough to save your sister. Will you continue forward with us?"

Aidan scented the foul stench of deceit when the giant shook his large head and gave his pledge to not steal the Goblets or hinder them in any other way again. Looking at Slaíne, he knew she had perceived Quick's intentions as well. "There's no way back to the House of Curses without a portal-maker, anyway," Aidan said after they had grasped forearms and shaken on their arrangement. "You won't be able to bring the Goblets back without us, Quick. Running off again could end up with you captured."

"Along with the Goblets," Slaíne added.

Quick nodded. "Quick knows. He knows."

CHAPTER TWENTY-ONE

Jinn

Here, wherever Jinn was, her second sight had fully opened. She was aware of the physical world, of her mortal shell lying in distress, the frantic wizard pouring spell after spell over it. 'It'. What a funny way to say 'soon-to-be corpse'.

She looked around, taking in the somewhat familiar terrain. Trees. Lots of trees. And large mountains looming in the near distance. The light in the sky was dimming, and a mist clung to her surroundings, making physical sight reluctant to come to her aid. So she turned to her foresight.

Jinn foresaw her brother mourning over her still form, which still clung to life. Hex was nowhere to be seen, but intuition led her to grab on to a crimson thread of light that was woven into the scene, and she followed it in her mind's eye. The scene changed to Meraude's tower, and she spied him at once. He stood out among the women warriors, taller than them all by a full head. Meraude was there upon the throne. Jinn gasped. "She found them all." This image wavered several times, and Jinn could almost sigh in relief; the future was far from being set in stone. She quieted her breaths so that she might hear the potential conversation.

"Please, milady," said Hex, "this is the only way to save her. Just a drop from all five and she will be whole again."

The mage queen's hair, Jinn was surprised to find, was streaked with white, and her eyes glowed silver. When she spoke, the room trembled. "What have you to offer in return?"

"I served your kind in the Great War. I can serve again."

At once the scene went black. Jinn opened her eyes and jumped. She had not seen the four elves that had appeared while she had been looking ahead. Jinn swallowed a scream as the four hemmed her in. "Where am I?"

"Mortal? Here of all places?" asked the tall one. "Aura's weak."

"A nearly dead Blest. A Sightful at that," said the warty one, looking her up and down. "Clingin' to some ill-gotten hope, if'n yous ask me."

The fattest one sniffed. "Reeks of Meraude."

The other three hissed and made a sign to ward off evil.

Jinn was turning in circles, trying to keep track of them all and where their cruel-looking hands were. "Please, I'm her daughter but I'm not with her. She—"

"What's going on?" asked a fifth, male voice.

But the elves did not move aside. Instead, they concealed Jinn from view. "None of yourn business, Salem," said the fourth one, the one who had not yet spoken. She'd said the last word as if it were a joke, but the others did not laugh. "Should we cast her out?"

"Wait," said the male voice, its owner pushing his way in. He was tall of stature, dark hair hanging down his neck in crazy waves. His expression lightened at the sight of her. "I've seen this woman in Aidan's thoughts. This is the Sightful who's been helping him."

The four elves looked at each other, their expressions inscrutable. "Let us be asking the other Sightful," said the tall one. Before the others could approve or protest, the she-elf snapped her fingers. "Mai Larkin. You're needed here."

"Where am I? How did you know me? What's going on?" Jinn backed away as the ring of elves opened up for her. She meant to flee, but the man Salem was in the way.

"It's all right. You're almost dead," he said, a knowing smile on his lips. "This is the Beyond."

Jinn blinked. "The – the Beyond?" She of course knew tales of the place all magical folk went when they died. Finding the tales to be true was rather a shock. Jinn stumbled backward, and the man caught her.

"Easy. It's all right. Truly. You'll like it here."

She thought of Quick mourning over her. "B-but I don't want to die."

"What's all this?" snipped a sixth voice, this one female, with a rasp. The small crowd parted farther still, revealing a woman a little taller than Jinn, with a shaved head and a slight gap in her teeth. "Ah, Jinn. I've been wondering when you might show your face." She turned to the elves. "It's all right. Her future was hard to see because of the wizard."

Again the elves hissed and crossed themselves.

But the other Sightful paid them no mind. "Jinn, listen to me." She took Jinn by the hands — so much as she could, as Jinn realized her own fingers and palms were nigh see-through. "If you want to live, so to speak, you must sever your ties with your mortal life now. Time runs short. Should they try to revive you with a Goblet or all of them, your odds of survival diminish greatly."

This was too much to take. Jinn looked around at the array of strange faces and began to shake. "I want to go back. I need to go."

"Tell her nothing," Larkin said over her shoulder, as though predicting an interruption. "The future is not yet set. Besides, she has enough information to make her decision."

"It's about to be made for her," Salem pointed out.

"Clings to life like a blight-fish to the hull of a great ship, that one does," said the warty elf. "Mayhaps a certain nymph queen could hurry along the dyin' process."

They all looked at Larkin, who shook her head. "No. Jinn here has a few more hours before it's too late. We shall leave this in the hands of fate." She gave Jinn an appraising look, as though to see how her words had landed.

Lights, but this was confusing. "I can't leave my brother behind."

No one responded, but continued to look at her, a mist rising up around them. One by one, they all were swallowed by it.

Jinn once again became aware of her body in the mortal realm. It was fighting to stay alive, thanks to her strong will to live and the wizard's intervention. But she knew there was only so much he could do. The magic he had accidentally thrown at her had been potent, meant only for restoring power to the house. As if in response to the thought, she felt her heart stop, and the mortal world faded, only to be brought back into sharp focus as Hex restarted it.

She looked at her skin. It was gray, cold. How much longer could she linger like this?

From the Beyond, she heard voices calling her, coaxing her to come back. But she couldn't relinquish her hold on life. There was still too much of it ahead of her, too much to live for. What would Quick do without her? Or, rather, what would she do without him?

The cold sank into her bones, into her soul. She shivered. The Beyond had seemed warmer than this. And here, drifting above her body, Jinn could feel pain. It would be ever so nice to rest, she thought. She watched as the distraught wizard continued to toil over her body. Why did he care so much? Jinn would never know unless she stayed.

A thread of gray light appeared to Jinn's left and she stared at it, her fingers itching to touch it. This was no thread she was used to, she knew. It would not lead to a vision from the future. The cord was her last tie to the land of the living, and it was rapidly thinning.

Hands shaking, Jinn reached for it, as though to preserve it, perhaps by knotting it or winding it into a ball. But it began to slip away from her. Feelings faded, and the Beyond called to her, pulled at her.

Jinn was too weak to resist. "I'm sorry," she breathed at last and, so tired, she severed the thread and let go.

CHAPTER TWENTY-TWO

Aidan

It was the middle of the night, two days after they had escaped, and Aidan had the distinct feeling of being watched. He had forgone sleep in favor of acting as lookout. Now, as the moon set, the feeling of a third presence looking in on them intensified, though he could sense no human Pull.

He thought of rousing Slaíne, whose snores filled the chill air, but he hesitated. Weariness clung to his bones still, an exhaustion that his change into wizardry had brought about. She continued to experience it as well, he knew, though neither of them complained aloud.

Quick stirred in his sleep, crying out softly before rolling over onto his side, sighing, and adding his snores to accompany Slaíne's. He had been silent the whole night, and Aidan hoped rather than believed they had talked sense into him.

Still, he felt like a monster for choosing as he had. But didn't the lives of countless magical beings outweigh the lives and happiness of a handful? Aidan shuddered, and his self-hatred grew.

You're being too loud, Slaíne thought at him. She groaned and sat up. At once her spine stiffened. "Someone's looking for us."

"I know," he said without annoyance. "I've felt watched all night long."

Slaíne swore at him. "Why did you nay wake me? Perhaps we ought ter move on." She rose and looked into the surrounding darkness. "Can you sense anything? Well, I mean, as far as Pulls are concerned?"

"No. Can you?"

"No." She looked back at him. "Ought we ter wake Quick?"

Aidan hesitated. The poor man had had a rough week and deserved all the respite he could find. "Let him sleep a while longer." When Slaíne started to dissent, he interrupted with, "If we determine the force is malevolent to all three of us, we'll wake him."

"An' if it's only a threat to you and me?"

"The wizard has had two days to find us. Maybe he's given up. Maybe all is well." He did not believe the words coming out of his own mouth, and he knew that his mate did not believe them either.

Quick had not spoken of any more visions. Aidan and Slaíne had kept a close watch over him, just in case, and had caught no hints he was being troubled further by foresight. But that did not mean something hadn't slipped past their notice. If Jinn were dead, they might not know.

Slaíne broke the silence with a yawn. "How far off are the nearest Pulls?"

"I can only feel strong Pulls within ten miles of wherever I stand. I'm assuming you're the same way. The only human Pulls I can sense now are here, in this camp." It was maddening, not knowing if they were headed in the right direction. Aidan thought he would be able to discern if Quick were leading them astray on purpose, but being lost was a whole different thing altogether. The thought stirred the embers of his temper, and he sat there seething over their helplessness.

The maps had done them no good. Inohaim Tower could be within eleven miles or eleven thousand and he would not know. Why did time seem to be slipping through their fingers like grains of sand, while their previous days had been like running through molasses? "How big do you think Meraude's army might be?" he asked. Perhaps he ought to have kept the question to himself, but he couldn't help it. And besides, Slaíne was aware of all or at least *most* of his thoughts now; there would be no hiding his irritation from her, that was for certain.

"Dunno. But will they be a problem for us, you think?"

Aidan was startled to hear the rhetorical tone. "Are you that powerful?"

Slaíne sighed. "Not this again. *We*, Aidan. Yes, we're that powerful." Apparently full of restless energy, she walked around their campsite.

"If we're that powerful," he said thoughtfully, "do we need to be so concerned about the wizard?"

She stopped and looked at him, eyebrows raised. "You got control of all your powers and have hundreds of years of experience under your belt?"

Aidan felt the heat of a blush spread across his face. "I see."

"Did nay think so. An' you're not the only one." Again she took to circling the encampment. "Not that we want ter have ter use all of our powers. Could be dangerous. We nay know everythin' we're capable of, yes?"

"Your point is taken," Aidan said, his temper rising before he could cool it.

Slaíne's eyes flashed brilliant blue in response. "Careful, love. We nay want to burn this place to cinders. 'Twould take buckets and buckets of rain to put out what damage we could do together."

That cooled Aidan's temper somewhat, and though it had not entirely dissipated, amusement began to creep up on him. "Buckets and buckets, you say?" He resettled himself. "Well, we are rainmakers, so that is not outside the realms of possibility."

The light faded from her eyes and she laughed. "Guess not. Rather do other things with ya, though, than put out fires."

"And what might that be?" he asked, feigning innocence.

Slaíne scoffed. "Oh, a thing or two. On second thought," she said, her expression mockingly thoughtful, "buckets and buckets of rain might make less noise." She looked meaningfully at him.

Aidan chuckled as he sat, and Slaíne settled down next to him. "He does snore," Aidan said after a time. "We don't want to wake him."

"Ha. Thoughtful for once, are we?"

It was almost possible to forget the presence he sensed watching them, searching for them, but not entirely. On the other side of the fire, Quick let out an almighty grunt, and Slaíne burst out laughing.

Aidan joined her. "On second thought, forget him. Forget everything, let's—"

He got no further. The feeling of being watched disappeared entirely, and a cold dread settled over their encampment as a red light exploded in the near distance.

Quick sat up with a cry. "Fire!"

"Get to the Goblets. He is not to have them, no matter the cost," Aidan said to Slaíne, jumping to his feet as Hex's Pull came to life in the near distance.

"Aidan, *you* get the Goblets. I have a better chance of fending him off."

There was no time to argue. Aidan did as she said, going with his better judgment yet against his heart as he ran for the three Goblets Immortal in the sack.

A flash of red fire shot at the Goblets, catching the parcel on fire. Hex appeared in the clearing and threw up a hand, effectively throwing Slaíne away from Aidan's intended path.

Aidan stood between the wizard and the Goblets, and hastily Called Slaíne to his side, faster than she would have been able to run on her own.

Hex eyed their joined hands warily. "Jinn's dead," he said to Quick. "Will you help me, or are you with them?"

There was no hesitation on the giant's part. He leapt to his feet and barreled toward Aidan and Slaíne with an inhuman bellow.

Aidan threw up a hand, and a wall of green flames erupted from his fingertips, encasing himself and Slaíne inside. *We need a plan.*

With a wave of his hand, Hex changed the flames from green to red, and the blaze slithered in toward them. The wizard stepped through the fire unscathed. "I'm sorry. But this is the only chance I have of bringing her back." But he moved no closer to the pair, the scent of dread and fear rolling off of him in waves.

Distract him and I'll think of something, Slaíne thought to Aidan.

"Quick, grab them," said the wizard, and the flames parted behind them. But his eyes kept traveling to Slaíne's and Aidan's hands.

For a moment, she let go of Aidan, but he quickly seized her by the wrist and would not let go. *Remember the ward?*

Hex had put up a hand for Quick to stop his approach. "Please. I don't want to hurt either of you, but I will kill you both if I have to."

Which ward? Slaíne thought back.

The red wall of fire that flew up between us when we were fighting. Our skin was touching, I believe. Aidan tensed as the wizard created a ball of red flame in his right fist.

Slaíne frowned. *Joined magic. Legends said that the wizards of old – the powerful ones that had been bound – could join their powers. It was somethin' awful.*

"Come, no one need die tonight," Hex said, the fire in his hand burning brighter still.

Aidan could feel Quick's Pull creeping toward them, and sent a wave of magic his way. He sensed rather than saw the man flying backward. *Guide me, on the count of—*

"Now," she shouted, throwing up her hand before her.

Aidan did likewise, as a painful burning stirred within his breast. Both of the soul-halves, hers and his own, writhed, and out of their hands shot a single golden spark.

Hex leapt away and circled around to where Quick stood, dazed. But the flicker of golden light followed him, rapidly growing brighter and larger. A wind picked up, and Aidan and Slaíne were lifted off their feet as a whirlwind of golden fire burst into life around them, raising the Goblets as well out of Hex's reach.

Cursing them, the wizard grabbed Quick by the arm, said something inaudible above the blaze's roar, and the pair disappeared in another flash of red light.

He's gone, Slaíne, he thought to her, for he did not think she would be able to hear anything either. He made to remove his hand from her wrist, but Slaíne Called him to her side and would not relinquish his Pull. *Think of Meraude. She'll find us if we don't stop this.*

"Let her," said Slaíne, her challenge echoing.

But Aidan was more accustomed to Pull manipulation than she was. Before she could sense his intention, Aidan Dismissed himself, landing in Nothingness with a strangled sound he had not known himself capable of making. It took him a moment, but soon regret washed over him. What had he been thinking, releasing that magic? They could have done anything together. As one, they were pure power. And now that he had tasted it, he wanted more.

Be careful, Aidan, said Salem's faint voice.

With a jolt, he brought himself back to Existence, and was devastated by the sight. Trees had been flattened for miles around and were smoldering gently in an unnatural breeze. In a pile of ashes sat Slaíne, her expression deceitfully calm and neutral.

He knew she had felt the same power, craved it as much as he did, but maybe she feared it more, because as soon as he started to suggest they try it again, she cut him off. "No. We can nay e'er do that again."

Growling, Aidan turned on his heel and began to stalk off into what were once the woods. He did not get far before a wall of blue light flew up in front of him, and he was forced to come to a halt. "What?" Aidan spun around, prepared for a fight.

His mate's eyes were glowing, but she continued to maintain her composure. "Come here, Aidan."

Aidan hesitated, but soon relented and stormed over to her.

Slaíne surprised him by throwing him to the ground, knocking the wind out of him. As soon as he caught his breath, she pulled him up again and hit him with a blast of cold, blue light. "We're dangerous, you an' me." And that was the last thing she said to him for the rest of the night, which they spent in the center of their mess, back-to-back, heartbroken, and terrified.

* * *

At the dawning, it was Slaíne who nudged Aidan awake. He had not thought himself capable of sleeping, not after what they had been through. Stupefied, he sat up and looked at the ruins surrounding them, which had at least ceased smoking. "How long...?"

But she was shaking her head. "Don't know how long we was asleep. Maybe hours, maybe more. There are human Pulls in the distance. I can feel 'em now."

"Then we'd best break our fast and move on." He Summoned the last pasty from Nothingness, broke it in two, and handed half of it to Slaíne. They did not speak as they ate, though they each knew what the other was thinking and feeling. A dull ache throbbed within Aidan's breast, a place where power had pulsed the night before. "It'll get easier," he said uncertainly after they had each taken a swig from a water bladder. "You'll see."

Slaíne gave him a knowing look. "An' what if it don't? How many people do ya think we might kill afore we figure it out, eh?"

He knew she was right. They were both wild and barely trained. It would take more than practice to master their combined magic; it would take time, instruction, and other things that Aidan did not want to think about just then.

"Do ya think he'll be back? Hex, I mean," she asked as they began picking their way around fallen trees and decimated underbrush.

"I don't know. He seemed rather terrified last night." *Of us,* he thought to himself in disbelief.

"Aye."

The going was nigh impossible, so great was the widespread destruction. After a mere ten minutes of pressing forward, Aidan stopped and Slaíne followed suit. "This isn't going to work."

"Drifting?" she suggested, though her tone was doubtful.

Aidan frowned. "No. I'm not well enough versed in that art, and it might take too much mental energy." He adjusted his grip on the scratchy new sack that contained the Goblets and reached inside.

Her head snapped up. "You think you can make another portal?" She watched as he removed one of the doorknobs from the sack and weighed it in his hands.

"Last time we were rushed for time and didn't know what direction to head in." He nodded north. "Quick was leading us in that direction, and in him I sensed no deceit. If I could at least take us ten miles in that direction, we might reach beyond this mess."

"Could lead us right into Meraude's army, though," said Slaíne, though she looked hopeful.

With a shrug, Aidan lifted the portal-maker to his eye and studied it. "Is there any magic you know of that might guide us?"

She was silent for a moment, chewing her lip as she watched Aidan lower the doorknob to his side. "What helped ya take us where you did the last time?"

"Instinct, mostly. A feeling that what I was doing was right or at least good enough."

Slaíne held out her hand. "Might I take a look?" When he hesitated, she laughed. "I ain't gonna try to use it, Aidan. You're the one with experience now. I just want to explore its Pull."

Sheepishly, Aidan handed the portal-maker over to Slaíne, who took it and held it up to her own eye. "There's some markings here. They're in Abrish." She squinted. "A bit hard ter read, but I think this one says 'north-west'." Slaíne handed the portal-maker back to him. "Might I see the others?"

"Of course." He removed the other two and gave them to her.

She held the other two, one by one, up to her eye and rotated them as she looked. "This one says 'south'," she said at long last, handing the one in her left hand back to him. The other she held up triumphantly. "This was the one you used last time, I reckon."

"Why? What does it say?" He held out his hand, but she did not give the other portal-maker to him. "What?"

"It says, 'heart's choice' and then some words written real small. A warning." Slaíne shook her head. "'Perliso synn emn': use twice, death follows."

Still unenlightened, Aidan cocked his head to the side and scratched at his chin. "Which could mean you die the second time you use it."

"Or the third time you use it," she finished for him. "An' we nay know if it's been used afore." She tossed it once into the air, caught it, and handed it to Aidan. "Not sure what we should do."

"And we're assuming 'heart's choice' means it will lead you to any destination you desire." Again he studied the doorknob, exploring its rather ordinary Pull. "I say we shouldn't risk it."

A moment passed as Slaíne seemed to be weighing the words in her mind. "Might I see it again?" She held out her hand, and Aidan obliged by returning the portal-maker. "I think I'll keep this. Just in case we're separated or somethin'."

Aidan nodded. He could see the wisdom in that. "Don't use it unless you're absolutely certain there is no other way out. In fact, why don't you take one of the others?" He began to hand her the north-east one, but she shook her head.

"I've a better feeling about the south."

So Aidan handed her the other one, though his suspicions had been roused. "What's south of here?"

But Slaíne did not answer. Instead, she pointed to the other portal-maker, the one that was labeled 'north-east' in Abrish. "Why don't we try that one? Quick was leadin' us north, anyhow." When she said it, she would not quite meet his eye, but Aidan was standing with the sun to his back, and it was a clear sky. The light must be bothering her.

"All right." Aidan Summoned the silver sword and handed it to Slaíne and Summoned the bronze one for himself into his left hand. They needed to be prepared, just in case he led them right to Meraude's doorstep, which was more than a slight possibility. The last time he had made a portal, his only thought had been to quickly get away. Now he had more time to focus. Setting his feet apart, Aidan closed his eyes and raised the portal-maker. It took a moment for the magic to begin to register with him, but soon possibilities began to shape in his mind's eye, something that had not happened the time before. Beyond the white hallway that awaited them sat the woods that they had knocked over the previous evening. From there on were more woods, clearings, a mountain, and woods again. He saw a sign: *Egethberem*, a name that sounded familiar but he couldn't place. "We'll try this one," he said, thrusting the portal-maker into the air before him.

A white door appeared before them, and beyond that sat another white passage. Aidan led the way in, closing the portal behind them. As before, the doorknob materialized on his side of the door, and Slaíne handed it to him.

"Where will we end up?" she asked in a hushed, almost reverent voice.

"Egethberem." He followed instinct down the straight and narrow hall that went on for eternity. With his destination in mind, he knew he couldn't go wrong.

They walked on for what felt like forever, and Aidan brought them to a stop, as his sword arm was tiring. "Do you need a drink?"

"Mm."

He took that as a yes and Summoned one of the water bladders. Instead of landing in his hand, the vessel fell past it and exploded on the ground before him, having clearly been cleaved in two. Aidan jumped back, and Slaíne screamed as the passageway trembled.

"I guess this sort of thing doesn't like Summoning magic," he mused. Again the ground shook.

"How much farther?" Slaíne asked as everything stilled.

Aidan pointed ahead with his wet hand. "Just a few more yards."

"Yer magic might've interfered with the magic powering the portal." Her tone was hushed, and when he looked back, her face had gone white.

There was an almighty groan, followed by a great ripping noise. "Come on!" he shouted, breaking into a sprint. He didn't need to look back to know Slaíne was fast on his heels.

Far behind them, Aidan was aware of the ground falling away. He urged Slaíne forward and fumbled for the portal-maker, which had begun to slip from his left hand.

"Open it!" she screamed again and again as the shaking intensified. Then the floor began to swing back and forth, back and forth like a perverse enclosed rope bridge. But if they fell, Aidan had a feeling it would not be ground they'd be tumbling toward.

"Hold this," Aidan said, tipping the bronze sword back to her, but she shied away.

"That magic don't like me."

Aidan swore and set the sword on the ground. He focused and, raising the doorknob, created an opening for the portal. The door thrust open into a blindingly bright landscape, which he did not have the opportunity to study. Aidan snatched up the sword and threw it ahead of him along with the Goblet sack, stepped outside, and then grabbed on to Slaíne right as the ground gave way beneath her.

Having the presence of mind to Dismiss the silver sword, she used her other free hand to cling to the doorframe, which was cracking. With Aidan's help, she pulled herself to the ground above, yanking her foot out of the abyss as the door began to crumble to dust.

Smoking, the now-black doorknob rolled toward Aidan and landed against his boot. They lay in a bed of creeping wintersnaps, which Aidan leapt out of before they could ensnare him, hacking with his sword at what clung to Slaíne with its tendrils. In the midst of the vicious plants sat a road sign that read: *WELCOME TO EGETHBEREM.* Aidan swore and spat at the post, and pulled his mate farther away from the scene.

As he watched, the blackened portal-maker was swallowed by the wintersnaps. There would be no retrieving it now.

"Doubt it still works, anyhow," Slaíne said, her voice shrill.

They needed to recover quickly, Aidan knew. The nearest human Pulls were a mere five miles in every direction, and it was uncertain if they would encounter friend or foe. Aidan Dismissed the bronze sword and tugged Slaíne by the hand, leading her away from the scene.

If only Quick had remained with them. He would have been able to say where they were and how far it was they had yet to travel.

Aidan Summoned another waterskin and they passed it back and forth a few times, indulging in as much water as their hearts desired. The shock of almost dying was slow in wearing off, and Aidan knew they must stay well hydrated...even though it meant they were now down not one but two bladders.

There were several animal Pulls moving in their direction from ahead, accompanied by two human ones. Aidan and Slaíne hid off the side of the road and waited for what turned out to be a horse and carriage to pass.

The ornate carriage remained closed, but there was a woman in the driver's seat, an odd sight. Aidan wished he could get a look at the occupant, but thought the better of it, and ducked the rest of the way behind the fallen tree they were hiding behind.

"Meraude?" Slaíne mouthed at him.

Aidan shrugged. *I don't think we're in Meraude's territory yet. But I think we're close.* The clip-clopping of hooves and the rattling of the carriage grew distant, along with the tug of the human and animal Pulls. They waited another ten minutes, however, just to make certain they wouldn't be seen from down the road.

"What makes ya think we're not already in her territory?" Slaíne asked as they chanced onto the dusty red road. The way through the woods was too crowded here with trees and bracken. To pick through it would be more perilous than taking the open road. Besides, there were plenty of places to hide, should any more Pulls approach them.

"I don't know. Call it a hunch."

Slaíne appeared annoyed, but she said nothing on that score as they continued onward. "Feels like I haven't et in years."

"Almost dying tends to do that to you."

They met no one for the next ten minutes of their journey, but the human Pulls were becoming many. Not enough to constitute a large town or an army, not by any means. As Aidan suspected as they passed through rusted iron gates, they were heading into a village. "Welcome to Egethial," he read as they entered.

If the villagers near the gate thought it strange for two dirt-caked and wind-whipped people to emerge from the road, they did not let on. Rather, the ones nearest the gate kept their heads down and minded their gardening in their small patches of land.

The farther in Aidan and Slaíne traveled, the more run-down the buildings became. Babies cried on older siblings' knees. Children sat around puddles, poking oozing mud with sticks or tossing rocks at passersby until their mothers yelled at them to stop.

Five minutes in, Aidan began to realize that they were being watched, but not outright. He could feel the curious stares boring into his back as they went, and turning quickly once and then again confirmed this suspicion as he caught many women looking on before going back to their work.

"Do you find it odd," said Aidan below his breath, "that we have yet to see any men?"

Slaíne nodded. "I don't like it. Somethin' ain't right here." She sniffed and raised a hand to her nose. "Reeks of despair."

"Papa?" called one of the small children from the doorway of a ramshackle building. She started to run toward Aidan, but a woman caught her before she could make it past their front garden.

Aidan gave her a polite nod, but the woman turned away and ushered the child back inside their hovel, shutting the door behind them. A chill went down Aidan's spine. "Let us risk no magic here."

"Makin' ya think of when we was attacked in Abbington?" Slaíne asked, looking up sharply.

"This place does have a backward feeling to it, don't you think?"

The village might have had a small population, but the buildings seemed to stretch on forever. Everywhere was disrepair, the sense of loss, and no men or male offspring that Aidan could discern.

Their footfalls were the only sound that could be heard around them, besides the occasional spade slicing through earth. In this part of town, the children did not play, most did not cry, but sat on cracked doorsteps staring blankly into the distance.

When Aidan thought he could take no more of the silence, he felt a human Pull approaching from behind. He froze and began to turn.

"Sir," said a low, raspy voice. "Sir?"

Aidan looked over his shoulder and spied an elderly woman with sagging jowls and leathery skin looking up at him with rheumy eyes. "What happened here?" he asked.

But the woman hushed him. "Not out here. She has her spies."

"Meraude?" Slaíne asked, excitement leeching into her voice.

The crone glared at her but motioned them both back toward the smallest shack Aidan had yet seen in this godforsaken town. "In here. Hurry." She ushered them inside the house – if one could call this shed a house – where they sat knee to knee and nose to nose as the woman tugged on a rope and pulled the door closed.

His nose wrinkled up of its own volition. The tiny room stank not just of human waste and sweat. Desperation radiated off of the woman in nauseating waves, and Aidan at once took to breathing in and out through his mouth.

"You have to be careful," said the woman, folding her hands. "Men are few and far between here. We're supposed to report any appearances to the Lady."

Aidan's eyes adjusted better to the darkness, and he saw that the woman was smiling. "This lady being Meraude, am I correct?"

The woman's smile fell and she spat, accidentally spraying her two visitors in the face. "I make no apology. That name here is lower than dirt."

"What happened to all the men?" asked Slaíne, drawing the woman's gaze. "Why are ya to report them to Mer— the Lady?"

"Men to her ladyship serve two purposes," said the woman. "Experimenting and…well, no delicate way to say this, but her breeders need men." Her wrinkled cheeks flushed like an apricot, and she would not look at Aidan.

"Breeders? What need have she of breeders?"

The woman sighed a long-suffering sigh. "To grow her army of Blest." She looked at each of them then lowered her voice further. "The men are all killed once they've served their purposes."

Slaíne blanched.

"The female Blest are raised by their mothers until they are Jolted into their powers, and then they are usually conscripted into her army."

Aidan's gaze sought out Slaíne's. "This sounds an awful lot like the Circle."

"There is hardly any difference," said the crone. "Only this one is run by magical folk for magical folks' supposed benefit."

"You know of the Circle?" he asked her.

The old woman cringed. "Sir, in these parts, everyone knows of the horrible things done by those men." She raised a gnarled hand in front of her, making a sign as if to ward off evil.

Slaíne was shaking her head. "I thought Meraude hated the Circle. Why's she copying it?"

"Power," said the old woman simply. "It corrupts anyone it touches."

Aidan avoided looking Slaíne's way at those words. He cleared his throat and said, "How far are we from Meraude? Do you have any maps we might use?"

"No maps to speak of. But you're not far from Inohaim Wood. It starts just west of town." The woman pointed over Aidan's shoulder. "You need to head farther north, but it's only about half a day's journey to reach Inohaim Tower from here, and Meraude's palace is about ten miles west of there." Her cloudy eyes narrowed. "You plan on walking straight into her waiting arms, do you?" She shook her head in apparent disbelief. "There will be no leaving there alive."

"Thank you for your discretion," said Aidan, meaning to crawl toward the door. His legs were cramping terribly in that confined space, and they needed to be on their way. The old woman had mentioned spies. The longer they remained here, the better the chances were that word of their presence would reach Meraude's ears, and they wanted her nowhere near Inohaim Tower when they attempted to destroy what Goblets Immortal they had.

The old woman put out a hand to stop him. "Let me make certain the way is clear first." Though it obviously pained her to do so, she crawled toward the entrance and pushed the door open.

Aidan was aware of the many human Pulls nearby, but didn't sense anything suspicious as he watched the old woman straighten up as much as she was able and limp toward the road. "We should reach our destination before nightfall. This is it, Slaíne."

She said nothing in response, but her eyes flashed as nerves and excitement pulsed between the two of them.

They started to crawl out of the hovel, but Aidan came to a halt and held up a hand for Slaíne to stop as well. There were raised voices in the streets. *Back up*, he thought at her. Through the crack in the door, Aidan could see the woman standing by the side of the road talking to two women in chain mail. *We've been had*.

Behind him, Slaíne laughed lightly. "Fight or flee?"

"We can't Dismiss ourselves or we'll leave the Goblets behind," he said ruefully. "Is there any magic you know that could cause a distraction while we run away?"

"The best distraction there is – fire." Before he could stop her, Slaíne threw a hand through the crack in the door, and a pulse of blue light flew out of her fingertips with a bang.

People began shouting and moving toward the building across the street, which had ignited, along with the two houses next door. "Put it out!" cried an elderly voice.

"Now's our chance." Aidan and Slaine crawled out of the hovel on their hands and knees. No one was paying them any mind, so they took off into the woods, leaving the people to put out the magical blaze themselves.

CHAPTER TWENTY-THREE

Aidan

After half an hour of running through the woods north of the town, they slowed their pace. Aidan Summoned a water bladder and passed it to Slaíne. "We're getting close."

She grunted in response and took a few large pulls from the vessel and passed it back. "Are we bein' followed? I nay can tell how close the Pulls are."

Aidan drained the bladder and Dismissed it. They would need to refill all their bladders the first chance they got. "No, I don't think we're being followed." He wiped his brow with the back of his hand. "There are some Pulls traveling parallel to us, but they are no closer than when we started out."

That seemed to alarm Slaíne, who looked at him wide-eyed. "Could they be from the village?"

"I don't know. We should keep moving, just to be safe."

Slaíne soared over some undergrowth that was hard to walk through and motioned for Aidan to do the same. She laughed when he hesitated. "Ya gotta learn some time, Aidan."

Aidan made a face. "This is no time to be messing about with powers I don't understand," he reasoned. "What if I went up and was unable to come back down?" The thought filled him with dread.

Again Slaíne laughed. "Ya mean like when you drank of the Drifting Goblet?" She pointed to the sack on his back, which contained the three Goblets Immortal.

He became aware of a small, nonliving Pull rushing toward him and Slaíne at eye level. At the last minute he managed to Dismiss what he discerned to be an arrow.

They looked at each other. "There ain't no one for miles, I thought."

Aidan nodded but held up a hand to keep Slaíne from making any sudden movements. Closing his eyes, he reached out and felt for other human Pulls. Like he had thought before, there was no one near enough to fire arrows at them, so he attempted to home in on smaller, nonliving Pulls. A few yards to the right and up ahead he sensed metal in a tree. With little effort, he Dismissed the object and Summoned it into his waiting hand. "I thought so." He weighed the arrow and examined it. It was rusted, as if it had spent many rainfalls in its hideaway. "This area is set with traps. We must be careful." He let the arrow drop to the ground. "See if you can sense anything metal."

"That ain't my specialty," said she, but closed her eyes anyway.

For the next ten minutes, they searched for and Dismissed many arrows and several traps set in the tall grasses. Aidan almost stepped in a rope snare, and if not for his abilities, would have found himself hanging high in the air from his ankle.

"I think that's the last of it," he said after some time. "We need to hurry if we want to reach Inohaim Tower before dark."

"An' we're just meant to place the Goblets in the Seeing Pool?" She threaded her left arm through his right as they tramped onward, still mindful of Pulls that could prove malevolent.

"That's what Salem said...or at least hinted at."

Slaíne swore. "We're gonna go on just his word, then?"

"Treevain alluded to the Seeing Pool as well," he reminded her, which earned him a dark look. "They want the Goblets destroyed as much as we do."

"We shoulda tried destroyin' them by other means first."

"The Romas tried melting the Warring Goblet down before giving it to me. There's protective magic there, Slaíne, something that will take a different sort of magic to destroy. We destroy them, and then we deal with Meraude."

They were silent for the next mile, each mindful of the handful of human Pulls they were approaching. Several times the two stopped to make certain there were no more traps or arrows before moving on again.

By the time they were within one mile of the nearest human Pulls, the sun was lower in the sky. They had maybe three hours of sunlight left, so they knew they must make the most of their time.

Aidan Summoned the silver sword and passed it to Slaíne, who swung it out experimentally. "There we are," he murmured, craning his neck back to get a better look at the tower that loomed over the trees in the distance.

"Do you think it's heavily guarded?" she asked.

As they hastened their steps, Aidan could swear the Goblets had begun pulsing with excitement or dread. Perhaps they knew their end was near. "I don't know. Meraude used the Seeing Pool to contact me in my dreams."

"Either she's a Sightful or has got a conduit."

Aidan raised an eyebrow at that. "What makes you say that?"

She gave him an incredulous look and said, "How else would she contact you in yer dreams?"

"Fair point." He held up his hand to stop her. There were Pulls moving about in the wood to their left, not a mile off. Slaíne and he would have to be quiet and quick if they wished to avoid detection.

After a short walk uphill, they reached the edge of Inohaim Wood, which opened into a clearing. In the center sat Inohaim Tower.

The fortification itself was like Aidan remembered from his dreams: tall, round, and made of what appeared to be one continuous slab of white marble. Seeing no one in the clearing, and knowing they would have to run at full speed, Aidan Dismissed his sword and knew Slaíne was doing likewise.

"Be mindful of small, fast Pulls once we're in the open," he said below his breath. "I'll Dismiss any arrows, should they fire upon us."

"I'll do my best ter help," Slaíne said, though she didn't sound very confident.

With one last look and feel for human Pulls around them, the pair ran out from their tree cover and hurried toward the tower.

Aidan felt human Pulls moving in from the sides, closing in behind him. They were armed, he sensed. An arrow came speeding toward them, and Aidan made quick work of Dismissing it.

Slaíne tripped, nearly taking him down with her, but they managed to right themselves as more arrows came flying their way. Again they Dismissed the missiles, and Aidan became aware that the archers were remaining where they were. No one was chasing them.

Is there anyone in the tower? Slaíne thought at him as they reached its base.

No, I can't sense any human Pulls within.

"Where is the blasted entrance?" she asked.

Another arrow came at them and another. Aidan Dismissed both. "Maybe it's on the other side." He held up a hand and Repelled three arrows coming at them. "Come on." The base of the tower was not extremely wide, so it did not take them very long to run around it. Thankfully, the archers made no attempt to approach them, but continued to fire intermittently. "The entrance must be hidden."

"Can ya sense it?"

A volley of arrows flew at them, and Aidan ground his teeth as he tried to Dismiss and Repel them all. A few of the arrows flew wide, while two escaped Aidan and managed to fly between him and Slaíne. Instead of bouncing off the tower's base, he noted, the arrows seemed to have disappeared. "I wonder...."

"We can't keep this up much longer. What should we do?"

"Can you Dismiss and Repel while I try something?"

Slaíne gave him an incredulous look. "I nay can do that. I've told ya I ain't hardly able."

"Then can you cause a distraction? Or use your other magic to give us some time?"

The archers had reloaded and let more of their arrows fly. Aidan Dismissed what was in their path, and then looked at Slaíne pleadingly. At last she nodded, and Aidan moved closer to the tower base.

There was a flash of blue light, followed by many screams as Slaíne's magical fire formed a wall between the pair and the archers. "That good enough?"

Aidan grunted his assent and closed his eyes. He reached out both with his mind and his hand, which he placed on the cold marble. It was difficult getting a good sense of the tower, as though some magic were blocking his abilities. He dragged his hand across the surface and then nearly stumbled through the invisible door he had found. "Got it."

Slaíne joined him and peered at the structure. "Here?"

An arrow flew through the blue flames and Aidan Dismissed it just in time. "Come on."

It was a strange sensation, walking through the invisible door. As they did, Aidan felt the human Pulls advance from the other side of the tower. More arrows came flying, and Aidan Dismissed them. He turned and made it another step when he experienced a burning feeling in his chest, and he lost all sense of the Pulls, human and nonhuman, surrounding them.

There was no chance to figure out why his abilities had been arrested, for more arrows soared toward them. "Hurry. Up the stairs. We need to get out of range."

"My powers," Slaíne cried as Aidan pulled her to the stairs, which they took two at a time.

"I know. Mine too."

It wasn't just his Summoning abilities. Everything else he had gained from Slaíne seemed to have retreated deep inside of him. "I think this is a trap."

"Ya think?" she snarled. "But what are we ter do about it?"

They slowed their frantic pace. At least no one was pursuing them, from what Aidan could hear or see as he craned his neck to look back around. "The Seeing Pool is a divot in the top floor of the tower." He paused and clutched a pang in his side, and Slaíne joined him. "I've been there before, in my dreams."

With a great huff, Slaíne blew a strand of hair out of her face and swiped at her brow. "Too bad we nay Summoned our swords."

A grim look was exchanged, and they moved on.

The narrow stairs wound their way up in a dizzying spiral. Nothing was to their right, and to their left was the slippery marble wall.

Several times Aidan tried but failed to feel the Pulls around him. It was disorienting without them, and once he stumbled and almost dropped the sack of Goblets from his back. "Well, that would have been a catastrophe."

Slaíne groaned. "We'll nay be in any shape ter fight, should we ever reach the top of this ruddy thing." She put out her hand, offering to take the Goblets from him for a time, but Aidan refused.

"No, I want to be the one to destroy them."

They straightened their backs, stretched, and then recommenced their climbing.

"Why must it be you?" she asked. "I could manage just as well as you could."

Aidan growled. "If I let you kill Meraude when we find her, will that appease you?"

She laughed. "*Let* me? Try an' *stop* me, is more like."

That made Aidan chuckle. "Indeed."

For the rest of the climb, they remained silent, pausing every now and again to catch their breath and rest. It might have been an hour-long climb, though Aidan doubted it. Having lost their abilities might have made the trek even longer and more arduous than it would have been otherwise.

Aidan hoisted the sack from off of his shoulder and switched it to his other hand. He noticed Slaíne was running a hand over her arms, apparently smoothing out gooseflesh. For a moment he paused, frowning.

"What?"

"Maybe you should do the destroying part, and I'll fend off any attacks."

Slaíne growled at him. "Right. Like I'm gonna let that happen. You destroy, I'll fend." Before Aidan could stop her, she moved past him.

They had reached the top of the tower, and where should have been a door leading into the top, there was a platform and a solid wall. Slaíne did not wait for him, but put out her hands and slipped through this invisible doorway, and Aidan quickly followed behind her.

Like in his dreams, Inohaim Tower's uppermost part opened up into a round, brilliant white room. There was the red floor runner running around and past the Seeing Pool in the middle of the floor, and at the other end of the roofless room sat a throne made of glass.

Meraude stood there, motionless, watching them. She was much like Aidan remembered from his dreams, though now there were white streaks running through her midnight-black hair. As they approached, Aidan became aware of several large women moving in on them from the sides, but instead of hindering their progress, the guards took to blocking the doorway behind them.

Beside him Slaíne stiffened, and her hiss filled the silence. "See her, lookin' so high an' mighty. I want to rip her throat out for all she's done."

"Easy," Aidan warned. "We don't have our powers right now. And we're outnumbered."

The mage queen's laugh flooded the room suddenly, and Aidan resisted the urge to cover his ears. He needed to get to the Seeing Pool, but a woman stood on either side of it, as if expecting him to try something.

"Long have I waited," said Meraude, her hushed voice full of reverence. "Tell me you have them all."

Aidan and Slaíne exchanged a look as he tried to communicate his thoughts to her. She might have been doing the same. Between the two of them, there was a dull buzzing sound, as though a bee were flying in and out of his ears.

"Walk straight toward the Pool," he whispered, trying to move his lips as little as possible.

"What?" Slaíne asked.

He shook his head, and took her by the hand, tugging her forward with him. "We don't have them all," Aidan said, which was the truth. Daring to glance left and right, he noted the mage queen's guards making subtle movements toward them. When he looked at them outright, the women stopped. Knowing he had a part to play, Aidan kept his eyes off of the Seeing Pool, hoping beyond hope that the guard's on either side of it would move. "Tell me how to bring my family back, and you can have your Goblets." That had been why Meraude had sent for him months ago, to find the Goblets Immortal, promising his parents and his brother, Sam, in exchange. His words sounded convincing enough to his own ears; he knew his family was dead.

To his surprise, the mage queen shook her head. "I'm afraid it doesn't work that way, Aidan Ingledark. You see, I know you're aware of their demise."

A shock went through his body at the words. "So, you *did* kill them."

The woman nodded. "Yes. I understand you found their bodies in a very unusual place," said she. Her hands smoothed out her dress and she prepared to take the throne, but paused. "It is my understanding that a certain Summoner left them there for you to find, to turn you against me. Mai Larkin always was a plotting fiend."

Aidan schooled his expression to remain neutral. "The seer—"

"Larkin was using you, yes. She had long hated me. When I killed your parents and your brother, she must have foreseen these events that are unfolding this very day, Dismissing the bodies to save them in order to Summon them and bait you decades later." Meraude raised a hand, and the guards around her stood at attention. "You need not come any closer, Ingledark. My ladies will take the Goblets from here."

The mage queen's guards moved away from the Seeing Pool, but the rest were quickly closing in on Aidan and Sláine. "This is it."

Sláine gave his hand a squeeze and let it go. "Meraude, you have much to answer for. I've long waited for this day as well."

Aidan broke away from his mate and ran for the divot in the floor, dodging the two guards coming for him. He made it several strides, before someone jumped him and hung around his neck. Aidan held the sack close to his body with one arm, and with the other he tried to pry his assailant's fingers away from his throat as he staggered forward.

From behind him, he heard Sláine putting up a fight. Without her abilities, he knew she wouldn't last long. Neither would he. If only he could make it two more large steps, then he could place the Goblets in the Seeing Pool, and it all would be over.

With a grunt, he flipped the woman off his back, but two more were coming for him. The first one, a tall girl, tripped the other, a smaller girl with closely cropped hair. Aidan tried moving around them as they fought and clawed at each other, attempting to be the first to get to him. Someone tackled him from the side, knocking him to the ground.

Aidan kicked his attacker in the stomach, effectively pushing her off of him. He rose, but the smaller girl with dark hair came at him, lashing out with a knife. Jumping back, he only just avoided being sliced.

There was a cry behind him, and he chanced a glance. Slaíne was being held by four women; a fifth was coming at her with a knife. Aidan's stomach lurched. "No, wait!"

Meraude held up a hand. "Bring me the Goblets, or she dies. It's that simple."

Aidan looked at the sack, which sat on the edge of the Seeing Pool. Just inches more, and his job would be done. But what would happen after? He nodded, hands raised, and moved toward the sack. *Meraude doesn't seem to know I could destroy the Goblets right here and now.*

The mage queen gave him a warning look. "No tricks, Ingledark. Egreet, Ing, step back."

He reached down and picked up the sack of Goblets, weighing them in his hands.

Go to the Seeing Pool. End this. It was Salem's voice he heard, and it was louder and clearer than it had ever been before.

Aidan stepped forward, and set the Goblets down in the Pool. Nothing happened.

"Bring them here, Ingledark."

Behind him Slaíne yelped.

"All right. It's heavy. Just give me a moment." *Why didn't it work?* Panic roiled in Aidan's stomach, and he reached down, his fingers inches from the Goblets.

The mage queen frowned and took the glass throne.

It felt as though a hand had grabbed Aidan from the inside of his chest and held his heart in its cruel grip. He wanted to run, to take the Goblets and find another way to destroy them. But he couldn't.

Pick them up and bring them to my servant, said Meraude's voice inside his mind.

Aidan spied the two remaining Goblets resting in the hands of a servant. She stepped forward, her eyes vacant. Unable to resist, Aidan lifted the sack and brought it toward Meraude. The Seeing Pool was in the way, and he could have gone around it, but he was no longer in control of his movements and stepped right into the middle of it. That is when the ground began to shake.

A great wind rose and swirled around the room, picking up the Goblets Immortal and lifting Aidan off his feet. There was a ripping sound, and the wound in his shoulder burned as the world faded and then disappeared around him. Weightless, Aidan floated in darkness. He could not move any part of himself, though he tried. *Is this Nothingness?* Again he attempted to struggle, and again he failed.

There were innumerable Pulls in the near distance racing toward him at an alarming speed. With a great flash of blinding light, the Pulls rushed past him, driving him forward and downward to what appeared to his family's estate, which had just sprung to life before his eyes. It was then, landing in a heap on the ground with the Goblets, Aidan realized he now found himself bodily in the Beyond.

"Hello?" he called out. His voice echoed and nothing stirred. Aidan picked himself up from the ground and took in his surroundings. "Is anyone here?" All his abilities as a wizard and a Blest had fully returned to him, and he crackled with pure power. He reached out and felt for human Pulls. There was but one and it was a ways away. The Pull was familiar, but it had changed somehow – or, rather, Aidan knew *himself* to have changed, being fully there in the Beyond.

"Am I dead?" he called out again, stretching out his hands before him. In truth, he had never felt so fully alive.

Behind him the Goblets pulsed. *Free us*, said five voices as one.

Aidan dumped the Summoning Goblet, the Drifting Goblet, and the Warring Goblet onto the ground. The other two, Enduring and Seeing, rolled toward them, as if moved by an invisible hand.

End our torment.

He shook himself. Salem's Pull was drawing nearer. Should he wait for the Endurer or get to work? Then he thought of Existence and knew time was moving forward without him. "All right."

First Aidan Summoned the silver sword from his cache in Nothingness, hesitating a moment as he was uncertain of how this would work – *if* this would work. He struck the Drifting Goblet, and a tremor ran up his arm. *Thank you, brother,* an ancient voice breathed as thunder roared overhead. The Drifting Goblet melted into a puddle, powerless. Trembling, Aidan turned to the next Goblet.

He ran the Seeing Goblet through, and, like the one before it, it sighed and murmured its thanks. The vessel disintegrated into a pile of ash, which was carried away on the wind, and in his mind's eye, Aidan beheld a brief vision of Meraude screaming in defeat.

The Warring Goblet rolled up against his boot, as if to say, *"I'm next."*

Aidan's whole body shook with fatigue as he ran the Goblet through. Again he was thanked. This vessel burst into green flames, which burned brightly as Aidan caught sight again of Existence, where a great army had gathered.

"Aidan, stay your hand!" Salem cried as he emerged from the mists. "Do not destroy the Summoning or the Enduring Goblets – not yet, at least."

With a shudder, Aidan allowed the silver sword to drop to the ground. "There you are. Where have you been?"

Of all things, the Endurer ran to him and threw his arms around Aidan. "You did it – you're finally here. Well, here in person and not just in spirit." He let out a boyish cry of delight.

Confused, Aidan patted him distractedly on the back. "Uh, yes. I am here. But what— Are you all right?"

It was discomforting to see the grown man crying. "I have waited so long to see you again, Aidan. I've sorely missed you."

"It's been a few weeks, I know, but certainly not a length of time worth mourning over." Was he missing something? He must be, for the other laughed and then began to cry again. "I think Slaíne's magic was blocking you out. I'm sorry for that."

Salem shook his head and pulled back to look Aidan directly in the eyes. "Never mind that. Haven't you ever wondered why I look so familiar?"

Aidan frowned. "Well, yes, but I've met many people on my travels, Salem."

"My name isn't Salem, Aidan," said the man, grinning knowingly. "I think you know who I really am, or at least can guess at it now."

The Pull was certainly more familiar, now that they both were in the Beyond physically. But, no, it was surely too good to be true. He looked the man up and down, a slow, incredulous smile taking over his face. "Sam?"

His brother clapped him on the back and let out a loud whooping noise. "Yes. Finally. I didn't tell you earlier because I thought it might make you want to come here too much, and we needed you in Existence."

"So that is how you knew all of those things about me. I should have known it was you."

Sam beamed. "And that's how I could reach you from the Beyond so easily, because you're my brother, and that blood-bond is strong. Strong enough to penetrate iron, that is for certain."

Aidan laughed, his heart lighter than it had been in a long time. "Would you care to do the honors?" He tipped the silver sword toward Sam, and nodded toward their two Goblets. "It's just Enduring and Summoning left."

His brother accepted the sword from Aidan and weighed it in his hand. "You do realize this blade belonged to the originator of the Drifting Goblet, don't you? It's the opposite of Melnine's blade." He swung it back and forth a few times, and Aidan was surprised to see how good he was with the blade. "Melnine being the originator of the Drifting Goblet, of course." He laughed. "How did you come upon it?"

"It came with Sláine," Aidan admitted. Pieces of information he had gleaned began to come together in his mind. "Melnine was her father, it would seem. Why are you cringing?"

"This blade is my opposite," said Sam. "It hurts a bit to touch."

Aidan thought he would hand the blade back over, but instead his brother tossed it onto the grass behind him. "Once the remaining Goblets are destroyed, we need to find a way to return to Existence. If that is even possible."

Sam shook his head sadly. "I do not wish to return, Aidan," said he, turning away from Aidan. "And I wish you wouldn't either."

"You're joking, right?" Aidan laughed once, a hollow sound to his own ears. When his brother did not turn, Aidan crossed his arms over his chest and shook his head. "Can't you come with me?"

"Oh, it's not that I *can't*. You are Death's Key, after all, and have made a passageway for the magical dead to reenter Existence. But why should I leave? And why should we destroy our Goblets, when they are such an easy and ready source of power?"

Aidan blinked back surprise. "We need to destroy all the Goblets, Sam, or Meraude—"

Sam cursed. "Forget about her. We have the remaining Goblets, few though they are. The legends say that whoever possesses all the Goblets has complete control of all life. We have all the Goblets that exist, therefore we can control the Beyond and the mortal realm. Don't you see, Aidan? The throne is just *one* means of control. The Beyond is a whole *realm* of possibilities." He turned, a maniacal glint in his dark eyes.

"This is madness. Brother, you must see that—"

"I mustn't see anything," said Sam. "You will still have abilities, should the Summoning Goblet be destroyed. Slaíne gave you quite a bit of her power, after all. But I – I will have nothing. My ability, such as it is, will be snuffed out like that." He snapped his fingers, and the sound echoed around them. Sam gave him a sad smile. "So, you see, if you want this sword, you're going to have to hurt me. And I know you would not hurt your only remaining relation."

As Aidan watched, Sam lifted the silver sword and bent it into a knot, the pointed end biting into the inside of a circle.

"Meraude has plenty of Endurers, I am sure. She had the Seeing and Enduring Goblets for goodness knows how long. She was breeding an army."

Sam shrugged and plucked the Enduring Goblet from off the ground. "If you must return to Existence, you must. I wish you would stay."

"So you will rule over all of the Endurers from here in the Beyond?"

He gave Aidan a smug look. "Not just Endurers."

Aidan sighed. Had he come this far to help one dictator fall so another might rise? *He's your brother. You thought he was gone for good, and now you're reunited.* He should feel happiness, joy beyond compare. Didn't he, Aidan, deserve it after all he'd been through? What harm would there be in leaving at least the Enduring Goblet? But the look in his brother's eye made Aidan cringe. Hardening his heart, he murmured, "I now know my curse."

Unmoved apparently, Sam shook his head. "And what is that?"

"It is to lose everything and everyone I love." And with that he shot a bolt of green fire at the Enduring Goblet.

Sam screamed and dropped the vessel to the ground, his hands smoking. "Aidan, what are you doing?"

But Aidan ignored him. He Summoned the bronze sword and plunged it into the Enduring Goblet. Aidan staggered backward as the very ground trembled. A crack formed in the ground beneath the vessel, and it, along with Sam, vanished before his eyes. "Sam!" Aidan cried, rushing forward, thinking his brother had fallen into the fissure. But it was only several feet deep, and Sam was nowhere to be found.

Now beyond weary, Aidan looked at the last vessel, the Summoning Goblet. Using his abilities, which seemed fitting, he concentrated on the sword and drove it through the metal cup with his mind.

Thank you, Aidan Ingledark. Your sacrifice shall mold the ages to come.... The voice continued to echo as Aidan sank the rest of the way to the ground, where he fell asleep.

CHAPTER TWENTY-FOUR

Jinn

Dying had been peaceful. It was difficult leaving Quick behind in Existence, but she had had little choice in letting go of life and joining the other magical dead in the Beyond. There was no night, no sleep here, as a dead person doesn't have need for rest and repose.

It had been only a few days since her demise, if her guess was correct. People avoided her for the most part, but she had heard and seen the army preparing…for what, she hadn't known until the portal opened in front of her.

One moment, there was a stillness, and the next the barrier between the lands of the living and the dead ripped apart.

Jinn stood in confusion, wondering what this meant. Before she could react, a great cry rose up from around her, and the army of magical dead charged at the great, glowing tear the size of five of the mountains back home. Not wishing to be trampled, Jinn ran with them.

The sensation of passing through the barrier was that of having woken from a long sleep: she was stiff and disoriented, but that only lasted for so long. She blinked rapidly and tried to make sense of what she was seeing before her.

The tear had opened around Inohaim Tower – a place she had only seen in visions – and where the magical dead appeared, there already stood a great army. The army was made up of women, their heads shaven.

Jinn kept running, dodging hands that would grab her and swords that would strike her down. She ran until she was huffing and puffing, and her bare feet were torn from the rough terrain. Around her, chaos reigned.

Meraude's army of Blest seemed unsurprised by the hags and elves and other Blest appearing out of nowhere and attacking. *She has the Seeing Goblet; she has Sightfuls in her ranks,* Jinn reminded herself as she tripped over a tree root. She needed to get as far away from here as possible.

Beneath her feet, the earth trembled. Unnatural yellow light flashed through the ranks of Meraude's soldiers, striking whoever got in the way.

Jinn could scarce draw breath.

At last she could run no more but collapsed by a great oak tree, panting. She had made it to the woods encircling the tower at least. Here the fighting wasn't so bad, though she knew better than to grow complacent.

Again the earth trembled, and Inohaim Tower shook considerably. That's when Jinn noticed a circle of people had formed around its base. Blast after blast of colorful magical light was being thrown at it, and Jinn realized they were trying to bring the structure down.

Metal clashed on metal. Jinn closed her eyes and stoppered her ears as she tried to look ahead, but before she could, she felt a large hand on her shoulder. With a shriek, she jumped to her feet.

"Jinn's alive!" said a familiar voice as she was swept up into enormous arms.

The air left her lungs in a great whoosh, and she swore her ribs would crack. "Quick?" she gasped. "How did you…? Where did you…?"

Red lightning flashed in the near distance as Quick laughed.

"Quick foresaw," he said proudly, setting her down. "Wizard helped. But Jinn is alive and—" He got no further before a ringing noise filled Jinn's ears. Quick stumbled and sank to his knees.

"Are you all right?" she asked, feeling suddenly weak.

Quick nodded. "No more Goblets. Quick and Jinn must keep moving, though. Tower will fall."

CHAPTER TWENTY-FIVE

Aidan

In his sleep, Aidan was vaguely aware of a battle, of the earth moving beneath the Seeing Pool in Existence. He knew he had to return, but he was so very tired. With a grunt Aidan shook himself awake and looked around. Sam was gone, whether to Existence or just out of the Beyond, he was uncertain.

Aidan reached out to feel for Pulls around him, but his Summoning abilities had fled. There no longer was the extra sense of what surrounded him and what he might do with it all. *That ability was destroyed with the Summoning Goblet*, he thought with a groan. He could not Dismiss himself into Nothingness from here, and then perhaps emerge back into Existence from there. *I've stranded myself.*

He staggered to his feet and looked around for something, anything that might give him a clue as to what he should do. But there was no one in sight. Perhaps there were books in the house that would tell him how to fix matters.

Aidan started to limp his way toward the grand house, only to collapse in exhaustion after making it five steps. He rolled over onto his back, defeated and despairing. *Good work, Aidan.*

Slaíne's soul-half writhed within his breast, and Aidan tried latching on to that, but the quality of their connection was different here. *I'm trapped*, he tried thinking at her. No response came.

The war, he knew in his soul, was raging between mortals and magic-kind in the land of the living. And he was helpless to stop it. "Death's Key," he murmured, repeating his unwanted title a few more times before sitting up with a start. Aidan looked at his shoulder where he had been stabbed by the nymph queen's blade, Nitchoo. With what strength he had left, Aidan ripped away part of his shirt and noticed that the patch of skin there had turned bronze and was glowing. Hopeful, he pressed on the months-old wound, which throbbed painfully.

One moment he was sitting in the Beyond, the next he found himself in Existence falling through the air. He landed back inside the Seeing Pool with a grunt.

It took his mind a moment to understand what he saw. The open throne room was empty, but for the bodies everywhere – none with flaming-red hair, Aidan was relieved to find – and Meraude on the throne. Her hair had gone pure white and had lost all its luster and beauty. Likewise, her face had shriveled, and she stared at him with haunted, hate-filled eyes.

"You stole my victory," said she through gritted teeth.

Without any of his new abilities, Aidan backed away as the madwoman rose from the glass throne and drew a thin, cruel knife from the sheath at her side. The tower shook beneath them both. Cries rose to them from the ground, as did the sounds of battle, and Aidan knew he must get to the stairs before she could run him through.

Aidan was still weakened from destroying the Goblets, so he had barely made it several paces backward when Meraude took a running leap and cleared the Seeing Pool altogether.

The mage queen landed, slashing out and nearly catching Aidan across the face. She would have struck him, had he not tripped and fallen over one of the bodies.

Aidan rolled out of the way as she came at him, and managed to kick her legs out from underneath her. This gave him enough time to get to his feet and limp toward the door. But something came whistling toward him, and Aidan let out a cry of pain as Meraude's blade took him in the back of his right shoulder. He fell toward the wall, but there was no real marble there to stop him, just the invisible doorway. Breathing hard, Aidan stared dazedly over the edge of the platform, which led to a several-hundred-foot drop.

He had only a moment's respite. Before he could regain his wits, Meraude was kneeling on his back, pushing the blade farther in and twisting it.

"Fool," she snarled. "Your mate couldn't kill me. And now you've failed as well."

Again the ground shook beneath them, nearly driving Aidan off the edge. Tears of pain blinded his eyes as he felt around for something, anything, he might use to defend himself with.

"A man started this. Now a woman will finish it."

Aidan screamed as Meraude pulled the blade from his shoulder and raised it and then drove it through his back, piercing him in the heart. The world went white as Aidan died, and the last thing he heard before he vanished was Meraude's horrible laughter.

★   ★   ★

As with any magical being that died, Aidan found himself in the Beyond. The wounds Meraude had inflicted had completely healed, and power once again rippled through Aidan's body.

He reached down and this time picked up the bronze sword, which he had left behind last time. Then he prepared himself before pressing the months-old wound on his shoulder. The Beyond faded, and Aidan found himself returned to the Seeing Pool. Again his powers had been arrested, but Aidan was no longer weak and weaponless.

An earth-splitting crack filled the evening air as Aidan moved toward the hidden entryway. He stumbled as the ground trembled, but righted himself quickly. He needed to get out of there before the whole tower collapsed.

But Meraude chose that moment to return to the throne room, her face white with shock. "How did you…?"

Aidan raised his blade and brought it down at her, but she managed to block the blow with the knife. With one hand he continued to press the bronze blade down on her, and with the other he managed to rip the knife out of the mage queen's hand.

With a pitiful cry, Meraude fell to the ground, the edge of Aidan's sword at her throat. She threw up her hands to shield herself.

Cries filled the air, and the tower shook mightily.

Slaíne had not materialized to share the victory with him, though her pulsing soul-half beat a powerful rhythm in Aidan's breast. *At least she's alive.*

"Spare me!" said Meraude. "I can make you rich beyond your wildest dreams. And powerful. If only you would spare me."

Here sat the woman, the murderer who had killed both of his parents...and Sam. Aidan swallowed, hard. This was his chance for revenge.

The mage queen licked her papery lips. "Please."

"Where is Slaíne?" he demanded.

"The she-wizard?" Meraude's eyes were rolling around in her head, so fast was she looking around her at the crumbling walls. "We haven't much time. You must help me out of here."

Aidan knew they hadn't enough time to get to the bottom of the tower before it collapsed. Even now, a crack formed in the floor and raced toward them. Something stirred inside of Aidan. As the tower shook one last time and turned into rubble beneath their feet, his new powers returned to him in full.

With a great cry, the so-called mage queen attempted to throw Aidan from her person. She spat and kicked and clawed at him, and much to his surprise, Aidan felt pity well up within himself. Perhaps he would have spared her, but the choice was not his. Meraude screamed her last as the fissure swallowed her. Though Aidan instinctively reached out to grab her, she slipped out of his grasp and disappeared.

It was his turn to free-fall. But as he raced toward the ground, Aidan realized something: where once things had been heavy, weighing on him from the power of Pulls surrounding, now all was light and airy. At a mere thought, Aidan soared into the air. Confident that he wasn't going to plummet to his death, he raised himself and slowly, if not gracefully, lowered himself to the ground.

All had grown silent. Aidan looked around him, his stomach churning at the sight of so many bodies. Most of them had shaved heads. All were women, from what he could tell.

A fog had formed in the chill air, and as Aidan moved onward, he had to pick his way around the dead. He could make out little in front of him, stumbling every now and then. Then, tired of continuing thus, Aidan floated toward whence came loud voices raised in glee, landing on the outskirts of a vast celebration.

Fires burned bright and merry where the mists had lifted. Nymphs danced around and through the open flames, shrieking and laughing raucously as hags warmed themselves around the next blaze over.

The nymphs stopped what they were doing when they saw Aidan and he tensed. He did not want a fight and did not have the strength for it. But the strange creatures merely nodded at him and then returned to their celebrating.

As for the hags, they cackled and sang in a strange tongue as meat roasted over their fire. Upon seeing Aidan, they made a sign as if to ward off evil, then quieted and were sober. Among them was Sam, now entirely mortal, and he gave Aidan such a hate-filled look that Aidan did not bother going over to explain himself.

The next six gatherings revealed faces of elves – none that Aidan had ever seen – and humans, ones that might have been Blest before. The elves nodded and began whispering among themselves, while the humans looked away.

Scanning for familiar faces, Aidan found none, and he no longer had the sense of anyone's Pull to guide him. As one lost, he wandered, noting that all the strange creatures he encountered were afraid. There were more nymphs, attracted to the fires; many more humans; several large, hairy creatures with one eye in the center of their foreheads; more elves and— Aidan paused. He recognized one of them.

Apparently the wretched creature had spied him as well. She rose from her position between two hags and approached Aidan slowly from around her campfire. "Thou hast accomplished no small feat," said the shifty-eyed elf, Treevain. "I should congratulate meself, an' I does. I does."

"What happened?"

"Opened the Beyond, ya did." She belched, and the air around her was perfumed with the stench of decay. "Freed us, as like. I see ya've managed ter get out yourn self, after ya destroyed the Goblets. Not as stupid as one might've thought." Here she laughed, a terrible sound that raised the hairs on Aidan's arms.

"I meant what happened *here*? I saw many bodies."

The she-elf shrugged, though her expression was far from casual. She looked rather smug. "Cleaned up after Meraude, we did. She's created a bunch o' Blest."

Aidan growled, and the creature took a step backward. "They were women, girls mostly, from what I saw. They were powerless once the Goblets had been destroyed."

Those in the near vicinity, Aidan noticed, were murmuring as they eyed him, before slinking away to join other parties of creatures. Treevain looked as though she wished to follow them.

"Calm yerself, Ingledark," said she. "Had to be done. They was wit' Meraude, see? She would have trained 'em to hate all magic-kind that's not Blest. Plus, not to mention the humans."

Aidan snarled at her, and the elf went still.

"Meant no harm, sir. But we can nay have the likes of them about. They'd poison us, so ter speak. Your mate, she did nay agree, but—"

Power crackled in Aidan's veins. Fury propelled him toward the elf, and he lifted the creature by her collar. "Where is Slaíne?"

Treevain clawed at her throat and made pitiable noises until Aidan let her drop. "I knows not. I knows not. Ask the other wizard. Him's what last spoke to her."

"*Last* spoke to her?"

But the wretch was crawling away. "Please, I mean no harm. I know nuffink."

Smelling the truth and desperation rolling off of the stinking creature, Aidan nodded and moved on. As he went, humans and creatures alike scuttled away and kept a great distance from him. There had to be thousands of them. Aidan would never find Slaíne in this mess.

Despair came easily, until he felt a hand on his shoulder. Aidan turned, ready to attack, but found himself staring at Hex, of all people. At first, Aidan was inclined to flee, but the wizard held up his hands.

"Peace, friend."

So *this* was the other wizard Treevain spoke of. "Do you know where Slaíne is?"

The wizard's expression was unreadable, as were his emotions. Hex motioned for Aidan to follow him to a red blaze, where sat two familiar figures. "Everything turned out better than we could have hoped for, Ingledark." He passed over a canteen from Jinn, and Aidan drank greedily.

When he came up to take a breath, Aidan observed, "I thought Jinn had— Oh, she did die, then?"

A shadow passed over Hex's face, and Quick groaned from his spot next to his sister. But Jinn laughed. "Yes. I was in the Beyond when you opened the portal, and I fled back to Existence with the rest of the magical dead."

"Sister not talk about death. No more death."

Aidan did not miss the look that passed between the wizard and the Sightful, though the giant seemed oblivious to it. There was something there, he mused, that he hadn't noticed before. But the thought only aggravated him. Where was Slaíne?

"It seems there was plenty of death today." Aidan's eyes slid back over to Hex. "Tell me she isn't gone."

Hex sighed. "Dead, no. Can't you tell from her soul-half? But, yes, she is gone."

Aidan frowned and repeated the word, trying to make sense of it in his head. "Gone? Where did she go?"

"She left you this," Hex said, conjuring a square of paper out of thin air. He would not quite meet Aidan's eye as he handed it over.

Hands trembling, Aidan opened the note and silently read:

Aidan,

For some time now, I've been worrying about the right thing to do. We have power, you and me, and it's almost too much. When we attacked Hex as one, it became clear that we are too dangerous together and that I had to do something.

I know you ain't going to like this, but we need to stay apart. At least for a while. Maybe forever, if that's what it takes.

Please know that I love you, will always love only you. But don't follow me. I do not wish to be found.

All my love,

Slaíne.

P.S. I saved Meraude for you to deal with. I hope you found the vengeance you wanted.

Aidan read the note several more times in quick succession, hoping to catch some hint of where she might have gone, a clue as to if she were serious in her admonition not to follow. What was she thinking? Slaíne couldn't mean it. She must mean for him to pursue her.

"Where are you going, Ingledark?" Hex asked, his voice full of too much compassion for Aidan's liking.

"She can't have gone far. Surely others have seen her. I'll...." Aidan stopped when Hex reached into the sack that hung over his shoulder and produced a portal-maker.

"This will take you home." He lifted Aidan's hand and pressed the doorknob into his palm.

Aidan shook his head. "I'm not leaving without her. And besides, I don't have a home anymore. I'll be hanged if I show my face in Breckstone again."

At that Hex chuckled. "Do you know how difficult it is for *magic* folk to kill a wizard? Never mind everyday *humans* trying it. You'll be all right."

"But Slaíne—"

"She has a portal-maker," said Hex. "I gave it to her, and with good reason. You two are entirely too dangerous with each other until one – or preferably *both* – of you are fully trained." His eyes narrowed. "Welch is in my employment again."

Aidan bristled at the mention of the shape-shifter. "Oh?"

"He can't kill you – or your mate for that matter – but he has instructions to keep an eye on you for the next five years." He replaced the portal-maker in his sack and brushed some invisible dust from his traveling cloak. "Still, I would keep wards up around my place, wherever I chose to settle." With that said, he removed the sack from his shoulder and handed it to Aidan. "There are some books in there to get you started."

Without acknowledging what had been said, Aidan accepted the bag and flung it over his own shoulder. He knew he would get no more out of the wizard. Then, with a nod to Jinn and her brother, Aidan pulled out the portal-maker Hex had given him and studied it and tried reading the small, foreign script in the early evening light.

"I made that one specifically for Breckstone," said the wizard. "It is good for one use, after that, it'll go black and cease working."

Aidan nodded and let the magic surge through him. Then, thrusting the doorknob into the air, he created a portal, and returned to the first place he had called home.

EPILOGUE

Ten years later

On the outskirts of Breckstone, in a wood that had once been called 'godforsaken' by the Romas who wandered the land, there now sat a small cottage. No stranger passing by would call it extraordinary by any means. "That is rather quaint," a passerby would say, to which a local might rejoin, "Ah, but do you know what lives there?"

The passerby would laugh in confusion, asking, "*What* lives there? Do not you mean *who*?"

At this point, the local man – or woman – would no longer be able to control their superiority of knowledge on the matter and would inform the stranger passing through the land that this very quaint cottage was in fact inhabited by the town's wizard. This information would always be followed by a gasp and then a stuttering response of fear.

"A wizard? Surely you jest. Those creatures are dangerous but have long since left the mortal realm."

Plied with some ale in the nearby tavern, the local person's tongue would relax, their courage would rise, and they would tell the tale of the lord who had been wanted for murder, ran for years in the wild, only to return decades later too powerful to be punished for his crimes.

"You don't say," the baffled passerby would say.

With a knowing grin, the local would say in a very low voice, "Ah, but I do. He runs the village now, and no one questions him. He's our representative to the magical world, and the magical world's representative to us."

Amazement and dismay would follow, for whoever heard of a

magical being allowed to rule mortals? It was outlandish. Dangerous. A complete outrage. Torches must be lit, and pitchforks sharpened!

But the protests and fearmongering would fall upon deaf ears. For though the wizard was not loved, he was not hated. Though he was powerful, he had not harmed anyone…well, not anyone who hadn't deserved it. He let the town folk be, for the most part, only intervening when trouble came their way.

Mighty useful. Mighty useful, indeed.

★   ★   ★

Aidan had finished with business for the week – watching over the town and keeping the peace when needed. His report to the Magical Council had been written up and, with a wave of his hand, sent to its recipients. There was no threat against magic-kind to be reported and hadn't been for a couple of years now. And the town had been quiet. Well, as quiet as it ever was. The Joneses had formed a plot against the Smythes after a prized goose had gone missing. All that had been required of Aidan was to give the Joneses a stern warning and the Smythes a talk about better patching up of their pens to prevent foxes from intruding. They'd been the only souls he had needed to talk to this week – this month, actually.

No more work or talking for this day or the next. He went to the side table and poured himself a mug of small beer. Without his ability to Dismiss, Aidan could no longer purify the water he meant to drink with a mere thought, so alcohol it was. He still distrusted the stuff. Becoming a wizard hadn't changed that. It certainly had changed everything else.

Memories of a different time rose up around Aidan like ghosts. Phantom pangs of old wounds also tormented him, as they did several times a day, making him wish that he cared more for drink than he did.

Every now and again, he would feel the tug between him and…the woman. It assured him that she was at least alive. Alive, but not with him. Without her, he knew he would never be complete, for she had the other half of his soul. "Not only my soul, but my heart." Cursing, he threw his mug into the fireplace, which sprayed him with gray ash. "Bah!" He waved his hand, and the glass cleaned itself up and tossed itself into the rubbish bin.

It did not do to remember. Remembering always brought regret. Should he have gone after her, all those years ago? His soul-half writhed somewhere in the great distance, and he shook his head. No. Loving her meant letting her go...even if she was being stupid. Some days, he thought he could hear her voice, a gentle lilt carried to him on the wind, as if to preserve – or destroy – his sanity. The sound usually sated him, but not today. Today he thought he heard singing, and it was louder than the usual kind he endured.

"A gent had me soft heart in his pocket
Tiddily do tra la day
A gent had me poor heart in his pocket
O it bled, and he did not do nothin'
Woe, woe, tiddle do tra la day

O me heart, he reft it in three small parts
Tiddily do tra la lee
O me heart, left berefted and wasted
Bled dry as paper, no love left for me
Tiddily do tra la la lee."

Aidan shook his head and picked up a book from the shelf in the corner of the room. It was a thick tome, one he had visited on many occasions, on the subject of herbs and their uses for medicinal purposes. There was a chill in the air that early autumn evening, so he started to light a fire the old-fashioned way. Reading by magical green light, he had found, was not nearly as comforting as by a natural one. Not that he needed the warmth or the light, what with his abilities and imperviousness to cold. Rather, it was an old creature habit, one he could not quite rid himself of.

Having set the book on the armchair where he meant to read next to the fireplace, he picked up the flint and struck it with a knife until the sparks caught his tinder ablaze. As quickly as he could without suffocating the small flame, he added more tinder and kindling and moved it into a standing teepee he had already made.

> *"Hello, hello, whence came you*
> *And henceforth do you go*
> *I am my sweetheart's lover*
> *And he bid me say hello."*

Aidan swore as the voice – a young girl's – continued to plague him. "Go away," he told what he had thought at first to be his imagining, but now realized was an actual child outside his window. The momentarily neglected fire sputtered to its death in the grate, so Aidan relented and lit it the magical way.

All was peaceful for a few beatings of his heart, so he thought it safe to sit in his seat and meditate over the flora of the middling lands. He conjured another cup of beer – this time in a metal stein – and, taking a sip, sat in his chair and propped up his feet.

"Your fire's green," said the young girl from the other side of the wall.

Aidan looked sharply at the window opposite him. For mortal eyes, it would have been impossible to properly see the child standing in the shade of the house and brush, but Aidan could make out every detail. She had unruly black hair framing a pale, heart-shaped face, and a smattering of freckles across the bridge of her nose and on her cheeks. At once Aidan sensed her magic.

"I said your fire's green," she repeated, backing away and leaving a smudge where her face had been pressed. The girl gave him a knowing look and then disappeared.

Aidan set his mug down on the side table next to his seat, closed his book, and got to his feet. If this were some sort of trap, he was really not in the mood for it. *Who would set a trap for you, Ingledark?* It was true that he had no friends, unless you counted Tris, but did he still have any enemies? *Not in these parts. At least, no enemies in these parts that are of the magical variety.* Warily he waited to see if the child would test his wards.

The doorknob rattled, and the lock he had set popped out of place, something Aidan had not been expecting. *No one should have been able to do that.* He tensed and reached for the dagger he always kept strapped at his side. The door swung open, and there stood the girl, her clothes dirty and patched, her brown eyes strangely intelligent as they bored into his.

"Oh, you're a wizard," said the child after a moment.

Aidan removed his hand from his dagger, sensing that there was no malice in this strange intruder. She was curious, and a bit lost, and that was all he could read on her at the moment. "May I help you with something?" he asked, perhaps a bit more brusquely than he had meant to, but he was unused to speaking to children and had no idea how to gauge his tone.

Without an invitation, the girl set foot over the threshold before he could warn her, but the ward did not harm her. "I thought most every wizard's magic was a red or blue or yellow."

"Someone is missing you," Aidan said, more to himself than to her. He went to the door to inspect his ward and was much surprised to find it still in place. By all magical law he knew, the child should not have been able to pass through it.

She laughed. "Mum lets me run wild. But I always come back." She had picked up his book of herbs and began pawing through it. "You do have a lot of books here. Might'n I borrow a few?"

Aidan raised an eyebrow. "You're not from around these parts."

"Mum says it's rude to read people without their permission," said the child without looking up from the words.

"And does your mother also warn you that it's dangerous entering a stranger's house?"

That made the girl laugh, and she looked up at him, her eyes dancing. "You ain't dangerous, not to me. How else could I walk through your wards?"

Aidan blinked. "So, you *did* feel them?"

"Yes, of course. I'm Samantha," she said, holding out one long-fingered hand. When Aidan hesitated, she laughed again. "I'm not gonna hurt you either. Your magic likes me, and I reckon mine likes yours too."

Still wary, Aidan nonetheless extended his hand and cold flesh met cold flesh as they shook. "Aidan," he said in way of greeting. "Your mother...." He gestured around vaguely.

"Oh, she'll find me. She always does. Like calls to like and all that."

Aidan nodded. "Right." *How does one entertain a child?* He shook his head in wonder as she took his seat and made herself at home. "Tell me, Samantha."

"You can just call me Sam. Everyone else does."

"Sam," Aidan said, nearly choking on the name, "where do you come from?"

But the girl seemed unwilling to answer and perfectly content to read from his book of herbs. So Aidan went to his kitchen, such as it was, and brought Samantha a steaming mug of tea and some biscuits that a grateful neighbor had brought him the day previous, and conjured another chair opposite her. He would wait until sunrise the next morning, and if the mother of this rather strange child hadn't arrived, he would set out looking for her.

"Here," he said, offering her the mug of tea and the biscuits.

Samantha eyed them curiously but made no move to take them.

"They're not poisoned, if that's what you're wondering."

She laughed, a spritely sound that raised the hairs on Aidan's arms. "Oh, I didn't think they would be. But, well, do men cook and bake and that sort of thing?"

"This one does," Aidan said, and she took the mug and plate from him. "Only, the biscuits are a gift from a neighbor this time."

"Hmm," said Samantha, levitating her mug in the air before her and shoving two biscuits into her mouth at the same time. "These are a little bland."

Aidan bit down on a smile that was trying to take over his face. "I'll be sure to tell the neighbor that. Then perhaps she will stop pestering me." He took the seat opposite and watched the fire.

For a moment they sat in silence, and Aidan thought it would be thus for the remainder of the evening until the mother arrived or the child fell asleep, but the girl set down the book with a startling thump and proclaimed herself to be bored. She took a large gulp of tea, and must have scalded her throat, because she let out a loud cough and swore a surprisingly colorful rainbow of profanities for someone so young, and turned pink. "Sorry. I'm not supposed to know those words."

Now Aidan did smile, and managed a weak laugh. It had been years since he remembered last having anything amusing to laugh about, a thought that rendered him quiet and pensive. "I won't tell your mother when she fetches you, if you won't."

Samantha grinned and this time blew on her tea before taking a more measured sip. "So, you live here all alone?"

Aidan tried not to bristle. "It is as you say."

"Must be lonely." Again she blew on her tea, took a sip, and then made the mug fly itself across the room, where it rested on a window ledge. "Mind if I save that for later?"

"Not at all."

"Not at all lonely or you mind not at all that I save it?" Her keen eyes bored into his and she shook her head. "Sorry. Mum always said it was wrong to read people. You're just really loud, 'tis all."

Aidan shook his head. He did not know what to make of this curious child…did not know what to *do* with her, was more like it. Where could her parents be? Whatever she said, the mother must be worried sick. He knew he would be, had he been missing a daughter. Pain swelled up inside of him, and he knew at once the girl had read it.

Thankfully, Samantha said nothing about his obvious pain, only giving him a confused look and hopping to her feet and going to the fireplace. "Green is so gloomy. I much prefer yellow." With a wave of her hand, the flames turned from jade to yellow, casting the room in a much more cheerful glow. "There. That's better. Ooh!" She went to his bookcase and pulled out a small tome with a bright orange cover. "I've been wanting to learn more about hexes. Could you teach me, you think?"

Aidan shook his head. "There are precious few who can cast a good hex, and it is getting rather late."

"I bet you can cast a powerful hex," she said after a moment of studying him. "You can teach me some other time. Or maybe tomorrow, if Mum says it's all right." Samantha gave him what she obviously thought to be a winning smile and set the book back among its fellows. "How old are you anyway?"

What a strange question to ask. "Forty-three, I suppose."

The girl shook her head. "You do not look it."

Aidan chuckled. "I suppose I am to thank you for that?"

"You look much younger and yet much older, so no thanks are in order." She picked at a spot on her blouse and looked around the room. "Where should I stay?"

That took Aidan aback. "Well, I suppose you could sleep on the floor. I have a feather bed around here somewhere." He turned and left the room, but he could sense that she was following him. It had been odd, losing his extra sense, the Pull that would inform him when someone was near. The only thing that alerted him to another's presence now was if they were magical, and as he was not around magical folk very often these days, it was oddly comforting to seemingly have the ability back.

"I can't sleep on the floor forever, you know. And since there doesn't seem to be many rooms here, you'll have to magic on another." She flicked her wrist and lit a candelabra in the corner of the room before he could get to it.

"You expect to be here long?" he asked, trying to keep the amusement and annoyance out of his voice. Young people presumed an awful lot. While he would not turn her out in the cold, he knew her parents must be nearby. And, if they were magical beings, they shouldn't have too much trouble locating their daughter. "Your mother should be here soon to collect you."

Samantha's brow puckered and she worried her lower lip. "You don't want me to stay?"

Now Aidan realized he was misunderstanding what was going on, that there was another hand at work here. He began to curse, but remembered himself to be in company and quickly hid his words in a cough. "Tris sent you, didn't he?"

"Who's Tris?"

"An old friend. He's been told to keep a lookout for magical folk and to direct them my way. Are you homeless?"

The girl's frown deepened. "I-I don't think so."

Aidan shook his head. No doubt the mother was a fabrication. Tris always knew Aidan had a soft spot for orphans and the homeless. Add the magical aspect on top of that, and Aidan was likely to find himself running an orphanage before long. Yes, this was no doubt Tristram's doing.

"I'll see about finding you a place to stay. But for tonight, you may sleep here. Is that all right?"

Samantha pulled a face but said nothing about her thoughts on the matter. "Couldn't you just conjure another bed?"

He did not want to regale the strange child with just how tired he was and how much energy that would take him. Instead he said, "If you need to stay more nights than one, I will make certain you have a bed. Satisfied?"

With a shrug, the girl ventured past him into the room, which was little more than a mostly empty storage closet. "Where have you got your portraits?" She began rummaging through a crate in the corner of the room, and came across a tiny box that Aidan knew to contain his mother's wedding ring. "Ooh this is lovely. Might I have it?" Before Aidan could answer that, no, she might not have it, Samantha closed the box and declared, "You have no portraits. Do not you draw?"

"I do not draw," he said. "It's getting later. Perhaps you'll want to calm down and—"

"When's supper?" she asked.

Bewildered, Aidan opened and closed his mouth a few times when, to his alarm – and relief – the front door creaked open noisily. *Who else might have got past my wards?* "Stay here," he said firmly to the girl, who started to tramp after him.

"But—"

"Do as I say, please." And with that said, Aidan plucked the dagger from his side and darted back into the main room.

The woman was standing by the fire, hood up and her back to the room. She was smaller than Aidan, though her presence seemed to fill the place.

Aidan froze, his soul-halves writhing. For a long while he could not speak, could not think. She did not turn, and neither did she speak, though he knew she was aware of his presence. At last he managed, "Am I dreaming?"

The very air crackled with the power coming off her, but it felt... controlled, like a well-trained steed. Perhaps not entirely safe, but not entirely feral either.

He could stand it no more, but covered the space between them in several large steps and spun her around to face him. Forever he stood there, staring at Slaíne, whose face had haunted his dreams all these years. Like Aidan, she hadn't aged a day, though her eyes seemed older than before, somehow. Just when he thought he couldn't endure another moment of this strange apparition, a small cry startled him out of his reverie.

"Mum!" said the girl, who had all but been forgotten. "I'm e'er so sorry for leaving you. But I found— Oh. Sorry."

The look Slaíne had given the child could have curdled milk. "Give us a minute, will ya, Sam?"

Samantha looked from her mother to Aidan, her expression confused. She retreated to the kitchen, where Aidan could hear her rummaging through his cupboard. "So."

Aidan shook his head and turned his back for a moment, trying to recover his composure. "You're not a bit of my imagining?"

"I can pinch ya, if'n ya need it."

He laughed once, a strangled sound.

Slaíne let out a deep sigh. "Look, Aidan, I'll understand if'n ya nay want to see me. I just— I needed to make certain you was all right. I know I waited long enough."

"Why?"

"I told you why then, Aidan. I was more dangerous and out of control before I received the proper amount of training. We woulda ended up destroying each other."

But Aidan shook his head. "That is not what I meant. Why are you apologizing?" No longer trying to hide his emotions, Aidan turned once more, and as their eyes met, her soul-half within his breast ceased to writhe and was still, calm.

She frowned and cocked her head to the side. "But you're furious with me. Don't say ya ain't, 'cause I can feel your anger."

Aidan nodded. "Of course I'm furious. You left me." He grabbed her and pulled her into his chest, hugging her as tightly as he could. "Promise me you won't ever do that again."

Slaíne rested her head against his heart and breathed in deeply. Her arms wrapped around him as well, and she squeezed. "I promise."

He pulled back so he could look at her again, both of them jumping when something shattered in the kitchen. "Is she ours?" he asked, amazement and sorrow washing over him.

"She's ours."

Aidan led her to the chair by the fire, keeping himself between the door and her, as though that could keep her from running away again.

I promised I'd stay an' I meant it, she whispered into his mind. Aloud she said, "We're not goin' anywhere, Aidan." *I love you.* Again she squeezed him.

"You must be exhausted," he said, kissing her brow, her cheek, and lastly her lips. They tasted of salt and tears, of hope and renewal and maybe a second chance. He surprised himself by pulling away first to sob once.

"I know," she said, touching his face, her own eyes shining with unshed tears. Again they flew at each other, desperate for contact.

Where were you? he asked, licking the line of her lips.

She opened her mouth to him, twining her fingers in his hair. *Overseas while I was taught to control my magic. The nymphs took care of Sam when I could not.*

Aidan nipped her neck and then soothed the spot with his tongue. *You trusted my child with nymphs?*

Slaíne laughed and then cried in happy surprise as Aidan swept her off her feet and into his arms. "*Our* child, Aidan. An' she were perfectly safe. Safer than she would have been with either of us."

Aidan conceded the point with a grunt. His temper alone had been out of control for the first seven years of his new life, and his magic was still a bit unpredictable. As the wizard Hex had once said, time would mellow his rage. Until then, perhaps he was not as safe for his daughter as he ought to be.

Slaíne, of course, could hear all his thoughts, and buried her face in his neck. "Let's nay worry 'bout that. She's stronger than you can imagine."

"Are you talking about me while I'm not there?" Samantha asked, peeking into the room. Her face was covered in biscuit crumbs, and a spoon had become tangled in her unruly hair.

Startled and unsure of how to behave with his wife around his new-found daughter, Aidan began to set Slaíne down, until she growled at him. "Sorry," Aidan said, straightening up with her once again, and the room filled with their laughter.

"Mum, don't growl at Papa. That's not how you should behave."

Slaíne didn't take her eyes off Aidan as she asked, "Let me ask your father. How should I behave?"

He would have known without the green light reflecting off Slaíne's face that his eyes were glowing. Magic pulsed in the air, and crackled all around them.

"Is it going to rain?" the child asked and ran to the window. "Odd. I don't think it's going to. But it feels like it."

"What do you think, Mrs. Ingledark? Is it going to rain?"

She grinned, her own eyes taking on a blue glow. "Buckets, husband. Absolutely buckets of it."

ACKNOWLEDGMENTS

Writing a book may be a solitary task, but publishing one turned out to not be so. There are so many people who worked with me to turn this labor of love into readable material, and here I'd like to recognize a few of them:

Thank you to Don D'Auria and the wonderful people at Flame Tree Press for believing in *The Goblets Immortal* books and blessing me so very generously with your time and efforts.

A shout-out to Ruthie Johnson and Julene Louis for being my indefatigable beta readers. Thank you for believing in me and giving me your honesty.

Thank you to my mom, Janet: your support and encouragement have seen me through some dark times. I can't believe I'm here but it is thanks, in no small part, to you.

Thanks to my street team for helping get the word out about my books.

And finally, a big thank-you to my readers. You've stayed with me this far, and I dedicate this final chapter of Aidan Ingledark's journey to you.

FLAME TREE PRESS
FICTION WITHOUT FRONTIERS
Award-Winning Authors & Original Voices

Flame Tree Press is the trade fiction imprint of Flame Tree
Publishing, focusing on excellent writing in horror and the
supernatural, crime and mystery, science fiction and fantasy.
Our aim is to explore beyond the boundaries of the everyday,
with tales from both award-winning authors and original voices.

•

Other titles available by Beth Overmyer:
The Goblets Immortal
Holes in the Veil

You may also enjoy:
The Sentient by Nadia Afifi
American Dreams by Kenneth Bromberg
Second Lives by P.D. Cacek
Thirteen Days by Sunset Beach by Ramsey Campbell
The Wise Friend by Ramsey Campbell
The City Among the Stars by Francis Carsac
The Haunting of Henderson Close by Catherine Cavendish
The Garden of Bewitchment by Catherine Cavendish
Vulcan's Forge by Robert Mitchell Evans
Black Wings by Megan Hart
Stoker's Wilde by Steven Hopstaken & Melissa Prusi
Stoker's Wilde West by Steven Hopstaken & Melissa Prusi
The Widening Gyre by Michael R. Johnston
The Blood-Dimmed Tide by Michael R. Johnston
Those Who Came Before by J.H. Moncrieff
The Sky Woman by J.D. Moyer
The Guardian by J.D. Moyer
The Apocalypse Strain by Jason Parent
Until Summer Comes Around by Glenn Rolfe
A Killing Fire by Faye Snowden
The Bad Neighbor by David Tallerman
Ten Thousand Thunders by Brian Trent
Night Shift by Robin Triggs
Human Resources by Robin Triggs
Two Lives: Tales of Life, Love & Crime by A Yi

•

Join our mailing list for free short stories, new release details,
news about our authors and special promotions:

flametreepress.com